Please turn to the back of the book for an
interview with Peter Clement.

Acclaim for Dr. Clement's previous medical thriller, *Lethal Practice*

"ER meets Agatha Christie as Buffalo doctor Earl Garnet is suspected of murder via a cardiac needle. Heart-pounding suspense, indeed!"
—*Entertainment Weekly*

"A single mysterious and grisly murder in the first chapter sustains this entire debut novel. . . . Clement doesn't make the mistake of substituting body count for narrative drive; the circumstances surrounding Kingsly's death and the motives floating around the hospital provide more than enough juice. Clement, a former ER physician, possesses punchy prose, medical know-how, and a knack for quirky details."
—*Publishers Weekly*

Please turn the page for
more rave reviews. . . .

D0965328

"Great debut novel—the story moves and carries the reader quickly from start to finish. Dr. Clement's background keeps the story authentic and urges the reader to continue on this heart-stopping suspense tale. Keep writing, Dr. Clement!"
—PATTY WACHTER
Harrisburg, Pennsylvania

"Dr. Clement writes like a seasoned pro! If his medical skills are as polished as his ability to relate them, I'd trust him anytime. Just enough medical detail to make it real, just enough suspense to keep me reading instead of doing other responsibilities. Great book and unexpected twist to the ending. I hope he writes more in the future."
—TISH MURZYN
Hartly, Delaware

"I loved it. I couldn't put it down. Very suspenseful!"
—MARY VECELLIO
Flint, Michigan

"An extraordinary medical thriller . . . contains plenty of believable scenarios with plenty of twists, suspense, and surprises. It kept me riveted all night long. I'm ready for more by Peter Clement."
—GINNY HIARING
Clarinda, Iowa

By Peter Clement
Published by Fawcett Books:

LETHAL PRACTICE
DEATH ROUNDS

DEATH ROUNDS

Peter Clement

FAWCETT GOLD MEDAL • NEW YORK

This book is dedicated to Vyta, Sean, and James, whose love makes all things possible.

A special thanks to my longtime friend and colleague in ER, Dr. Brian Connolly, for his support and advice. And a special thanks to my agent, Denise Marcil, for her generous help with this book that went far beyond what any writer could hope for.

A Fawcett Gold Medal Book
Published by The Ballantine Publishing Group
Copyright © 1999 by Baskerville Enterprises, Ltd.

Fawcett Gold Medal and colophon are trademarks of Random House, Inc.

www.randomhouse.com/BB/

Library of Congress Catalog Card Number: 98-96764

ISBN 0-449-00450-3

Manufactured in the United States of America

First Edition: March 1999

10 9 8 7 6 5 4 3 2 1

PART ONE

Incubation

Chapter 1

10:00 A.M., Tuesday, October 21

She looked dead. Her flesh was mottled purple and white from not enough oxygen and loss of circulation. But as I stepped up to the stretcher where she was lying, I could hear her breathing—gurgling noises, each ending with a whimper—and I could see the muscles between her ribs suck in and out as she struggled for air. Her skin felt warm despite its ghastly appearance and had a sour acrid smell, the aroma of sweat saturated with lactic acid. Brown fingertips betrayed years of smoking. At the touch of my hands she half opened her eyes and stared about her with quick darting movements. Her pupils were wide with terror, dilated by the flood of adrenaline that goes with dying, and her gray hair splayed out wild and tangled over the pillow. The worst was when those black eyes glared at me. Even in her agony, gasping and unable to move or speak, her expression seemed to say, *You sent me home.*

I smothered a rising wave of alarm and guilt as I placed two fingers at the right side of her neck. "Pressure?" I asked, trying to sound in control. I could barely palpate a pulse in her carotid artery.

"Eighty over zip, Doctor," replied the nurse who was at the patient's head. She was applying a translucent green oxygen mask and attaching the tube to a hissing wall outlet. "I just took it. And the pulse is one-twenty and irregular." She'd already wired the woman to a cardiac monitor. The erratic beeping accompanying the rapid squiggle on the screen above me was far from reassuring. "I think it's atrial fib," she added, as she watched me study the tracing. She was right.

When I didn't reply, she asked, "Aren't you going to cardiovert it?"

Her tone made it clear she thought I should try to shock the heart back into a normal rhythm. I shook my head. "It may be the result of the shock and not the cause." I forced myself to concentrate to keep thinking this through.

Two other nurses trying to start IVs in the woman's arms crouched at opposite sides of the table. Bags of saline had been suspended in readiness from overhead poles. "Got it," announced Susanne Roberts at my elbow. She was the head nurse and, like me, a twenty-year veteran of these desperate struggles. Without waiting for instructions, she reached up and adjusted the valve in the clear tubing that dangled from one of the bags of fluid. She then stepped around the foot of the bed and came to the aid of her much younger colleague, who'd just muttered, "Damn!"

The nurse at the head of the table reached past me to clip an oxygen monitor to the tip of one of the patient's fingers. Yet another machine began beeping behind me. "O2 sat's only eighty percent," she commented grimly, meaning the blood oxygen level was dangerously low.

"The first person free," I said, "get me a twelve-lead cardiogram, and I want a portable chest stat. Get someone else in here to draw bloods and catheterize her."

"Routine bloods are drawn and gone, Dr. Garnet," Susanne informed me as she started the second IV, "and X ray's been called." Then she nudged her flustered helper and quipped, "Even if he is chief of ER, I hope he knows enough to want blood cultures because I ordered them as well."

This time I barely managed a curt nod as I quickly slipped my stethoscope into my ears and listened to the woman's heart sounds. Susanne gave me a puzzled little glance.

Normally I welcomed her sassy wisecracks and joined in the fun. It was how we kept the rookies relaxed.

I moved the stethoscope to the lower right side of the woman's chest. Barely any air moved in her lungs. What little flow there was wheezed and crackled as it passed through—what? Fluid? Pus? Both? A listen on the left revealed more of the same. She was in warm shock, probably caused by sepsis—an overwhelming infection spread into the blood stream—with pneumonia being the most likely primary source. Yet I continued to check elsewhere. Stepping around the tangle of ECG wires Susanne was hooking up, I palpated the abdomen and examined the lower extremities. Nothing. But when I moved back up to the patient's head and flexed her neck, checking for stiffness and evidence of meningitis, her eyes still followed me and I had to endure that stare again. *Look at what you've done to me!*

I shuddered but kept myself focused on treating her. "Okay, everyone, this is an infectious case, septic shock, probably from overwhelming pneumonia of some kind, and isolation is in force." We were already wearing masks and gloves as a general precaution. Isolation meant donning surgical gowns for additional protection against bodily fluids and discarding all this protective gear in a bin at the door whenever we left the room. Such measures were intended to protect us and the other patients in the rest of the hospital. Hopefully. The circus I was about to create wasn't conducive to the confinement of deadly microbes.

People were running in, fumbling with back ties on their half-done-up masks and gowns.

I kept giving orders. "Keep the IVs open, raise her legs, but give me vitals every few minutes. We don't want to overload her. And get me an inhalation therapist fast. We need to intubate this lady and help her breathe *now!*"

But my words sounded hollow. When I turned to speak specifically to Susanne, I found it hard to look her in the eye. "When whoever you called to take blood cultures gets down here, have him culture and Gram-stain everything else as well—sputum, urine, CSF, even stool—and repeat the blood cultures again in thirty minutes if we get that far." While talking, I was already struggling into a green OR gown I'd gotten from one of the racks where we kept gear for dirty cases. "Get one of our residents to do the LP," I added, praying that no one would see through my phony show of calm.

The lab tech arrived with a basket of tubes and swabs.

I stepped to the top of the bed behind the woman's head and flipped off her oxygen mask. She'd started to cough, and yellow foam was seeping out between her lips. Mercifully her eyes were now closed. "Get whoever's on call for ICU and ID," I said over the rising voices. I grabbed a rigid suction catheter from the wall beside me and opened the valve that activated it. "And tell ID if they don't get here fast, we'll choose their antibiotics for them." Infectious disease consultants, by definition, never liked our choice of treatment, even when we got it right. Today I knew I needed their help.

I put my gloved fingers into the pus streaked with blood flowing from her mouth and scissored open her teeth. Through the thin latex I could feel the debris was thick and warm. How could I have allowed her to get like this? Whatever I thought of her, she was one of our own. With the recriminations, I broke into a sweat.

"Let me culture that gunk before you suction it out," ordered the lab tech who'd just finished drawing off the bloods. He pushed by me, took a sterile cup and gingerly scooped up a glob of the stuff as it rolled out the corner of her mouth. He'd mount a dab of this sample on a glass slide and color it with violet and iodine solutions, the ingredients of a Gram stain. In twenty minutes he'd have it under a microscope and know what was killing her. He then plunged several long Q-Tips into the pool of secretions welling up at the back of her throat. Her whole body bucked as she gagged and choked while he poked about. Small yellow droplets flew onto the front of my glasses. When he withdrew, thick strands of the purulent sputum dripped from the ends of the swabs. These specimens would be plated onto various types of agar in which the organism would be grown to determine what antibiotics, if any, it was sensitive to. "That'll do it," he said, sliding the cultures back in their containers of charcoal growth medium and sticking labels on them.

I stuck the catheter into the woman's mouth. The unsightly debris vanished noisily up the tubing. She still bucked at the stimulation, but less than before. I focused my thoughts enough to verify there was no evidence of tonsillitis or discoloration of her mucous membranes to suggest a toxic shock syndrome. But would she tolerate intubation without sedation? My hesitancy disgusted me.

"I've got it, Earl," said a familiar voice at my side, and Dr. Michael Popovitch reached across me, a laryngoscope in one hand, an orange endotracheal tube in the other. Even if he hadn't spoken, the pepper-and-salt beard sticking out from the corners of his mask and the unmistakable pear-shaped physique under his surgical gown made him instantly recognizable. He was both director of teaching and my associate chief in ER, but more important, he was also my friend.

"Thanks, Michael," I said, moving out of the way.

He slipped the curved steel blade of the scope alongside her tongue, opened her airway to illuminate her vocal cords, and slid the tip of the curved rubber device into the woman's trachea. She immediately heaved and blew out some more of the yellow slime that was clogging her bronchi, then fell quiet. As he started ventilating her, the inhalation therapist ran up and took over. Michael stepped back, then led me by the arm away from the table to where we wouldn't be overheard.

"Earl, what the hell's the story with this lady? And are you okay? Christ, you're pale, you're sweating—" He suddenly looked horrified. "Oh my God! You haven't got chest pain have you?"

I took a breath. "The story with this lady, Michael, is that her name is Phyllis Sanders, she's in her fifties, and she's an OB nurse at University Hospital. Eighteen hours ago she presented here with a slight cough, minimal fever, and a touch of diarrhea. I assured her she only had the flu and sent her home."

The rest of the resuscitation raced on around me. Residents eager to do procedures rushed into the room grabbing needle sets and ripping open packets for central lines. Michael hastily reined them in and orchestrated their frenzy into specific tasks. The beeping sounds from the monitors and the shouted orders for blood gases and LP trays seemed distant.

She needed antibiotics. But I couldn't organize all her symptoms and signs to point to a likely organism and make the choice clear. All that pus suggested a gram-positive coccal infection, probably pneumococcal, but other parts of the pattern didn't fit, nagged at me, hinted at something unlikely and atypical. Or was I just trying to let myself off the hook . . . make it seem more complicated than it was to justify my screwup?

A sudden stench in the room told me someone had gotten a stool sample. Even though her source of infection was obviously in her lungs, the emergence of drug-resistant infections in many U.S. hospitals made screening her feces for VRE, vancomycin-resistant enterococcus, mandatory and routine.

I wasn't waiting for ID. "Hang up two grams of ceftriaxone in one IV, and one gram of erythromycin in the other," I told Susanne as I saw her get off the phone. I'd cover a mix of possibilities for now.

"ICU is ready for her as soon as you can get her up," she reported as she wrote out my order and handed it to one of the orderlies she'd stationed at the door to act as runners.

We got Phyllis Sanders's pressure to rise a bit, started the antibiotics, and snapped a portable chest X ray before whipping her off to ICU, where they would put her on a respirator. We even managed to slow down her heart with a bit of intravenous digoxin. The X ray confirmed my diagnosis of pneumonia—her entire right lung and part of the left were whited out by the infection—but by then the woman had drifted off into a coma. Her blood results, when I finally got them, were a disaster of falling white counts, rising liver enzymes, and increasing renal failure.

Michael had tried to be supportive when he'd gotten over his initial surprise at my declaration, assuring me he was certain I'd acted reasonably, but his reassurance hadn't helped. Even when he looked at my notes on her chart from the previous day's visit and said he couldn't see how he'd have acted any differently, I replied, "Given what happened, I should have kept her."

"On what grounds?" he challenged. "A little bit of temperature? Look at the resident's workup. For once we can be thankful about their habit of ordering too many tests. Apart from a slightly elevated white count and a sodium of one-thirty-three, everything else was normal, including the physical exam. Christ, the guy even ordered a chest X ray, which frankly I wouldn't have done. From his note, apparently there wasn't much on that either."

"A bit of COPD from smoking, and a minimal horizontal line in the lower right lung we thought was either old scar tissue or atelectasis," I interjected, précising the report from memory. We were huddled in a quiet corner of the nurses' station, a large central room with huge windows looking out on the rest of the department. I kept watching over Michael's shoulder for ambulances in triage or new patients in the surrounding bed areas, but for the moment the city of Buffalo had given us a breather and ER was quiet. Our residents seemed to be handling whatever few cases the nurses had brought in. "Obviously that little mark was the start of infection and was a lot more significant than we thought," I added, sounding pathetically morose even to myself.

"Bullshit!" Michael said, loud enough for anyone in the station to hear. A young medical student looked up from her computer screen, but no one else paid him any mind. He immediately lowered his voice, but not his intensity. "If a radiologist says that film suggests anything more than what you called it, he's a liar. No one could predict that little mark was brewing into what she had today, certainly not without a previous film to compare it to—which, by the way, makes me wonder why she came here to St. Paul's instead of the staff health service at University Hospital."

"She was on vacation, St. Paul's was closer to her home, and she said she didn't like everybody at work knowing her business anyway," I answered, only giving part of the reason. In fact she had phoned in ahead of time and found out I was on call. "I work with his wife," she'd announced at triage, putting everyone on the defensive. She'd increased the level of discomfort even further by proclaiming, "And my son's the chief technician for the labs at her hospital." By the time she'd done the same routine with the resident who'd initially assessed her—browbeating him into ordering more tests than he might normally have asked for—anyone who went near the woman resented her. I only learned all this from the clerks and nurses after I'd sent her home. But I'd already taken my own dislike to Phyllis Sanders.

"I know Janet, Dr. Garnet," had been her greeting when I'd appeared at her bedside to review her case with the resident.

Dr. Janet Graceton is my wife, an obstetrician at University Hospital. I met people all the time who announced they knew her, had had their children delivered by her, thought the world of her, but this had been different. I felt I'd had my chain yanked.

"I've heard so much about *you* as well," she'd continued in a high whiny voice. Sitting up in her hospital gown, her arms crossed in front of her chest, her gray hair pulled tightly back into a bun, she'd seemed rigid, held in. She'd forced a smile, but it had looked like a reproach as her forehead frowned while her lips turned up. All the while her eyes seemed to say *Are you going to disappoint me too?*

I'd resented her immediately and had been particularly repulsed by her attempt to use her acquaintance with Janet to manipulate me.

When she'd told me her son's position and then added, "He's worked with your wife too, you know," I'd barely kept the irritation out of my voice. Go do your wheedling for special treatment in someone else's ER, I'd been thinking while explaining she'd nothing much wrong with her.

"How long did you say she'd been sick?" Michael asked, snapping me back from my thoughts.

"Only a day," I answered, trying to keep my words steady and not sound defensive. "She'd had a slight headache when she woke up that morning, then the temperature and diarrhea."

"It doesn't sound like much to bring a nurse into ER. I wonder if she chose Saint Paul's over her own staff health service because they had her number there and knew she was a malingerer?"

"Maybe," I answered, not admitting that was exactly what I'd suspected as I'd firmly insisted she could go home. "Obviously she wasn't malingering this time."

Michael gave me a smile and clapped his hand warmly on my shoulder. "You made a solid call, Earl, given what was there. Hey! After all your years in the pit, you of all people should know you can't beat yourself up over every disease that turns nasty." He finished signing off his part of today's resuscitation, handed Sanders's chart back to me, and added, "When this case is reviewed, everyone will agree with me." He then strode briskly out of the station and over to where a new ambulance case had been rushed into triage.

He'd meant to support me, but the mention of a case review unleashed once more the sense of dread I'd been trying to control. All unexpected return visits trigger investigations to identify possible slipups. I'd instigated the mandatory checks myself when I'd first become chief over eight years ago. But not all physicians at St. Paul's Hospital had appreciated my setting up an arena where their errors were dissected and laid bare for critical scrutiny. Whenever I had a case on the schedule, more than a few of these doctors turned up hungry to settle old scores. This time they might have a point. As I signed off my own notes, my memory of yesterday's encounter kept playing over and over. Had my resentment at the woman made me miss something?

Chapter 2

I spent the next five minutes trying to make sense of a rambling history given by an earnest medical student about an old man who seemed to hurt everywhere. I ended up suggesting he discuss the patient with Michael.

"Dr. Garnet," called the ER clerk from her work area on the other side of the station. "It's bacteriology on line three, about Mrs. Sanders."

I grabbed the desktop telephone beside me and punched the third button. "Garnet here."

"Dr. Garnet," said the technician, his voice obviously excited, "it's staph. Clusters and clusters of gram-positive cocci on the Gram stain of her sputum."

"You're sure?" I questioned, surprised. "It's not just strands of pneumococci heaped together?"

While both these organisms are gram-positive cocci, that is, when treated with Gram stain reagents they stain blue and appear round under a microscope, pneumococcal bacteria line up in strands and pairs whereas staphylococci tend to occur in clumps and to resemble bunches of grapes. I'd been expecting pneumococci.

"It's out of a textbook," he replied, "like a goddamned vineyard. I'm keeping the slides for our teaching file. All the other cultures are being plated out now."

He was as excited as a kid with a new toy. Staph pneumonia was unusual, and bacteremia from staph pneumonia was outright rare. In all his enthusiasm he seemed to have overlooked that he'd just given Mrs. Sanders a one-in-three chance of dying.

"Do you know if it's a hospital- or community-acquired infection?" he asked eagerly.

It was a good question despite the macabre exuberance. Hospital-acquired staphylococcus was apt to be resistant to the antibiotics we'd given her. One strain in particular, called MRSA, or methicillin-resistant staphylococcus aureus, responded only to vancomycin.

"She's a nurse at University Hospital," I replied. "I suppose we'll have to assume resistance until we get your culture and sensitivity results."

"Thanks for the great case, Doc!" he said before hanging up.

I was left shaking my head.

I called ICU and informed the charge nurse about the Gram stain result. She told me ID still hadn't seen Sanders, so I ordered vancomycin—just in case.

"Do we stop the erythromycin?" she asked, not unreasonably. If the pneumonia was caused by staph, erythromycin wouldn't add anything to the treatment already in place, except an increased chance of side effects.

But I hesitated.

"Dr. Garnet?" asked the nurse, after a few seconds of silence.

Something still didn't fit. I couldn't pin it down, but one thing I'd learned not to ignore in ER was an uneasy feeling that I was missing something.

"No," I answered slowly, "leave it until ID sees her, and have them call me here when they do. They'll probably change all my orders anyway. By the way, has anyone talked to the family yet?"

"There's no answer at the woman's home. Her chart from yesterday says she's widowed—Sanders's her maiden name—but the next of kin is her son, a Harold Miller, with the same phone number. Did he send her in?"

"No, according to the ambulance sheet a neighbor found her this morning and dialed 911." I hesitated before giving my next suggestion. But it had to be done. "Her son's in charge of lab technicians at University Hospital. You might try for him there. Tell him he can reach me in ER."

After I hung up, I glanced around the department, confirming that Michael and the residents still had things under control. I stepped over to a set of corner shelves where we kept reference texts. While most of the residents used the computer to access material on any given topic in emergency medicine, I still preferred the written page. As chief of the department, I could assure we had both.

Despite the Gram stain result identifying staphylococcus, there were simply too many features of this case that seemed unusual. I pulled the middle volume of a medical text published by *Scientific*

American—a large three-ring-binder format that was updated monthly—and found the section on pulmonic infections.

Looking at the differential diagnosis of pneumonias in a systematic outline relaxed me. The bits and pieces of various syndromes suggested by Sanders's symptoms suddenly seemed to settle into an organized pattern. The thickness of her sputum and the presence of blood was indeed consistent with the more common pneumococcal infection that I'd been expecting to find, but pus was also a hallmark of how staph infections released toxins that destroyed tissue and so created abscesses. The bloody sputum could have been the result of noncardiac pulmonary edema—a condition in which shock and sepsis break down the membranes lining the tiny air sacs through which oxygen normally passes into the blood. The result is a leaky-lung syndrome in which these same little sacs are flooded with blood-tinged serum.

The article reiterated that staph organisms were carried in the nostrils of up to fifty percent of hospital personnel, a well-known statistic, and that this was the most common nosocomial, or hospital-acquired, source of this infection with elderly or immunocompromised patients. In the update, however, was a new statistic. The incidence of serious drug-resistant organisms in U.S. hospitals, namely, MRSA or VRE, was now up to forty percent.

This creepy piece of data made my skin crawl. I immediately felt the urge to wash my hands.

But the next chapter, while reassuring about my personal safety, reinforced my suspicion there was something strange about Sanders's being infected at all. Healthy adults only developed pneumonia from staphylococcus after some event, like an influenza infection, made the lung susceptible. The expected pattern was a flulike illness for at least five days and then the classic symptoms of life-threatening pneumonia we'd seen in Sanders today. The one-day prodrome she'd presented with yesterday wasn't part of the picture.

Peering at the small print through the bottom part of my glasses, I suddenly realized the yellow droplets from Sanders's sputum were still dried on the lenses. "Shit!" I exclaimed. The same medical student who'd overheard Michael's profanity gave me a disapproving look. "Sorry," I muttered, and rushed out of the nurses' station. Illogically, I held my breath while running to a utility room. There I whipped on a pair of gloves, dropped my glasses into the deep sink where mops were cleaned, and emptied half a container of concentrated cleaner on them. My eyes were red with the fumes by the time I finished rinsing them off. On returning to the nurses' station, I smelled like a recently scrubbed toilet.

"Phew!" said Michael, who was standing over the open book I'd abandoned on the counter. The section on pneumonias must have caught his eye. "What are you using for aftershave?" he kidded, but his laugh sounded a little nervous.

"Smart-ass!" I stepped by him to put away what I'd been reading.

"Hold it," he cautioned, and pointed to a section I hadn't looked at yet.

There, in a succinct paragraph, was exactly the prodrome I'd been looking for.

> *The pneumonia is preceded by a one day history of myalgia, malaise, and a slight headache after an incubation period of 2 to 10 days. Gastrointestinal complaints, especially diarrhea, may be present, and orthostatic dizziness has been reported. The cough is initially nonproductive.*

I looked up to the title of this section. It was Legionnaires' disease.

Little Gary Rossit, the chief of our infectious disease department, was the biggest son of a bitch in the hospital. Whenever he could use his considerable knowledge about communicable illnesses to humiliate his fellow physicians, he did so with relish. Perhaps it was his way of paying back the rest of the world for being taller than he was. I always suspected he simply enjoyed being mean. That his considerable skills also helped desperately ill patients get better was why most of us put up with him.

"Look, Earl, just because you booted the case yesterday, don't think overdiagnosing the same symptoms today and ordering every antibiotic you can think of is going to let you off the hook."

I felt my face flush with anger. We were outside the isolation cubicle in ICU, a well-lit glassed-in room located against a back wall of the department. He'd just finished pulling off his cap and other protective wear after seeing Mrs. Sanders, and his wavy black hair was sticking up in tufts. I had to resist grabbing one of them and lifting him off the floor by it.

"I've ordered the lab to test for *Legionella*," I told him, gritting my teeth to help me keep my temper. Special culture and staining techniques that could take up to three days were required to isolate the hard-to-detect organism. Even then, none of the tests was one-hundred-percent sensitive.

"Where's your reference to justify even thinking of those tests," he asked belligerently. "There's no literature on Legionnaires' preceding staph pneumonia."

"Show me literature on staph pneumonia and bacteremia after a twenty-four-hour prodrome in an otherwise healthy adult," I shot back at him.

We glared at each other for a few seconds. The resident in charge of ICU who'd been listening from a few feet away started to fidget.

Then Rossit shrugged. "No wonder we're way over budget," he muttered as he walked over to a large desk near the central nurses' station where he began writing his consultation note. Behind him were dozens of monitors and screens arranged on a wide curved console—a flashing array of fluorescent tracings, blinking numbers, and squiggled readouts. Every now and then an alarm bell would softly sound and get the attention of a nurse. Sometimes she'd readjust the monitor. Other times she and her colleagues would rush into one of the many curtained cubicles that lined the room and perform some procedure on a patient, out of sight. Occasionally there would be a cry or moan, but ICU was generally a quiet place where conversations were hushed and pain was monitored, measured, and medicated until it was endured without a whimper. Somewhere on the blinking wall of screens in front of me were the numbers that documented Mrs. Sanders's agony.

The resident hesitantly approached and asked, "Dr. Garnet, what do we do if he discontinues the erythromycin?"

Erythromycin was the treatment of choice for *Legionella*.

"Ignore him," I answered none too quietly. "He's only a consultant giving an opinion."

I watched the little man flinch, sign off his brief entry with a flourish of his pen, then rise and start back toward me. He was shaking his head and trying to smile, but it was his turn to look flushed.

"At this stage, Garnet, I think she's SOL, whatever we do. Our next discussion about her will probably be at Death Rounds, when we'll have the benefit of an autopsy and not have to endure some cock-and-bull scenario cooked up by you to assuage your own guilt. And by the way, chum, you did miss something yesterday that justified keeping her." He abruptly wheeled about and walked swiftly toward the exit. As he hit the metal disk that activated the sliding doors, he glanced back at me. His bristly mustache, stocky body, and short legs usually reminded me of a video game character, but there was nothing comic in the triumphant glare he gave me before he stalked from the room.

Looking embarrassed, the resident was tugging at her stethoscope. "Excuse me, Dr. Garnet, but I have to round on the other patients," she said nervously, then rushed off to one of the cubicles.

I exhaled, trying to release the knot that was quickly tightening in my stomach again, and forced myself to go over to the desk where Rossit had left the chart. Cursing the little man's hostility, I quickly reviewed the notes from yesterday's visit, yet couldn't find what he'd inferred—and what I'd been dreading—that I'd missed something basic. I was about to dismiss the accusation as a cheap shot when my eye fell on a circled passage in the nurse's notes.

2 P.M. Patient discharged home by Dr. Garnet. Reported feeling dizzy on standing but complaint passed when sitting. Patient taken to front door in a wheelchair and helped into a taxi.

Orthostatic dizziness—the nurse should have recognized it was significant and taken the woman's pressure standing. We would probably have picked up a drop and known she was becoming unstable. At the very least we would have started her on an IV to rehydrate her and observed her vital signs. We would have had her here when she decompensated, and earlier administration of antibiotics would definitely have increased her chances of survival.

Sanders herself must have known the dizziness was of concern. Had she protested, insisting that someone should take her pressure again, but only increased the antagonism of her nurse? Had she been ignored and hustled out the door in a wheelchair?

In any ER, the attitude of the chief sets the tone. Kidding and teasing aside, I knew my staff usually took their lead from me. Even though we'd all found Sanders tiresome, it was up to me to make sure my own attitude and dislike of the woman hadn't implicitly signaled that the patient was a crock and that her complaints weren't to be taken seriously.

Rossit was right. I'd missed a key sign of orthostatic hypotension that was clearly there to be found. Worse, I'd probably assured no one else would find it either.

I literally fled from ICU.

Chapter 3

Seeing patients was going to be difficult. As I headed down the stairwell from the third floor, I thought of signing out to Michael until I felt more collected, but the idea of sitting around and dwelling on things unnerved me even more.

When I arrived in ER I took Susanne to a quiet corner and explained what I'd learned. The expression on her face quickly registered the same anxiety I was feeling.

She groaned. "Oh no. Who was the nurse?"

In my confusion upstairs I hadn't bothered to notice.

"Sorry, but if you go over the chart, her note is now plenty obvious. Rossit was kind enough to circle it."

"You're kidding!"

"You know how he is. Nailing the mistakes of others is a blood sport to him, and I'm afraid he can't wait to wipe the floor with me over this one. The trouble is, in his eagerness to have my hide, he's likely to smear everyone else in the department who went near Sanders."

"Chiefs make for especially good hunting, do they?" she asked harshly, obviously angered by the prospect of Rossit's legendary troublemaking hitting so close to home. "Christ, the man's a menace. He makes everyone in the hospital want to cover up mistakes instead of learning from them."

I gave a little laugh. "That's exactly what some physicians think about my mandatory reviews of unexpected return visits."

I must have sounded as miserable as I felt.

Her eyes widened in surprise. "Earl Garnet!" she exclaimed. "How can you even think of yourself in the same category as a louse like him. You're fair in those reviews, and everyone knows it, even, I suspect, the ones who resent having to look at their own errors. You help physicians be better doctors, Earl. Rossit doesn't care about that. He's vicious, pure and simple, and everybody knows that, too!"

17

Susanne hardly ever called me Earl, except when we happened to meet at a social function outside the department. At work, even after all these years, she insisted the chain of command be evident and clear to all our staff. The practice was one of the many fundamentals she adhered to that ensured we ran a tight ER. Realizing the damage Rossit could cause had obviously rattled her.

Still, I appreciated the spontaneous outburst of support. "Thanks Susanne," I said, trying to sound a lot less worried than I was, but her frown deepened.

"Are you sure you want to work? It's not that busy, and you could do the light cases."

"Sanders had been a light case," I muttered without thinking.

Susanne started, then slowly nodded. "Yeah," she said quietly. "I know what you mean."

In ER, the so-called little cases were the sleepers—the ones that occasionally hid something rare but lethal. For most competent physicians, the sicker the patient, the more straightforward the treatment. The already dead—a cardiac arrest—were the most routine cases of all.

"The shape I'm in right now, Susanne, I'm probably safest in resus." I left her standing there with a doubtful look on her face as I headed toward the triage desk to find the sickest patient we had.

For the next twenty minutes, a bad asthmatic in severe respiratory distress kept me busy enough to push away any thoughts of Sanders and Rossit, but when I got to more routine cases, those thoughts, always present at the back of my mind, came to the fore. Each time I began listening to a person's complaint and attempted to seem empathetic, I felt like a fraud. I kept imagining Sanders's eyes. Remembering her expression. *Are you going to disappoint me too?*

Then her son phoned.

I'd been sewing up the lip of a five-year-old girl who'd been dancing on a slippery staircase in her stocking feet.

"Dr. Garnet," the clerk had summoned, poking her head in the door of our minor surgery room. "There's a Mr. Harold Miller from University Hospital on line three inquiring about the Sanders woman."

"I'll be right there," I said, tensing.

I finished my suture and got to a phone. "Mr. Miller, it's Dr. Earl Garnet. No doubt you're calling about your mother?" I kept swallowing, but my mouth was dry.

"Dr. Garnet! I was in the medical library at the university, and our lab secretary reached me only a few minutes ago. A nurse from your ICU called and said you'd admitted Mother with a diagnosis of pneumonia and septic shock?" His speech was fast and clipped. He sounded tense, but I couldn't tell if he was also angry.

"I'm afraid she's very ill, Mr. Miller. I'm glad you're on your way," I said as evenly as I could. I hated having these conversations on the phone, especially this one. Without seeing the face of the person I was talking to, I couldn't fully judge the impact of my words. I wasn't going to lie, but I didn't want to let something slip out that would hand my head to his lawyer, either.

"But Dr. Garnet, what happened? I talked with her around ten last night. She said that she saw you yesterday afternoon and you told her everything was okay, that it was just the flu."

"You saw her last night? And she was all right?" I'd assumed she must have deteriorated from the time she left ER. If she was still apparently not too sick after ten, she must have gone septic in less than twelve hours.

"No, I didn't see her," he answered. "I phoned her at home from the hospital. I was on call for the night. She sounded like you said, like she had the flu."

Then wham, the kind of virulence we shouldn't see in an otherwise healthy woman in her fifties. I suddenly felt more compelled to explain that riddle than to try to avoid being sued. Perhaps I'd do both.

"Mr. Miller, I apologize for questioning you on the phone about this, but your mother's infection puzzles me. It's not typical, and perhaps you can help us find the answers. Do you want to meet me in ICU?"

"Sure, but what do you mean 'not typical'?"

"The prodrome was unusually quick."

"What did the Gram stain show she has? Come on, Dr. Garnet, what are you not telling me?"

Damn! I'd really wanted to do this face-to-face, but I didn't want to cut him off. He was sounding increasingly alarmed.

"I'm afraid the Gram stain of her sputum showed staphylococcus," I said as calmly as I could.

"Staph!" he exclaimed, incredulous. "My mother has a staph pneumonia?"

I listened to him breathing a few seconds as he presumably digested the odds against his mother's survival. As a chief technician, he'd certainly have enough medical knowledge to know how grave her prognosis was. "Look, Mr. Miller, come over, and let's talk here—"

"Do you think it was hospital acquired? You know she'd been on vacation for five days." His voice was becoming much more agitated, but he seemed determined to continue on the phone. "Don't leave me hanging," he ordered.

I had to reply. "Yes, I *was* worried that it was a hospital-acquired organism," I began, "and that she might have MRSA, so I covered her with vancomycin." Let him satisfy his immediate need for answers, I decided. It might help him prepare for seeing his mother so ill. "Even with her being on vacation," I continued, "she could have been carrying dormant organisms from the hospital in her upper respiratory tract, as you're no doubt aware. Have you had any recent problems with staphylococcus infections at University Hospital?"

"Not lately, but we have had MRSA in the past. I know because I'm on the infection control board, along with your wife, Janet."

I cringed at his innocent use of Janet's name. It was like an unwitting rebuke, and I prayed he'd never know how I'd resented his mother for making the same reference yesterday. "Your mother said she was in good health until the morning of her first visit here. As far as you know, was that accurate?"

"Yes. She hadn't anything wrong with her that I knew of, apart from her smoking."

"Might she have minimized a five-day flulike illness? Ignored the symptoms? Not mentioned them to you?"

I heard a gentle chuckle. "Dr. Garnet, my mother never minimized anything." His voice relaxed a little; it was lower, less strained. Perhaps having a clinical discussion, even over the phone, was helping him get over his initial shock.

So I continued with my questions. To be honest, I found myself especially wanting to know the details of what had happened to her after I'd sent her home. That her son had talked to her so many hours after I'd discharged her and she still wasn't very sick somehow made me feel less guilty. "Last night, did she complain to you about dizziness?"

"Not really. She said she felt a bit unsteady. But I assumed it was the usual lightheadedness that went with the flu. Why?"

Careful now, I thought before answering, still not wanting to hang myself legally. "Her prodrome, and this may be off the wall, well, it suggested another not so common but very bad infection."

"What are you talking about?" His voice rose sharply.

Damn! I was upsetting him again, I thought, as I tried once more to calm him. "Mr. Miller, please, it's all supposition right now. Come over, and we can talk further, right after you see your mother."

"What rare and very bad infection?" he demanded, his anger now clearly evident.

Great choice of words, Garnet, I cursed to myself. "Mr. Miller, I repeat, I have no proof, and ID thinks I'm nuts even bringing it up—"

"Answer me!" he snapped.

"It reminded me of Legionnaires' disease," I finally admitted.

"Oh Jesus!" he said, and hung up on what sounded like a sob.

I'd retreated to my office, a cubby hole located in a back corridor away from ER. My secretary, Carole Lamont, had phoned in sick for the day, so thankfully I was alone.

I sat at my desk without the lights on and wondered what else I could do wrong. A small window in the outside wall was too grimy to see through, but it let in a little gray illumination. The effect was positively cheery compared to my mood.

I'd botched Sanders's first visit. My attempt to comfort her son was worse than a disaster. Instead of reassuring him as I'd hoped, I'd frightened him even more with my questions and talk of Legionnaires' disease. Why hadn't I just kept my goddamned mouth shut?

Because I was increasingly impatient to know everything about this infection that had tricked me.

Maybe Rossit was right. My guilt was making me overcompensate and screwing up my judgment.

I'd better warn ICU that Mr. Miller was on his way over, nicely primed, I thought, reaching for my phone. Stewart Deloram, their chief, would have to deal with him personally. If there was any hope of settling him down, Stewart could do it. I'd learned firsthand when I'd once been a patient of his how supportive he could be. Perhaps, despite the mess I'd made of things, Miller could still trust the ICU staff enough to help him cope with what lay ahead for his mother.

"Dr. Deloram is in the main auditorium attending an administrative meeting," his secretary announced.

"Shit!"

"I beg your pardon!"

"Sorry. I just remembered where I'm suppose to be. I'll find him there."

I ran out the door and headed for the huge reception hall. The meeting I'd forgotten in my preoccupation with Sanders was a doozy. The boards of St. Paul's Hospital and University Hospital had decided it would save money if they completely amalgamated the administration of the two institutions. The gathering I was rushing to was a combined assembly of all chiefs to begin the process of naming a common chairperson for each clinical department. It was the political equivalent of sudden death. For weeks now administrators and department heads at every level had been squaring off and vying to keep their turf. There'd be winners and losers, and needless to say, the struggle for ascendancy was sometimes outright nasty.

I had mixed feelings about it all. The losers would remain department directors in their own hospital under the authority of an absentee chairperson. In my case, if I lost out to my counterpart at University Hospital, I'd still be in charge of ER at St. Paul's and there'd be a whole lot fewer meetings. But without the mantle of being chief, I'd have no way of protecting emergency services from loopy policies adopted in other parts of the hospital. In a time of cutbacks, I'd had my fill of them.

I hurried through a double set of doors and entered a noisy group of about a hundred people. They were standing, talking animatedly, and balancing paper plates of cocktail wieners and glasses of variously colored juices—the luncheon fare of austerity. Our home crowd was still decked out in their lab coats; the visitors wore suits. Obviously the formal part of the assembly was over.

I immediately started looking for Deloram. A few of my acquaintances razzed me for being late and joked that I'd already lost my job, but they didn't seem very merry. I also greeted a few friends of Janet's whom I'd met at various University Hospital functions, but I didn't stop to talk. I found Deloram at the edge of the crowd near the stage, conversing earnestly with Sean Carrington, the chief of surgery. Whereas Deloram was medium sized, dark haired, and meticulously groomed, Sean was tall with permanently tousled red hair and a bushy mustache—a sort of Yosemite Sam in a white coat.

"Earl!" he greeted me enthusiastically. "What say we settle this nonsense like the old gladiator movies. Pair us off right here, using wienie toothpicks—'We who are about to die' and all that stuff."

In spite of my problem, I couldn't help but grin. The man always tried to keep us laughing.

"Sorry, Sean, but I need Stewart here for an emergency," I announced, stepping up and gently taking Deloram by the arm to steer him toward a nearby doorway.

"Of course," said Sean, turning away. "I was just going back to the food table."

"What's up?" Deloram asked as soon as we were out of earshot.

I hastily explained all about Sanders, and my bungled attempt to talk to her son. "You'd better hurry," I concluded. "It won't take him long to get here."

"I'll handle him," he said curtly, handing me his unfinished plate of wieners and some kind of green juice. "Try not to worry," he called over his shoulder as he rushed out the door.

I was left eyeing the remains of his lunch, wondering if I should eat something. The increasing tightness in my stomach said no, and I dumped everything in a nearby bin.

I did rejoin Sean at the food table, where he was busily loading up with brownies. Other people were starting to leave, and thankfully Rossit was nowhere to be seen.

"They should take those out of your pay," I teased, pretending to grab at Sean's plate.

"What pay," he mumbled, his mouth full.

"Seriously, what happened here today?"

He swallowed a few times. "No specific appointments yet. But Hurst made it pretty clear he intended to give up the chair of some services in order to keep anesthesia and internal medicine chaired by St. Paul's."

"Terrific!" I groaned, not surprised. Paul Hurst was a former surgeon and now our VP medical and acting CEO. He pretty well ran the hospital the way he liked. The two chiefs of the departments in question were wimps he could easily control. Sean and I, however, challenged him whenever we felt he was out of line and were right enough times that he couldn't fire us. "Obviously he's found a new way to cut us down to size," I added.

"Oh, what makes you think that?" replied Sean, pointing to draw my attention to the center of the room. There was Hurst, tall, gray-haired, and pale as always, laughing heartily with Arnold Pinter, the diminutive chief of internal medicine. Arnold usually slouched, and from a distance he reminded me of a field mouse on the lookout for hawks, except today. He was grinning broadly and looking as happy as I'd ever seen him.

The two men suddenly caught sight of Sean and me watching them. As if to underline my suspicions, they immediately stopped smiling, turned, and walked away with their heads huddled together.

"Maybe they're afraid we can read lips," Sean commented.

We made small talk after that, but I sensed he was worried. For all his clowning around, I knew that he loved being a surgeon, and that being chief of surgery was his passion.

Minutes later the page came booming over the PA.

"Dr. Garnet! Call ICU immediately! Dr. Garnet! Call ICU!"

It was loud enough to momentarily hush the room, but conversations started up again as I ran for a wall phone. In my rush I dropped the receiver while punching in the familiar numbers. It was Deloram who picked up.

"Earl?" he asked, obviously expecting my call. I could hear shouting in the background.

"What the—"

"He beat me here, Earl, and what's worse, the nurses had shown him the chart, as a professional courtesy. The note Rossit had circled practically jumped out at him, and he's livid. Worse, he wants to transfer his mother out of here and back to University Hospital. The trip's out of the question—she's too unstable—but I can't talk sense to the man."

Christ, I thought. Then I saw a familiar head towering above all the others in the room. "Stewart, there's someone here Miller will listen to. Cam hasn't left yet. Tell Miller he'll be up in a minute!" I ordered, hanging up without waiting for his reply.

I made my way through the thinning crowd toward the blond-haired, slim man I'd spotted. In his mid-thirties and dressed in a navy blue sports jacket, tan pants, and a light blue shirt open at the collar, he resembled more a movie star than what he was—chief of the Department of Infectious Diseases and director of laboratory services at University Hospital. In any group he was a head taller than the rest and had to continually lean down to hear what others were saying. That he spent a lot of time surrounded by physicians and residents was a tribute to his brilliance. And unlike Rossit, he was every bit a gentleman.

I'd met him several times with Janet and had even been lucky enough to be seated near him at several of her hospital dinner parties. His funny stories were legendary. More pertinent was that he was Miller's ultimate supervisor.

Having no time for niceties, I pushed through the circle of people around him. "Excuse me, Cam," I interrupted, drawing irritated stares from the people I jostled. Cam himself smiled and said, "Hi, Earl. How come your lovely wife isn't here? We could make her chief of everything and solve—"

"I'm sorry, Cam. We've got a big problem in ICU with one of the nurses from your hospital. It's an ID case, and we need your help fast."

His smiling face immediately became serious. "Of course," he replied. "Excuse me, everyone; it's back to reality." There were appreciative chuckles from his audience as he strode away with me and we headed toward the door. I almost had to run to keep up. I talked as we went.

"Her name is Phyllis Sanders, and of course you know her son, Harold Miller."

"Harold? Certainly I know him. We just named him our director of laboratory technicians. He's very conscientious. His mother works in OB doesn't she?"

"That's right. She's in her fifties, smokes, but otherwise has no major risk factors. I saw her yesterday in ER and sent her home with what seemed like a mild, one-day history of the flu. She'd been on vacation and lived nearby, so she came to us instead of going to your staff health service. Unfortunately, she was returned to us by ambulance this morning in septic shock due to pneumonia."

We swung through the doors to the stairwell and started up. He took the steps two at a time. He showed no reaction to what I'd just told him.

"The Gram stain showed staph," I puffed, "but the short prodrome bothered me." We swung around the first landing and continued toward the second. "It reminded me of something else. ID here thinks I'm crazy, but . . ." I had to stop speaking for a few seconds to catch my breath while we continued to run. Cam was half a staircase ahead of me. "It made me think of *Legionella*," I said, far too loudly.

He stopped in midstride.

"Pardon?" he said, turning to look down at me as I caught up to him.

"I know it's foolish, Cam, but when you see the labs and review her initial symptoms . . ." I trailed off.

I'd expected him to be bemused, skeptical even, though not as rude as Rossit had been. Instead, he was staring at me as if he'd seen Banquo's ghost.

"Cam, are you all right?" I asked, dismayed at the shaken expression on his face.

"It's not foolish at all, Earl," he said finally. "If you're right, and frankly I hope you're not, then she'd be the third perfectly healthy nurse from our hospital in the last six months to have contracted *Legionella*."

Chapter 4

It was my turn to feel astonished.

"But that—that's impossible," I stammered after getting over my initial shock. "It's against the odds. And Janet's said nothing about *Legionella*'s being a problem at your hospital. Besides, we'd all have known about—"

"That's what's so bizarre, Earl," he interrupted, turning and continuing up the stairs. "We *don't* have a problem with *Legionella*. We checked everywhere, for each case, and there was no source we could find. Neither nurse had been involved in treating patients with *Legionella*, no other staff members had the disease, and no pools of the organism could be found in water distribution sites throughout the building. Believe me, we looked, especially after the second case. We had to conclude they weren't nosocomial infections."

He stopped at the third floor landing and held the door for me. He obviously knew where our ICU was. "The really creepy thing is the timing," he added. "Those two nurses also developed their symptoms shortly after going on vacation."

"What?" I exclaimed, stopping. "Go on. You're kidding me."

"I'm afraid not. The first became ill five days after leaving work, the second within seven days of the start of her holiday." He gestured we should continue walking.

"Did they vacation together?" I asked, starting along the corridor.

"No such luck. There were snide jokes about shared hot tubs, but in fact they didn't even know each other. One worked in ICU; the other was an OR nurse. Nothing in common whatsoever, and they were away at different times. The second case spooked us so much we even had an ID team check out her home and where she vacationed, but again, there was nothing. That's why I hope you're wrong. It's going to shake up a lot of people at our hospital, including me, if this is a third case."

He pressed the metal disk outside the sliding doors.

"Did they recover?" I asked.

"One died. The ICU nurse not only survived but is back on the job," he answered, lowering his voice as we stepped into our own ICU.

It was quiet. Deloram was leaning against a desk in the nursing station, his arms folded. Beside him stood a young man dressed in a green isolation gown who I presumed was Harold Miller. He had closely cropped blond hair and, though of medium height, broad shoulders and a compact muscular physique that was evident even with the loose clothing. He immediately looked up as we entered. Beside him was little Gary Rossit.

I felt my stomach turn. Rossit looked furious to see Cam on his turf.

"Harold," said Cam, quickly striding up and putting his hands on the man's shoulders. "I happened to be here and heard about your mother. I just wanted to drop by and offer my support."

Miller mumbled, "Thank you."

Rossit seemed about to protest.

Cam gestured to him, "I've always said Dr. Rossit here is one of the best ID experts in Buffalo. I'd trust him to care for me or a member of my family anytime." He glanced around and found a place to sit down. "What do you think of this case, Gary?" he asked.

Rossit's ego was as big as his mean streak. Praise from the likes of Cam stopped him cold. "Why, I, well . . ."

"Let's take a look at the chart," suggested Cam as he pulled up another chair and invited Rossit to sit beside him.

Deloram grinned and winked at me from behind Rossit's back.

Miller stood very still watching the unlikely Mutt and Jeff pair of infectious disease specialists huddle over his mother's records and talk quietly together.

I didn't know if I should say something to the man or leave him be. I wasn't even sure if he'd read my identity badge and knew who I was. While I hesitated about what to do, he slowly turned and looked up at his mother in her isolation cubicle at the far end of the room. Its interior was more brightly lit than the rest of the unit. He watched her lying there, a tube in every orifice, wired to total life support, and said quietly but very coldly, "It reminds me of a glass coffin, Dr. Garnet, right out of the Snow White story she used to read to me when I was a kid. Dr. Rossit says you put her there. I *really* don't want to talk to you. Just get the hell away from me."

* * *

"You can't do that, Michael!"

"Can't I? With two other nurses contracting *Legionella* in the last six months!" he said incredulously.

We were alone in my office where I'd taken him so we could talk in private. Michael had handled ER alone without a problem while I'd been running around about Miller. What he wasn't coping with very well was Cam's revelation.

"I accredited that hospital a month ago," he continued. "There was no mention of *Legionella* in the minutes of the Infection Control Committee then. If those sons of bitches think they can cover up . . ."

I let him rant. His tirade wasn't bothering anybody, and I was still trying to shake off what had happened in ICU. Miller's cold anger wasn't a surprise, nor was Rossit's quick attempt to stir him up, but both were unnerving. Rossit must have heard them paging me and—like a shark catching the scent of blood—rushed over to see if it was about Sanders.

"Why shouldn't I check them out?" Michael demanded, grabbing my full attention.

"Because they'd say it was an abuse of your powers as a hospital accreditor for the state of New York," I answered. Accreditors were the medical equivalent of tax auditors. They checked out hospitals to assure they complied with the clinical and academic standards necessary for public safety. Only the most credible physicians were chosen to render these judgments, and Michael Popovitch was chosen more often than most. By convention, they always assessed hospitals other than their own to protect themselves from retaliation by their colleagues and administration should they issue a particularly critical report.

"Nonsense!" he scoffed. "I worked on the Sanders case. Nosocomial infection is suspected. She's a nurse at University Hospital. Doesn't that give me cause to alert them to a possible problem? I'll call Cam tonight. If he's as forthright with me as he was with you, I'll offer to look at the charts of those other two cases. I'll tell him that at this stage it could be kept informal. Believe me, with the jockeying for primacy going on between the two hospitals because of the amalgamation, he'll jump at the chance to settle this privately. The last thing University Hospital wants right now is a public review of a *Legionella* scare."

"I don't know, Michael—"

"A follow-up visit's in order here, Earl, and if your tests for *Le-*

gionella are positive, then University Hospital is going to get hit
with a full official visit from our team. Who knows if they're as
clean as they think? One teaching hospital I visited that claimed it
had never had *Legionella* had missed the diagnosis in fourteen percent of its nosocomial infections. We found the organism in two-
thirds of the hospital's water supply sites—drinking water, shower
water, whirlpool bath water—"

"Cam assured me they'd checked all that," I interrupted.

"Hey, Earl. He's the best, but he's under the same kind of pres-
sures to cut costs and cover up bad news that we are. Besides, the
organism's even harder to find in water than it is in sputum, and the
tests are costly. Bottom line, Earl, there's something really screwy
going on over there, and it could be dangerous for anybody in the
place, patients or staff."

I knew he was using me as a sounding board, to test just how
defensible his twisting of the rules was going to be. But instead of
continuing to try to dissuade him, I found myself wanting him to
go, to find out what I'd been up against in the Sanders case after
all. And I found myself thinking of Janet. "Yeah, I suppose you're
right," I answered.

I drove home in the rain around 6:00. I wanted Janet to be there. I
wanted to hold our baby son, Brendan. I wanted sanctuary.

What I got at the back door was our fifty-pound poodle, Muffy.
As she leaped and wiggled for attention, I managed to get by her and
into the kitchen. The house seemed quiet. A note on the kitchen table
from Amy Hollis, our live-in nanny, informed me that she'd gone to
bed early, that Brendan had been fed, bathed, and put in his crib, and
that Janet had phoned to say she'd be at a meeting until 10:00.

The only one thrilled to have me to herself was Muffy. I hooked
up her leash and took her outside. She normally loved walks, but she
hated rain. We were back in no time.

After drying her paws and giving her a biscuit, I headed upstairs
to the baby's room. Though it wasn't completely dark outside, I
turned on the night-light when I reached the side of his crib. He was
lying on his back, his little fists up by his head. I never tired of
watching him, even in his sleep.

Unable to resist, I reached down and picked him up. He was still
so small and weightless that I held him easily in one arm as I pulled a
rocking chair over near his bedroom window. He gave a few little

grunts, moved his fists around, and found his thumb. Three half-hearted sucks, and he was back to sleep. I sat with him listening to the rain until the last gray light of evening had turned to night.

Then I put him back in his crib, had a bowl of soup, and climbed into bed to wait for Janet.

We had started making love in our sleep, unconsciously moving against each other, becoming aroused, until I awoke already in her, both of us thrusting and straining to climax.

"God, where did that come from?" whispered Janet afterward, rolling over to lie against me.

I was flopped on my back, still trying to get my breath. It wasn't the first time we'd made love since Brendan was born, but it had felt like it. The fierceness had surprised me.

"We gotta have sex more often," I said. "That was incredible."

Janet gave a throaty chuckle. "Three A.M. feedings and a live-in nanny make that kind of hard. But pent-up lust *is* nice."

"I didn't even hear you get home."

"You're the perfect obstetrician's spouse, Earl. You can sleep through anything."

"Do you think *we* woke anybody?" I asked, listening for sounds from the baby's room. There were none.

"Do you think we made him a brother?" asked Janet, nestling her head against my chest.

"Janet!"

"Hey, you didn't exactly give me much warning, you know. I may deliver babies, but I can't change the rules of nature, especially that one about how they're made." She raised her head and looked at me, resting on her elbow and cupping her chin on her hand. In the moonlight from our bedroom window, I saw her smile. "You aren't ready for the next one? What's so hard on you about having another baby, apart from having a little fun with me?"

"I thought you might want to wait a little bit."

"Really! I may be your tall sexy blond, but I'm also forty-one, and it's family time if you really want all those other little Garnets we talked about."

I grinned. "No argument from me there, ma'am. Just let me know when and where you next need my services, and I'll be ready."

She giggled, then lay down and snuggled up at my side. "Can you fifty-year-olds do it more than once a week?" she asked slyly.

"Forty-eight, smart-ass."

"And a half," she corrected sleepily, laying her thigh over my groin.

"Do you think Amy will hear us?" I whispered, feeling encouraged.

"Earl, I think she knows we do it."

"I love you, Janet," I declared, suddenly clinging to her, trying to keep away thoughts of the hospital. Damn it! I thought, don't rob us of this.

"You just want my smart ass," she murmured into my ear while sliding on top of me and straddling my hips.

Brendan started to cry.

Three A.M.

I groaned. "Oh no."

I did the night feedings.

Twenty minutes later I was sitting in our darkened living room holding Brendan and listening to him smack up the remains of his bottle. Even by the streetlight I could see his brilliant blue eyes as he kicked and punched with his pudgy little limbs, then grabbed the rubber nipple and noisily finished gorging himself. I settled back on the couch, refusing to be distracted by my worries, and tried to enjoy the spectacle. His funny small fingers were practically holding the plastic container.

"I gave birth to him; you can feed him," had been Janet's decree on the division of labor. Her real worry was being called away from him all the time for deliveries. "Besides," she'd added, "don't guys your age have to get up at night anyway?"

Nearly six months old, Brendan was sleeping through most of the time, but occasionally, he got an urge for the good old days. And I didn't mind, not even with tonight's interruption.

The phone rang, and I snapped up the receiver. If it was for me, I didn't want Janet wakened needlessly.

"Dr. Garnet here."

"Oh, Dr. Garnet, it's the case room at University Hospital. I'm sorry to bother you, but we need Dr. Graceton."

"No problem. I'll get her for you."

But already Janet had picked up the bedside extension. "It's okay, Earl. I've got it."

I hung up, then sat watching Brendan suck at the dregs of his feed. I was putting him over my shoulder to burp him when Janet descended the stairs in her OR greens, obviously having been called in for a delivery. Even in that shapeless garb, she was a terrific-looking woman. She finished hooking up her hair into a ponytail with an elastic band, then walked over to take Brendan from me. "I've got twenty minutes. Why don't you make us some coffee?"

Brendan replied with a loud burp and spewed out some formula onto Janet's shoulder. "That's okay, my little angel," she said. "This outfit will see a lot worse before the night's out."

On my way to the kitchen, I had to step over a large, dark mound in the hallway that gave a low growl. Muffy had gone into a sulk when Brendan arrived and moved out of our bedroom into the downstairs hallway to sleep. Tripping over her was now part of the nighttime feeding routine.

Five minutes later Brendan was asleep on the couch between Janet and me. It was 3:40. Muffy had deigned to come and lie at our feet but wouldn't look at the baby.

"Longest mope I ever saw," said Janet, reaching down to ruffle the drooping ears.

"Are you going to be back for breakfast?" I asked, hoping for a chance to talk.

"No, I'll stay at the hospital. I've got a lot to do today."

I felt a twinge of disappointment but wasn't going to say anything. Janet looked straight at me. "Cam told me what happened with Phyllis Sanders, Earl. The meeting tonight was an emergency session of his Infection Control Committee. My, you certainly set the cat among the pigeons. Even your buddy Michael Popovitch showed up later, as an observer. He got Cam on his cellular halfway through our session—calling about Sanders—and got himself invited over. The trouble is, none of us came up with anything."

I looked at her, astounded. "Why did he act so quickly?"

"He had to. Whether Sanders has staph pneumonia with an unheard of prodrome, or the equally unlikely combination of *Legionella* and staph, the nosocomial implications have to be looked at. Besides, he's really spooked, like the rest of us, by the mystery of why and how the nurses got sick only after they left on vacation. Two cases might be a troubling coincidence, but he couldn't sit on a third."

I didn't know what to add. "Did he tell you about Rossit?" I asked, after a few seconds.

"He mentioned it, privately, and told me not to worry. But I'd like you to tell me what happened."

* * *

I must have talked for five minutes. The whole time Janet cradled Brendan and stroked Muffy's ears. Even my admission of how I'd resented Sanders didn't change her expression. She simply listened and let me unburden myself. I felt knots I didn't know I had let go in my stomach.

When I finished, she kept staring out the window. I waited for her to say something, but she remained silent. "Janet?" I asked, starting to feel uneasy.

"They were all bitches," she said in a faraway voice.

"Janet!" I protested, not believing what I'd heard.

She turned to me, suddenly becoming animated. "You're right, Earl. It's a terrible thing to say, even to think, and that's why no one has seen what those three nurses have in common."

"C'mon Janet, you can't call—"

"Earl, Phyllis Sanders has always made people resent her. Doctors and nurses at University Hospital have been resenting her for years without your giving them permission to do it."

"Janet!" I protested again but smiled in spite of myself.

"She's exactly like the other two nurses in that regard. I know, because time and time again my patients have complained to me about all three of them."

I listened without another word. I had no idea where she was going with this.

"You know the kind of nurse who makes a patient feel humiliated for needing help, who seems to resent their demands, particularly the emotional demands put on them by those in their care. I'm not talking about the occasional loss of patience; we all have those. I mean systematic cruelty in little ways—delaying giving a bed pan, holding back pain medication, leaving someone on a toilet too long, accusing someone who's afraid or in pain of 'being a baby.'"

I winced. I'd had to reprimand some of my own staff for such behavior, and they weren't all confined to nursing.

"Sanders had some nerve invoking my name," Janet continued. "I've forbidden her to go anywhere near my patients in the delivery room. The second timers insist on it."

"So what are you suggesting?" I asked, feeling uneasy again.

"I'm suggesting that they're women who make people angry."

I sat there stunned. "My God!" was all I could reply at first. What she was implying couldn't be. "You think that someone is deliberately infecting them?"

She sighed and gave Muffy's ears an extra rub. Brendan smacked his lips, and Janet smiled down at him. "It's crazy, I know. But, well, maybe I had those kind of crazy thoughts for a reason."

If there was one thing I knew about Janet, she always had a reason, for everything.

She looked up from watching the baby. "Did you ever hear rumors about the Phantom of University Hospital?" she asked, her smile for Brendan quickly fading.

"The what?" I said, not believing I had heard her correctly. "Come on; give me a break."

She flushed. "Hey! Don't laugh. It was serious at the time."

"Janet, what the hell are you talking about?" I still thought she was kidding.

She sighed again and stared out the window. "A few years ago there were some incidents that were brought to the attention of the ID committee. They were little things, but the staff was worried. People would suddenly have unexplained but explosive vomiting and think something had been slipped into their food or coffee, but nothing was found. Another time an orderly came down with a brief bout of bradycardia, dizziness, asthma, and diarrhea. He was sure he'd been poisoned but couldn't prove it. There were other occurrences, all brief, all nonspecific, and thank God, nothing serious or fatal."

"Were they poisoned?"

Before answering she put Brendan over her shoulder and let him nestle there. "We were only responsible for checking that it wasn't something nosocomial, but as far as I know, the events were never explained by anyone else either."

"Hence, the story of a Phantom," I surmised.

"You got it. People started joking to each other to be good or the Phantom would get them."

"Wait a minute. You're not saying these victims were like your nurses."

"Let's just say there wasn't a lot of sympathy for them."

"Did they ever suspect anyone in particular?"

"I'm afraid not."

"Is it still going on?"

Janet looked up from adjusting Brendan's blanket. "After what's happened in the last six months," she answered, "that may have become a very scary question."

Then the phone rang. Janet grabbed the receiver and answered, "I'm on my way," without waiting for the caller to speak. She handed me Brendan and was gone.

Chapter 5

Most ER doctors learn to sleep when and where they can. Normally I would have grabbed another hour and a half before heading back to St. Paul's. But after what Janet told me, I knew my sleep was finished for the night. I returned Brendan to his crib, poured myself a second cup of coffee, and stared out the living room window. Over the tops of the nearby roofs and trees I saw a flash of lightning in the distance. I counted about ten seconds before I heard a low roll of thunder.

I kept trying to dismiss Janet's suspicions. There was no way I could conceive of by which *Legionella* could be transmitted to an individual and be made specifically to infect him or her while sparing others. That the victim could also be kept unaware of the attack seemed even more impossible, if they had been unaware. The OR nurse had died. I had no idea if she'd been able to answer any questions before her death. Certainly Phyllis Sanders was in no condition to talk, whether or not she turned out to have *Legionella* as well as staph. The likelihood of her impending death went through me like a pain.

I assumed Cam had questioned the ICU nurse who had survived. Yet, if Janet was the first to consider the infections were deliberately inflicted, then Cam hadn't known the right questions to ask. What would be that nurse's response now if she were prompted to consider the infection as an attack?

She'd think we were loony was my instant reply, because whatever unsavory personality trait the three nurses had shared, the possibility they were all victims of a resurrected phantom stopped cold at the same unsolved puzzle I'd started with—how could each of them have been infected?

I got a third cup of coffee and mulled this over. Maybe it couldn't be done. Maybe Janet was wrong, and the three women being nurses who were obnoxious was a fluke. To be honest, if anyone besides Janet had tried to suggest such a wild idea as a murderer being behind the *Legionella* mystery, I'd have laughed in his face. Yet there I was, unable to toss off the idea and not at all comfortable with the logic that it could not be done simply because I couldn't figure out a way to infect three women. Janet's instincts were too often proven right.

She possessed a rare gift—a brilliant intellect combined with plain common sense—that made her judgments sound and her insights something I'd learned to listen to or ignore at my peril. In University Hospital, where her quick mind and clinical accuracy were legendary, she was regarded as a treasure and was especially known for her ability to look at the same symptoms and signs her colleagues had seen and to think what no one else had thought.

They were all women who made people angry. The words kept rolling through my thoughts like the ever-increasing thunder overhead, and were joined by another idea. If she were right and the *Legionella* cases were somehow part of a macabre vendetta being carried out at her hospital, then asking questions about those cases could be dangerous. Should I warn Michael?

By the time the rain began to pelt against the glass panes in front of me, my stomach was churning on enough caffeine for the entire day.

Dawn was little more than a gray smudge in the east when I started out for St. Paul's at 6:15. The downpour was deafening on my car roof. It had soaked Muffy in the moments she'd taken to do her business in the lane, but she'd enjoyed the extra toweling I'd given her drying her off. When we'd finished, she'd playfully pranced about my feet, then had pawed at a rubber ring that was her favorite toy, inviting me to throw it. I'd bought her off instead with a dog biscuit, but as she'd watched me go upstairs to check on Brendan before I left, the sudden droop in her ears and sad-eyed stare from her brown eyes had left no doubts about what she'd thought of the deal. The object of her jealousy had still been sleeping off his early morning feed. He'd not even stirred when I'd gently stroked his head. Before leaving, I'd given a gentle tap on the door of the nanny's third-floor bedroom to warn her she was back in charge.

As I drove, the deluge increased and the wipers worked more like paddles trying to keep the windshield clear of water. By the time I reached the entrance to the expressway for downtown Buffalo, I found myself leaning forward straining to see the other cars ahead of me. We were all poking along at low speed, and the sign on the visor reminded me I was likely to be killed by the air bag if I had a collision while driving hunched up in my current position.

I pulled over and called St. Paul's on my car phone. As I was waiting on the line, the battering from the rain suddenly became so noisy that I could barely hear when someone finally answered, "ER, Mrs. Cooper speaking."

"Mrs. Cooper, it's Dr. Garnet," I shouted over the din. "I'm on my way, but for the moment I'm stuck in the storm; it's too hard to see so I pulled over. How are things there?"

"We just got an MVA that should have done what you did," she answered in a faraway voice. "Apart from that it's quiet, but if the storm keeps up, we're liable to get a lot more of the same." *MVA* referred to a victim of a motor vehicle accident. Through the window I could make out a few cars that were on the side of the road like myself. The rest formed a line of red taillights crawling up the expressway ramp, but overhead most of the vehicles already on the highway sped past in a swirl of blinding spray, giving credence to her grim prediction.

"Who's on?" I asked, wondering if we had enough veterans lined up to handle the possible carnage.

"Dr. Kradic's in with the MVA now. We're not sure who's taking over for days. It was suppose to be Dr. Popovitch, but he left a message that he'd signed out his shifts to a number of the other doctors until the end of the week. Apparently he's doing some kind of emergency audit at University Hospital. Your secretary's supposed to give us the revised schedule this morning."

"Shit," I muttered. I'd wanted to see Michael before he started poking around over there. I'd decided to warn him about Janet's suspicions.

"Pardon, Dr. Garnet. I didn't hear what you said."

"It's nothing, Mrs. Cooper, just me thinking out loud. Tell Susanne I'll be in as soon as I can."

I rang off and quickly dialed Michael's home number.

"Don't you two know the rest of the world sleeps now and then?" yawned his wife, Donna. She was a fun lady, about five years older than Michael, and had good-naturedly put up with my phone calls at atrocious hours for over a decade. She was also twenty weeks pregnant and a patient of Janet's.

"You think I'm a sleep disturber?" I answered. "Just wait until your own little bundle of joy arrives. My interruptions will seem like the good old days."

"Michael's already left, Earl," she answered with a chuckle. "He's headed to University Hospital but said he wouldn't be at any one extension once he got there. He told me to page him if I needed him."

"Thanks, Donna," I said. "How are you doing?"

"Janet says great. But it will be a relief to get the amnio over with." Donna was referring to a scheduled amniocentesis—the withdrawal of amniotic fluid from her uterus through a long needle—routinely done on pregnant women who were thirty-five or older. The fetal cells floating in the fluid would be examined for chromosome defects—particularly 21 trisomy, or Down's syndrome. I remembered Janet's and my own worry waiting for the results. The incidence wasn't common, but at one in two hundred, it wasn't so rare as not to cause concern.

"I know what waiting for that can be like," I commiserated, unable to change the odds for her. They were obviously on her mind.

"You men," she snorted. "It's us who get the needle, not you guys."

I laughed, appreciating her way with troubles—beating them back with wisecracks—and added, "Now you sound like Janet."

"Thanks. I'll take that as a compliment. Say hi to her for me." She hung up.

Gusts of wind were buffeting the car as I called locating at University Hospital.

"Hello, Dr. Garnet," the operator said. "Shall I find Janet for you?"

"No, I actually need one of my own guys who's doing an audit there—Dr. Michael Popovitch."

"At this hour?" she queried.

I glanced at my watch and saw it was only 6:35. "He may not have arrived yet, but would you try him anyway?" I asked. The rain peppering the sides of my car made it clear I wasn't going anywhere for the moment.

She was back on the line in less than a minute. "Security at the front desk has him signed in, but he's not answering. Do you know where he is? He may not be hearing the page."

There were a number of possibilities where he might start—labs, staff health, the medical records department—but at this hour there wouldn't be any secretaries or clerks around to help him. He may have chosen instead to log onto the hospital computer at a charting station in one of the many doctors' lounges, taking advantage of the early hour before the system got too busy. "No," I answered, "he could be anywhere. Would you mind trying again later?" I gave her my cellular number.

Visibility was still lousy, and the drumming sound of the rain was unrelenting. Should I drop by UH and try to find him? I wanted to get to St. Paul's as soon as possible. I wasn't scheduled to see patients this morning, but my job as chief meant I was the ultimate backup—twenty-four hours a day. While all our physicians were competent to manage patients, not everyone—especially not rookies—could manage the department in a crisis. Without knowing yet who was coming in for the day shift, it was better I be there in case Mrs. Cooper was right and the load got heavy. One pileup, and we could be overrun.

But the thought of Michael poking around UH completely unaware of Janet's suspicions left me uneasy. Besides, the hospital was less than ten minutes away, and unlike St. Paul's, which was downtown, it could be reached easily without using the freeway. I swung back out onto the road, bypassed the on-ramp, and headed toward a route Janet had taught me through quiet, still-deserted city streets.

Driving onto the large grounds of University Hospital was like a trip back to the turn of the century. The sprawling stone institution, built in the towering gothic style favored by Buffalo's early industrialists, had initially been a county hospital housing both the mentally and physically ill. It was surrounded by sweeping lawns under ancient shade trees that once had occupied a small army of gardeners and groundskeepers. Now many wings were shut down to save money, and the land was being auctioned off to developers.

The hospital itself had been acquired by the university in the fifties, and the acute care portions had been renovated, rewired, and brought up to snuff for the sixties. The high risk areas—ER, ICU, the case room, and the ORs—had all been updated repeatedly since. But changing times, economies, and ideology had led to the gradual closing of the psychiatric portions of the building. Now they remained dark and unused, cold gray structures with bars on the windows that made me shudder. Janet once told me that some of the basement rooms in these sections had earthen floors, and the places where inmates had been chained to the wall were still visible.

Cars were numerous as people were arriving to make the 7:00 start of sign-out rounds—the routine by which patients in hospitals the world over are handed off to the day shift. I used my university ID to get into the parking section for physicians, then ran for the front entrance with the rest of the staff—mostly nurses, residents, and orderlies, alongside the occasional doctor huddled in his or her lab coat. The rain wasn't as heavy as before, but I managed to get pretty wet anyway. Searing flashes of lightning crackled overhead, and glancing up, I saw a light mist had wrapped itself around the upper stories of the hulking building. No wonder they've got a phantom, I thought, rushing through a massive arch that supported a pair of gargoyles at its corners. While they guarded the doorway from up there, down here two overweight security officers manning a metal detector were doing the best they could to keep evil from entering the premises.

The high-domed foyer and marble floor inside belonged to the era when grand train stations had rivaled cathedrals and rail travel had held the height of promise for the city of Buffalo. The evocative construction had been a deliberate tribute to the railway barons who had provided the bulk of the money to build the place. Today, ironically, the structure was an unwitting memorial to what had been the real pride and joy of those same barons—the once magnificent Buffalo Central Station, now abandoned and disintegrating into ruin, along with so much else in the East Side section of the city.

My leather soles slipped on the polished stone floor while others around me flapped umbrellas and shook off the water from their soggy overcoats. Pocketing my glasses, which had immediately steamed up, I headed over to the house phones and dialed locating.

"This is a surprise," commented the operator, realizing I was calling from inside the building. I didn't often have cause to visit. My counterpart in ER here, William Tippet, was an insecure man ten years my junior who seemed to get nervous anytime I came around. As a result I stayed away as much as possible, and he kept joint meetings about our shared residency program to a minimum. It didn't help any that the residents called him Wild Bill Tippet behind his back.

"Yeah, it's even a surprise to me. Did you ever locate Dr. Popovitch?"

"Yes, I got off the phone with him a few minutes ago. We gave him your number, but he called back and said you weren't answering."

I'd left my cell phone in the car, not wanting to use it in the hospital. He must have just missed me.

"He's now up in the records department for staff health. He said to put you through if you rang again. I can get him if you want, or are you going there in person?"

"Just tell me where it is, and I'll find him myself." I got directions—third floor in one of the rear wings—and started out.

The bustle of activity in the corridors was familiar to any teaching hospital. The clinicians who had been running alongside me moments earlier were now striding through the hallways followed by groups of sleepy-looking residents, interns, and medical students.

Already the question-and-answer routine of clinical teaching had started. "What's the most common cause of fever two days postop?" I heard one staff man snap as he swept by at the head of his procession. "Pneumonia!" called out someone a short distance behind him. "What kind?" continued the staff man. "Right upper lobe, from aspiration," came an answer from a bit farther back in the line. "Any other ideas?" I couldn't hear the reply as they moved out of earshot. The medical students hustling along at the rear were recognizable by the shortness of their clinical jackets and the number of reference manuals they kept stuffed in their pockets. Some were trying to thumb through the well-worn texts for answers as they hurried to keep up with the rest.

Surgical patients from all over the hospital were being taken by stretcher to the OR for their early morning rendezvous with the knife. There was a lineup of them outside the elevator. Most were already beyond fear, snoozing under the effects of their preoperative sedation, but a few chatted nervously as they waited with the orderlies who were wheeling them to their fate. I used the stairs to save time.

As I climbed, the door on the landing above me pushed open and yet another group of students in lab jackets started down the steps toward me. Their instructor was still out of sight behind them, but I could hear his voice.

". . . most still don't order enough blood cultures or the right screening tests to reliably detect bacteremia . . ."

I'd reflexively stepped aside to let the group pass when I suddenly recognized the voice at the same instant I saw the broad-shouldered figure in a white coat follow the others through the door.

"You'll find out a lot of doctors aren't knowledgeable in their use of lab tests—" Miller was saying when he caught sight of me pressed against the wall. He froze, his mouth open in midsentence;

then his eyes narrowed, becoming hard and hurt looking. He swallowed once and started down, saying nothing to me as he passed. "Like I was saying," he continued, "as lab technicians you'll often feel frustrated at the tests ordered by doctors . . ." He didn't look back as he descended the rest of the stairs and strode out the door below.

When he and his entourage were gone, I let my breath out. I hadn't even been aware I'd been holding it. I felt a wave of perspiration prickle out of my skin. The pain in Miller's eyes had been frightful.

Staff health turned out to be on the same floor as administration in this hospital. It was easy to tell which was which, even without following the arrows and signs. I knew I was headed for the section without the lush carpeting and oversized offices. The clinic was also the only area where some people were actually at work. If this hospital was like St. Paul's, the gurus of management wouldn't make a showing much before 8:00.

At the front reception desk in the waiting room, clerks were busily sorting charts and preparing for the day. In the hallway behind them I could see nurses running in and out of a line of doorways carrying equipment trays, presumably stocking up the examining cubicles. A young man with crutches hobbled up to one of these nurses, who showed him into a room.

Before stepping up to the counter, I had to pause.

Miller's single accusing stare had left me shaken. Feelings of guilt, regret, and disgust over my decision to send his mother home had flooded through me. I had to compose myself, force a smile, and keep control of my voice to speak with an assurance I definitely didn't feel.

A clerk looked up from her work and, seeing me standing in the entranceway, asked, "Do you have an appointment?"

"No, I'm Dr. Garnet from St. Paul's Hospital. I'm looking for Dr. Popovitch who's supposed to be here doing an audit," I explained, walking up to her.

Her smile vanished immediately. "I'm sorry," she said, frowning disapprovingly, "but Dr. Mackie told me we were only to let Dr. Popovitch and Dr. Graceton in to see our records."

That caught me by surprise. "Janet's here?"

The lady's frown deepened. "Not yet, but Dr. Mackie called a few moments ago and told us to expect her as well. He didn't say a word about you or anyone else. It's quite irregular as it is, you know, looking at staff medical files even if it is a part of a hospital audit. If you are to be given access to our confidential records, I'm afraid it will be only on orders from Dr. Mackie."

"Look, I don't want to see any charts." I lied, but I had to reassure her. "I simply need to speak to Dr. Popovitch for a moment. It's business. We're colleagues at St. Paul's and—"

"It's okay, Madge, he's harmless," said Janet's voice from behind me. I hadn't heard the elevator. She must have come up by the stairs the same way I had. She swept toward us, the crisp lab coat she wore over her wrinkled greens flowing after her like a cape. "Believe it or not," she added, reaching me and fingering my own sodden coat, "this bedraggled specimen happens to be all I could come up with for a husband. Earl, meet Madge. She runs this place—has all the malingerers pegged even before the nurses and doctors get to them."

The transformation in Madge was instantaneous. "Oh my gosh, you're Janet's husband. You should have told me, Mr. Graceton, I mean, Dr. Garnet," she gushed, beaming me a warm smile. "I've heard so much about you." Then she flushed and turned to Janet. "I'm terribly sorry about being so abrupt, but when he asked for Dr. Popovitch—"

"Hey, think nothing of it, Madge. I treat him like that all the time." Janet chuckled, putting the poor lady at ease. "I'll take responsibility for him," she further reassured her, leading me by the arm through a nearby unmarked door.

"Nice meeting you, Madge," I called over my shoulder, letting myself be dragged along, presumably into the records department. The smile I got back from Madge let me know that the woman had no doubt Janet would keep me in line.

"What are you doing here?" I asked as soon as we were out of sight and walking through rows of filing cabinets.

"I phoned Cam this morning and got him to assign me to work with Michael. I figured it was the best way to check out what we were up against." She sounded nonchalant, but I felt a stab of alarm at her revelation. To have rousted Cam out of bed and then insist on taking time from her busy practice to work on the audit meant that her Phantom idea must be disturbing her as much as it disturbed me.

"Did you tell Cam about what you thought about the three nurses—"

"Of course!" she cut me off, sounding annoyed. "The silly man told me I was nuts. He actually ordered me to keep my mouth shut about it, as if I didn't know enough not to panic the whole hospital. He certainly won't listen until we get some solid proof about what's going on." She was leading me around a corner and toward a small table where I could see Michael studying a chart.

He looked up at the sound of our approaching voices.

"Does this guy know?" I asked, smiling at his surprised expression when he saw me.

A few minutes later, we'd also failed to convince him.

"Listen, you two," he replied, frowning deeply, "how the hell can *Legionella* be transmitted at will? And the idea that it's being used as a weapon in some weird vendetta is crazy! Beyond crazy! I'm surprised at both of you," he scolded. "The last thing we need are sensational rumors."

The three of us were huddled together around his table—more a desk meant for two—and we were speaking in terse whispers in case Madge or anyone else entered unexpectedly. Michael kept looking nervously over his shoulder, apparently more worried about being overheard than about what we'd said. At one point all of us thought we could hear someone in the rows of files behind us. Thinking it was Madge or one of the nurses, we immediately hushed up, but when I went to check, no one was there.

"And so what if all three women had complaints against them," he continued to scoff. "That puts them in the same company, unfortunately, with a lot of doctors and nurses." Turning to me he added, "Christ, when you're away and I'm acting as chief, there's at least one letter a week against someone or another in our department who was stupid, callous, or rude."

"Michael, these women were systematically cruel," countered Janet. "Cruel in a way that's hard to catch, easy to deny, and almost impossible to prove. But the patients know, Michael. They're the ones who clued me in. Over and over, they told me the same basic complaint; they were made to feel humiliated, helpless, and a burden in a hundred nasty little ways by those three nurses."

"So they were women who pissed patients off. Hell, like I said, that's apt to get them reported, not killed," snapped Michael. He was becoming increasingly impatient. "Aren't there other nurses your patients haven't liked? They didn't get *Legionella*."

"These nurses pissed people off in a certain way," Janet shot back, her frustration equally obvious.

"So why haven't these three got a high number of complaints

against them in common? That at least would be something objective to link them together."

Janet leaned forward and stabbed at him with her finger. "Michael, I'll bet you've had similar trouble with lots of residents who, when they're angry about something or somebody, take it out on their patients—maybe they rip a dressing off a little too aggressively or catheterize someone too roughly—then say, 'What did I do?' You know the game they're playing, Michael, and so do the patients, but let's see you prove it. Most of my ladies didn't even bother making a report. They simply vented their anger and swore they'd sign themselves out the next time one of those three came near them."

Michael threw his hands up. "Janet, do you know what people will say if you keep on with this? 'Next you'll be claiming a patient tried to kill those nurses with *Legionella* instead of registering a complaint against them.'" His sarcasm was blistering even though he continued to whisper.

Janet's eyes flashed. It was time for me to intervene. "Hey, Michael," I quickly admonished, "what the hell's the matter with—"

Janet waved me quiet. "What I'm *saying,* Michael," she whispered back at him through clenched teeth, "is that three women have all come down with mysterious infections neither you nor anyone else can explain. One of them's dead, one's dying, and the only thing the three of them have in common is they like to punish patients!"

Michael startled us both by slamming his hand down on the table. "What *I'm* saying, Janet, is that Earl can't afford this kind of talk!" he thundered.

She jerked back from him, stunned.

He glared at me. "Don't you realize how much trouble you're in? Hell, half of last night's shift at St. Paul's does. I found out when I got home from Cam Mackie's meeting and discovered I had an urgent message to call Susanne." He took a breath and then exhaled it slowly as he used to do with cigarette smoke before he quit. "Rossit seems to be coming down on you a lot harder than you initially realized," he stated. His frown deepened, but from what I now suspected was concern, not anger.

"Susanne told me about the run he took at you in ICU," he continued, speaking low and quickly, "and that you'd both put it down to his usual troublemaking. But by evening her nurses were hearing rumors that you were going to be charged with everything from missing vital signs through diagnostic errors to overprescribing antibiotics. Susanne was alarmed to the extent she thought you should be warned, yet felt uncomfortable calling you herself. I told her I'd speak to you this morning, but I've been lying awake half the night, unable to figure a way you can respond to what Rossit's mounting against you. Besides that, I've already heard rumors here that the woman's son, Miller, is equally stirred up and hostile as well. So for God's sake, man, going overboard with crazy stories about phantoms is the worst thing you can do for your credibility right now!"

I was staggered by the alarm in Michael's voice. It was in such sharp contrast to his easy reassurances yesterday that all would be well. Nor had I expected Rossit's lighting into me to grow into his leveling such damning broadsides against my reputation. That kind of assault was beyond the usual way he'd lit into others who'd misjudged an infection. Even Harold Miller's being so outspoken about my incompetence shook me up, though God knows the man had cause.

Taken together, all this bad-mouthing served as a supreme wake-up call. Rossit's antics in ICU yesterday—his criticisms and threats of a hostile case review—were suddenly more chilling, more credible than they'd first seemed.

Michael grasped both my shoulders and broke me out of my thoughts with a little shake. "I warn you, Earl," he said, his voice sounding strained, "if you persist with this nonsense, you'll hand Rossit and Miller your own head on a platter!"

I glanced over at Janet. She now appeared more startled than angry.

Chapter 6

I pulled away from the parking lot of University Hospital and started driving toward St. Paul's. The wipers slapped the rain back and forth more easily than before, like a pair of metronomes keeping time as I batted my thoughts around.

I glanced in my rearview mirror and decided I'd learned a lot during my visit to the gray building that was receding into the mist. I certainly had a whole new understanding of how much trouble I was in. I also had to admit that it was clearly going to be difficult to pursue Janet's suspicions about the Phantom and protect myself from Rossit at the same time.

Particularly galling was that I'd absolutely no idea why Rossit was singling me out for such particularly vicious treatment in the first place. Damn him anyway, I thought, wondering how much damage the spiteful little man could do. To be honest, as much as I'd always considered him a loathsome nuisance and a nasty troublemaker, I'd never really believed until now that he'd be able to cause lasting harm to a physician of my standing.

Working ER—being there day after day and pulling the tough cases through year after year—gives a doctor a certain status in a hospital. In my case I'd come to take it for granted that I didn't have to prove myself anymore. I knew my clinical judgment and diagnostic skills carried a certain weight with my colleagues, and I was used to them turning to me for help when they or their patients were in trouble.

In other words, for years I'd presumed my track record gave me immunity against having to defend myself in front of the likes of Rossit.

Apparently not anymore.

Could he actually help Miller convict me for negligence in a court of law? Miller's behavior on the stairs and his mouthing off had made it pretty clear his bitterness hadn't subsided any. Might the conviction lead to suspension, even a withdrawal of hospital privileges? I shivered and again felt a cold prickle of perspiration on my back.

I focused on threading my car through the traffic to get to St. Paul's as fast as I could but seemed to hit every red light on the way. Listening to the wipers tick off the time only increased my impatience at each stop.

Michael had held fast to his theory that the *Legionella* cases must have originated from a source or case in the hospital that had been overlooked or missed. As lightning continued to send cracks through the morning gloom, part of me wanted to agree with him, wanted to dismiss the alarming possibility of a phantom as little more than a troubling fantasy fueled by thunderstorms, lack of sleep, and too much caffeine.

But I couldn't. Each time I recalled Janet's unyielding insistence that the three women had been attacked, my fears for her own safety made my stomach clench like a fist. Michael's arguing with her about a lack of proof had only increased that foreboding. He no more had proof for his position than she did for hers. Until *he* found hard evidence of an undetected source of *Legionella*, connected the three nurses with that source, then explained how they'd all contracted the disease just before leaving on vacation, I was going to find Janet's suspicions impossible to ignore.

But my reasons for taking her suspicions seriously weren't going to be enough to persuade others. No one would believe a murderer was on the loose simply because Janet had seen a trait of cruelty common to the three victims which everyone else had missed.

Except, of course, the killer.

Predictably, Janet and Michael had equally frustrated my concern for *their* safety. "If you're probing the work of a maniac, it could be lethal," I'd argued.

Michael had scoffed some more, and Janet, once again seething at him, snapped, "With reactions like that, who else *but* me could do the job?"

For my sake, they had at least promised not to fight anymore and to be careful. I'd ended up trying to ward off visions of someone prowling after them as they worked.

Michael *had* readily accepted Janet's help. No matter how much their perspectives differed, there was a lot of work to do. Charts of the infected nurses, charts of the patients those nurses had come in contact with, records outlining the ID investigation into possible sources of the *Legionella* organism—all had to be reviewed. But Michael rejected my offer to stay and look through files with them.

"Are you kidding?" he'd exclaimed. "A lot of people were edgy about letting *me* snoop around."

"You know, amalgamation paranoia," Janet had added, sounding resigned to agree with Michael on this point. "If you got caught, they'd shut down the audit and call us all spies."

As if to underline their caution, when I'd stopped at Madge's desk to use her phone on the way out, I'd noticed a stack of files placed beside me with a piece of paper bearing Michael's name on top. Waiting for St. Paul's to answer, I'd been trying to see what the top folder contained, when a red-faced woman in a nurse's uniform had whipped the entire pile away from me and off the counter. "Well!" she'd exclaimed and huffed off. Even Madge had protested, "Dr. Garnet!"

"Sorry!" I'd pleaded, putting down the phone. "Force of habit. I always check my charts when I'm on hold in my own office. I didn't see anything—honest! Hey, Madge, please don't tell Janet!" I'd added, backing out of the room and trying to act the harmless husband that Janet had introduced me as.

I smiled, recalling this performance, then quickly lost patience again as I missed yet another green light. But instead of once more sitting there and fuming over the slow pace, I thought of a call I could make. I dialed the number for our ICU.

"It's Dr. Garnet," I announced when one of the nurses answered. "Could you tell me the status of Phyllis Sanders, please?" Had she survived the night was my real question.

"One moment, I'll give you the doctor who just saw her."

I braced myself. Normally a nurse would simply give me the report. Passing me on usually meant bad news.

"Dr. Rossit here," snapped the unpleasant voice.

Shit!

"Uh, it's Dr. Garnet, Dr. Rossit. I just wanted to have the nurse give me a rep—"

"She's as good as dead, Garnet. Calling in and wringing your hands over a near corpse isn't going to make you any less negligent. And it sure isn't going to make any difference when this case is reviewed. I promise you I'll take care of that personally!"

He was practically screaming, his voice crackling through the receiver and sounding ten times as venomous as what I'd endured yesterday. I could even hear him breathing hard over the noise of the rain. Christ! Susanne and Michael had been perfectly right. No matter how bad his reputation was, this was definitely over the top. Nailing me to the wall must be pretty lusty stuff for the little prick. A nasty afterthought flashed through my mind. Maybe his loathsome practice of hunting doctors who'd screwed up was the man's substitute for sex—the result of small equipment.

"Rossit, either keep this professional or get off the line and put somebody on who can!" I ordered. I knew that he'd had his own problems with the ethics committee as a result of other witch hunts he'd launched and been reprimanded several times for unprofessional conduct. However he planned to get me, I could at least make sure he was going to have to do it by the book.

I listened as his breathing slowed down. "Now, Rossit!" I insisted. The light changed. I had trouble concentrating as I picked my way through the traffic. There was still no reply. I was about to hang up in disgust when I finally heard him say, "What do you want to know?"

I want to know how she is, you asshole, I nearly screamed, but instead I replied coldly, "How are her vitals?"

"Not much change. Her systolic's floating around ninety, the central pressure's still down, and despite the ventilator, she's increasingly hypoxic with respiratory acidosis. Did I mention her bicarb's falling by the hour? You can guess the rest—low white count; rising BUN, creatinine, and liver enzymes; decreasing urinary output—like I said, she's kaput."

My anger at his callous description was quickly replaced by a sense of hopelessness. Rossit had described the laboratory findings of unchecked septic shock and circulatory failure. Her immunity was being wiped out, her respiratory function was deteriorating, and she was sliding into complete renal shutdown. I knew it was unlikely she'd ever regain consciousness. "What about a trial of rifampin?" I asked, knowing it would probably be a futile measure. Rifampin was an antibiotic initially used decades ago against TB. Some recent articles had suggested it was effective in nonresponsive cases of *Legionella*.

The unguarded suggestion absolutely ended our truce. "Christ! You hand out drugs like candy!" he exploded.

"What!" I exclaimed.

"It's hot dogs like you who are mostly responsible for drug-resistant infections in the first place!" he screamed. "From the beginning of this case you've shown a clear tendency to overuse antibiotics, and I intend to order a full chart review of your prescribing competency. Such abuse is the main cause of virulent new strains—"

I hung up on him.

I arrived back at St. Paul's at 8:15. Casualties from a five-car pileup on the expressway inundated ER.

"We need you in resus!" Susanne said, rushing by me with bags of blood under her arm.

"Dr. Garnet," called the clerk from the nursing station, waving a phone at me. "Dr. Carrington wants to know if you need him down here."

"Yes!" yelled Susanne, answering for me over her shoulder.

I was pulling off my wet coat and running to catch up with her. "What have we got?"

"Six casualties, two critical, this one's the worst," she summarized as we entered the tiled, echoing room where we managed major trauma. The chatter and noise matched the confusion. Residents and nurses in surgical greens were circled around the pale lifeless body of a middle-aged man, busily sticking him with needles and attaching him to a web of tubes, catheters, and monitor wires. A high white cervical collar immobilized his head and neck while a respiratory technician struggled to pass a ventilation tube through his nose and on down into his trachea. Yet another tube, this one transparent, was sticking out of his upper left side and draining pure blood into a bottle under the stretcher. These were all lifesaving procedures, but to the uninitiated, the scene might have been a tableau depicting the agony of torture.

"He's in shock with a flail chest on the left," continued Susanne. "X rays have just been taken, but we don't have the developed films yet. I added a pelvis; there's blood at the mouth of his urethra, and we can't get a catheter up more than a few inches. OR's notified, and ortho and urology were called as well as Dr. Carrington."

She'd just told me the man had broken enough ribs to detach a section of his chest wall from the rest of his rib cage. I could see the piece—like a deli side of ribs the size of my hand—still held in place by muscle and sinew, flopping in and out uselessly as he tried to breathe. Shock meant he was bleeding from somewhere, and with blood pouring out of his chest cavity, the source could be a lacerated lung, a major vein, or even a ruptured aorta. The trickle of blood from the man's penis suggested a severed urethra, probably caused by the jagged ends of a pelvic fracture. Susanne's clinical savvy was better than any other nurse's.

"You should have been a doctor," I told her, not for the first time, as I quickly finished gowning and gloving up.

"Who'd be here to tell you what to do then?"

"Speaking of telling me what to do, thanks for calling Michael last night."

She blushed but smiled her acceptance of my rather awkward acknowledgment, then moved in to hang up the blood she'd brought.

Expressions of profound loyalty and deep friendship could hinge on an instant in ER.

Seconds later I strode up to the head of the gurney and took over the intubation from the struggling technician.

For the next short while the harsh world of blood, sinew, and broken bones chased away any thoughts of Rossit or shadowy notions of a phantom killer. It was particularly satisfying when I secured the man's airway, an intubation far too difficult for the tech, especially after I'd had to step aside during Sanders's intubation less than twenty-four hours ago.

Once the patient was properly ventilated, I started firing the questions—the tools of teaching since the time of Aristotle—to focus the residents on what needed doing next. "Okay, gang, where's he bleeding?"

While they shot back answers about the left lung, I rapidly palpated the sternum, auscultated the rest of the chest, then tossed out more questions. "Is he still in shock?"

"Seventy-five over zip," answered one of the nurses.

"What about this chest tube pouring blood?"

"Clamp it?" a young man across from me answered hopefully.

"Good show." I grinned, moving on to palpate the abdomen and to select my next pupil. "Did anyone clear his cervical spine?"

"We took X rays, sir," replied a young woman on my right. "They're not back yet."

"Did you do a rectal?" I asked her.

She flushed above her mask. "Not yet."

"Now I'm going to show you where else this guy is bleeding out on you." I slipped on some lubricant and inserted my index finger through the man's anus. I felt a prostate bobble as free as a floating olive in a martini.

I slipped out and let her perform the same maneuver. Her eyes widened as she confirmed a transected urethra for the first time.

Then I squeezed the pelvis. Both halves slid free of each other and gave a sickening grind.

I stepped back, "Your turn."

More wide eyes.

"Bottom line, folks: this patient needs a surgeon."

The nurses busied themselves recording neurological signs, and I slipped yet another needle catheter into the man, this one through his belly to check for free blood in the abdominal cavity. Negative.

Sean ran into the room as I was flipping X rays up on the viewer, and together we confirmed our clinical impressions. "Let's go!" he cried, reaching through a forest of IV lines and grabbing the head of the stretcher himself to lead the rush to the elevators. The nurses had piled portable monitors and an oxygen tank onto the bed between the patient's legs and were still securing drainage bottles when they started off. The respiratory technician was on the bed itself, straddling the patient's chest with her knees, bagging as they all went out the door and disappeared down the corridor.

I stood for a moment in the empty room, savoring the triumph that always follows a successful resuscitation. This is what I do and do well, I thought. There was no other job in medicine I found sweeter than saving a life. But the delicious glow of accomplishment was quickly being replaced by a spreading sense of dread because two days ago I'd sent the wrong woman home. Foul play at University Hospital may have started the infection. Missing it was my fault.

I looked around that room where over the years I'd experienced incredible miracles and witnessed unspeakable losses. The litter of a major trauma case that inevitably ends up on the floor—the torn boxes, the wrappings, the needle covers left lying in spatters of blood and pools of various other fluids—suddenly made the place seem forlorn. I've had two decades on this stage, I thought, my mouth going dry. I had to swallow repeatedly before I could allow myself to think the unthinkable—that I could lose it all.

The call I'd been dreading, but expecting, came early that evening. I was still in my office finishing resident evaluations when Stewart Deloram reached me.

"I thought you'd want to know she died half an hour ago."

I sighed into the mouthpiece but said nothing.

"Earl?"

"Sorry, Stewart. I knew it was likely, but still . . ."

After a few seconds of uneasy silence, he said, "I hate to have to say this now, but you've got to watch out for Rossit. He was like a vulture dancing around her body. I know he's usually bad-mouthing someone or another, but I'm afraid he's after you big time on this, worse than the usual mischief he gets up to. Frankly, he scares me."

I listened, not knowing what to reply. Although it was only confirmation of what I already knew, his words caused my stomach to tighten.

"He's gotten the post arranged for tomorrow morning," Stewart continued, sounding as miserable as I felt, "and somehow he's gotten the case on the schedule for Death Rounds this coming Monday."

"What!" I was speechless for a moment.

For us as healers, Death Rounds are our crucible, our place to be judged. There the pathologist's scalpel has cut into the disease that defeated us and revealed whether we'd been right with our treatments, probings, and tests or we'd been wrong and our patient died because of our mistakes. It's a rigorous arena where verdicts are rendered starkly and accepted without excuse. Some doctors shunned the process, but I couldn't have continued as a physician without it. The alternative would be agonizing: to lose patients over the years yet never know for sure if I'd killed them or served them well.

But a case usually didn't reach Death Rounds until weeks after the autopsy. Preparing and processing the various slides took time, and the backlog in pathology had tripled after Hurst's repeated budget cuts. "But they won't have tissue samples back by then!" I exclaimed, totally disbelieving what he'd said.

Stewart sighed heavily before he replied, "Either Rossit's managed to get some kind of priority, or he figures he doesn't need slides for a lynching."

My breath caught midway, and my mouth went dry. Rossit's launching such an assault on my reputation was bad enough, but it was another matter altogether that he was somehow able to pervert the most serious of hospital forums to his purpose.

"Stewart, what the hell's going on? How did he get pathology to agree to that?"

"I don't know. Maybe it's the amalgamation."

"What do you mean?"

"Hell, you know these days it affects just about everything everyone does," he said, disgust thick in his voice. "Everybody's suddenly got an agenda to protect his own turf. Maybe that's why Rossit's doing what he's doing. He's got to know he doesn't stand a chance of winning the ID chair against the likes of someone as reputable as Cam Mackie. Probably he's trying to grandstand this case to show up Cam, suggest yet another hospital-acquired infection in a nurse at UH and that the ID department there was missing something . . ." he trailed off, said nothing more for a few seconds, then conceded, "but as to why pathology would go along with such an early date, I've no idea." He sounded finished, then added, "Nor, for that matter, do I understand why he's so rabid about nailing you for negligence."

His last word made me wince. My silence must have given Stewart a clue as to its impact.

"Hey, Earl," he quickly reassured me, "I don't agree with the guy at all; you know that, and I'll say so, publicly, at Death Rounds."

"Thanks, Stewart, I appreciate it." But his declaration sounded forced, and I was feeling more and more alone.

"One other thing," he interjected. His tone seemed even more uneasy. "I called Miller earlier this afternoon when it was clear his mother was preterminal. He was here when she died. He was certainly expecting her death—he took it very quietly, then signed for the post—but I got the feeling that despite his exterior calm, he was even more angry than he was yesterday."

More of what I already knew. My stomach obediently tied itself into a new set of knots anyway. "You think he's going to sue?" I asked, cutting to the point of Deloram's warning.

I heard him breathe out again but wondered if it was from his relief at having finished the unpleasant duty of giving me a string of bad news. "I think you can count on it" was his quick reply.

I got locating to track down Janet at UH and told her the news.

"I'm sorry, Earl," she said softly.

She didn't have to say anything else. As physicians we both knew that a patient's death, even an expected death, could force us to confront things we'd rather not—our futility as doctors, our own inevitable demise, the frailty of a human life. But in this case, I was feeling a pretty high octane mix of guilt over my part in whatever killed Phyllis Sanders and rage at whoever might have murdered her in the first place.

"I want to hold you," Janet said quietly.

"Thanks, love," I answered, swallowing hard. Like a match added to what I was already feeling, her sudden tenderness had ignited an urge to cry.

"Do you know how Miller took it?" she asked after a few seconds.

I told her what Stewart Deloram had said.

She stayed silent again, then quietly told me, "Michael and I saw Miller today, just before noon, while we were checking out ID procedures in the lab. I was surprised he was there at all, but he said he preferred to work and keep his mind occupied. He admitted then he knew there was little hope, but while it was strained between us, he wasn't overtly hostile to me. Now Cam was there too, so Miller might have been being careful, keeping his anger under control and out of sight from his boss. Yet as time goes by and his grief runs its course, his judgment of you may be less harsh," she said, sounding hopeful. I couldn't tell if she believed what she was saying or was simply trying to comfort me.

"What's Miller usually like?" I asked, flashing on the tormented look he'd given me this morning.

"Brash and bright. Hell, he's more up-to-date on the latest in clinical testing techniques than most physicians, including myself. He's always badgering us to use the lab more appropriately, sometimes to the point of annoyance, but he's usually right."

"I overheard him this morning, on my way up to staff health. He was bad-mouthing incompetent physicians to his lab students. Does he often talk like that, or was that diatribe inspired by me?" I found it hard to keep from sounding angry.

"First of all you're not incompetent," said Janet dryly.

I snorted, skeptical of her attempt to set me straight but then immediately felt a few of the knots in my intestines untangle themselves while I waited for her to answer the rest of my question. Lady, you do know how to play me.

"Unfortunately, it's probably a bit of both," she finally said. "He's obviously pretty raw about his mother right now, but he also has a reputation for being a bit critical of doctors, especially when he's teaching. His father used to be an obstetrician here. It was before my time, but the rumors are that Miller senior was an alcoholic and a womanizer who lost his license. Apparently he also died as a result of alcohol, in some kind of drunken fall. Most of us figure that's why Harold's the way he is, overcompensating for the mistakes of his old man. I hear he even once applied to medical school but was turned down. He probably still feels he'd be a better doctor than most of those he sees around him, and who knows, maybe he's right. In any case, he seems to have found a real niche for himself in laboratory sciences. And having a stickler for excellence around the place is nothing to complain about, so we try to take his dedication with a certain grain of charity."

"But with that kind of background he's liable to sue simply to make an example of me. Hell, he hardly needs Rossit to stir him up."

"Possibly," she said, her voice neutral. It was a tone she always resorted to for telling hard truths. "But don't jump to conclusions yet about what he may do."

Good advice, but tell that to my stomach, I thought, as I felt it start to rearrange itself again. "It still sounds like I shouldn't expect much," I commented glumly.

"Earl, I want you to do something for me right now." Janet's sudden sharp tone snapped me out of my morbid worries. "I'm down in the basement archives, where they keep old records. No one's here, and I want you to come over. I've dug out the records of all the staff who were attacked by the Phantom two years ago. Michael still doesn't take me seriously, but neither of us found a shred of evidence today that can explain the infections. I'm sure I'm right about this, Earl. I want you to look at the charts with me. Maybe you can find what I'm missing."

It was after 7:00 when I once again pulled into the grounds of UH. The weather hadn't changed much since my visit that morning. It had stopped raining for the moment, but the mist had graduated to fog and now descended all the way down the walls of the building. The dimming effect, added to the dusk, had been enough to trigger the sodium lamps. Inverted cones of yellow light illuminated the gray haze that drifted through the parking lot and the many footpaths surrounding the hospital. In a few weeks it would be fully night by this hour, after we'd all adjusted our watches and stopped saving daylight for yet another year. Maybe I wouldn't do it this time; I hated surrendering to winter darkness.

As I walked to the front doors from my car, the air felt cool against my face, and I enjoyed a few brisk lungfuls before flashing my identity card at the sole security guard. A dozen other people carrying bouquets of flowers and food baskets entered the large vaulted lobby with me, but the huge echoing chamber seemed empty compared to the rush I'd seen at the start of the day.

A woman with two children, each of them clutching a small bunch of roses, studied a map of the hospital mounted on the wall. A massive directory listing the locations of all the hospital departments was hanging beside it; there was no one else around to give directions. A nearby glass booth marked INFORMATION was dark and had a handwritten sign taped on the door, BACK IN THIRTY MINUTES.

I'd already called home to say Janet and I would be late. Amy, our nanny, was having dinner with Brendan.

"He likes the spinach, and I prefer the carrots," she'd told me as I'd listened to his happy cries and smacks in the background. "But if you two don't hurry, we'll eat all the applesauce and leave you the yellow stuff. Neither of us likes that."

Then she'd held the receiver up to his ear and I'd gotten to say, "Hi, Brendan," and listen to him gum the mouthpiece.

I found the archives on the directory and learned they were in the subbasement by the old psychiatric wing. Terrific, I thought, studying the map and figuring roughly how to get there.

The elevator took me down two floors and let me out in the middle of a long deserted corridor that seemed to run forever in both directions. While lit with occasional overhead lights, the passage had an arched low ceiling, giving it more the feel of a tunnel than of a hallway. There wasn't a soul in sight, and after the elevator doors closed behind me, the place was silent as death.

"Jesus, Janet," I muttered under my breath, setting out in what I thought was the right direction after my study of the map, "could you have brought me anywhere more creepy?"

The air in the passage was absolutely still, the result of being two floors below ground. The stone walls and ceiling only added to the sense of weight pressing down from the hospital above. I wasn't usually claustrophobic, but this place made the basement hallways at St. Paul's feel absolutely spacious.

I came to an intersection. The archives should be off to the left, but that hallway didn't look as used as the one I was in. It was certainly less well lit, and the lights were spaced farther apart. The corridor to the right was in complete darkness. The air at its mouth had a damp musty smell, and a sign hanging from the arched ceiling warned, DANGER! OFF LIMITS TO ALL PERSONNEL. I stared up that dark passage and wondered if it led into the old abandoned asylum. Shivering, I turned left.

The floor was concrete, and my shoes made muffled tapping sounds as I walked. There were occasional doors set in the stone walls, and what would be behind them besides storage rooms I couldn't imagine. I passed two more intersections, then turned right at the third. The microfilm archives should be at the end of the corridor.

But I came up to a blank wall.

Shit! The map had indicated left at the first intersection, past two corridors, and then right, exactly as I'd done. I should be standing in front of a door marked HOSPITAL ARCHIVES. Instead it was beyond a doubt the proverbial blank wall.

I retraced my steps a bit, trying the doors that I'd passed on my way down the corridor. Most were locked, and those that weren't simply opened into musty rooms stuffed with everything from boxes to old beds and shelves of outmoded clinical equipment.

This place needs a garage sale, I thought, poking into yet another disorganized storeroom.

"Janet!" I called, not feeling very hopeful. Did I get turned around when I got off the elevator and start out in the wrong direction to begin with? It was the only explanation. I'd retrace my steps back to where I started, then follow the same routine heading the other way.

I turned left out of the passage I'd been exploring and strode toward the series of intersections I'd passed on the way in. Far up ahead I could see where the corridor I was walking along extended into the darkness. Toward what—rooms with earthen floors and the remnants of chains in the walls? I'd be glad when I found Janet. The complete silence and stillness of the air in the place was oppressive enough without imagining what kind of horrors had been carried out there in the name of psychiatry.

I passed the first intersection and quickened my pace. The rapid clicking sounds of my shoes matched my heartbeat as I walked. I kept my eyes on the darkness ahead, knowing that's where I'd turn right and be back near the elevators.

I passed the second intersection. In spite of telling myself to calm down, I was nearly running now.

Suddenly, in the murky archway I'd been watching, I thought I saw movement—a shadow against a black background stepping away from the light.

"Janet?"

There was no answer. I started to slow up, not taking my eyes off that dark corridor up ahead.

"Who's there?"

Still no answer. I was stopped now, listening to my own breathing and trying to see into that blackness farther back in the archway.

"All right, this isn't funny. Who's there?"

Silence. Complete stillness, except the sound of my own breath. I started to back away, keeping my eyes on that corridor. I had seen something. I was sure of it—a form in the dim light at the entrance way.

I was all the way back to the intersection I'd just passed when the lights went out.

I couldn't see a thing. I didn't hear a sound, not even my own breath anymore. I was suddenly holding it in the stillness of that place. The complete absence of light pressed against me. For a second I felt dizzy, unsure of where was up or down. When I finally exhaled, the sound startled me, it seemed so loud in my ears. I tried to inhale through my open mouth, to make as little noise as possible. Whoever was up ahead remained completely silent.

Then I heard the steps.

They were a softer sound than my own shoes had made. A kind of padding sound, like a paw or a foot wrapped in cloth.

I wanted to scream at whatever was advancing toward me, but I didn't dare give away where I was standing. Instead I crouched down and removed my shoes. I'd been about a hundred feet from the mouth of that corridor when the lights had gone out. The padding noise came steadily toward me. How far away now I'd no idea. I reached blindly out to my right side trying to feel the wall. Nothing. I stood and took a step toward where I thought the wall would be, holding my shoes in my left hand and groping ahead with my right. I still felt nothing.

The soft sound kept coming up on my left. I took two steps ahead, then three, four. Still nothing. I must be in the intersecting corridor, I thought, trying to fight off panic. I quickly took four more strides into what I hoped was the side passage, then stood completely motionless, attempting to take controlled breaths through my open mouth. I slowly turned back toward the sound of the approaching steps. Would whoever it was turn the corner and touch me? Or go by, heading straight off down the passage in the direction I'd just come from?

I could feel my heart pounding, and the sweat in the small of my back was like ice. The padding was very near, almost passing in front of me. Then it stopped.

I didn't breathe, didn't move, didn't even blink in that complete blindness. But I could hear whoever was there breathing. It was little more than the sound of air moving in that totally stagnant place. For those seconds my ears rang in the silence between his breaths. If my stomach gurgled, I'd be discovered. I didn't know there could be such absolute quiet.

Then the padding began again, moving off to my left and receding in the distance. I still didn't move, but strained to hear the fading sound, every last soft puff of it.

When I was sure I couldn't hear anything more, I felt for the wall on my right, then worked my way back to where the passages intersected, my hand telling me when I was at the corner. I stopped and listened for any sound from the left but again heard nothing. I immediately turned right and felt my way along the wall as quickly and as quietly as I could. I couldn't see a thing and kept blundering into recessed doorways as I rushed to reach the next corner and the corridor to the elevators. I didn't think I heard any padding steps coming after me, but I didn't stop to make sure. I could tell I was getting near the final intersection because I started to smell the damp musty air.

Had I missed the turn? I wondered in a flash of new panic. Had I blundered straight into the passage where the figure had come from and into God knew what? The odor was cloying in my nostrils. It seemed so much more pungent now than before, like wet earth. Had I missed the turn? Just when I was about to stop and reverse direction, my fingers slipped around the corner I was looking for.

I paused and listened. Nothing.

I made the turn and headed for the elevators. I switched the shoes to my right hand and felt along the wall at my left so as not to go by the sliding metal doors in the dark. I kept trying to be quiet but was practically running again as I barreled ahead in the darkness. As I remembered it, there were no obstacles to speak of that I'd crash into.

Suddenly, way up ahead, there was a break in the blackness—a small round white light set in the wall I was hurriedly feeling along. The elevator button.

I redoubled my pace, keeping my eyes fixed on that tiny light, still fumbling with my left hand on the wall at my side. I was almost there—another twenty feet—and was about to run for the doors when I felt my fingers slide over the top of another human hand.

Before I could scream, it had seized my forearm and yanked me forward. I now rocketed toward that tiny light, head first. I felt another hand grab me behind the neck and further propel me straight at it. It got as big as a train light right between my eyes as my head crashed into the metal door frame. After so much darkness the white explosion in my brain was spectacular.

Chapter 7

The patient seemed to be doing well, at least that's what a man's voice kept saying.

"... going to be fine, just a concussion ..."

It must be somebody pregnant, because I could hear Janet sounding very worried. "Oh thank God!" she said. "For a second I was even afraid he was dead, finding him lying down there in the dark."

No, it couldn't be Janet's patient. "He's" don't have babies. But I couldn't get my eyes open to see whom she was talking about. Whom had she found lying in the dark?

Then it came back in a rush.

The figure, the padding footsteps—someone had knocked me out.

My eyes flew open, and I sat up. "What happened!" I demanded, ignoring the ache in my head and trying to focus on the two faces in front of me.

"Oh, Earl, what a relief!" said the blur on the left. It was Janet's voice again.

"Whoa there, Dr. Garnet, lie back," ordered the man's voice, and the form on the right moved closer. I could feel his hands pushing gently but firmly on my chest. "You're okay, but it was quite a hit. You've been out more than five minutes, as far as we can figure, and we want to do a CT."

"Janet! What happened. Did he hurt you?" I asked anxiously, turning again to the shape on my left. "Who was it?"

My vision suddenly cleared in time to see her warm smile fade and the concern in her gaze slowly turn to wide-eyed amazement.

"Pardon?" was all she said.

"Someone jumped me in the dark and knocked me out," I explained, puzzled by her response. "It must have been whoever was chasing me. Did he hurt you?"

"Oh my God," she exclaimed, suddenly looking alarmed and

turning to the young man beside her who I could now see wore a clinical jacket.

"Oh boy," he uttered, moving back from me. "He's really confused. I better get my staff man." He turned and walked out of the curtained cubicle I was lying in. From the sounds around us—beeping monitors, shouted orders, the spring and click noise of an ambulance stretcher having its legs extended—I knew they'd gotten me to ER.

"I'm not confused!" I protested to Janet. "What's he talking about?"

She gave me a smile as phony as Bre-X. "Now just relax, Earl," she said, patting my hands and looking as if she were about to cry.

I took her hands in mine." I'm all right, Janet," I told her emphatically, sitting back up. My head hinted otherwise, but I ignored the pain.

"Wait a minute," she protested, pushing me back onto my pillow. I was wearing a neck collar, so my head and trunk flopped down in tandem, like a wooden doll's.

"Ouch." I winced, the change in position setting my head throbbing again.

"You're not to move, Earl," she cautioned, her tone of voice intense and full of concern.

"What happened" I asked again.

When the lights had gone out, Janet told me, she had come out of the archives department and felt her way back to the elevator. The room actually was in the opposite end of the subbasement; I'd taken the wrong direction to begin with, as I'd belatedly realized. She'd been fumbling her way along in the dark like I had, but at a lot slower and safer pace. When she'd heard a thud in the dark ahead of her she'd been frightened but had continued to approach the elevator door, albeit more slowly. She'd become terrified when she tripped over my body. She had only realized it was me after she'd gathered her wits and pressed the elevator button. When the door opened, a shaft of light had fallen across my face. She'd checked my vitals, then gotten help, and everyone, including Janet, had assumed I'd tripped in the dark and knocked myself out.

When she finished speaking, I lay there, feeling her fingers stroke my head, thinking. Should I tell her what had really happened? It would scare her terribly, as if she wasn't worried enough as it was. "What did they tell you was the matter with the lights?" I asked instead.

"The maintenance people said a circuit breaker had closed down for some reason," she answered, clearly puzzled by my question. "When I ran for help to get you up here, one of them went to check the panel. He turned the lights back on, no problem."

"Was that panel in the abandoned passageway leading under the old psychiatric hospital?"

"I think that's what he said. I know he went up that way, but frankly, I was too worried about you to pay much attention to anything else. Why?"

"And the lights stayed on? They didn't short out again?" A faulty breaker would likely blow a second time, but a single timely outage would suggest a hand at the switch.

"No, they stayed on," she said, once more sounding a bit alarmed and looking over her shoulder. "Where's the damn staff man?" I heard her mutter.

I had to tell her. She had to know for her own safety.

"Janet, there's a point to what I'm asking. It's not brain damage. I've got one more question. Are there other corridors leading back to the elevator from the asylum end of the subbasement besides the one we were in?"

"Earl, what are you going on about?"

"Janet, I'm okay," I insisted, grabbing her arm, and then I explained what had happened.

When I finished, she didn't say anything for a few minutes.

Tears welled up in her eyes. Her lips quivered a few times. "Are you sure it wasn't an accident? Maybe you tripped, and the force of the fall only made you think you were pushed."

I hadn't imagined the hands on my back and neck, I thought, but said nothing.

"And are you sure it was a person you heard when the lights went out," she asked, "not a rat that came on down the corridor in the dark? I hear there are some big ones under the old asylum, and maybe—"

"If it was a rat, it was a two-legged one," I interrupted, speaking as gently as possible. No matter how shaken she was about my being attacked, I couldn't let her deny and rationalize away what had happened. From now on there would be no more illusions about the need to be careful. "I could hear whoever it was breathing, Janet," I added, nudging my point home while recalling those endless seconds with a shudder.

She sat on the edge of the bed, staring off at the curtains, then absently brushed back a golden strand of hair from the side of her face. I watched her lovely familiar profile as she stayed quiet with her thoughts.

I could only guess at what she was thinking. Her greatest weakness was her absolute belief in her own invincibility—her long hours, her defiance of fatigue, her relish to take on cases none of her colleagues would touch—all that made her great and yet could lay her low. She'd been so sure someone had killed those nurses; still, it was completely within her character to be equally incredulous that the very same evil might strike back at her or at someone she loved.

She looked paler than usual, and under the harsh fluorescent lights the fine lines of her forehead, jaw, and neck gave her the delicate appearance of a porcelain figurine. So vulnerable, I thought, with a sudden rush of apprehension for this strong woman who was such a force in my life.

The muscles around her lips tightened, and she turned to speak. "All right, here's what we'll do," she began, sitting up straighter, appearing to take charge. "Michael's right about one thing. Until we have proof that there is a killer behind the *Legionella* cases, you can't afford to be telling wild tales about a phantom." But her voice had a brittle edge to it that occasionally broke and belied the determined expression on her face. "Even if we told somebody what happened in the subbasement tonight, they could dismiss it," she continued, speaking more quickly, almost to herself. "They'd say that the person you saw was some derelict who'd snuck in and was trying to use abandoned parts of the old asylum as shelter or that the person who shoved you into the elevator had simply acted reflexively, to protect himself when you barged out of the dark, and then panicked, running off when he saw you were hurt." She was speaking ever more rapidly, as if racing through her thoughts aloud, her tone harsher. I didn't like the desperation I heard. "And who knows, maybe that's what happened after all—oh, Christ I'm stupid!" she exploded, angrily snapping off her own train of thought. "I've probably gotten us both into something that's way over our heads—something that at the very least needs the police. And for the life of me I don't know how we're going to get a single shred of evidence to make anyone believe us."

The words poured out of her, like the tears that started down her cheeks. I'd rarely seen Janet cry. I sat up, rather awkwardly, and put my arms around her. At first I felt her stiffen—she hated losing control—then she hugged me back, hard. I felt her body start to heave as she lost the battle to contain her sobs, and I felt my own tears roll down my face onto her slender magnificent shoulders. I held her like that until her crying ended and I felt her body relax against mine. She never noticed when the resident came through the curtain with his staff man, and I waved them away.

"I guess I don't have to tell you I'm scared," she sniffled when she spoke again, "especially after what happened to you tonight. God, I'm sorry, Earl, to have been so blind."

"It's okay," I reassured her. "You were the least blind of all. No one else even thought of the Phantom."

"Yeah, except you warned me about what might happen if we got close." She pulled away and reached into her lab coat pocket for a tissue. "But if that was the Phantom and my looking at those charts was what brought him down on us, then there must be something in those records that can help us find out who he is," she said slowly, starting to sound less shaken.

"Hold it, Nancy Drew," I said. "As your trusty sidekick, I've had enough knocks on the head for tonight."

She smiled, gently ruffled my hair, then laughed and gave me another hug. The closeness felt good, but from my experience in ER I knew the relief we were both feeling at that moment was the kind that always follows a near miss. It was part of the shock, and temporary. Already, as I hugged her back, I was thinking, This guy probably gives out worse things than bumps on the head, things like *Legionella*. "Janet, who besides me knew you were going to look at the old files on the Phantom cases?" I asked, still holding her.

Janet's expression strained again when she pulled away, and once more her eyes filled with worry.

"No one. I was tired of being scoffed at."

"So only Cam, Michael, and I heard your Phantom idea?"

She nodded.

"Have you seen a lot of any one person today, someone who could be watching your movements?"

"No," she answered quietly.

"Then how did he know you were there?" I asked, not expecting an answer. "Or could we be wrong in assuming whoever it was had gone down there tonight to find you? Maybe the person was there for another reason, and I disturbed him, wandering around."

"Wait a minute," Janet said. "Are you changing your mind and saying that getting attacked tonight had nothing to do with the *Legionella* deaths, that those crazy excuses I made up might be true?"

"Not at all. Whoever turned out the lights came at me and somehow was waiting back at the elevator for me. And that judo push propelling me into the door was certainly no panicky grab. At the very least the person didn't want me snooping around. I'm just suggesting that maybe it wasn't connected to your going over files on victims of the Phantom."

"So apart from making me feel less guilty about that knock on your head, where does that leave us? You're not seriously suggesting your figure in the dark has nothing to do with the *Legionella* cases?"

I didn't answer right away. The menace I'd felt from that hideous encounter was not at all in doubt, but if pressed, I had to admit I'd only assumed the attack was connected to the nurses, especially with Sanders's death fresh on my mind. But I couldn't rule out the possibility that I'd stumbled onto a completely unrelated creep.

"It would be a pretty big coincidence, but you're right. It's a possibility the attack tonight had nothing to do with the Phantom or *Legionella*."

My admission left us looking glumly at each other across a spread of white bedsheets. They reminded me of blank paper—a tabula rasa—waiting for answers that wouldn't come.

It was an odd sort of letdown. If the attack was an unrelated fluke, then Janet hadn't threatened anyone, wasn't in any immediate danger, so far, but might be completely on the wrong track. In that case, we were probably no closer to discovering why two nurses had died and certainly weren't any nearer to stopping a lunatic who could kill with *Legionella*.

Even more frustrating was that we had to live with the other possibility: we somehow had threatened a killer.

After a few moments, Janet raised her head. "I need you here, Earl. You're the only one who believes me, and I'm certainly not getting anywhere working with Michael. You've got to get yourself officially named to his investigation. Then we can start from scratch, together, and maybe you'll see something I've overlooked."

"Don't worry," I told her, trying to sound more confident than I felt. "If Michael doesn't listen to me, you can tell Donna on him. She'll make him behave."

We got out of University Hospital's ER by midnight. The CAT scan and a series of staff doctors declared that apart from an already forming bruise, the blow hadn't done me much damage. On our way

home Janet agreed she'd do no more prowling around until I could
be with her. We again considered making a report about the attack to
the police and again decided against it. Even if they believed me,
which, despite Janet's skepticism, they might, the crime they'd be
investigating would be simple assault and nothing else. Besides,
creating a fuss for the hospital would only make it harder for me to
get the access I wanted to their records.

Later, in bed, I lay awake listening to Janet's breathing and pic-
tured that sinister figure in the hallway. Despite our second-guessing
why he'd turned out the lights and come after me, I couldn't stop
thinking he was down there because Janet was checking into the *Legionella* cases and digging out the old files on victims of the Phantom. What would he have done to her if I hadn't come along?
Possibilities out of a nightmare flooded into my thoughts and burned
away all possibilities of sleep. I got up, went downstairs to the living
room, and paced to control my fears. No one, I swore, not Michael,
not Cam, not anyone at University Hospital, was going to keep me
from protecting my wife.

But after putting a few miles on the carpet and tripping innumerable
times over Muffy, by 3:00 A.M. I still had no plan. That was when I
remembered Phyllis Sanders's autopsy was scheduled for 7:00.

During twelve hours on a slab in the morgue the flesh of the dead
becomes yellowed and white as the blood slowly drains toward the
back and pools in the skin behind the head, shoulders, and hips.
There it clots, suffusing those resting spots with large purple
blotches—a telltale pattern of how the body was initially lying after
death. Pathologists call this pattern dependent lividity, and it can reveal whether a body subsequently was moved into a different position and, if so, suggest foul play.

Phyllis Sanders had obviously spent an undisturbed night on her
back. She now lay naked on the dissecting table under the harsh light
of the operating lamp, awaiting her final medical procedure and
hopefully a definitive diagnosis as to the cause of her death, if the
purely medical cause of death could be called definitive. In her case,
the possible cause of the cause—a dim figure in the shadows—
wouldn't be discovered here.

Her eyes were closed, her cheeks were slack and hollow, and her
mouth was a gaping hole. Her gray hair lay splayed out over the glistening steel of the table's surface and hung off its end, reminding me
of how she'd looked in ER. I found myself wondering how they'd

protect those long strands for the mortician if they planned to include her brain in the post. The standard cutting procedure would involve an incision across the top of her head from temple to temple and pulling the front half of her scalp forward over her face to expose the skull.

I was dressed in greens, mask, and gloves and pacing impatiently, having been in the chilled room for ten minutes and wondering what the delay was. On the steel counters surrounding me were the rows of tubes and glass beakers that would hold specimens of her various bodily fluids. Other bottles filled with colored liquids stood waiting to receive tissue samples from her major organs. Spread out near the deep sinks at the end of one of these counters was an array of large Tupperware containers, each half filled with formaldehyde, where the major organs themselves would be placed once they were removed in their entirety. The overhead vents hummed and did their best, but even through my mask the familiar fumes of the preservative stung my eyes and bit into my nose. Every now and then I also got a whiff of the unmistakable odor of early rot.

Scalpels, probes, pickups, forceps, bone cutters, and a rotary saw lay neatly arranged on a steel cart placed near the woman's chest. This being an ID case, a plentiful supply of swabs and culture sets were on a separate tray within easy reach. All that was needed was a pathologist.

Finally I heard the sound of approaching voices coming from the changing room on the other side of the doors to the autopsy suite. As the conversation grew louder, I realized a heated argument was taking place.

"I don't give a goddamn about whatever juice you managed to pull from upstairs! Down here you're on my turf, this is my case, and it's my policy that any attending physician or resident not only can be present but should be encouraged to be present at an autopsy of his or her patient—"

The doors swung open and the thin figure of Len Gardner, already in full protective gear, strode into the room. Of medium height and build, he was in his early fifties. He should have been chairperson of his department but was far too frank and honest to have any political support at St. Paul's. "Oh, hi, Earl," he commented cheerfully, winking at me over the top of his mask. He gave his head a little nod in the direction of whoever was following him, the corners of his eyes wrinkling merrily with the smile I couldn't see. Then he suddenly stared at my forehead. "Hey, that's quite a bruise. What happened?"

"I hit a door in the dark," I mumbled.

In huffed Gary Rossit, also fully garbed, but the visible portions of his face and neck were deeply flushed. The effect made his head look like a round beet enclosed in a cap and mask. "Garnet's handling of this case is under review, and I insist you comply with my wishes and bar him—" He broke off when he saw me, his forehead flushing even redder.

I felt my own face grow warm. "You wouldn't be trying to keep me away from the post, would you Dr. Rossit?" I snapped. Having caught him in the act of doing exactly that, I was furious. But I gritted my teeth knowing my mask at least partially kept him from seeing how well he'd succeeded in making me livid.

He glared back up at me, his pupils widening as I watched.

"You are both welcome to stay," Len interjected sternly, giving us a precautionary glance that made it clear he wouldn't tolerate his domain being used as a battleground. He reached overhead and snapped on the microphone to record his running commentary of the autopsy. Rossit eyed the device, the blacks of his eyes growing even bigger, but kept silent. Whatever he had to say against me, I guessed he still preferred it said behind my back and off the record.

Apparently satisfied that we would behave, Len stepped to the business side of the table, picked up his scalpel, and looked down at his subject. "The patient is a fifty-seven-year-old female with no external markings except needle punctures at the documented IV sites—the right and left forearms—below the junction of the lateral and middle thirds of the right clavicle, and at an arterial line inserted in her left wrist. The central line has been left in place for verification of position."

This initial inspection included documentation that the various lines had been properly inserted in her veins. Antibiotics injected outside a vessel would simply collect in the surrounding tissue where they'd pool and fail to reach the site of the infection.

"Likewise the endotracheal tube has been cut and the lower end left in place . . ."

Len grasped her windpipe between his thumb and third finger at the thyrocricoid—a tiny area in the upper end of the trachea covered by a thin membrane—and brought the tip of his scalpel blade down to make a vertical slice. As the skin and tissue parted, the orange tube so expertly inserted by Michael two days ago came into view. I recalled my own hesitancy trying to intubate her, which had necessitated his taking over.

". . . incision through the cricothyroid membrane reveals a properly positioned endotracheal tube . . ."

And so it went: the preliminary to what we were all here to see—her lungs.

Len's scalpel made a sweeping cut from her upper right chest across to her sternum and down to her pubis. Her flesh pouted open along the path of the blade, the cleanly sliced edges forming a bloodless trench the color of sushi. He made a similar cut above her left breast, joining his initial incision and completing a Y that would allow him access to both thoracic cavities and the abdomen. His expert use of the blade had penetrated not only dermis but also more than half an inch of glistening subcutaneous fat. Abandoning the knife for a large pair of tissue spreaders—an instrument resembling scissors with curved blunt probes instead of blades—he deftly widened and deepened the fleshy trench along its length. In the thoracic region it took him seconds to reveal the white striations of sinew and the pearl gray sheen of underlying bone. Working lower down over her belly, he brought into view the darker gray of peritoneum—a fibrous sheath holding back her intestines and other contents of her abdominal cavity. He continued to give succinct explanations of all he did, the easy flow of technical jargon consistent with his years of experience.

"Double glove if you haven't already. I'm going through the chest wall," Len advised us.

Both lungs were liable to be full of pus. The extra layer of latex was protection against an incidental tear midst such septic material. Rossit and I complied, reaching for the dispenser box at the same time; then we both impatiently insisted the other hurry up and use it first. I caught a glimpse of us struggling to pull rubber over rubber in our reflection from the glass doors of a nearby cabinet. Positioned back to back, we looked like dualists gloving up to mark off twenty paces. I heard Len muttering behind his mask—something about rectal orifices.

Len picked up the rotary bone saw—a hand-sized tool fitted with a two-inch round saw blade—and switched on the motor. He bent over his patient again and touched the top of each rib with the whirling saw blade, making only a partial cut so as not to disturb the structures underneath. At each contact with bone there came a high-pitched whine, not unlike a dentist's drill, that made me cringe.

While Rossit and I watched, he reached for his rib cutters, stainless steel shears any florist or chef would die for, and finished snipping completely through the ribs. Their freed ends sprang upward, allowing access to the lungs.

"Good God!" he exclaimed, stepping back from the cloying stench that rose out of the open cavity, staggering all of us, even with our masks.

Swallowing and trying not to gag, I peered at the right lobe. The surface, already blackened by years of cigarette smoking, was blistered with abscesses—some of them open and draining. The entire organ was floating in a yellow pool of debris similar to what I'd suctioned out of her airway two days ago. The left lung appeared much the same, with the exception of the top half of the upper lobe.

"She must have been breathing and oxygenating through that until she died," pronounced Len, pointing at this partially spared segment. His voice lost its practiced neutrality. He spoke slowly, clearly shaken.

The extent of the spread of the infection and the degree of tissue damage we stared at was truly alarming. Len nevertheless picked up his scalpel and proceeded to prepare the trachea, lungs, heart, and esophagus for removal en bloc. Identifying each major vessel and structure as he cut, he freed, then lifted this large dripping assembly from the chest cavity and placed it on an adjacent smaller table equipped with a drain. As he went to work on her right lung, removing it from the rest of the dissection, I swallowed a few more times and managed to ask, "Have you ever seen an infection this aggressive before?"

"No," Len answered quickly, then added, "except . . . well, at least not recently, not in patients who weren't immunocompromised somehow, and even then, not as completely unchecked as this. . . ." His voice trailed off, and the lines in his forehead formed into deep vertical furrows as he looked up from his work. "But I saw cases somewhat similar during my residency in the early seventies, when methicillin-resistant staphylococcus first emerged, before vancomycin became the treatment of choice. Those pneumonias went fast too." He looked back down and resumed his cutting. "But you had this lady on vancomycin, didn't you?"

"Among other things," I stated quietly, glancing at Rossit. I hoped the mere mention of what I'd ordered wasn't enough to start him on another diatribe about my use of antibiotics.

"Any signs of resistance so far, Gary?" Len asked without looking away from the incisions he was making.

Rossit darted his eyes my way, then just as abruptly looked back across the table. "The organism in her sputum was coagulase positive, confirming staph aureus, and the preliminary disc diffusion screen suggested methicillin resistance," he admitted to the top of Len's head. The way he coldly rattled off the technical terms indicated he resented being made to reveal that vancomycin seemed to have been the right choice after all.

Well, well, I thought, feeling a flash of satisfaction. Rossit would be forced to put his attack against my prescribing patterns on hold, at least until we received confirmatory tests.

He admitted as much when he added, "But that procedure isn't as accurate as the minimal inhibitory concentration method using a full twenty-four hour incubation and broth dilution." This mouthful of terms made him pause for breath. "Any *intelligent* comment about Dr. Garnet's choice of therapy will have to wait until tomorrow," he concluded sarcastically, finally looking at me.

"Yeah, yeah, Rossit," I shot back, "and heaven help me if the *minimal inhibitory concentration method* doesn't validate the use of vancomycin! Get a grip, Gary! You'll probably end up having to admit it was a reasonable call."

"The erythromycin, even rifampin—was there any antibiotic you *didn't* think of?" he retorted.

Len was ignoring our spat.

". . . slicing through the hilum, severing the main stem bronchus, pulmonary artery, and divisions of the pulmonary vein, thereby completing the removal of her right lung . . ."

He lifted the sodden organ, placed it on several pieces of paper towel, then cradled it in his gloved hands and set it on a balance for weighing. After recording the reading, he sliced open each of the lung's three lobes, spreading the meaty halves and inspecting their interior. His hands moved slowly, so as not to spray any organisms into the air.

Suddenly his running commentary ended in midsentence. He stood frozen, transfixed by what he saw.

His unexpected reaction immediately made Rossit and me shut up, and we both strained forward to see what he'd found.

Across from me I heard Len whisper, "Holy shit!" Rossit muttered something else on my right. But my eyes were fixed on the horror in Len's hands.

The inside of the lung was virtually destroyed. Its entire central structure—arteries, veins, and airways—had been converted into a brownish black mush. No circulatory pathways remained that might have carried antibiotics to the sites of the infection. But even if they had, the destruction of tissue visible to the naked eye meant the airways leading to alveoli, the microscopic sacs where life-giving oxygen passed into the blood, were no more. What little tissue had survived was confined to the periphery of each lobe. It had a reddish color—the sign of diffuse inflammation—and was coated with blood-streaked bubbles, a result of the leaky lung syndrome I'd suspected during her resuscitation. In the middle section of the lobes were more dark cavities where the abscesses we'd seen penetrating the lung's surface first developed. Any remnants of tissue still intact around these holes had a coating of yellow slime.

I stood mesmerized by what I saw and didn't realize at first that Len had resumed speaking.

". . . the congested tissue appears diffusely inflamed and exudes a serous sanguineous fluid in the outer segments. Slightly deeper is extensive evidence of early cavitation. Most of the central parenchyma and vascular structures, however, have been replaced by liquefied necrotic debris—"

His voice wavered, and he stumbled over the dry terminology, which, while accurate, belied the enormity of what had happened to Phyllis Sanders.

"The debris gives the appearance of two infectious processes, one causing a diffuse lobar pneumonia, the other a more consolidated infection, with evidence of phagocytic tissue destruction more typical of staphylococcal organisms—Jesus Christ! What the hell's going on here?" he finally broke off and simply stood staring down at what defied his attempt at a cold clinical description.

For a few seconds no one spoke.

Then I realized what I'd heard—*two processes.*

"Could it be *Legionella*, Len, followed by staph?" I blurted out, clearly startling him out of his fugue. I glanced at Rossit. He was simply standing there, repeatedly swallowing, with his eyes riveted on the open lung. *Two processes.* Try and rip into me for mentioning *Legionella* now, Rossit, I thought, almost giddy with the possibility of suddenly turning the tables on the obnoxious little man.

"It's something plus staph," Len replied grimly after a few more seconds. "It'll take a microscopic examination of tissue samples to determine the exact sequence for sure." He paused, looking back down at the grisly specimen he still held. "But one thing's certain," he went on, his voice regaining its usual authority, "staphylococcus wouldn't get this big a toehold on an intact lung, even a smoker's lung, without some process first attacking the pulmonary tree and making breaks in the lining through which the staph could penetrate."

"Like *Legionella*?" I repeated.

"Really Garnet," interrupted Rossit, "will you drop your obsession with bizarre scenarios—"

"I think *Legionella* is a hell of a good clinical suggestion, Gary," declared Len, placing the lung in one of the plastic containers, then stepping around from his side of the table and coming to stand over a considerably startled looking Rossit. "Dr. Garnet was incredibly astute to recognize from the beginning we might be dealing with two separate organisms here," he continued, his usually taciturn voice rising. "And as for 'bizarre scenarios,' this case is already bizarre!" he bellowed.

I could see Rossit's chin flutter overtime under his mask—whether trying to swallow or find words, I couldn't tell. His forehead and neck flushed an even deeper crimson than when he'd first seen me at the start of the autopsy. He made a few more attempts behind his mask at whatever he was trying to do with his mouth, then spun around and strode from the room.

Len stood with his hands on his hips, somehow looking bigger as he watched the vanquished little man disappear between the swinging doors. "Like I told you, Rossit," he muttered, "here you're on my turf, and this is my case!"

"I wish I'd done that," I said cheerfully, stepping up and patting him on the back. "Just watching you felt terrific."

"Oh, Earl," he exclaimed, turning and looking at me, as if he'd forgotten I was in the room. "Sorry for the outburst."

"I want to thank you for standing up for me," I told him. "I was beginning to fear I might not get a fair hearing. Rossit's been on my case big time since I . . . well . . ." I paused and looked over at Phyllis Sanders's corpse. Staring at her eviscerated trunk with the severed rib ends bent outward, I felt a sudden letdown and realized whatever petty little battle I'd won here just now with Rossit hadn't really mattered, because no matter what else Gary Rossit might try to pin on me, what I had to answer for in Death Rounds wouldn't change.

". . . since I sent her home," I finally said, trying to keep my voice from betraying how morose I felt, putting my guilt into words. Her disfigured body made me remember how she had stared at me in ER. *Look at what you've done!*

Len stepped back to the autopsy table. There was a great deal of work to be done yet.

"Don't worry," he answered, beginning to cut free the left lung. "That little bastard won't use me, this department, or Death Rounds to railroad you or anyone else if I can help it. That's why I put him on the spot—a reminder that questions about the management of this case could be asked of him as well as by him. If we're right and there are two major infectious processes here, he's not only going to have to explain why he didn't catch on but why he was haranguing the one physician who did. And if our tissue samples confirm *Legionella*, you're going to come out of this looking like a genius," he declared enthusiastically as he carefully placed the left lung on his scale.

A genius with a dead patient, very possibly a murdered patient. Dare I tell Len?

All I had were Janet's remarkable observations and a creepy tale about a figure in the dark. In medicine we called such evidence anecdotal. Interesting and sometimes considered, it usually didn't count for much.

Better stick to the plan, I thought. Get into University Hospital as soon as possible and find some real proof. An idea suddenly occurred to me. "Is this infection unusual enough for us to warn UH about it right away?"

He didn't answer immediately. "It's the possible combination of organisms that's strange here," he finally replied. "I've seen *Legionella* by itself kill in twenty-four hours, and staph pneumonia can certainly be lethal within forty-eight hours, but having them together? I never heard of it."

"But should we warn UH about what we found now?" I repeated, hoping that an alert about two such serious organisms would force University Hospital to allow Michael to add people—including me—to his investigation.

Len stared over at the right lung lying in one of the Tupperware containers. "Not right away," he said at last. "At least not until we get full culture and sensitivity results, and not until I see tissue samples under a microscope. If we are dealing with MRSA or *Legionella* or both, then immediately state health gets involved, and they'll be jumping all over UH and St. Paul's in a big way. To raise all those alarms with everyone just on the appearance of her lungs . . ." He shrugged, then added, "But I've got to admit—so much tissue damage so fast . . ." He shook his head and went back to slicing off the different specimens he'd need to solve the riddle.

Damn! Maybe I should haul Michael in here myself, I thought, force him to look at the telltale organs, and let them frighten him into listening. But the gory things weren't finished with me yet. A terrifying question shot through me like a chill. Was this what the person who'd come padding toward me in the dark had intended for me? Or Janet, if I hadn't come looking for her? Might her lungs have ended up like the specimens in front of me, infected and devoured from within?

I wanted out of the autopsy room. I wanted to get away from Phyllis Sanders's remains and call Janet. Maybe she shouldn't even be at UH working until we had figured out what was going on or unmasked whoever was prowling around in the subbasement. Then I remembered all three nurses became ill while away from the hospital and felt even more at a loss what to do.

But I slowed my breathing and forced myself to focus instead on a final question I had meant to ask Len. It had nothing to do with Janet, but I still wanted to know.

"How did Rossit get you to give this case such an early date in Death Rounds?" I asked him point-blank.

He looked up from his cutting, an annoyed frown underlined by the top of his mask. "For Christ's sake, give us some credit, Earl!" he ordered gruffly. "Rossit did. He knew we wouldn't go along with him, so he convinced somebody else whom we had to listen to."

"What do you mean?" I asked, truly puzzled.

"Hey, I'm supposed to be the guy around here with no political smarts, but even I could figure that one out."

"Len, what the hell are you talking about?"

"There's one other person in this hospital who was hot to put you on trial for this case, and Rossit knew we couldn't refuse him."

"Who's that?" I asked, my mouth going dry.

"Your good friend Paul Hurst, our acting CEO. Hurst ordered us to put Sanders on Death Rounds for Monday."

Chapter 8

"It's only a presumptive diagnosis, Janet, until we get confirmation by culture results," I told her over the phone. I'd gone back to my office after the autopsy and finally tracked her down between deliveries in the UH birthing center. "But Len Gardner is certain there was a preliminary infection prior to the staphylococcus, and *Legionella*'s a good bet."

"How'd Rossit like that?" she asked, her sarcasm evident.

"Speechless!"

"Does that solve your problem with him?"

"Not really. I found out he's linked up with Hurst to nail me at Death Rounds."

"What! How'd you find that out?"

I told her about the call Len had gotten from Hurst.

"Jesus Christ," she exclaimed. "Rossit and Hurst—those two lizards deserve each other. But if you were right about the diagnosis, won't that shut them up?"

"It'll take some of the steam out of Rossit, but I did send the woman home, Janet. He'll push that to the max, and whichever way you dress it up, at the very least I made a lethal error in judgment. As for Hurst, well, you know how dangerous he can be if anyone or anything threatens the good name of St. Paul's. He'd love to get rid of me at the best of times, so I'm sure he'd be particularly willing to throw me to the wolves over this."

Complete silence was Janet's answer to that reminder. Hurst had once gone as far as to make me a suspect in a homicide investigation at St. Paul's to divert the police from discovering some of the more sleazy secrets in the place. As things turned out, the real killer was eventually discovered, but I'd exposed just how ruthless Hurst could be in pursuing whatever he thought would protect the hospital's reputation and his place of power. We'd been wary enemies ever since and probably would remain so for life.

"It stinks!" Janet said vehemently, interrupting my gloomy musings. "How can Hurst get away with that kind of crap? Why don't all the other wienies who call themselves chiefs over there stand up to him? Are you and Sean the only two with . . ."

Her outburst went on for more than a minute. Whenever she sprang to my defense like that, it meant she thought I was in a lot of trouble. But right now I was a whole lot more worried about her safety than my career.

". . . more women on that council of yours would put an end to his smarmy nonsense—"

"Janet," I interrupted, "the only important thing right now is what's going on at your hospital. I'm even beginning to think it's dangerous for you to continue working there." I hadn't intended to blurt out my worst fears. But I kept seeing Sanders's corpse, and I couldn't shake the sounds of that creeping figure in the dark. My pacing the carpet last night hadn't helped either. I'd imagined enough "what if" nightmares for a Wes Craven festival.

"Earl!" she exclaimed, sounding appalled, "I *couldn't* leave my practice!" Her silence made me feel I should have known better. "Besides," she added in a much softer voice, "those nurses became ill away from the hospital."

Startled to hear her echo my own thoughts from earlier that morning, I reexperienced the same panicky fear I'd had then; there was no safe place for her. I felt my courage collapsing in a rush.

"Don't think I haven't taken precautions," she quickly added, "and Cam's insisting everybody in the hospital pay strict attention to isolation procedures until this business is sorted out."

I wasn't at all reassured, and Janet must have sensed it.

"Look, Earl, there's nowhere we can run to," she persisted. "Our best chance is to see if we can find out how those two women were killed. There's got to be a common link, someone with a connection to all those cases."

It sounded hopeless. "But you couldn't find it. That may mean it's not there."

"I won't accept that until you go over the files of the Phantom's victims with me." Her voice was getting a clipped edge to it that warned she was digging in her heels.

But out of fear, I could be stubborn too. "Hell," I persisted, "if there was something incriminating in those files, they may have been stolen last night."

"They're fine. I checked first thing this morning after I had the same worry."

The thought of her going back down to that basement, even during the day, abruptly refilled my head with nightmares.

"Janet! I thought we had a deal! You agreed you wouldn't do anything alone—"

"Relax. I had security accompany me to open the room."

I tried another tack to dissuade her. "Well then, if those records held such incriminating evidence, don't you think whoever's behind this would have taken them last night to keep you from looking at them anymore? Maybe the fact he left them is proof that further checking is pointless."

"Maybe he couldn't risk going back to get them, what with all the excitement you caused down there and electricians prowling around the place," she replied sweetly.

I knew I wasn't going to budge her. Her determination was steel once she made up her mind about something important. Clearly she'd decided we were continuing the hunt.

She listened to my silence for a moment, then added, "Earl, I know last night scared you, deeply, just as it scared me. And the autopsy today must have been gruesome for you. I can only guess at how all that has left you terribly frightened for me."

She paused, giving me time to mutter, "You got me pegged again, lady."

"But I'm not being stupid," she continued, ignoring the wise-crack. "One thing I've done today is broadcast that Michael and I found nothing. I've told everyone here that the investigation was a complete waste of time and that's why I'm back at work. Even what happened at the elevator, I said, was the result of your imagining noises and having a panic attack."

"What!" I couldn't believe I'd heard her right. "Janet! You didn't," I protested. "I don't want people at UH thinking I get panic attacks. I'm a chief of ER, for Christ's sake. Wild Bill Tippet will have a field day teasing—"

"Well excuse me!" she interrupted, laughing. "One minute you're worried about my life, but the next, your reputation takes a little ding, and you get all upset!"

She'd gotten me. "I'm not upset," I objected, feeling foolish. But within seconds I'd joined her in laughing at myself. With one yank of my own ego she'd distracted me out of my fear. For a brief moment I felt my anxiety lessen a notch. God, she knew how to handle me.

"Good, because it's a small price to pay," she concluded. "Now, whoever's behind the infections won't see you or me as a threat."

Still pretty thin protection, I thought. But thanks to Janet, I was a little calmer. Maybe I *was* prone to panic attacks. If so, Janet was a better remedy than Ativan any day.

"Have you talked to Michael yet?" she asked in a firm voice, making it clear we were switching away from the topic of her safety. Part of her remarkable spirit was her capacity to not dwell on a problem that nothing more could be done about for the moment. "Things we cannot change," she would repeatedly remind me when I bogged down in worry that was futile. It was one of the ways she had of finding enough courage for us both.

"No, I'm phoning him right now," I replied. Determined to match her bravery, I added, "Either he lets me in officially, or I do a B&E on all your records tonight."

"Not alone you won't!" she snapped. "Our deal goes both ways."

"Hey, just kidding," I answered. "There's no way I'd go back into that basement by myself." But I'd thought about it if Michael balked on me and if that's what it was going to take to identify a murderer. Along with the return of my nerve came resignation. Until this killer was caught, neither Janet nor I could be safe. I said good-bye, then tried to reach Michael through locating. They couldn't find him.

By midafternoon I'd worked through the usual menu of a busy day in ER—heart attacks, asthmatics, hemorrhagic shock, and a half dozen complaints of abdominal pain. The MVAs had kept rolling in, a few strokes arrived, and the psychiatric emergencies—some of them violent—were many, due to the storm. Between these big cases were the legions of minor problems, everything from colds to VD. But it was a good thing no one asked me the patients' names. I'd like to think I'd been kind and reassuring, yet in the heat of restoring breath, restarting a stalled heart, or replenishing lost blood, I remained obsessed with Janet's safety.

I returned to my office again and again to try to reach Michael but each time had no luck. I kept wondering if I should head over to UH after my shift to look for him. Sitting at my desk, puzzling over what to do, I absently flipped through a pile of mail my secretary had left for me. Most pieces—notices of various meetings, bureaucratic

shuffles, receptions— I tossed into the recycling bin. I'd scrupu-
lously attended all these things in my greener years but long since
learned they were a total waste of time. However, today a memo intended to summon me to a special meeting at 4:00 that afternoon of
hospital physicians, the chiefs, and Hurst regarding "the pending
amalgamation and the growing dissent of the medical staff at St.
Paul's" caught my interest, especially the sole item on the agenda: a
threat from physicians to withdraw services if the merger process
continued.

Maybe Hurst had finally gone too far, I thought. He could play us
off one against the other individually and had done so successfully
for years, but perhaps with all the doctors angry at him at once about
the same thing, he'd be in for a rough ride. Maybe some of the wienies Janet had alluded to were finally going to stand up to him.

My phone interrupted this fantasy. Hoping it was Michael, I answered before the first ring was complete. "Yes?"

"Dr. Garnet?" was the startled response. I recognized the voice of
one of the residents.

"I'm sorry, I thought you were someone else," I explained. "What
can I do for you?"

"Well," she started, sounding embarrassed. "We're all waiting for
you in the classroom. You're supposed to give us a talk at three
today?"

Shit!

I quickly glanced at my calendar and saw I was scheduled to
give the residents a session on "The weak and dizzy patient in ER"
from 2:45 until 4:00. My watch said I was already a quarter of an
hour late.

"Yes, on dizziness, right? I'm just getting my notes together," I
lied. "Tell the others to have a coffee and I'll be with you in five
minutes."

We plan such seminars weeks in advance, and it was a topic for
which I'd already built up quite a file of teaching cases. I'd even
planned on including Phyllis Sanders's story to demonstrate the importance of checking for orthostatic hypotension and at least ensure
others would learn from my mistake. But today the whole thing had
slipped my mind.

I'd need her chest films, I thought as I headed for the door. They
were probably still in pathology. Len would have used them to cor-
relate the radiology findings with what he discovered in the lung itself. I decided on the run that I'd pass by the morgue and retrieve

them before meeting the residents. Damn Michael anyway! Why couldn't I reach him? Not knowing if he'd now agree to let me help Janet was one of the reasons I was so distracted.

I descended a back staircase to the basement and came to the dimly lit corridor leading to the dissection room—and halted. I always found it oppressive walking through this passage, set apart from the busier and newer sections of the hospital. But after what happened last night, I felt my heart start to pound and my respirations quicken. "Not again," I muttered. I'd had the same reaction going into the post early this morning but had overcome it. I stood there a moment, once more trying to slow my breathing. No way was I going to give credence to Janet's cover story by giving in to the flutterings of panic I was beginning to feel.

I fixed my thoughts firmly on getting the X rays and meeting my residents, brought my respiration back to a respectable rate, and stepped into the corridor. To tell the truth, it was nowhere near as cramped or as old as the one at UH—the initial construction of St. Paul's began in the late thirties—but it still pressed in on me. I had to concentrate to keep from thinking that the lights would suddenly go out or that someone was waiting for me in the darkness at the end of the passage. It didn't help any that the tangle of pipes, conduits, and ducts just above my head seemed coated with sixty years of dust and spiderwebs. Every now and then I could hear scurrying noises from deep within this jumble, but in all the time I'd been coming down here, I'd never seen for certain what lived up there.

I passed the heavy wooden doors of the walk-in freezer where bodies were kept pending an autopsy or a pickup by a funeral home and peeked into the brightly lit room where we'd been working earlier. The empty tables, counters, and floors were gleaming from a recent cleaning, but no one was there.

The adjacent changing room was also empty, so I walked farther down the hallway toward the pathologists' and secretaries' offices. Len's cubicle was one of the first in a long line of doors. I could see a light under the sill, so I knocked and let myself in. "Hi, Len, sorry to disturb—"

It wasn't Len in the office. I immediately recognized the broad shoulders and closely cropped blond hair of Harold Miller who was standing in front of Len's desk with his back to me. As he turned at the sound of my voice, I saw he was holding a sheet of paper with the format and familiar outlines of the human form used for our autopsy synopses. He seemed mildly surprised to see me, but returned his gaze to the document in his hand and went on reading it.

"Mr. Miller," I said, appalled to have barged in on the last person I'd have either expected or wanted to see here, "I'm sorry, but I was looking for Dr. Gardner."

"So was I," Miller answered without looking up.

I felt uncomfortable just standing there.

He added, "I was here arranging the release of my mother's body to the funeral home and wanted to know what he'd found during the post." He still didn't look up.

I started backing out of the office when he suddenly tossed the paper he'd been reading onto Len's desk, looked me directly in the eye, and said, "I see you were probably right all along about there being two infections."

"Pardon?" I asked, not immediately catching on.

His expression remained frozen, revealing neither the hurt nor the anger I'd seen in his face the morning before.

"It's in Dr. Gardner's preliminary report on Mother's autopsy this morning," he explained, gesturing with his thumb back toward Len's desk.

"You took it from his desk?" I asked, dismayed, then quickly feeling foolish. Reading a person's notes on his mother's autopsy might not be too polite or appropriate, but it was a hell of a lot less an offense than sending a sick woman home from ER.

"I'm sorry about your mother's death, Mr. Miller; I truly am," I said, but on hearing my own words, I immediately felt overwhelmed by their inadequacy. *It reminds me of a glass coffin, and you put her there,* echoed in my memory. Nothing I could ever say or do would make up for what he'd lost on account of me.

He remained silent.

I turned to go.

"Once it was too late to help her, you were pretty damn on, clinically speaking," he called after me.

I kept walking. This kind of encounter wasn't going to end well no matter what I said. There was no way it could.

He followed after me.

"You certainly impressed me more than the others," he continued, hurrying up and striding along beside me. "As a lab tech I get a pretty good take on a physician—who knows what to order, who follows through, who's up-to-date—that kind of thing."

I stopped and turned to face him. "Look, Mr. Miller, I know this must be one of the worst periods in your life. I don't think this kind of conversation is going to help—"

"Doctor Garnet, I don't expect any help from any conversation with you or any other doctor here. I only expect the simple courtesy of your standing there and hearing me out," he stated.

The blank expression on his face canceled out the hurt look in his eyes that I remembered from the morning before on the stairs. Neither did he seem to be angry. I felt pity for him, and he was right about one thing; the least I could do was stand there and listen.

"Do you want to come to my office and talk?"

"No, here is fine," he said.

I only now noticed we were standing opposite the freezer doors. I hoped he wouldn't realize how near we were to his mother's body.

"In fact, I may be able to help you," he continued.

"What?"

"I'm only a lab tech, Dr. Garnet, but I keep up with the literature, especially diagnostic testing and screening procedures; this is more than a lot of physicians I work under do. Dr. Gardner's comments in his report indicate that the staph infection hadn't seemed to respond at all to the vancomycin you'd been astute enough to order. Rossit's still trying to verify whether the strain was methicillin resistant, but there's another form of resistance that nobody seems to have thought of."

To talk so clinically about his mother's case seemed to me an eerie kind of defense against grief.

"Three months ago," he continued, "the CDC published an advisory to screen staph infections that failed to respond to vancomycin for evidence of decreased susceptibility to that drug as well," he told me, his voice taking on an easy authority that I wouldn't have normally expected from a laboratory technician, even in a less-charged setting.

The CDC is the Centers for Disease Control in Atlanta, staffed by the national experts on infectious diseases. I knew about the advisory; I'd heard the residents talking about it. It had been published in the *Mortality Morbidity Bulletin*, an excellent bimonthly report exposing troublesome new medical puzzles or twists in the presentation of old familiar problems that had recently killed or maimed patients somewhere in the world. I had about a year's worth of issues piled up in my office, waiting to be read.

"What are you getting at?" I asked, intrigued.

"I'm saying the staph organism that killed my mother should also have been tested for decreased susceptibility to vancomycin. Dr. Mackie has had me update our own techs on the new protocol for such cases already. But according to my mother's hospital chart and the autopsy synopsis I just read, that hasn't been done here." He studied me for a few seconds, as if waiting for my reaction to his remarkable pronouncement. When I neither said nor did anything, he added, "The test still should be ordered, for obvious public health reasons."

As he watched me further, I felt uncomfortable again and couldn't decipher what he was watching me for—a response to the information he'd revealed? A recognition of his knowledge and intelligence?

And then he completely disarmed me. "You see, Dr. Garnet," he said with a sudden gentleness, "I couldn't help her when she was still alive. But I want her death to be handled properly. I want whatever killed her identified and tracked down, by the book. If her death were to point out the need for screening to prevent the same infection from hurting anyone else, well, at least that's something . . ." His words trailed off, and tears welled up in his eyes. He spun around and walked away.

I finished my seminar with the residents a few minutes to 4:00. I'd been so distracted after my run-in with Miller that I'd nearly left pathology without retrieving Sanders's X rays, which was why I'd gone down there in the first place. I'd had to rush back to Len's secretary and have her dig out the films, but the effort was worth it. Seeing those lungs nearly whited out by infection so soon after a seemingly benign initial visit had a profound impact on my protégés. That radiographic image taught them more about the perils of missing postural hypotension than hours of listening to lectures or reading textbooks ever could.

Back in my office I made a quick check with University Hospital. Locating still hadn't heard from Michael. I left yet another message for him to phone me right away.

I put my hands behind my head and leaned back for a stretch. The bruise on my forehead had begun to throb and it hurt to move my neck, but with less than four hours sleep, only coffee for breakfast, and no lunch, I figured I should be grateful that I didn't feel worse. Nevertheless, I groaned aloud when I stood up.

The notice for Hurst's meeting with the hospital physicians was lying on my desk where I'd left it. Should I go? I didn't have much stomach for politics at the moment, but in all honesty, I was increasingly too preoccupied with worry about Janet and waiting for Michael's call to be much more use in ER. The encounter would at least be a distraction, I thought, and besides, maybe I could help give Hurst something else to think about besides dumping me as chief of ER.

Before leaving, I took a few minutes to hunt up my copies of the *MMB*. I was curious about the article Miller had quoted, both as to its content and as to how accurately he had interpreted it. Also, I had to admit I wanted to discover something else a lot less scientific. If the man who held my career in his hand was capable of discerning a balanced medical argument, maybe he'd give me a fair shake.

Flipping through my pile of back issues, I quickly spotted the title I was looking for—"Interim Guidelines for Prevention and Control of *Staphylococcus aureus* with Reduced Susceptibility to Vancomycin." The article itself was brief, and I took it with me, stuffing it into my lab coat pocket as I hurried from my office and headed toward the auditorium.

A special meeting of Hurst and all the physicians at St. Paul's was rare. Hurst could barely abide the interference of regular hospital committees into the way he ran St. Paul's. And doctors were usually loath to get involved in hospital politics. They barely had time for the day-to-day issues in their own departments—scheduling, teaching, doing shifts, and the never-ending struggle to keep their clinical skills up-to-date. Speak of downsizing or budgetary restraints and their eyes would roll upward. "That's what chiefs are for," my own staff would say, "to protect us from having to deal with all that garbage."

Stepping through the large oak doors at the rear of the steeply raked amphitheater, I was struck by the size of the turnout. The place was packed, every seat taken and the aisles lined with clinicians in lab coats sitting on the tiered steps. They were a vociferous lot, sounding more like a fight crowd waiting for the start of a match than a group of professionals.

The place was a great choice of venue, for the doctors. Six hundred seats in a steep curved bank towered above Hurst and his band of cronies—all of whom were bunched together on the small stage below. I could tell the man knew he had trouble from the large number of board members he'd brought with him. I recognized most of them from previous social functions, but they'd looked a lot more comfortable then than they did now sitting on folding metal chairs and peering up at the noisy ranks of white coats above them. There had even been a touch of theater in the lighting. While the stage was harshly lit, the spectators were in semidarkness. Hurst kept squinting at us while shielding his eyes, but I doubt if he could recognize a specific face. As I sat on one of the upper steps, the single word "trial" popped into my mind to describe the spectacle—the kind of trial in which the jurors render verdicts with stones.

Someone in the second row stood and made his way toward the podium. Even before he stepped into the spotlight, his frizzy red hair and large physique gave him away. "I'd like to call this meeting to order," said Sean into the microphone, igniting a round of applause, cheers, and whistles. Some of the board members clutched their briefcases to their chests and looked nervously at one another. Hurst, his face always a pale shade of gray, scowled disapprovingly at us and looked positively ill under the overhead lights. His forehead had an unhealthy sheen in the glare.

More than a decade ago a heart attack had brought an end to his surgical career, but since then he had found his niche in administration. During my tenure as chief over the last eight and a half years I'd watched him become more and more obsessed with his pursuit of absolute authority over the hospital. He was ruthless in cutting budgets and trimming deficits, and in a world where hospitals were subject to hostile takeovers and closure, the board loved him for it — called him dedicated. Clinicians had other names for his management style and either feared him, submitting to his decrees, or held him at bay, challenging him whenever he risked patients' lives in his drive to get them out of hospital quicker and sicker—to save a buck.

The enthusiastic clapping became rhythmic, and a few voices took up the chant "No! No! No!" They were joined by more and more until the entire room was booming with the defiant shout.

Hurst sat back in his chair, made a pyramid of his fingers, and tapped his lips, seemingly keeping time with the protest all around him. His eyes were fixed on the floor and he remained motionless, but I knew that pose from previous encounters; he was livid.

The other board members were shifting uneasily in their chairs, whispering to each other, and shuffling their feet, all the while looking repeatedly at Hurst and then back out at the crowd in front of them. They seemed as astonished by his immobility as by our raucous behavior. Finally Sean held up his hands and spoke again into the microphone, "Okay everyone, come to order now, settle down . . ."

The room gradually grew quiet.

"Fine," said Sean brightly. "Let's get right to the point. We, the clinicians of St. Paul's hospital, are here to issue an ultimatum to you, Dr. Hurst," he said, turning and gesturing toward the stony-faced former surgeon, "and to the members of the board," he added, opening his arm farther to include their part of the stage, "who, I may say, I'm glad to see have joined us and have turned out in such numbers."

Sean was smiling and speaking as pleasantly as if he were honoring the visitors. Some were obviously confused by such effusive politeness in a hostile encounter and returned his smile, then checked themselves and retained the same severe expression Hurst had adopted.

"As far as we are concerned, there will be no merger of our clinical departments with UH. This whole operation has been engineered by accountants and managerial gurus, with all the decisions coming from above. That approach may make sense in companies," opined Sean, again turning toward the board members, most of whom were CEOs of their own corporations and industries in Buffalo. "It would even be a sensible way to amalgamate the administrations of our two hospitals, which, by the way, the majority of us here would support."

I wasn't sure, but I thought I saw Hurst flinch at the mention of merging his control of St. Paul's with the CEO of another institution.

"But clinical departments aren't like companies. Academically and professionally each of us is his or her own CEO when it comes to taking care of a patient. We have the ultimate responsibility for that life; we cannot and will not surrender that autonomy. Neither will we allow our departments to be reorganized by anyone but ourselves. We're the ones with the competence to assess how our clinical units best work to deliver safe and timely care, not some time-and-motion expert. And we will not accept that our departmental leadership be parceled out to another institution. That's a formula to guarantee a department won't make its needs heard at the budget table. Shutting us up isn't going to save money, Dr. Hurst; it's only going to lead to misinformed decisions, misspent funds, and a patient clientele denied the equipment and resources it really needs. Do whatever you want with the other services in the two hospitals—laundry, catering, distribution, and supply—they seem perfect things to merge. But our clinical departments must retain full thickness."

There were immediate murmurs of approval from everyone in the audience. Hurst suddenly flushed. The board members looked puzzled, clearly not familiar with the term that had caused such a buzz around the room.

"Full thickness" was a surgical expression known to all the doctors in the amphitheater, including Hurst. It referred to a skin graft that restored all levels of tissue. Sean meant that our clinical departments and departmental leadership would remain completely intact, chiefs included, or there would be no deal.

"I needn't remind you," concluded Sean, "you can merge and amalgamate all you want, but you need physicians if you want to have a hospital." With that comment he walked from the podium and took his seat.

The applause from his colleagues this time was long and loud, though decorous, as befitted the seriousness of what we were faced with. Sean had lifted our opposition to the plan from petty worries over turf to the vital connection between saving lives and solid medical representation at the level of financial planning. Some of the board members were whispering to one another and nodding. A few reached into their briefcases, pulled out notebooks, and were busily writing. Hurst hadn't budged, and he was no longer tapping his lips with his fingers. But his eyes looked molten with rage.

Stewart Deloram, who had been sitting beside Sean, stood up, seemed to sway a few minutes, then recovered his balance and strode to the podium. I recognized a few other chiefs in the front row, who over the years had been willing to oppose Hurst when it had been necessary. Sean must have recruited the lot of them to help him lead today's effort. I wondered why he hadn't approached me, since we'd been so effective joining forces for these battles in the past. The proof of our successes was the enmity of Hurst that we'd incurred in the process, and without a doubt we were certainly considered his two most vexing chiefs.

I glanced over at our old adversary again. He still seemed to be smoldering in his chair since the board members had obviously responded positively to Sean's opening remarks. Watching him fume, I quickly got a pretty good idea why Sean hadn't included me in his offensive this time. If he'd heard about the Sanders case, he probably figured I had enough trouble as it was.

"To the members of the board, welcome," said Stewart when he reached the microphone. He broke off to cough into his hand, then continued, turning to face his guests but pointedly ignoring Hurst. "I'm Dr. Deloram, chief of Intensive Care at St. Paul's. My job today is to help you better understand our grave concerns over the way this merger is shaping up. In a minute, I'm going to let you ask questions or say anything ..."

As Stewart spoke, he kept having to clear his throat and turn away so as not to cough into the microphone. He must be getting a cold, I thought, and noticed he looked a bit pale under the stage lights. I absently gazed around the audience and spotted here and there some of the chiefs Hurst had in his hip pocket. They were slouched down in their chairs, probably hoping their master wouldn't see them but no doubt just as scared of what their own department members would do to them if they'd skipped the meeting.

Stewart had another coughing fit, took a sip of water, and went on speaking.

"... but let me first ask you, if you were a patient in our ICU, who could best assure that the equipment and personnel needed to pull you through were there? An accountant? An absentee chief looking out for his own department at UH? Or a chief who was present ..."

Then I saw Rossit sitting a few rows ahead of me leaning forward with his chin resting on his hands. Even in the half light I could see the continual movement of his jaw muscles. He mustn't be too happy with something, I thought, watching the familiar chewing motion.

Stewart finished speaking with an apology to his audience for sounding so wretched, joked about being a shoemaker poorly shod, then croaked an invitation for questions.

"Jesus, someone should send him home to bed," I muttered to no one in particular while watching him give his microphone to one of the visitors on the stage who'd raised his hand. This man had his chair closer to Hurst than the rest, and I'd noted he hadn't been among those nodding and taking notes at the end of Sean's remarks. He, like the others, seemed vaguely familiar.

"Thank you, Dr. Deloram," he began, "but I feel compelled to explain why this merger is necessary ..."

There were groans and the sounds of shuffling feet throughout the auditorium. We'd had these explanations ad nauseam, and the familiar phrases were like Sominex. "Partnerships," "greater efficiencies," "better clout with HMOs and regular insurers"—the mantra went on against the rising mutter around me. "Can it!" "Give it a rest!" "Christ, not again!"

But this speaker seemed undaunted by the hostility he was incurring. In fact, he seemed encouraged by it, raising his voice and bulldozing on while the volume of the protests around him increased. ". . . their bargaining power means lower rates, and that means less income for the hospitals . . ." I suddenly recognized him. He wasn't a member of the board but one of the hospital lawyers. He'd once accompanied Hurst to a meeting with other lawyers to discuss the hospital having been named in a lawsuit against ER.

I quickly looked over at Hurst. He was in the same fixed position as before, his fingertips at his lips, but his eyes were roving over the increasingly unruly audience and he was starting to smirk. Suddenly he placed his hands on the sides of his chair and appeared to be about to get up. But he paused halfway out of his seat, and as I watched, his expression changed. He raised his eyebrows, dropped open his mouth, and, bringing his hands up from his chair, raised his palms to the heavens—a perfect parody of shock and dismay. But that little smirk had given him away.

"Excuse me!" I said, rising from my place on the stairs. "I want to know who you are, sir." I pointed at the man with the microphone. He stopped in midsentence and stared at me. "Yes, you," I insisted. "Tell us who you are!" I continued to point at him. But out of the side of my eye, I could see my outburst had been in time to catch Hurst still halfway out of his chair. His white face instantly went crimson, but he slowly sank back into his seat.

"Are you a member of the board?" I persisted, continuing to face the startled lawyer.

"Me?" he asked, glancing nervously at Hurst.

Everyone had gone absolutely still, the doctors probably more than a little uneasy about what I was up to and no doubt wondering whether I would embarrass or hurt their attempt to win over the board members. The businesspeople themselves looked puzzled, and one of them volunteered, "This is Norman Baker, an attorney for the hospital. His law firm is representing St. Paul's in the merger." His tone of voice clearly implied he hadn't a clue why there would be anything wrong with the lawyer being here.

"I simply want us all to know who he is," I countered. "As a member of the law firm handling the merger, he obviously has a vested interest in the process quite different from that of the board members," I explained.

"Now just a minute!" exploded Baker.

"Dr. Garnet!" roared Hurst, leaping out of his chair.

"Relax, Dr. Hurst," I interjected before he could get started. "And you too, Mr. Baker. This meeting was called, among other things, to allow the physicians to express their deep concern over the merger, not to give yet another lawyer another chance to lecture us on why legal takeover specialists think it's a good idea. That the board is also present to hear these concerns, and hopefully to ask questions about them, gives added value to this meeting. It's simply too good an opportunity to waste—an opportunity to assure that the choices made in the coming weeks are fully informed choices. What better way to assure that the best possible decisions will be taken for the future of St. Paul's?"

I'd only intended to stop Hurst from scuttling the meeting. I'd been sure he was going to engage in a show of mock outrage at our rudeness in front of the board and then lead the lot of them out of there. He knew full well how fed up we all were with proclamations from above, and he certainly could predict how we'd react to yet another harangue about why the merger was good for us. I even suspected Baker had been told to deliberately try to antagonize us to give Hurst the excuse he needed. I'd seen Hurst pull similar stunts and engineer his acts of indignation before but had learned to keep an eye out for that little smirk which always preceded them.

But what I hadn't counted on was the applause that followed. Even some of the board members rose to their feet and clapped. Hurst remained seated, his hands once more in the shape of a pyramid and his fingers rapidly tapping his lips. But there was no trace of a smirk now as he glared up in my direction. Baker leaned forward, whispered in his ear, then picked up his briefcase and stalked off the stage. Around me my colleagues went on clapping. I caught Sean's eye as he stood at the front of the stage. He raised his arms, joined his hands over his head, and pumped the air with them like a triumphant boxer. Then, still smiling at me, he used his right index finger to point at his temple and make little circles—the universal sign that he thought I was crazy.

I might have found Sean's gesture more humorous if I hadn't seen Rossit arrive at the front of the stage at that moment and exchange a few words with Hurst as he pointed toward where I was sitting. The two men then looked in my direction, while Hurst nodded and spoke into Rossit's ear.

"A regular pair of Iagos," I muttered to myself. When Hurst

turned to leave through a door down at the stage level, I watched Rossit push his way back to the foot of the aisle I was in and start up the steps toward me, scowling the whole way.

As he jostled past, he snarled, "Fuck up this merger, Garnet, and you'll make yourself a lot of powerful enemies!"

I was halfway to my feet and trying to control an urge to run after the little bastard and pummel him. He had reached the top of the stairs when I heard a crash on the stage below and someone screamed. I whirled in time to see Stewart Deloram fall onto the podium, toppling it over, and roll off it onto the floor.

Chapter 9

Six hundred doctors and nobody moved for the space of a few heartbeats. Then about a hundred of us tried to take charge.

I sprinted down the steps two at a time but was so stiff I nearly took a tumble myself.

Stewart was being swarmed by his rescuers.

"Get a stretcher!"

"Is he breathing?"

"Get a pulse?"

"Get back!" Sean was yelling as he knelt at Stewart's head.

Elbowing my way through the circle of white, I could see Stewart himself struggling to sit up. His face was the color of paste, and glistening dots of perspiration spread across his forehead.

"Lie back, Stewart," I commanded, pushing gently on his chest and reaching for his wrist. The front of his shirt was damp with sweat, and his pulse, difficult to feel, was rapid. I noticed blood starting to pool on the floor from a gash behind his ear. Sean grabbed a packet of tissue from his lab coat pocket and applied pressure to slow the bleeding. There was also a stench of feces in the air.

"Let's get him to ER!" I yelled. "Call them for a stretcher stat!"

"This'll need a few sutures," added Sean calmly.

My main concern was for Stewart's vital signs. Still coughing, he seemed to be breathing okay, but clearly he had a low pressure. He moaned, looked around with a puzzled expression on his face, then reached for his head with his right hand. "Hold it, Stewart," I restrained him. "You fainted and have a cut there. Do you feel pain anywhere else?" I knew he was in his late thirties, so a heart attack was unlikely but not impossible.

"Earl," he said weakly. "What happened?"

I repeated, "I think you just fainted. Do you have pain anywhere?"

"Only my head," he answered, reaching for it again.

95

"Hold it, Stewart," said Sean. "I've got to keep pressing until we sew you up in ER."

Stewart obediently but weakly let his hand flop to his side.

"Stewart, do you have a history of heart trouble or of any other medical problems, like diabetes, ulcers, or lower GI bleeding?" The differential for dizziness and fainting snapped into my head—cardiac, metabolic, vascular.

"No, nothing, Earl, just this cold, and—Oh Christ!" he exclaimed, raising his head and looking down with disgust at the wet crotch of his trousers.

"Don't worry about it," I tried to reassure him. "It happens." But not usually with a simple faint. With a seizure or a full cardiac arrest, yes, but I hadn't seen any shaking movements and he'd obviously had a pulse from the moment I got there.

"I've had diarrhea since a few hours ago." He groaned. "It's part of this flu I picked up, but this is embarrassing."

He'd not been coughing on the phone last night, I thought.

"I only felt dizzy when I got up to speak," he continued. "Until then, apart from the usual muscle pains and a slight headache, I didn't feel that bad, for a cold."

His words sent an icy shiver up my back.

The stretcher arrived, and as we hurried toward emergency I kept my fingers on his pulse while Sean kept up his chatter as he continued pressing on the laceration. "You know, I usually let the students practice on cuts like this. You're getting pretty VIP care for a simple case of the runs, what with two chiefs taking . . ."

But my insides were turning to ice. "While Sean's doing his artwork, I'm going to run a few tests, Stewart," I told him breezily when we got to ER, hoping my *everything's-going-to-be-all-right* tone kept him from realizing what I was suspecting.

Two days ago I never would have thought about it, because until two days ago, it would have been impossible. But any doubts I had that I was overreacting vanished moments later. As we worked on Stewart, starting IVs, drawing bloods, and rechecking his vitals, I happened to glance up and saw Rossit standing at the door, looking on. The expression on his face looked as grim as I felt. There was no trace at all of the hostility and anger that had been part of whatever game he'd been playing over the last few days. In fact, if I had to put a name to what I saw in his black unblinking stare, it would be fear.

Well, this is a change, I thought rather bitterly, knowing full well that he'd resume our hostilities whenever it next suited him and I couldn't ever drop my guard against the little troublemaker. But for that moment I was willing to bet we both expected the same results from Stewart's tests—a low white count, a low sodium and albumin, and a near normal chest X ray.

"I don't have to explain it, Michael, and I don't have any more time for this kind of crap." Locating had finally found him for me in the general records department at UH. Our conversation was not going well. "I've just admitted Stewart Deloram to his own ICU with a presumptive diagnosis of *Legionella*, I could have been killed last night by whoever came after me in the subbasement, and I don't even want to think about what he might have done to Janet if I hadn't come along. Now when the hell are you going to admit there's something more going on than a missed water sample?"

"Is Stewart going to be okay?" he asked, refusing to answer my challenge.

"Who knows. He's loaded to the gills with erythromycin and the infection's early, but it's alarming as hell he could even have contracted *Legionella* in the first place. And if it is *Legionella*, we're also just seeing the prodrome. The pneumonia won't develop until tomorrow. So far there's no evidence of staph."

Not only had Rossit and I agreed there were no clinical indications for more antibiotics at the moment, the real irony was that he and I had then stood side by side and lectured the residents about the perils of overprescribing and cautioned them to rein in their urges to throw everything at an infection "just in case."

Michael stayed silent, then asked, "Could Stewart have gotten it taking care of the Sanders woman?"

"Michael, you know secondary person-to-person spread has never been recorded," I snapped back. "Now *you're* inventing unheard of scenarios and all the while dismissing Janet because she's dared to suspect something you'd never heard of!" I was losing patience by the minute with his stubborn refusal to admit what we might be up against.

"Earl, calm down. I meant could an accidental aerosol of *Legionella* have been created from a problem with the ventilation or from incomplete sterilization of equipment used on her."

I took a deep breath and lowered my voice. "They're checking that out now, but so far there's been no evident breech of isolation and sterilization procedures."

"But it's possible," he persisted.

"Not probable, Michael. Stewart's young, healthy, even less likely than those three nurses to contract *Legionella*."

"Are they checking where he lives—"

"Yes, Michael, yes! You realize you're going down the same blind alleys they already went down at University Hospital?"

This at last shut him up. But in the silence between us, I realized something.

I didn't know why or where it happened specifically; perhaps it was last night when someone tried to crack my skull open. Or was it witnessing the utter devastation of Sanders's lungs this morning? Or maybe it was seeing Stewart fall victim to an inexplicable infection a little more than an hour ago. But over the last twenty-four hours I'd passed from considering that a killer was possibly on the loose to absolute certainty that I was in pursuit of someone very real, very clever, and very evil. Perhaps it was the impossibility of making anyone else believe that murder had been committed that had made me so sure.

I'd begun to feel Janet and I were battling a superb defense—a protection set up by a killer who knew how the medical community would interpret and investigate these infections and deaths. A killer who was convinced that fidelity to science would practically forbid any investigator from thinking the infections were deliberately inflicted. It was as if the very bizarreness of the infections was a taunt, a tease, an arrogant flouting of the murderer's method—a demonstration of the murderer's certainty that no matter how strange or inexplicable the infections might be, adherence to accepted medical thought would prevail, and no one would ever suspect the killer's existence because no one would dare contemplate that murder had ever been done.

Paranoia? Maybe, but that reaction described Michael's behavior perfectly and Cam's and probably anyone else's I could think of whom we might try to tell about the Phantom.

I was so lost in thought, it took a few seconds to realize Michael was talking to me again.

" . . . but Janet's been telling everyone what happened in the basement was just a panic attack."

"That's only a ruse," I answered, suddenly feeling hopelessly tired.

"I didn't know you got panic attacks."

"Will you forget goddamned panic attacks!"

"All right! All right! You don't get panic attacks. But didn't you hear *anything* I said yesterday about what this kind of Phantom talk could do to your credibility? Besides, Janet doesn't exactly seem to be sharing your worry anymore. She's broadcast all over the hospital that our audit is a waste of time, which, by the way, I don't particularly appreciate. Just because I don't buy her Phantom idea, we still have to find a source of—"

"Damn it, Michael!" I was snapping again. "I told you it was a ruse!" Once more I took a few seconds to try to calm down. "Have you talked to her yourself today?" I asked through clenched teeth.

"No, I haven't seen her at all. But she's obviously been feeding the gossip network," he replied brusquely, letting me hear how miffed he was with her.

"Well if you had, Michael, she'd have told you she's only saying that stuff to fool the creep who attacked me last night into thinking she's backed off." The receiver might have been Michael's neck, I was squeezing it so hard. I relaxed my grip and watched the blood rush back into the skin around my knuckles. Still, I couldn't let go of my fury with him for being so thick. "You didn't see that woman's lung. It made me scared for anyone at University Hospital, including Janet and you. Now I'm scared about what's going to happen to poor Stewart. And I'm going to stay scared every time Janet goes to work and every time she comes home and goes near the baby." I let my frustrations pour out of me. "Better yet, Michael, put yourself in Janet's position. You don't think she isn't frightened, at least if not about herself, then certainly about Brendan?" Then I let fire my final shot. "Whether you're right or, God forbid, she is—and I'm more and more convinced she is—you could at least give Donna and your unborn child the same concern."

I heard Michael grunt like he'd been hit, then listened to him breathe for several seconds. "Ouch," he finally answered. Then added, "God, how could I be so blind!" A few more seconds passed. "I'm such an asshole! Donna's right, I've got the sensitivity of a runaway truck once I get my head set on a clinical problem." He was speaking more and more rapidly and sounding increasingly chastised. "Damn, I'm sorry Earl; I just never clued in on how this might be affecting Janet and you personally. Will you forgive me? And will Janet? Oh my God, Donna will kill me for this if she ever finds out I was so insensitive. I'll find Janet and apologize to her myself. No! Better yet, I'll send her flowers in the morning and then apologize. For God's sake, don't let her tell Donna."

While his self-reproach built up steam, I recalled something about jackasses and two by fours, but now that I had his attention, I pushed. "Michael, it's time to cash in all those markers you've chalked up with the accreditation board and get me named to this audit. Or threaten Cam if you have to. Tell him we're sitting on another presumptive diagnosis of *Legionella* related to the Sanders case. Impress on him that I'm his best chance of finding answers before culture results make the outbreaks official. If he still isn't moved to cooperate, tell him I'm going public by noon tomorrow unless I've got carte blanche to find out what's going on over there."

Michael's silence was encouraging. Figuring I had him cornered, I hung up before he could change his mind.

I heard sirens approaching. There were at least two, maybe more. If they were all ambulances heading to our ER, I knew I'd be called to help within minutes. I was starting for the door and pulling my stethoscope out of my lab coat pocket when I noticed the *MMB* article slide out with it and fall to the floor. I paused to pick it up, glanced at the summary on the first page, then started to slip it back into my pocket. Had Miller been accurate in his précis of it? The blended wailings of the sirens were closer but no ambulance was here yet. Neither had Susanne run in to fetch me. I had a moment still.

Unfolding the article, again I skimmed through it. The brief synopsis described a case report from Japan of the world's first-ever infection by a methicillin-resistant, vancomycin-inhibiting staphylococcus organism. The key word was *inhibiting*. It ultimately succumbed to vancomycin but only at very high doses. What had made this case alarming, the authors stated, was that in the past, organisms on the way to becoming fully resistant to a specific antibiotic had often demonstrated this inhibiting effect first. Historically, the emergence of a fully resistant strain of these organisms almost invariably followed, usually within two years. Should the same pattern repeat itself this time, the resulting staphylococcus bacteria, resistant to both vancomycin and methicillin, would be virtually untreatable. Any new antibiotics that might be useful were at least two or three years away from use in humans. The authors then brought the issue even closer to home. The first vancomycin-inhibiting strain of MRSA in the United States was reported by a hospital in Michigan, a second by a hospital in New Jersey. In both cases the organisms had responded to large doses of antibiotics, and no outbreaks anywhere in the world had been reported since.

One of the sirens had become much louder than the rest. Suddenly it cut out, and seconds later I heard the vehicle roar into the ambulance bay.

Getting ready to leave, I flipped over to the last page. A single item in the final list of recommendations was what I was looking for. Exactly as Miller had reported, in a case like his mother's, in which a staphylococcal infection had failed to respond to vancomycin, the organism should be rechecked for this new trait of reduced susceptibility. There was even a hot-line telephone number at the CDC where any instances of the strain were to be reported immediately.

I tossed the article onto my desk. The rest of it looked rather technical and would require more time than I had at the moment. I had a hell of a lot more to worry about than some theoretical superbug coming at us from the other side of the world two years in the future.

But as I was heading out the door and running toward ER, on impulse I thought, why not call bacteriology and ask that vancomycin be included in Rossit's special sensitivity tests already under way for the Sanders case? According to the CDC, the minimal inhibitory concentration method he was using—a determination of the times a culture of the organism can be diluted and still resist a given antibiotic—was the only reliable way to screen for the inhibiting strain. Rossit would probably be furious at me for meddling with his lab studies, but at least the gesture of adding the antibiotic to the group being checked might please Miller. After all, if Rossit hadn't been so busy bad-mouthing me, he could have kept St. Paul's up-to-date on this latest protocol for staph infections himself, the way Cam had done for University Hospital. I asked the clerk at triage to phone in the order.

The next hour I spent working with every available resident and doctor in ER resuscitating a dozen seniors suffering from smoke inhalation. Their residence had burnt to the ground. The culprit responsible for the fire, an eighty-year-old man repeatedly caught smoking in bed, was brought in later—a charred corpse held together by a body bag.

As I was filling out his death certificate, our telephone clerk transferred a call to where I was sitting. "Bacteriology department for you Dr. Garnet, line three."

It was a technician.

"Dr. Garnet, I'm sorry to bother you, but the clerk told me you wanted the staph organisms from the Sanders case checked for an inhibitory effect on vancomycin?"

"That's right."

"Well, I thought I'd better tell you, it's already been ordered."

"Really? How come that's not on her chart?"

There was a pause. "Gee, Dr. Garnet, I hope I'm not in trouble." Another pause. By now I recognized the voice of the technician who'd done the initial Gram stain on Sanders's sputum sample and who'd been so excited about finding staphylococci. "You see, it wasn't exactly an order," he continued, sounding sheepish. "It was actually more a suggestion from Dr. Mackie over at UH. He phoned yesterday morning, said he'd consulted on the case, and recommended we do the test since Harold's mother wasn't responding to treatment. It's the routine in his department, and should be here too if you ask me."

"Did you check with Dr. Rossit?" I asked, glad this innocent couldn't see my wicked grin.

The complete silence on his end of the line answered my question. Finally the young man dared to say, "You know how *he* is, Dr. Garnet. Besides, Dr. Mackie's going to be the new overall chief soon, isn't he, when the merger goes through?"

Not if Rossit can help it, I felt like warning him, for despite the popular expectation that Cam would prevail on merit, I'd seen hospital politics favor the Rossits of this world all too often. Ambition was an easier currency for boards and CEOs to manipulate than the harder mettle that resided in a man like Cam. I tried to keep my voice neutral when I replied, "You must have inside sources that I don't."

I'd been about to hang up when the tech said, "Dr. Garnet, I wonder if I could ask you a favor?"

I immediately felt my guard go up. "Yes?" I replied cautiously. Over the years, as a physician and a chief, I'd been asked a lot of favors. Most had been legitimate, but some, especially those from people I didn't know, had been embarrassingly inappropriate and some had been outright illegal.

"Well, since you were going to order it anyway . . ."

"Would it help your peace of mind if I put my name on the order?" I volunteered, chuckling at the simplicity of the request.

"Would you? That'll be great! The test probably won't come to anything, but I never know what Dr. Rossit is going to be angry about, especially these days."

Another little sin on my tab wouldn't matter much, I thought while hanging up.

*   *   *

Before leaving that evening, I dropped in to see Stewart. It was an eerie feeling gowning up to visit him in the same glass chamber in which we'd put Phyllis Sanders.

At first Stewart appeared in surprisingly good spirits and seemed more intrigued by how he could have contracted *Legionella* than frightened by his infection. But as we talked about the conventional investigations into the organism's source—I'd no expectations they'd find anything—I soon discovered Stewart's underlying fear when he began to cough from the effort of speaking. As his hacking made him progressively short of breath, his eyes filled with alarm, and he asked, "Do you think when the pneumonia comes I'll get as bad as she was?"

"Of course not Stewart," I bluffed. "Early treatment's the key to a mild and uneventful course. And remember, she had a secondary staph infection as well."

He looked away without saying anything more and stared through the glass walls of his isolation room into the dim light of ICU. The gray semidarkness of evening was visible through the large outside windows behind the nurses' station. He knew as well as I did that evolving respiratory conditions get worse at night. And as a physician, he knew what could go wrong. I figured he had to be thinking of the *Legionella* cases he'd seen in the past. It would have been impossible for him not to remember chest X rays he'd viewed that had shown the lungs whited out by the disease. He'd certainly have seen the remains of the infection at autopsy often enough, though I thanked God he hadn't witnessed the particular horrors of Phyllis Sanders's post today. Even with antibiotics on board, he had no way of knowing for sure what lay ahead for him.

All the while I desperately wanted to ask Stewart some leading questions about who might have done this to him. But should I? In his vulnerable state, he might not be as skeptical as his colleagues, and talking about the Phantom could needlessly add to his fears.

"Stewart," I began, choosing my words carefully, "if the infection is related to the Sanders case, then your exposure had to have happened in the first hours after her admission. Was there ever anyone around you using an aerosol at that time?"

"No, I went through all that with Rossit."

"Do you use any nose sprays for allergies?"

"Again, like I told Rossit, no."

"Did anyone visit Sanders from UH on that first day?"

"Visitors? Besides her son? No. She was in no shape for visitors. You know that. Unless you consider Cam Mackie a visitor."

"Was anyone else here, during those hours—an orderly, a nurse, someone dressed in isolation garb you might not have recognized—who shouldn't have been?"

"What do you mean?"

"Could some unauthorized person have come in here and been around you and Sanders, and you not have realized it? In my own department all sorts of people in greens come and go—they're almost invisible—without my noticing it."

"I don't know. It's possible I suppose, but we're a lot smaller and more controlled than ER. The nurses would be pretty quick to ask anyone they didn't recognize what he or she was doing, especially if someone tried to get into this room," he answered, sounding a little morose and looking around him. I suspected he still couldn't quite believe he'd ended up a patient in his own domain.

"Is there anyone who you've seen around a lot outside of here who may have been following you or want to do you harm?"

"What!" He stared at me, an expression of amazement creeping over his pale face.

I immediately backed off. "Nothing, forget about it. I was just kidding—a bad joke about how shit disturbers like you and Sean could expect Hurst to keep an eye on you. You guys really got him nicely at the meeting today."

He looked puzzled but seemed to accept the question as a failed attempt to make him laugh. I decided that I couldn't ask him anything more without scaring him silly or leaving him convinced I was crazy.

When I stopped at the nurses' station to check his chart, I learned everyone working in ICU had gone on oral erythromycin as prophylaxis against *Legionella*, despite Rossit's best attempts to assure them it wasn't necessary. Not a bad idea, I thought. Maybe Janet and Michael should do the same thing.

All the way home I kept wondering how someone from UH could have gotten near Stewart and infected him without his knowing. Despite his protests to the contrary, I was sure he'd be as oblivious as I to the legions of anonymous hospital workers who were around us every day. They could come and go like ghosts or like a phantom. I began to feel overwhelmed again by how nebulous our killer was. Might it be impossible to ever pull him from the shadows? Could he go on forever, moving undetected through the faceless echelons of a hospital, and continue to murder?

I felt a little less hopeless when I remembered Cam had been with Stewart and Sanders during those critical hours. Maybe he had recognized someone he knew from University Hospital, someone he might normally pay no heed to at UH but who may have stuck out in his mind because he or she was at St. Paul's. I'd ask him tomorrow.

It was only at the entrance to my house that I asked the big question. Why was Stewart chosen as a victim? I couldn't think of any conceivable motive pertaining solely to him. Then a nasty possibility concerning myself popped unbidden into my head. Perhaps it was a demonstration, a show of power, a message from the killer that he could get anyone he wanted, including people on my turf, and I couldn't do a thing about it.

The relief Janet showed when she learned I'd soon be with her at UH quickly evaporated when I told her what had happened to Stewart. She was also as disturbed as I was about the implications of the attack. Like me, she no longer included an *if* during our discussions of the killer.

I related the rest of the day's events during our dinner together, although it felt more like a debriefing than table talk. I wanted to make sure I hadn't overlooked anything significant.

Janet was quiet afterward, then said, "There is something that doesn't add up. It's Rossit. Why would he want the amalgamation to go ahead?"

I'd been too preoccupied about Stewart to have given much thought to Rossit's peculiar antics at the meeting. "How do you mean 'doesn't add up'?"

"Whatever he's cooking up with Hurst, given the likelihood he'll lose his job as chief to Cam once the merger goes through, I'd have figured he'd be cheering you on, not threatening you or anyone else who was trying to stop the amalgamation."

I leaned back as I thought more about Rossit. "He may not be as completely out of the running against Cam as everyone thinks," I finally answered.

"What?"

"Politics can be screwy, and Hurst might figure it would be easier to make deals with a self-serving guy like Rossit than it would be with Cam."

"That sucks," Janet said.

"It supersucks when you think he's probably making the same calculation about every chief, including yours truly, and will only support those he's sure he can control."

"Christ!" she muttered, downing her drink—club soda, in deference to both recent and planned efforts at keeping Brendan from being an only child.

"If Rossit thinks he's got some kind of arrangement with Hurst," I resumed, "then he might see the merger as an opportunity and not a threat."

Janet received this observation with raised eyebrows, leaned back, and seemed to savor it for a while. "I see what you mean," she finally allowed.

I picked up my own drink, a Black Russian, acknowledged that the rules of pregnancy weren't fair by raising my glass to Janet, then swirled the ice, took a sip, and added, "What *I* don't get is Rossit's extraordinary ardor in trying to nail me for the Sanders case. It's gone way beyond his usual mean streak, and for the life of me, I can't see how my downfall could benefit him."

Janet had winced at the word *downfall*. "Has he ever teamed up with Hurst before, during any of these other vendettas he's carried out?"

The image of Rossit and Hurst huddled together, whispering and pointing toward me, sprang to mind. I shuddered, then answered, "No, at least not that I know of."

Janet settled back in her chair and twirled the stem of her glass with her left hand. "So," she began, holding out her right thumb, about to start counting something, "Rossit has outdone even his own smarmy standards in his attempt to crucify you." She held up her index finger alongside her thumb. "He's even recruited Hurst's help, an unusual step for him, to get you into Death Rounds almost immediately." Her middle finger joined the other two. "And he's a fan of the merger, as though against all odds he has some trick up his sleeve whereby he could prevail over Cam." Four fingers were now in the air. "Hurst's support could be part of that trick, but Rossit's got to know my hospital's going to fight as hard as yours to dominate the merger. He's got to be counting on something more than Hurst's getting his wish list to help him win the day." The fifth finger she pointed at me, with an expectant look. It was my turn to provide a piece of the puzzle. "What could be Rossit's additional hidden trick?" she asked.

Our problem solving often proceeded this way, an idea at a time, layer by layer, back and forth. But usually the topic was interpreting a work of art, where to go on vacation, or how to redecorate the house. Yet it seemed as good a method as any to help unlock whatever might help us get a grasp on our killer who no one else even suspected existed.

And unlock something it did. Another inconsistency, a big one that Stewart had noticed, flew into focus. I sat up and snapped my fingers. "Janet, you're a genius. If Rossit needed another trick, something more to assure his advantage over Cam, why did he keep ridiculing my diagnosis of *Legionella* in Sanders's case?"

"What do you mean?"

"Look. One of Cam's most important responsibilities as chief of ID is the control of hospital-acquired infections. He'd already been unable to explain two cases of *Legionella* involving nurses from UH. What better way for Rossit to undermine Cam's credibility than to discover a third? By doing so, Rossit could imply that University Hospital had a recurrent problem with the deadly organism and that Cam couldn't solve it. A scare about uncontained *Legionella*, if it became public, would frighten away patients, shatter public confidence in UH, and be a disaster for the hospital's contracts with HMOs. With the potential for such a catastrophe tied to Cam's reputation, the board might hand the chair to Rossit instead."

I stopped for breath and took a big gulp of the Black Russian. Janet frowned, whether at what I was saying or at my wolfing down forty-proof alcohol, I was too caught up by what I was thinking to pause and ask. "So why wasn't Rossit shouting the possibility of *Legionella* from the rooftops since day one," I continued in a rush, "or at least since first thing this morning in the light of our autopsy findings? The case should have been like a gift to him, the 'extra trick' you said he needed to 'win the day' over Cam. Instead of ridiculing me for suggesting *Legionella*, he should have been encouraging me to confirm the diagnosis." I caught my breath. "But it was almost as if he'd wanted to suppress any mention of the organism. Why would that be?"

Janet grimaced, then shook her head. "I've no idea," she said quietly.

We sat for a while without speaking, Janet frowning at the rising bubbles in her drink, me slumped back in my chair and letting my eyes roam around the cozy dining room. We ate here with the lights low and candles lit whenever we managed to be home for dinner at the same time, to claim at least a little tranquillity despite our insane schedules. The little flames from the candelabra bathed the room in a soft glow that was particularly calming. While they flickered and reflected off the rich mahogany surface of our table and the surrounding furniture, I found myself looking at a chess set we kept on a nearby buffet for the occasional after-dinner game. The candlelight projected shadows of the chess pieces against the wall and made them move and sway as in a dance. The effect was eerie, as though some tactical strategy that defied my understanding were being played out while I watched.

Just as when I played Janet, I thought idly. She always beat me. Her moves inevitably caught me by surprise and seemed to anticipate anything I could throw at her. Like the Phantom, she too was a master of defense.

I continued to watch the shadows of the chess pieces on the wall, letting my thoughts move with them, this way and that.

The Phantom's only slipup so far was that he hadn't counted on someone like Janet making the connection between the three nurses.

The turrets of a castle appeared and receded, followed by the shape of a horse's head, followed by the flicker of an afterthought.

Perhaps he had after all.

If he was such a master tactician, surely he'd have taken into account that someone might see what Janet saw, link the three nurses together, and become suspicious about what was happening. Wouldn't he then have been circumspect enough to try and prevent that from happening?

"Janet," I said, startling her, "if you hadn't known Sanders had *Legionella* but thought she simply had a staph infection, would you have made the connection between her and the other two nurses?"

She thought a minute. "I don't know. Maybe, maybe not. It certainly wouldn't have leaped at me the way it did when you mentioned *Legionella*. Why?"

"Because maybe I missed something. I haven't given much thought to where Phyllis Sanders might have contracted staph on top of the *Legionella*," I continued. "I simply assumed she must have already been carrying the organism like a lot of hospital workers unknowingly do, harboring it under their nails and up their noses. I knew the bacteria wouldn't have penetrated into her lung and taken hold if the *Legionella* hadn't first created breaks in the protective surface of her bronchi, but I never once thought that the staph infection had been anything but a fluke. Now I'm not so sure. What if he's also found a way to infect his victims with staphylococcus?"

"What! Why would he want to do that?"

"To vary the infection. Such a strategist would have been wary that a third case of *Legionella* could tip his hand and lead to someone figuring out the connection between his victims, exactly the way it did with you. He still had to use the *Legionella* to set up the staph infection, but once the staph became an overwhelming pneumonia and all that pus became apparent, it was reasonable to expect no one would think of *Legionella*."

Janet stared at me, as if daring me to go the next step.

I took the dare. "Obviously, however, the killer would be vigorously opposed to anyone who did think of it."

Janet became very still. "You're not serious?"

"The killer would behave toward me exactly as Rossit has from the beginning—doing everything in his power to suppress a diagnosis of *Legionella* in Sanders."

She looked astonished at what I was saying. "My God!"

"His 'hidden trick' might have been to infect personnel at UH, knowing full well how it would reflect on Cam. But two things went wrong. She came to St. Paul's, instead of going to her own ER, and I found the *Legionella*."

After days of snapping at mists and shadows, I felt I'd finally clamped down on real flesh and bone. I sat perfectly still, astonished that I'd actually come up with my prey, horrified by what I thought I'd uncovered.

"There's one problem," Janet said in a cool quiet tone that was scalpel sharp. She immediately seized all my attention. Over the years I'd learned it was the voice she reserved for disagreeing with a colleague's opinion when her own diagnosis was bad news—an unexpected cancer, a fetal deformity, or an unpleasant secret that her sharp intellect had discerned.

I braced myself.

"How do you explain his selecting only people who punished patients?" she asked.

I couldn't.

Chapter 10

That Friday morning I was driving into St. Paul's an hour later than usual. It was stop and go on the so-called freeway, and as far as I could see, row on row of taillights, three abreast, blinked the on-and-off rhythm of our progress toward the stumpy skyline of downtown Buffalo. A few shafts of sunlight penetrated the otherwise leaden sky and roved over the city like silver beams searching out first one building, then another. I didn't mind the slow pace much, because I had a lot to think about.

Janet and I had talked long into the night about Rossit. "You're simply pinning motives onto the parts of his behavior you can't explain," Janet had declared. "Apart from giving me nightmares, it does nothing."

"But that's exactly how you started with the three nurses," I'd protested.

"Earl, don't take this personally, but you're just not as good at intuitively seeing things as I am" had been her reply.

I'd nearly slipped an ice cube down the back of her dress. Then I'd come up with another possibility, equally dark and troubling.

"What if Rossit has resurrected the Phantom, taught him whatever is the lethal ID technique that's being used here, then put him to work seeding infections at University Hospital? That way the motive would be Rossit's, but the killings would still have the hallmark of the Phantom, selecting victims who were punishers."

"Still a problem," Janet had promptly replied in that same cutting tone. "Why would Rossit have his Phantom infect Stewart Deloram? And from what you described, Rossit seems as shocked as you are about that infection."

She had me stumped again. "Maybe the monster he's created is out of control," I'd mumbled.

At that point she'd declared, "You've been watching too many horror movies," and had ordered us to bed.

110

Before obeying I'd called ICU to check on Stewart.

"He's coughing more and experiencing some increased difficulty breathing. But his pressure's holding," his nurse said.

"If he's awake, say hello from me."

Then we'd overslept until 7:00—a rare event, only possible because neither of us had gotten called . . . by Brendan or our hospitals.

I crawled through an interchange where I turned onto the Kensington Expressway, but the switch in routes didn't let me drive any faster. I spent five minutes passing a golf course, then another five contemplating an adjacent cemetery. I wondered if it were some kind of weird retirement package. I halfheartedly listened to the radio and continued to brood over my thoughts from last night.

There was no denying Janet's observations. Just as I'd learned to trust her insights, I'd grown to respect those same instincts when she declared something didn't make sense. But I couldn't ignore my own intuition either, whatever Janet thought of it. Maybe parts of my ideas about Rossit were right, I thought. Maybe I had only some of the motives wrong, or the motives right and some of the players wrong. In the light of day I had to admit that the idea of Rossit recruiting a murderous Phantom to advance his career was a bit much. Surely there'd have to be a hell of a lot more at stake for someone to be that crazy, even Rossit.

After I finally reached the exit ramp, I inched toward the hospital through congested streets and listened to the news, the weather, the sports scores—it took one block for each—and then a business report. Some spokesperson for the Buffalo Chamber of Commerce prattled away for five minutes about the booming economy, low unemployment, and billions in investment that the business community hoped to attract to the city in the coming years. Except nobody can get to where they work, I muttered, leaning impatiently on my horn after a delivery truck blocked my way. A cacophony of other horns joined in. I winced at the noise and thought that maybe the bunch of business leaders at the meeting yesterday could do something about traffic.

I recalled the sight of them all sitting there behind Hurst and smiled at how I'd thwarted him and Baker, the hospital lawyer. Except the forces behind the merger were nothing to smile at. There had been a lot of power on that stage and a lot of money. It was the kind of board hospitals liked to have these days—made up mainly of CEOs, best suited for the business of medicine, and loyal to the chain of command. This usually meant they saw the hospital CEO as one of their own and would back him to the hilt.

"Hurst's kind of people," I said aloud, breaking the monotony of the traffic noise, and wondered if our little revolt yesterday would really accomplish anything. Again I thought of Hurst huddled with Rossit, and Rossit's angry warning. *Fuck up this merger, and you'll make yourself a lot of powerful enemies.* I don't know why he was so worried about my little speech having any lasting effect. Seemed to me he should have also given the same advice to the other six hundred doctors in the room.

Unless it was exposing the Phantom that threatened the amalgamation or at least Rossit's own interests in it, or Hurst's, or others like Hurst. If I were going to consider other motives, the merger itself represented a huge opportunity for power and money. The resulting complex would have an operating budget of half a billion a year. That was a lot of influence and a lot of motivation for a whole new group of players. Hurst and his cronies would be wanting to come out of the amalgamation process with the upper hand and as much control as possible over the new venture. It was a pretty heady prize, but was it dazzling enough someone would commit murder for it? I found myself revising who might have recruited whom and set off on an even more macabre chain of thought. What if it were Hurst, or Hurst and members of the board, who had recruited the Phantom to help destabilize University Hospital, to give St. Paul's a huge advantage in the amalgamation? Rossit might have been persuaded, in exchange for the promise of the chair, to develop and then teach the Phantom the infection technique. Later, when things went wrong, he would have been ordered to prevent Janet and me from exposing the Phantom at all costs.

Loud honking behind me made me realize I was still stopped after the light had turned green. I hit the accelerator, sped across the intersection, then immediately was back in my stop-and-go routine, not unlike the way I was thinking over my latest bizarre scenario. While there was enough power and money at stake to make a motive for murder seem feasible and the ghoulish scheme was consistent with Hurst's and Rossit's recent behavior to discredit me, it still failed to explain why Stewart Deloram had been infected. Besides, I figured Janet would be about as enthralled with a conspiracy theory as she had been with the monster-out-of-control idea. "Now it's too much *X-Files*," I could imagine her saying.

I quickly snapped back to reality at a few minutes before 8:00

when a bulletin cut into the regular chatter on the radio. "The administration of St. Paul's has just announced a temporary closure of its emergency department due to some unscheduled maintenance problems. Ambulances are currently being rerouted, and the public is advised to use ER facilities in other hospitals until the situation is rectified. And now back to the weather. More rain will be . . ."

"What the hell?" I muttered, reaching for my car phone. It rang before I could start punching in the number of ER. "Garnet here," I answered briskly.

"Have you been told what's up?" It was Susanne.

"Not a goddamned thing! What the hell's going on?"

"We don't know. The radio announced we were closed about the same moment Hurst's office called looking for you a few seconds ago. His secretary said to get you pronto!" As Susanne spoke, I could hear the PA in the background asking a string of names, all of them chiefs, to report immediately to the boardroom. "What do they mean, 'unscheduled maintenance'?" she demanded, obviously upset. "There's nothing broken here."

"I've no idea. I'll call Hurst's office right now. I should be arriving in five minutes, traffic permitting."

I one-handed the steering wheel, kept an eye on the road, and managed to dial a bakery before I finally got the number right for Hurst's private line.

Busy!

The light at Main and High Streets was unusually long. I kept pressing my redial button, my frustration rising as each repeated attempt ended with that same annoying buzz. The light changed, and once again I shot across an intersection only to get ensnared in yet another tangle of cars halfway up the next block. Stone and brick office buildings loomed over me on each side of the street, adding to my sense of being blocked in. Exasperated, I called back to ER. The clerk passed me to Susanne immediately.

"I can't get through to Hurst. Do you know what's up yet?"

"No, but somebody's really spooked," she reported, sounding shaken. The change in her voice from minutes earlier was alarming. "All the patients in the department are suddenly being moved to an empty ward that was closed down during last year's budget cuts. And get this. We've all been ordered not to leave ER, while every orderly transferring patients is wearing gloves and a mask. Somebody better tell us damn quick . . ."

As her words continued to come in a rush the radio suddenly

caught my attention again. " . . . My, the gremlins are certainly plaguing Buffalo's hospitals this morning. We have news of another closure. This time University Hospital is advising all its obstetrical patients that the delivery rooms and attendant wards are going to be out of service until at least this afternoon. Any of their patients who go into labor during . . ."

"Susanne, I've got to hang up. I'll be there in minutes." I cut her off, not even having heard her last few words. I did some more one-eyed, one-armed driving while punching in the number of Janet's case room.

"Just a minute, Dr. Garnet," answered a clerk who sounded as rattled as Susanne. In seconds Janet was on the line. "I've no idea what's up. Patients and babies are being taken to another wing in the hospital, the orderlies and nurses accompanying them are wearing gloves and masks, and it's scaring the shit out of everyone." She sounded furious.

"No one's told you anything?"

"Nada! We're waiting for Cam now. Waiting, hell! We've been ordered to stay here until he comes."

My car was finally nosing into the entrance of St. Paul's. "Did you hear they've done the same thing with my ER?" I asked while cutting off a red four-by-four with tires as big as my car and slipping into one of the few remaining parking spaces ahead of it. The driver honked angrily and roared off to another part of the lot.

"Oh my God. You don't think—"

"I don't know, Janet." I cut her off. "I've got to run. I'll call you as soon as I learn what's happening here."

My mounting sense of alarm made me fumble my car keys and drop my briefcase while I hurriedly locked up. The elements—Janet's case room, my ER, and people in both places running around in gloves and masks—had only one thing in common, Phyllis Sanders. Thoughts of more *Legionella* victims swept through me like a chill as I ran for the entrance to emergency. On the other side of the lot I could see the huge red RV still circling, presumably trying to find a spot.

Everyone in the department immediately surrounded me.

" . . . some official from the state health board took our patient lists from Monday until now."

" . . . ordered a call-up of all our staff that have worked during the last five days."

" . . . labs called and said we're going to get our hands, fingernails, and noses cultured."

The barrage of comments was coming from a group of twenty doctors, clerks, nurses, and residents who were all understandably angry, some quite wide-eyed with fright and a few already wearing masks and gloves.

"Look, I don't know anything more than you guys do," I said, pushing through them and moving toward the nurses' station, "but if you'll let me through to a phone, I'll find out."

Orderlies wearing protective gear were wheeling patients on stretchers past us and out of the department. Susanne was trotting alongside, reassuring, "It's just a precaution, until they get some maintenance problem checked," but the patients looked bewildered anyway. A security guard at the door pointedly stopped Susanne before letting the others through. "I wasn't going to leave!" she said impatiently, pivoting away from him and striding back to the nurses' station. "By what authority can they keep us here?" she demanded when she got up to me.

"I don't know," I answered her. On my way in I'd already been warned by a security guard not to try to leave. He couldn't tell me why and had refused to say what would happen if I did. I turned to the clerk. "Where's this state health official who took your patient lists?"

"Search me," she said. "He wouldn't come near us without gloves and a mask on. He even put the books in a plastic bag. Are we quarantined or something?"

Without answering, I stepped over to the counter behind us and grabbed a phone. I finally got through to Hurst's secretary.

"Oh, Dr. Garnet," she said, her voice drenched with disapproval. "Dr. Hurst definitely wants to speak with you."

As I waited on the line, through the windows of the nurses' station I saw a group of men and women wearing masks, gloves, and gowns enter the department carrying baskets of culture tubes. Some I recognized as our own lab techs, even with the protective gear, while the others, about a dozen in all, were strangers to me. Four of them went immediately into the resuscitation room. The rest walked up to Susanne and started talking to her and pointing to the cubicles where we normally see patients.

Hurst finally came on the line. "Well, Garnet, you really put your foot into it this time," sneered that familiar harsh voice. "If you'd spent nearly as much effort attending to emergency cases as trying to sabotage my efforts to run St. Paul's—"

"What the hell's going on?" I roared.

Out in the hallway Susanne, the rest of our staff, and the lab techs all swung around to stare at me.

"I suppose you'd better join us," continued Hurst on the phone, "but you're about as welcome as the plague. I trust you'll wear suitable clothing to protect the rest of the hospital from being contaminated further by your carelessness!" He slammed the phone in my ear.

"Up yours," I said into the dead line, taking out my fury at him by banging down my receiver as well.

Susanne and her group turned away from me and started talking earnestly to one another, occasionally looking over their shoulders in my direction. I was about to walk over and see if the newly arrived techs knew what was happening but was interrupted.

"Who's Dr. Earl Garnet?" boomed a loud male voice from near the triage area. The group with Susanne went quiet again. I instinctively moved to leave the nurses' station and identify myself when I stopped midbreath on seeing the man who wanted me. Big was not a good enough description. The man filled the far end of the corridor. He was bald, black, and laden with half a dozen metal suitcases, one under each arm and a pair in each of his very large hands. He was dressed in a yellow-and-black jogging outfit that looked more expensive than one of my best dress suits, and on his feet were a pair of well-worn hiking boots that gave him a military air. I figured he could have worn pink bunny slippers and I'd probably still have had an urge to salute him. He was that kind of man. I was relieved to see him smile when I went into the corridor to greet him. A gray mustache accented the friendly expression he fixed on me. "Dr. Garnet?" he asked politely.

"Yes," I said, walking toward him and offering my hand. As I got closer, I better appreciated the mass of the man's shoulders hunched over by the weight of the cases he was carrying. I could also see some lines around his eyes that suggested he was nearer my age than I'd ever have guessed from his superb physique.

He too was wearing latex gloves but didn't free one of his hands to shake mine. "Excuse me, Dr. Garnet. I'll just set my equipment over by that row of stretchers against the far wall," he responded, stepping by me and striding to the nearest gurney where he hefted his cases onto the mattress. He quickly snapped open the smallest one, took out a stack of surgical masks and a box of latex gloves, then went back to where Susanne and the staff had gathered with the technicians. "I'm Dr. Douglas Williams," he introduced himself in a voice that could reach the cheap seats in Carnegie Hall. He needn't have bothered raising the volume. He'd had everyone's attention since he entered the department. "As a precaution, until we find out what's going on here, would everyone please put on masks and gloves from this fresh supply. Don't use the ones in your ER as they may be already contaminated." As he spoke, he distributed the protective gear he'd brought as nonchalantly as a waiter might pass out hors d'oeuvres at a cocktail party.

"What have we been exposed to?" asked one of the nurses nervously, breaking the silence and igniting an immediate echo of the same question from everyone standing in front of him.

"I know this is upsetting," he answered, handing the remaining gloves and masks to Susanne and quickly raising his hands to quiet the sudden outbursts of questions, "but we're making sure the department hasn't come in contact with a resistant form of staphylococcus again."

"Shit! All this for an MRSA case?"

"Why the extra fuss? We never evacuated patients before."

"Or closed ER for that matter."

Susanne frowned at me as Williams pressed on with his reassurances. "That's right; it's nothing you haven't handled before," he said, almost managing to sound bored while he looked around at everyone and smiled. "We're just using a stricter protocol this time." He caught my gaze and held it, still smiling, but I felt I'd gotten a direct order to bite my tongue. "Now," he continued, looking directly at the group of technicians, "some of you are from state health and some are from the hospital, but for this job you'll work my way. Do nasal passages, hands, and fingernails—all of them on everybody." He stepped back to retrieve another of his suitcases as he talked. "I want you to use these to get under the nails and scrape," he ordered, pulling out sterile packets of thin, wiry culture sticks normally used to insert up the male urethra and culture for VD. A few of the men in the room winced. "Dr. Garnet, I'd like to speak with you in your office," he ordered, handing me a mask, slipping one on himself, then offering me some gloves. "And I could sure as hell use a coffee," he added, indicating with his large hands that I was to lead the way. "Some jerk cut me off in the parking lot and I spilled the one I had all over my dash."

* * *

"Do you think they'll buy it?" he asked me as soon as we were behind closed doors in my office. We'd grabbed two coffees from a pot the nurses kept brewing twenty-four hours a day. In here he seemed to think it was safe enough for us to lower our masks and load up on caffeine together.

"Not for long," I warned. "There's too much experience out there for anyone to believe you'd close ER simply because we treated a case with MRSA. Better we level with them now if you want to keep everyone calm and cooperating. Better yet, you can start by leveling with me." I moved to sit behind my desk and offered him one of my visitors' chairs. Standing, he made my office look puny.

"What have you been told?" he asked bluntly, settling into a seat opposite me.

"Not a goddamned thing!"

"Hey, don't get pissed at me. I was rousted from my motel about forty-five minutes ago because I happened to be in Buffalo heading up a university field trip to trace botulism in ducks," said Dr. Williams curtly. "I don't even belong in the Hospital Infections Program, but when your ID guy—Russet?"

"Rossit," I corrected.

"Yeah, Rossit. Well, when he called Atlanta on our hot line about the culture results at 6:45 this morning, they rousted the program director—"

"You're with the CDC?" I interrupted. "How come you didn't say so?"

"Because then everyone would know this was the big deal it is and really get scared shitless."

"Have there been more *Legionella* cases?" I asked, sick with imagining that the Phantom must have unleashed his organism on a large scale in both hospitals. Maybe my notion of him going berserk wasn't so crazy after all. Janet at least had been right about this being out of a horror movie. "How many?" I braced for the answer.

"What?" snapped Douglas Williams. He was so startled by my question he nearly sloshed his coffee into his lap again. "What are you talking about, *Legionella*?"

Another chill was starting a slow crawl up my spine. "Why are you here?" I asked, not answering his question and keeping my voice as steady as I could

He spotted the *MMB* article I'd left lying on my desk, frowned, and tapped it with his forefinger. "We're here because of this," he answered, seeming puzzled by my own confusion. "On the reports they faxed me, you're listed as the doctor on record who was astute enough to order the sensitivity rechecked by the minimal inhibitory concentration method. You obviously suspected something."

"What?" It was my turn to nearly slosh my coffee.

"The vancomycin sensitivity test you ordered on the staphylococcus organism in a patient named . . . Saunderson?"

"Sanders," I said without thinking. My voice sounded far off. My throat was too dry to swallow. "My God, we've got a vancomycin-inhibiting strain."

But it couldn't be. How could the Phantom have been involved with such an exotic organism? It was too rare, too improbable. Even testing for it had made sense in only an academic way, and the most compelling reason for me had been Miller's peace of mind.

While my thoughts raced, I grew even more queasy. Williams was continuing to look at me as if I were nuts. "Holy shit," he said, running a large hand over his shiny head, "you really don't know what's happened this morning?"

It was still an effort to keep my voice steady, but I tried. "I presume it's another vancomycin-inhibiting strain of MRSA from the patient Phyllis Sanders, like they had in Tokyo, Michigan, and New Jersey."

He looked at me and swallowed.

My queasy feeling graduated to the burn of bile rising in the back of my throat.

"I hate to be the one to break the news to you, Dr. Garnet," he began, speaking quietly, "but what your ID man discovered this morning in the test you ordered seems to be the superbug itself—a staphylococcus organism completely resistant to everything."

My instinctive reaction was more denial. Now I was sure there'd been an error. A too zealous lab tech must have misinterpreted the culture results. Then came fear, like nausea, waves and waves of it, despite my best effort to resist the realization sweeping over me. A killer with a superbug? It wasn't possible. The organism was some theoretical nightmare in an article. How could it be here?

"March out in front of your troops," Williams was instructing me, "and cheerfully be among the first to get cultured." But I was having difficulty focusing on what he was saying. I barely noticed he was out of his seat and leaning over my desk until I felt him lever me out of my chair, his left hand wrapped easily around most of my upper arm.

"The organism's unstoppable?" I asked, my own voice sounding distant and shaken. It was a silly question, born out of my refusal to accept what I'd just heard. That aspect of a superbug needed no repeating.

But Williams, obviously unaware of the full implications of his bombshell, ignored my incredulity and instead marched me back toward ER, instructing, "The key to getting through an operation like this is bluff—big, bold-faced lying bluff—that you are calm, in control, and not feeling a shred of panic. We have to make sure that not a single bacterium of that organism has passed onto one of your staff or is lying in wait somewhere in your department. Until then, ER is closed. So plug in your happy voice, Chief. Your surgical mask will hide how miserably glum you really look."

The scope of what he was setting out to do so staggered me I could barely grapple with how the Phantom figured in it all. "Dr. Williams, there's more you have to know. Something much graver is going on here than you suspect—"

"Hush! No talking in front of the children," he whispered curtly as we joined my own staff assembled in the area that several technicians had set up to conduct testing.

Soon a good five inches of a ten-inch Q-tip was up my nose and moving through places I didn't know I had way in there.

"Don't move, Dr. Garnet," ordered a steely-eyed woman glaring at me over the top of her mask.

My eyes were streaming with tears while she finished probing my left nasal passage. "Just give me a minute before you start on the right," I heard myself beg, but my mind was swirling with other thoughts, rushing ahead, unbidden, to grasp the terrible new dimensions of killing that such an organism implied.

The technician sighed, rammed the swab she'd been using into its container, and splashed the charcoal medium back up onto the front of her gown. "This is going to take forever," she complained to Williams. In a far corner about a dozen of her previous victims were commiserating, identified by their red eyes above their masks, some of them still tearing. Obviously I wasn't the first to complain.

Williams nodded toward the unhappy group and told the woman in front of me, "As soon as they've recovered, start getting them organized to help take cultures with you. We're going to need everyone on the ER staff to pitch in given the huge number of patients we'll be calling in for testing."

My God! I hadn't thought of this bacteria breaching isolation precautions and reaching the public. The idea sent a veneer of cold sweat down my back.

The technician nodded, coolly uncapped yet another long Q-Tip, and eyed my nostrils. After she'd finished reaming the other side of my nose, scraping under my nails, and swabbing the backs and palms of my hands, I immediately reapplied my mask and gloves.

"We ask all ER personnel to remain on the premises and in isolation garb," Williams announced, "until Dr. Garnet and I return from some serious paper shuffling upstairs in the boardroom." Murmurs of discontent protested this order, but he kept on speaking, his massive voice easily rising above the angry muttering. "Today's exercise is going to include the call back and screening of hundreds of patients. Since all of you will assist with the taking of these samples, I suggest you get ready." He turned toward the door, crumpled up his empty Styrofoam cup and lobbed it twenty feet into a wastebasket located in an empty examining cubicle. At the entrance we paused to remove our protective gear, dropping everything into a large cardboard drum. Activating the automatic doors, he flashed his ID to the security guard stationed outside in the corridor. "Dr. Garnet's with me!" he snapped.

"ER personnel have to put on clean protective gear to go into the rest of the hospital, Dr. Garnet." The guard gestured toward a cart stacked with masks, gowns, and a box of gloves. Such precautions, called reverse isolation, were meant to protect the rest of St. Paul's from anyone in ER already infected.

"Okay, Chief, take me to your leaders," quipped my escort when I'd finished dressing.

Some of the people we passed in the hallways gave me curious glances. Even in a hospital, anyone outside a work area with gloves, a gown, and a mask in place was a little unusual. "You might as well hang a goddamned bell around my neck," I muttered to Williams, but he ignored me.

A few colleagues, recognizing who I was despite the mask, stepped up and asked what was going on.

"Oh, we seem to have a problem with MRSA again," I told them breezily, trying to hide my own anxiety and increasing my pace so as not to give them time for more questions.

"But why did you close emergency?" one of them called after me.

I turned, shrugged, and, walking backward a few steps, said, "Hey, it wasn't my idea. Someone must have overreacted."

In my heart, I desperately hoped someone had. I kept recoiling from visions of what a serial killer could inflict with this microbe. Again, I grasped at the straw of human error. "Maybe there's a more likely explanation, like a mix-up in the lab," I exclaimed, resuming my stride alongside Williams. "After all, it's so improbable that the staphylococcus found in Sanders is some dreaded strain foreshadowed by an outbreak in Japan. Shouldn't we redo the culture first—"

"Of course," he cut me off with a wave of his hand. "A whole crew's on the way here from Atlanta not only to do that but also to double-check and reconfirm everything about the woman's infection, both here and at University Hospital where she worked. City and state health officials should already be on both sites setting up what we'll need. But if you don't mind my asking, if you were suspicious enough to order the test in the first place, why are you so skeptical about the results?"

"Someone else thought of the test. I simply agreed to sign the order" was all I answered. I was suddenly reticent to tell him the heart of the matter. After all, blurting out that the organism which ate away Sanders's lungs was not only unstoppable but also in the possession of a maniac wasn't exactly going to establish my credibility with the man. Better to be cautious about how I broach the subject of the Phantom, I decided, and said instead, "It's too fantastic." I continued, "Even the *MMB* article implied that if such an organism did occur, it wouldn't happen until two years from now. How could it have gotten here from Tokyo so fast?"

"Those authors actually said *within* two years. Full resistance to an antibiotic has developed in some bacteria only three months after the emergence of an inhibitory strain. And distance is no barrier to an organism these days. Jet travel's just like an overnight shipping service for bugs; it can carry them from point *A* to anywhere on the planet within twenty-four hours. But this one probably didn't get here from Tokyo."

We joined a large group waiting for the elevator.

"What do you mean?" I demanded.

"I thought you said you read the article."

I felt my face redden as I shook my head and admitted, "I only glanced at it."

"Have you heard of the process called conjugation?" he asked.

Again I shook my head.

He folded his arms in front of his chest and began to explain. "Different types of bacteria in close proximity can pass genetic material from one organism to another. The nightmare scenario described in the article was a vancomycin-resistant enterococcus, VRE, passing its gene granting vancomycin resistance to methicillin-resistant staph. One of these genes—VanA—has already been inserted experimentally into the DNA of *Staphylococci aureus* in a laboratory. Though the researchers were using recombinant DNA techniques—adding specific enzymes to break the DNA strands of the VRE organism to isolate the VanA gene, then inserting that gene into the DNA strands of MRSA bacteria—their success in creating the superbug in a test tube strongly suggests the potential for the same transfer to occur naturally in real life through conjugation."

He paused, like all good teachers do when they're about to deliver a punch line.

"The circumstance by which it could happen in humans is chillingly simple," he continued, looking down at me. "Both VRE and methicillin-resistant staph organisms can reside side by side in the human intestine. Since conjugation is a process occurring all the time, sooner or later it would release the specific genes conferring resistance in VRE, including VanA, and then incorporate these DNA fragments into the DNA of the methicillin-resistant staph organism. The next time this person didn't wash his hands after wiping himself, the new bug would be in circulation."

When the elevator door opened, nobody moved to get on. I'd been so intrigued by Williams's description, I hadn't noticed that the dozen or so people who were waiting with us had gone silent. His voice had easily carried to every one of them, and they were responding by backing away from me in my isolation outfit. The closure of ER and the transfer of patients by orderlies wearing ID protection already had the hospital buzzing. Rumors of this conversation would be like kerosene on fire. "Well, thank God we don't have anything like that here," I declared loudly, stepping into the elevator. "Makes our little MRSA case seem routine."

I think I sensed the group relax a little, but not one of them got in the car with us.

"That was a slick recovery back there," Williams complimented me after we'd reached the floor where the boardroom was located. "There's enough possibility for panic as it is, without my setting it off. We can't afford any; there's so much to be done in the next hours and days." We were trudging over the beige pile that stretched everywhere throughout the administration suites. "I keep forgetting how my voice carries. Comes from working with ducks; they don't care what I say." He glanced at me out of the side of his eyes and snapped his fingers. "That reminds me. I cut *you* off back in ER to keep you from scaring your own staff. You mentioned something much graver going on here than I suspected. It sounded serious."

I'd already decided there was no way I could convince him here and now that Sanders was murdered. Besides, the containment exercise we were rushing into had to be carried out anyway, and knowing about the Phantom wouldn't change how we'd do the screening.

We turned a corner and approached a massive set of double oak doors which, reaching as high as the ceiling, guarded the inner sanctum of the boardroom. The thought of those closed minds behind that set of doors only reinforced my decision. "It's complicated," I told him. "I'll talk to you about it later, when we have more time." To make him believe anything, I'd need him alone, and I'd certainly need him away from Rossit and Hurst. And I'd need him in a very private place where we wouldn't be overheard or interrupted.

He shrugged. "Okay. It has to wait. Right now our job is to keep *these* turkeys in line," he instructed, jerking his thumb toward where we were headed. "Administrators are always the biggest obstacle in any hospital outbreak—denying, blaming, covering their asses— like they can bluster the bugs to death." Without breaking his step, he banged the tall panels open and strode through the high arched frame like a one-man assault team. "Morning!" his loud voice thundered even before the noise of the doors hitting the wall could die down. "I'm Dr. Douglas Williams from the CDC, and as of now I'm in charge of this investigation."

Everyone standing around the room immediately froze. Rossit and Hurst, who'd apparently been talking together, gaped at Williams. A half-dozen men and women I didn't know—presumably the local city and state health officials Williams was expecting—stood with coffee cups suspended at various distances from their mouths.

"If you'll all please sit down, we have a great deal of material to cover," Williams added, lowering his voice but not his authority. The chiefs present, eight or nine of them representing the areas most affected by the scare, quickly began taking their seats. Sean was there for surgery and gave me a wink, but the usual twinkle in his eye was missing. Len Gardner, already sitting at the long mahogany table in front of a stack of documents, presumably records of the Sanders autopsy, smiled and nodded his greeting. Arnold Pinter, chief of internal medicine, looking more startled than usual, scrambled to find a chair near the far end where Hurst regularly sat and hunched down in his seat. The outside officials and the remaining chiefs from obstetrics, gynecology, anesthesia, geriatrics, neonatology, and pediatrics quietly found places for themselves.

I surveyed the expectant faces staring back at Williams. It looked to me as if he most definitely had his turkeys in line.

Except Rossit. "This is an extreme pleasure and a surprise to have you here, Dr. Williams," he gushed as he rushed up and grabbed the man's big right hand, trying to pump it with little effect.

While I watched, a frown began furrowing its way across Williams's massive forehead.

Rossit took no notice and persisted, "I had no idea our problem would rate such a distinguished world authority as yourself." Turning to the men and women around the table, he explained, "Dr. Williams is a genius at studying the transmission patterns of an infection and determining if a particular vector—rodents, fleas, ticks, that sort of thing—is behind its spread among humans. Why, his work in the Southwest on the Hanta virus . . ."

While Rossit lavished on the praise, Williams glowered down at him and appeared increasingly annoyed. I couldn't help thinking that if he'd plucked Rossit up and put him on his shoulder, together they would have resembled the strong man and Tom Thumb from old circus posters.

"Let's get to work!" Williams commanded, gruffly putting an end to Rossit's blatant attempt to suck up to him.

The little man flushed and his chin began its familiar chewing motion, but he took his seat without uttering another word.

Fueled by my earlier speculation about Rossit, I found myself studying his face. Normally I would have dismissed his obsequious behavior as simply another try to win some political advantage or other. But this morning, the possibility of a darker agenda sprang to mind. If Rossit did know the secret behind Phyllis Sanders's death and was trying to keep it hidden, wouldn't he be eager to get into Williams's good graces, I thought, and attempt to influence the investigation that might expose that secret?

Chapter 11

An eight-hundred-bed teaching hospital like St. Paul's employs more than three thousand people. A challenge, a threat, or a clear and present danger to any community of that size can mobilize its citizens into actions beyond their daily routine. Usual jobs take on an added importance, and the change is evident immediately in the corridors. The pace of walking is quicker, carts of supplies arrive at their destinations faster, conversations are briefer and limited to orders or instructions. There's a snap to everything. Even more unusual, meetings are kept short and to the point.

Not long into our own session with Williams, we were interrupted by the technician responsible for screening in ER. She reported that at least a dozen of our staff had symptoms of colds—runny noses, sore throats, coughs—but none of them was very ill at the moment. Williams nevertheless ordered these people quarantined and asked that I assign some of my emergency physicians to check them out. We both agreed they probably only had the flu, but if they had any purulent nasal discharge or sputum, we would have to sample it, Gram-stain it, and look at it under a microscope to make sure they weren't actively infected by staph. Even if these slides were negative, showing no evidence of gram-positive cocci in clusters, this group still had a problem. Flu, or influenza, was also known to inflame and damage bronchial airways enough to let staphylococcus penetrate into the underlying lung tissue, just as the *Legionella* had done in Phyllis Sanders. Anyone with the flu who as a carrier was also harboring the fully resistant superbug was vulnerable to developing a full-fledged infection by the fatal organism. Along with everyone else, they would have to wait forty-eight hours for their culture results.

I insisted on leaving the meeting and personally delivering Williams's verdict to the affected people in ER. I tried to reassure them that we were simply taking precautions but watched uneasily, fearing the worst for them, while they bravely made cracks about being off to Club Med and were led away into one of the wards previously closed by Hurst. As an added precaution, I advised the physicians who would be examining them to make sure no one had signs of a *Legionella* prodrome.

They were debating how to decolonize anyone found to be a carrier when I returned upstairs. The usual measures involved little more than repeatedly cleansing their hands and nails with bactericidal soaps and applying copious amounts of mupirocin ointment, a salve normally used for cuts and scrapes of the skin, to the mucous membranes of their noses. Unfortunately, these treatments were notoriously ineffective in eradicating nasal carriage sites.

"With the new strain, they may have no effect at all," Williams advised solemnly. Incredibly, there were no other conventional decontamination techniques to help modern hospitals deal with carriers. "If any of your personnel do prove to be harboring the superbug, we might try some experimental alternatives, albeit unsavory ones," he added. "For example, slipping a tube through the mouth, up over the back edge of the palate, and into the posterior nasopharynx, then flushing a concentrated saline solution or bactericidal soap anteriorly through the passages would, theoretically, lavage the organisms out the front of the nose."

The thought of it made me gag.

Williams then decreed that we'd have to screen all patients who'd been in the ER since Monday, including the friends and relatives who accompanied them. I knew from our statistics that four days' worth of ER visits was nearly eight hundred patients, most of them having had at least one other person with them. "Are you aware of the work hours and resources we'll need to culture sixteen hundred people?" I demanded, my eyes locked directly on Hurst. I didn't want him giving us only half of what we'd need.

For my trouble I was told to set up forty culturing stations in the hospital auditorium and to man them with my remaining staff from emergency—doctors, residents, nurses, aides, orderlies, technicians, and clerks—who were not showing any symptoms of the flu. But they were to continue wearing protective garb, in case there were any carriers among them.

"Of course the cost of screening emergency department personnel and patients will be paid out of your ER budget," Hurst declared, avoiding my stare. He turned toward Rossit and muttered something behind his hand.

When Rossit replied, his voice was just loud enough for me to hear snippets of what he was saying. ". . . if he'd treated the goddamned *Legionella* . . . might have avoided this mess . . ."

I felt my face flush all the way into my ears as I controlled my anger.

ER itself would remain closed until cultures taken from all the sites tested on the premises proved negative and the facility had been washed down with bactericidal soaps, just for good measure.

The meeting concluded with everyone dispersing to carry out dozens of tasks. Off-duty personnel from the rest of the hospital were summoned to help process all the specimens we would be collecting. Additional microscopes and culturing equipment had to be scrounged up from all over the city. Since bench space in the bacteriology lab would be overcrowded with people doing Gram stains and plating cultures, tables were set up in the corridors where rows of technicians prepared to examine hundreds of slides under the many borrowed microscopes. Volunteers were found to keep the records straight, sort the collected data, and enter the results into computers.

Yet as I watched so many of my colleagues mobilize against this organism, I was increasingly haunted by the fact that none of them knew it could be wielded by a killer. My resolve to make Williams see what I feared we were really up against grew by the hour.

But in the committee, we continued to lie. Our cover story explaining the massive screening effort was particularly disingenuous. "We're evaluating existing isolation practices, making sure none of our patients or visitors in ER are at risk, by testing our response to a recent case of methicillin-resistant staphylococcus." Maybe, technically, it wasn't exactly a falsehood, but it sure as hell wasn't the truth, and I felt dirty each time I repeated it.

Finally, Williams attempted to limit outside publicity. "No bulletins over the airwaves," he insisted. "Better we initially contact everyone we can by phone, keep the explanation low key, but stress they are obliged to come in to St. Paul's by order of the health department." We recruited every secretary in the hospital to do the telephoning, and by 9:30 we were organized enough to begin calling in the first groups of patients.

All in all, logistically, it was an impressive response, but the truth remained that in an age of miracle drugs we were reduced to fighting this bacteria with little more than the weapons our forefathers used against pestilence—soaps, salves, and isolation.

* * *

Her eyes tearing, her face grimacing in pain, she was trying to pull away from me. "Mommy!" she screamed. I got the culture swab out of her nose just as she started to sob uncontrollably.

"What are you doing to her?" cried her mother, sliding protective arms around the little girl's chest and head while glaring angrily at me. The child's name was Cynthia, she was six years old, and she'd had the misfortune of being in our ER for a sore throat the same day Phyllis Sanders had been admitted. She was in her mother's lap, and they were both seated in front of me at one of the culturing stations. The testing of hands, nails, and nostrils—one swab per site—took minutes. The reassuring and comforting took forever. After an hour I'd barely managed to take samples from six people.

"I'm sorry," I said to her mother. Then, facing the little girl, I cajoled, "Cynthia, you're a brave young lady. I know it's unpleasant, so take a little break before we do the other nostril." While I talked, I inserted the swab I'd just taken into a tube of charcoal culture medium.

"No, I don't want it," cried Cynthia, burying her face in her mother's shoulder.

Her mother cradled her head and rocked her slightly. "Couldn't we leave it, Doctor? You've got samples from me, and after all, you said the chances of us getting it were remote. Why hurt her again?"

"We must get one more, I'm afraid," I told the mother. To the back of Cynthia's head, I added, "A few more seconds, and I'll be through. You know, when they checked me this morning, I yelled twice as loud as you did."

She peeked out at me.

"And I've got special friends in the cafeteria who will give ice cream to anyone braver than me."

She studied my eyes. Being masked, gowned, and gloved, my appearance didn't lower people's anxiety any, but Cynthia must have seen something she liked, because a minute later I had my samples. "My name's Garnet," I told Cynthia's mother. "Tell the cafeteria to put the ice cream on my tab."

"Can I tell them I was braver than you?" asked Cynthia eagerly, exuberant now that her trial was over.

I laughed. "You sure can."

"When will we know the results, Doctor?" asked her mother.

"The cultures take two days. As I said, it's unlikely we'll find anything."

"But what happens if you do?"

"Oh, usually they use bactericidal soaps for the hands, and there's an ointment that can be applied topically for organisms found in the nose," I replied casually, trying to sound matter-of-fact.

"Thank you, Doctor," said Cynthia's mother, appearing comforted as she turned toward the exit and followed her daughter, who was already skipping happily out the door.

I finished labeling my specimens from Cynthia and summoned the next person in line. An elderly black woman with a cane slowly made her way to my table. "Hi, I'm Dr. Garnet," I greeted her, "and I just need to take a few cultures. Rest assured there's nothing to worry about. Now, if you'll tilt your head back . . ." As I explained the procedure and set to work, I thought, Lord help us if anyone becomes infected and these people find out how they were lied to.

Other problems were already starting.

The quarantined group had initially been cooperative, concerned for their own safety and not wanting to endanger their families at home. But then Rossit had begun insisting they have their noses lavaged right away without waiting for the culture results, contrary to what Williams had suggested. Suddenly the cover story that we were simply checking the effectiveness of our MRSA containment procedures was no longer sufficient to ensure everyone's submission, even to the reasonable measures that Williams had intended. First there was a murmur, then a howl of protest against our authority to violate their personal liberty, subject them to forced confinement, and impose treatments on them without their consent.

"Rossit's a fucking idiot!" Williams bellowed when I alerted him to the trouble.

Or a saboteur, I thought.

Williams and I went into the ward where the suspected carriers had been isolated and tried to calm them down, assuring them Rossit wouldn't be allowed to lavage their noses, but it was too late. Teams of lawyers had already been summoned by the parties on both sides of the argument, the employees' union and the department of health. They descended on St. Paul's and went at each other tooth and nail somewhere upstairs.

"Nobody talks to reporters but me," Williams growled at a hastily reconvened session of our special committee. Rossit didn't attend.

But shortly afterward a very hostile media arrived, probably alerted by one of the individuals unhappy with the quarantine. Soon local news bulletins were also ripping into the validity of the health department demanding that citizens submit to the tests being done at St. Paul's.

The call-in shows were the worst. "Civil liberties versus state health. Is Big Brother now Big Doctor? When the men and the women in the white coats take 'knowing what's good for us' too far . . ." one commentator blared. Everyone in the auditorium heard him over a portable radio that a nurse had brought in. Williams happened to be there at the time, giving an interview to a newspaper reporter in an attempt to add some balance to the debate that was raging.

"Turn that crap off," he yelled, then walked away shaking his head, looking more worried than I'd seen him so far.

By early afternoon the open revolt against compulsory compliance, stoked by the local broadcasters, was resulting in fewer and fewer patients agreeing to come in. Yet even when the whole operation was threatening to collapse, Williams persisted with his order that we keep the lid on what was really happening. "I'm afraid the panic would evacuate the hospital," he warned, "and patients too unstable to be moved could die."

"But evacuation's illogical," others on the committee protested.

"So's panic," retorted Williams. "You've seen the media zoo here today. Imagine how they'd play up an unstoppable organism that can kill in forty-eight hours and is carried unknowingly in the noses and on the hands of hospital personnel. The first impulse of patients would be to sign themselves out, and family members would insist on it. Do you really think you could control that kind of hysteria with clinical logic and measured reassurances?"

As uncomfortable as I'd been with his deception, his stark prediction of what a candid disclosure might unleash left me even more alarmed.

But then the entire exercise was salvaged in a totally unexpected way by pure luck and a nasty bit of gossip.

Small groups of patients were still responding to the call-up, enough to keep some of us busy despite the hue and cry, and a young resident was taking cultures at a table situated near my own. Suddenly he turned to some of his colleagues who were waiting for subjects and declared rather loudly, "I don't for a moment believe what they're telling us."

Smart lad, I thought, continuing to take swabs from a young girl's fingernails.

"In fact," he continued, "I just read an article that might explain what they're really looking for."

He instantly had my attention. His buddies looked interested as well, and any patients within hearing distance visibly perked up. I also noticed a reporter with a microphone who'd been trying to get interviews look over from where he'd been reading his notes.

"It's staphylococcus all right, but a new MRSA strain."

I was about to throw down my culture swab, run over, and quickly whisper that he keep his theories to himself when he pronounced, "It's a nasty, virulent bug recently reported in Ontario, Canada, that infects thirty percent of its carriers. I'll bet some Canadian shopper has brought it down here."

I sighed my relief and went back to culturing fingernails. The so-called Ontario strain had been around for years, was causing a problem just over the border in Toronto but fortunately hadn't been reported here yet. Most important, it was sensitive to vancomycin.

But seconds later the reporter had his microphone in the resident's face, beaming while the young doctor expounded with absolute certainty about the Ontario strain of MRSA. "Oh yeah," a few of the other residents added, proceeding to corroborate that they'd either read about or had attended a lecture on that same organism. Some nurses who also had overheard the conversation quickly joined in the interview, expressing their own alarm and explaining they had friends caught in Williams's quarantine. In the ensuing discussion the residents reassured them that while aggressive, this bacteria was still sensitive to vancomycin and could be treated.

Soon a rumor about the "Ontario strain" swept through St. Paul's and rapidly established itself as the official "secret" reason behind the patient recall and the need to quarantine some of the personnel. By 2:30 the rumor had been on the news, frightening people enough to come in, but, since the newscaster stressed the organism could be treated, the panic that Williams had feared was avoided. By 3:00 compliance was soaring, but the lawyers upstairs, I was told, continued to wrangle.

"I couldn't have planted a better story if I'd tried," Williams commented, grinning in relief when we finally had a private word together late in the afternoon. We were standing in the corridor outside the auditorium. Patients were arriving, everything at the testing stations was running smoothly for the moment, and there was a lull in the incessant demands on both of us. I'd asked him to meet me, determined to convince him about the connection between Sanders and the other *Legionella* cases.

But it was not to be.

"Dr. Williams," Hurst interrupted from twenty feet away. He strode up to us, ignoring me but taking Williams by the arm. "Your CDC colleagues have just arrived from Atlanta. They're waiting for you upstairs," he informed him curtly.

Williams excused himself and quickly walked toward the elevators. Hurst waited until the man was far enough down the hall not to hear. Then he glared at me and said very softly, "My only consolation in this mess that you've caused is that I'll finally be rid of you." Then he pivoted and hurried after Williams.

"That's about what it was like here, except mothers with newborn babies are a whole lot more panicky," Janet said over the phone after I'd described my own day's activity. I'd called her during a break for supper. As a member of the Infection Control Committee at University Hospital, she'd received the same confidential briefing about the superbug that morning as I had and had spent the day taking cultures much as I had done. She was tired, her voice sounded strained, and like me, she was frightened.

"What about the rest of your staff members?" I asked.

"Much the same as at St. Paul's—a few women showing symptoms of what is probably the flu are spending forty-eight hours here in a closed ward as a precaution until the cultures are finished. But we got one break. For the past few months since the *Legionella* cases, Cam had stepped up screening programs for all possible hospital-acquired infections, and the most frequent testing was for MRSA. All the personnel on the obstetrical unit were checked five weeks ago and everyone was negative then, including Sanders. That meant she'd only been a potential risk as a carrier going near patients and other staff for the three weeks before her vacation."

"That also narrows when she herself was infected," I added. "If we traced her activity in that period, we might get some idea as to how she contracted either *Legionella* or staph."

"Yeah, if we can ever get any of these CDC types to consider she was murdered. That kind of 'tracing' needs a lot of work hours."

"Did you talk to any of them about the *Legionella* cases?"

She sighed. "Not yet. And there's no way anyone's going to consider anything today but the superbug. I figure we'll have a better chance when the initial screenings are done and everyone's sitting around waiting for results. But I think Michael's finally as worried about the connection between the three nurses as we are. He attended our ID meeting this morning. After Cam dropped the bombshell about Sanders's staph organism, Michael leaned over and apologized for rejecting my scenarios simply because they were bizarre and previously unheard of. He looked quite shaken and asked where the records of the Phantom's previous victims were. I've been too busy reassuring mothers and culturing tiny noses to see how he's doing."

I felt a flash of alarm. "Should he be down there alone?"

"Hey, I still can't tell that friend of yours anything. I asked him the same question. He laughed, and said, 'No Phantom's going to make a move with the CDC all over the place. These guys are like the cavalry,' " Janet mimicked, catching the impatient tone Michael used when anyone opposed him. "I suppose he's right," she added, sounding nervous.

Maybe, I thought, maybe not. The cavalry wasn't looking for the Phantom, didn't even know he existed, and that could still leave him room enough to be dangerous, especially if all the scrutiny was making him feel threatened.

Janet interrupted my thoughts. "Right now I've got to get back to work. By the way, my secretary told me there was a bunch of flowers in my office this morning. I never got there to read the card. Did you send them?"

"No." I laughed. "They're part of Michael's apology."

"Ah, too bad. And here I was ready to meet you in the parking lot, as a show of my appreciation, and fool around with you in the back of your car. We would have worn masks, gloves, and gowns, of course, but nothing underneath."

By 9:00 P.M. we were finished screening for the day. Attempts to reach those who had been missed were to be continued on Saturday. The dozen people with the flu who were in quarantine had finally accepted the wisdom of their being there, though none were aware yet that they were waiting for cultures of an untreatable organism. But what to do with all the rest of the staff while we waited the forty-eight hours for our culture results was less clear.

"If they are carrying the organism somewhere—under their nails or secluded far up a nostril—and they go home to infants or children who might have a cut or scrape on their skin, then they theoretically could be putting those children at risk," Williams had explained gravely during our morning session.

A flash of alarm had shot through my chest as I immediately thought of Brendan. Had I already exposed him?

"I suggest a second facility be set aside for those staff members who may wish a voluntary quarantine," he'd continued, "away from those already at risk."

It had probably been an overreaction, but I'd immediately called Amy and ordered her to bathe Brendan for an hour, scrub the rails on his crib, and hot wash every article of clothing, bedding, toy, or anything else that might touch him. Then, after thinking about it more coolly all day, I decided to play it safe in a more logical way and told Janet that I was staying in the hospital. But once I was alone in the barren room, outfitted with nothing more than a bed and mattress rolled out of storage, I felt so forlorn I nearly changed my mind. The musty, stale odors of a disused building permeated the ward, though it had been hastily cleaned and just as hurriedly heated. Not many people had accepted Hurst's accommodation, but occasionally in the interior stillness I heard the hollow sound of someone's cough or a toilet flush. Outside a storm was brewing again. The wind rattled panes of glass and whistled through gaps in the wooden frames around the windows; those noises didn't help my mood any. Yet instead of running home from that stark place, I lay there and forced myself to arrange the fragmented thoughts I'd been struggling with all day into some kind of logical perspective.

It seemed clear to me that natural conjugation couldn't have produced the superbug in Sanders. I remembered reading or hearing somewhere in premed statistics that random chance virtually never was responsible for two rare events occurring simultaneously. The odds against a new organism selecting Phyllis Sanders as its first victim over the nearly four billion other souls on earth were just that—four billion to one. The odds of an organism appearing by chance for the first time ever on the planet in the middle of a deliberately inflicted *Legionella* infection—in itself a previously unheard of phenomenon—were ludicrous beyond consideration. For these two extraordinary events to have happened in the same individual, something had to have made them happen together, and the obvious "maker" in this instance was the killer. But how to convince Williams of this? Or anyone else?

Whoever this killer was, I suspected he had to have access to a genetic laboratory with the capacity to alter the gene structure of bacterial DNA or at least to the end products of such a place. Nobody at St. Paul's that I knew of, not even Rossit and certainly not Hurst, would normally have the opportunity to even get near that kind of esoteric equipment let alone possess the skills to use it. I'd have to ask Janet if she knew of anybody at UH with that kind of expertise. I also had no idea if any work of that nature was being done at the university and would have to check there as well.

Droplets of rain pinged against the windows. In the harsh reflection of the overhead lights they looked like oblique scratches being slashed across the pane.

I thought of Michael's suggestion that the Phantom would have already retreated into the darkness with the arrival of the ID experts. I doubted it. No one else even knew he existed, and we'd spent the day carrying out a drill never intended to trap him. Our running about probably seemed to him as if we were scrambling around on a web of his making, the pattern unknown to us, while he lurked at its edge, out of sight, waiting, and gloating.

I was startled by a sharp sound. Was it a rap on my door? A product of the raging storm outside? Or something . . . someone I wanted to avoid?

I'd taken off my protective gear. Instead of putting everything back on to see if somebody was there, I called out, "Yes?"

No answer.

I immediately thought of a dark figure and the sound of breathing. "Who's there?" I yelled again, trying to remember if I'd snapped the lock shut or not. As I got off the bed I quickly looked around for some kind of weapon, but the room held nothing, not even a phone. Feeling both foolish and increasingly frightened, I picked up one of my shoes and held it up in the air by the toe while I started to creep forward. I was holding my breath, and all I could hear was my own heart as I moved my hand toward the lock. I froze midway. The handle was slowly turning, the door opening.

"Shit!" I muttered, scurrying backward, my shoe still held on high, until my back pressed against the wall behind me. Standing in the dark corridor was a tall slender figure wearing a surgical mask, gown, and gloves who was taking off a lab coat.

Janet gave a low chuckle and said softly, "Now that's no way to greet a lady who's come to offer you a little affection." She stepped into the room, then came toward me, dropping her coat as I put down my shoe.

"You scared me half to death," I whispered, slipping my arms around her. I quickly discovered she'd dressed exactly as she had promised, the feel of her naked body under her greens making me catch my breath and quickly igniting my hunger for her. We kissed greedily. As I slid my hands lightly over her back and down between her hips, she stood on her tiptoes, letting my fingertips feel her heat and readiness, even from behind. Her own hands reached for mine, then glided them up across her stomach to circle around and touch her nipples, already erect from my kisses. We continued to propel our desire for each other with our hands, our mouths, and our words. By the time we were on the bed, she was trembling. She slid me into her with a deep thrust that unleashed a long low growl from her throat; the sound and feel of her seared through me like lightning. While outside the storm surged and shrieked, we writhed, rode, and urged each other up ever higher waves of ecstasy, until, fused in a glorious instant, we lifted ourselves over the top and descended, clinging together, into the freeing, pulsing release that comes to souls whose joining is blessed by love and driven by a healthy dose of lust.

"I don't suppose this place has room service" was Janet's first comment after we had breath enough to talk.

"I wouldn't even drink the tap water. It's brown with God knows what from the pipes."

"Well," she exclaimed, throwing off the covers and hastily starting to pull her greens back on. "This lady of the night is going back to UH where I can at least have a shower."

Outside the storm continued as intense as ever, the wind buffeting against the windows and peppering the panes with rain so driven it sounded like particles of sand blasting the glass.

"By the way, I may have at least one piece of good news," she informed me as I watched her continue dressing. "Harold Miller was at our ID meeting this morning. He'd come in after Cam had notified him at home about the organism that killed his mother. Cam made a point of stressing to us that the only way this organism could be stopped was by decolonizing it from contaminated surfaces in the hospital and from human carriers. He was looking right at Miller when he reemphasized that once this particular bug took hold clinically, there wasn't anything anyone could do to stop it. Obviously he was calling on us to be vigilant, but I also got the impression he was specifically telling Harold to stop tormenting himself with the idea that his mother might have been saved if you hadn't sent her home."

I winced, but I was also relieved that at least Cam seemed to be on my side. His support might prove important if Miller took me to court. "So what's the good news?" I asked, immediately regretting how harshly I threw the question at Janet.

"Hey, I'm not the bad guy here, and neither are you," she reproached me gently as she finished pulling on her white lab coat over her otherwise revealing garb.

"Sorry, Janet," I said, reaching for her hand.

She sat down on the side of the bed and continued to speak while stroking my head. "The good news is that after the meeting, Miller came up to me and asked that I tell you he's sorry for reacting so harshly. He didn't say anything more and he's of course still looking pretty shaken about his mother's death, but I think he may be seriously reconsidering his initial anger toward you. In fact, he seems instead to be focusing that anger more toward the organism we're up against. He insisted on coming back to help set up all the screening that had to be done, and the man worked like a demon all day, pitching in with taking samples whenever he wasn't running off to deal with some snag or other in the lab. I suppose it's his way of striking back at what killed his mother." She leaned over me, gave me a soft kiss, her lips still full from our lovemaking. "So you see, as I told you, things might work out with him after all," she whispered.

I felt a mix of relief, surprise, and puzzlement. "But if I'd clued in that first day, hit her with a dose of erythromycin before the staph took hold—"

She silenced me by gently placing her fingers on my lips. "Stop beating yourself up. Wait until they find out in Atlanta about the incubation and prodrome of this bug and if anything you might have done would have made any difference." Then she got off the bed and let herself out of the room.

By noon Saturday, we had taken culture specimens from most of the remaining patients who were recalled for screening. We had not yet reached about fifty cases but would follow them up by home visits.

By Saturday evening, preliminary culture results showed no vancomycin-resistant organisms in either staff or patients but suggested the possibility that a few of the hospital workers were carrying MRSA. Some of them were already under quarantine. Those at home were called in, and they all were subjected to bactericidal soaps and intranasal mupirocin ointment.

By Sunday afternoon, all the cultures taken on Friday were confirmed to be negative for staphylococcus resistant to both vancomycin and methicillin. And there wasn't any evidence of the vancomycin-inhibiting strain that had been discovered in Japan. The only positive findings were confirmations of the MRSA carriers already identified by the preliminary results. The ER itself was given a clean bill of health and would open that evening.

All in all, as far as the men and women from Atlanta were concerned, it was an unbelievably good result. The superbug they'd been anticipating with such dread had come out of nowhere, claimed a single victim, and then vanished without a trace, at least without the sort of trace that could be detected by culturing nooks and crannies of rooms, sundry pieces of equipment, and the hands, nails, and nostrils of anyone who'd been near Sanders. At a 4:00 P.M. wrap-up meeting, everyone was clearly buoyant with surprise and relief.

"We lucked out," the gray-haired chairperson of their hospital infection group kept saying, slapping his colleagues on the back and congratulating them on a well-run operation. Rossit and Hurst watched this good cheer nervously at first, then seemed to realize that they were now likely to end up looking good, given how the operation had gone, and tentatively joined in the handshaking. For me, just getting to shed the protective gear we'd been stuck in for over two days was a cause for celebration. Particularly annoying had been the way my mask trapped the humidity from my breath, constantly steaming up my glasses.

I found Hurst's demeanor toward me controlled and cold as usual. I hadn't seen him since he'd muttered his threat to be rid of me, but there was no evidence this evening of the overt malice I'd felt then. I had to admit, the more I'd thought about the encounter, the more I'd found it puzzling. Hurst rarely attacked me or anyone else directly, let alone announced his intention to do so. His preference was to sandbag his adversaries from behind the scenes, in ways that were easily denied and hard to prove. I would have expected him to simply let the blame for the Sanders case give him the excuse he needed to dump me as chief, without ever having to confront me directly. Had the angry words slipped out spontaneously, spurred by his fury about all the negative publicity for St. Paul's? Or had he deliberately tried to rattle me, as some sort of distraction? His steely expression gave me no answers.

Williams was nowhere to be seen. "Probably back with his ducks," one young woman from the CDC team told me jokingly when I inquired where he was. Her crack at his expense produced a few other laughs from her colleagues, but I doubted they were mocking him. Rossit's recognition of him two days ago, even with all the obsequious antics, had suggested there was much more to Williams than some obscure study of botulism in ducks.

The chairperson from the CDC called the meeting to order, but while some of the group excitedly reported on the work already under way in Atlanta to isolate VanA genes from the organism's DNA, and others outlined the myriad studies that would be performed on the cultures and autopsy specimens taken from Phyllis Sanders, I was thinking of *Legionella* again.

I'd dropped by the labs just before the meeting. Over the weekend the protracted process of special cultures and immunofluorescent staining procedures that I'd ordered on Sanders's sputum had finally produced a positive result, but the result had gone unnoticed in all the excitement.

If I could just get this group to consider the *Legionella* cases in their investigation, I thought, it might be a first step in getting them to realize what was really happening. When the discussion focused on how the CDC labs planned to investigate the aggressiveness of the superbug and determine which factors might predispose carriers to becoming infected, I passed my results around the table and challenged, "What about the fact that Phyllis Sanders also had *Legionella* before the superbug took hold? And what about there being two other unexplained cases of *Legionella* at UH in the last six months? I take it you're also aware that the physician caring for the Sanders woman himself came down with a presumed case of *Legionella* a few days ago, though his cultures aren't ready yet. Are you going to look at this pattern?"

Rossit and Hurst immediately scowled at me. For interrupting? Or for touching on what they preferred no one look at too closely?

The distinguished chairperson from the CDC frowned as he regarded me from his end of the table. "What you're raising are serious issues, of course, but I assure you the CDC is not here to deal with a few cases of *Legionella*. Your distinguished and most competent local ID authorities can and will guide you, as they always have, on such *routinely* reportable infections." I presumed his emphasis on the word *routinely* was a not so subtle way of saying don't bother him and his superstars with small potatoes. That stuff he *obviously* left to underlings.

A young man wearing red suspenders to which a Buffalo Public

Health ID badge was pinned seemed suddenly to recognize his role and piped in, "We'll certainly be looking into those cases, Dr. Garnet. And I can assure you and the rest of this group that we'll be spending some time at University Hospital, since Phyllis Sanders worked there. We've already suggested to Dr. Cam Mackie that *all* personnel at UH be screened immediately for staphylococcus, just to take no chances. Perhaps we can look into rechecking the place for *Legionella* at the same time, although Dr. Mackie assured us they'd already done that. Sanders could have acquired the *Legionella* anywhere. Whatever the case, I must tell you that we are most satisfied with Dr. Rossit's measures in response to the unfortunate *Legionella* case involving your own ICU director."

Rossit beamed. Both he and Hurst had also seemed pleased about the attention University Hospital was scheduled to get.

"Of course we will be determining the infectivity of this bug," the chairperson said, bringing the discussion back to the big issues that he was here for.

I tuned out the doctor-speak about the percentage of carriers likely to come down with the disease—as high as thirty-three percent in other strains—and thought about the Phantom. I shivered. We had to track him down . . . had to.

After the meeting broke up, I was dying to get home and see Janet and Brendan, but I had a few more jobs to do. I managed to get the telephone number where Douglas Williams was staying from a member of the departing CDC team, claiming I wanted to thank the man for the help he'd given us on Friday. Then I went up to the library, plugged into the computer Med-Line program that indexed all major medical publications, and punched in the key words "infectious diseases," "patterns of occurrence," "vectors," and the name "Dr. Douglas Williams." This particular search program summoned a list more than three pages long of abstracts of articles. Glancing at the titles, I picked a few that particularly interested me, had the librarian dig them out, and spent the next hour reading. I learned a lot about what the man was good at from reviewing his previous work. I began to have a glimmer of hope that his expertise might be a whole lot more helpful than the CDC's.

Finally I stopped by ICU, but Stewart was sleeping. The nurses assured me he was stable and promised to tell him I'd dropped in to say hi.

* * *

The phone woke me near midnight that same evening. I was in my own bed at home, but at first I'd briefly thought I was back in that accursed room at the hospital where I'd spent the last two nights. I fumbled with the receiver, heard a nurse from St. Paul's excitedly identify herself, and shook myself out of a deep sleep to concentrate on her words.

". . . yet he's febrile, in acute respiratory distress, and shocky, just like the Sanders woman," she exclaimed, "but he won't let us intubate him until you get here."

I instantly thought of Deloram. "You mean Stewart's going shocky?" I blurted out, immediately wide awake and sitting bolt upright. "But he was stable when I—"

"No, Dr. Garnet, I'm calling from ER!" she exclaimed, her voice suddenly cracking with what sounded like barely controlled sobs. "It's Dr. Popovitch. He was brought in by ambulance a few minutes ago. He's septic, wheezing like hell, and everyone's afraid he's about to shut down his airway and have a respiratory arrest. But he's refusing to let anyone intubate him until he can talk to you. Please hurry. He's so hypoxic he's out of his head. He keeps insisting someone has deliberately infected him."

My drive into St. Paul's was a blur of rain, speed, and gut-tying fear. Michael, septic, in shock just like Sanders, the nurse had said. How could he have let anyone near enough to infect him? Was he going to die like Sanders? Who was next?

Half the time I couldn't see through the torrents pouring over the windshield despite the wipers, but there was little traffic, and each time I thought of Michael's arresting before I got there I went faster. The car shuddered and pulled from side to side as the wheels plowed through deep collections of water lying across the road. My hands strained to control the steering wheel but I refused to slow down.

"Damn your stubbornness, Michael!" I yelled as spray roared up against the underside of the car. But it was myself I blamed. Why hadn't I screamed my bloody head off days ago and forced everyone to face what Janet had suspected from the beginning? We might have frightened off the Phantom. Why the hell had I even listened to Michael's concerns about my credibility and what Rossit could do to my career?

The car nearly careened out of control as I sped down the off ramp and flew through the deserted downtown streets. Don't die,

Michael. Don't you damn well die, I swore, tears welling up in my eyes and blurring my vision even more.

He stopped breathing seconds after I ran into the resuscitation room. I think he might have seen me as I burst through the door. His bearded face was lolling, his eyes were bulging as he stared in my direction, and one of his arms, hanging down off the stretcher, rose limply toward me, then dropped back. Despite a forest of IVs pumping him with fluid, the vascular collapse from sepsis had left his huge body looking as if it were made from glistening rolls of paste. Circled around him, a silent group of green-clad residents and nurses in protective gear stood alongside their neatly arranged trays of tubes, scopes, and ventilation equipment, waiting to resuscitate him from what was clearly an imminent arrest.

His eyes seemed to slide toward this array of instruments that would soon be in him and his facial muscles jerked into what appeared to be a look of terror, but it was the start of a seizure accompanying the complete halt of his respirations. It quickly spread through the rest of his body, curling and uncurling his limbs into cruel shaking spasms, then dropping him like a lifeless doll.

The team was already on him. They struggled to pry open his jaws still clamped shut in the seizure's aftermath. While pulling on my own protective gear, I watched the monitors as his pulse dropped to thirty and his oxygen levels plummeted. Alarm bells started going off one after the other as other vital signs fell.

"We can't get his mouth open to intubate," yelled an anesthesia resident in panic.

Another resident at his side was trying to shove a tracheal tube into Michael's nose and attempt a blind intubation down through his nasopharynx. In his nervousness, he forced the delicate maneuver, failed to get the airway, and produced a hemorrhage. It didn't last long. The near dead don't have the blood pressure it takes to bleed. All the monitors were flat but for an occasional heartbeat.

The nurses were beside themselves, screaming useless instructions.

"For Christ's sake, get a tube in him!"

"I've lost his pressure. Pump him!"

"What about atropine for the bradycardia?"

But what he needed was an airway and ventilation. I finished snapping on my gloves, stepped to the head of the stretcher, and shoved aside the residents. "Give me a soft nasal pharyngeal tube," I ordered the nearest nurse. She handed me a flexible six-inch hollow piece of latex the size of my little finger. I added some lubricant and slid it easily up the nostril that wasn't bleeding. I felt it readily curve down along the contours of the nasopharynx and its tip push past the base of his tongue, which had fallen back to block his airway. There was a slight rushing noise through the near end of the tube that was still sticking out of his nose. His chest muscles and diaphragm were reflexively starting their movements of breathing again, now that the way to the lungs was open. But the effort was weak. We helped him out with a ventilating bag, the residents pressing the mask to his face to avoid leaks while I forced oxygen through the nasal tube, into his airway, and filled his lungs. His pulse and blood pressure rose immediately, the seizure in his jaw broke, and his mouth dropped open, the muscles slack. Within minutes we had him intubated the regular way, on a respirator, and ready for ICU.

The nurse who'd spoken to me on the phone led me into the corridor outside the resuscitation room. Her eyes were red, and she still was having trouble keeping her voice from shaking.

"Will he make it?" she asked.

"I hope so" was all I could tell her.

Then she started to cry and turned away. "I'm sorry," she said, fumbling for a tissue, "but I've never had to resuscitate one of our own before. And Michael's such a powerhouse here. It's hard to see him like that . . ." Her voice trailed off, and she had to use her tissue again. "He was barely able to talk more than a whisper," she continued when she had control over her tears, "and even then, he could only gasp out a word at a time. As I said, he was obviously delirious. But he was desperate to speak with you. He got increasingly afraid he wouldn't hold out until you got here and begged for a pen and notepad." She reached into her pocket and handed me a folded piece of paper.

I thanked her, quickly turned away, and unfolded what was a scrawled message. *The Phantom is real. Check the charts! The pattern!*

PART TWO

Prodrome

PART TWO

Probate

Chapter 12

A glance at my watch told me it was 1:00 A.M. I was at a loss what to do. I wanted to know what charts Michael had been checking—wanted to see them for myself—but didn't even know for sure which charts he meant. Janet said on Friday he'd gone to look at the records of the Phantom's first victims—the same records Janet had wanted me to see the night I got attacked in the subbasement. But he'd done that a couple of days ago. Had he found something else in the meantime? Had he been poking around during the weekend?

"Dr. Garnet," one of the nurses said, touching my arm.

I was leaning against the wall just outside the resus room, still staring at Michael's note, lost in desperate thoughts.

"Dr. Garnet," I heard her repeat, "we put Dr. Popovitch's wife, Donna, in the grieving room, to give her some privacy. She came in with him in the ambulance and is obviously upset. Could you speak to her about her husband?"

At that moment an orderly wheeled Michael out of resus and down the corridor toward the elevator that would take him to ICU. He was completely still, the tube protruding from his mouth distorting his lips and cheeks into a grotesque sneer that made me think of the rictus of death. "Oh, Michael, my poor friend," I said softly, watching the winking lights of the monitors recede up the dark passage.

I tried to prepare what I would say to Donna as I crossed the waiting area. Even at this hour there were more than two dozen people in the place, waiting either to see a doctor or to receive lab results and the final verdict of their examination.

When I opened the door to the grieving room, Donna looked up, saw me, and said, "No!"

"He's alive, Donna," I quickly told her. "We got him full of IVs; he's breathing on a respirator and being pumped full of erythromycin as we speak." I walked over and put my arm around her shoulders, continuing to talk, afraid to give her time to ask questions. I didn't trust my usual capacity to hide from a family member how frightened I was for his or her critically ill loved one. "He'll be in ICU and you can see him there in a few minutes. But remember, he'll be sedated to keep him comfortable on the respirator. When he gets a bit better . . ."

While I talked she stared at me, her brown eyes brimming with tears. Black curls, cut off at shoulder length, framed her attractive face, but fear had driven away the flush of pregnancy. The contrast between dark hair and pale skin left her looking ghostly. "What does he have, Earl?" she interjected. "And tell me straight what it means, especially if there's any risk for the baby."

In other words, cut the crap. I took a breath and leveled with her. "We presume he has *Legionella*," I told her solemnly. "Healthy adults like you shouldn't get it. There's never been a case recorded of person-to-person transmission, so you and the baby are in no danger."

She seemed to sit up straighter, swallowed, and tremulously asked, "Isn't that what killed the nurse from UH whose infection he was investigating?"

"She had two infections, Donna, one of them a very virulent form of staphylococcus. It's not the same with Michael. His airway wasn't full of pus when we intubated him. We'll do a Gram stain on the scanty bit of sputum he does have just to be sure, but I'm certain it will be negative, unlike what we found in the nurse." A little later, so as not to scare her more now, I would suggest she be screened for staph, simply as a precaution.

"But this morning, he just seemed to have a cold," she said, shaking her head and looking at me as if I were to provide answers about how he could have become so ill.

But the answer I had—that someone had deliberately infected him—wouldn't do her any good. "Donna, was he complaining of any symptoms on Saturday?" I asked instead.

"No, not at all. He spent the day at UH going over records. He even seemed fine Saturday night, though I thought he was preoccupied by whatever he was looking into."

"Why? Did he say anything?" I asked eagerly.

"No, it's just that he was quiet all evening. Normally we play cards or watch a movie, but he insisted we go for a walk instead. If he said three words the whole hour we were outside, I couldn't tell you what they were. We just strolled along, and when I asked him what was the matter, he simply told me that the audit wasn't going the way he'd hoped and that he'd have to go back in to UH on Sunday."

"How sick was he this morning?"

"Not very. He had a mild cough and complained of a bit of diarrhea, but neither seemed like much. The only thing unusual was his being concerned about it at all. He never takes care of himself, even when he's obviously too ill to work. So when he said he was going to pick up some antibiotics, I was pretty surprised."

"Did he?"

"Yes, I've got them here." She reached for her purse. "Then he came home in the middle of the afternoon, went to bed, and told me if he wasn't feeling better by morning he was going to check into ER as a patient. That shocked the hell out of me, because he still didn't seem too bad. I actually kidded him that he was going soft in his young middle age and that I expected better stuff when I robbed the cradle." She was fumbling for the pills and starting to cry. "Maybe if I'd checked on him sooner, he wouldn't have gotten so bad. But I let him sleep, and only when I went to get into bed around eleven, did I realize how wheezy and hot he was. When I could hardly wake him up, I called an ambulance." She sobbed, handing me a container full of red-and-black capsules, then groping back in her purse until she found a handkerchief.

I recognized what those capsules were without looking at the label—erythromycin.

While I comforted Donna and let her finish crying, my thoughts were racing. Michael must have suspected as early as Sunday morning that he'd been infected with *Legionella*. But he couldn't have been all that sure. Otherwise he would have admitted himself to emergency for IV antibiotics then, not simply put himself on oral erythromycin. What pattern in what charts had he subsequently seen that convinced him there really was a phantom? Or had he seen something previously and only later realized what it meant? In fact, maybe the pattern didn't strike him until he was on the way to ER by ambulance. If he'd been as certain about the Phantom earlier in the day as he obviously was when he arrived in ER, wouldn't he have told me, or Cam, or someone? Slowly a horrible possibility dawned on me. It might have been his own progression through a vague prodrome to the brutal characteristics of respiratory distress and septic shock from *Legionella* that had finally convinced him there was a killer—when he knew beyond all doubt what he had and that he had become a victim of the Phantom.

Damn your skepticism, Michael, I thought. Despite his belated willingness to look at records for traces of a murderer, his stubborn doubts that anyone could transmit *Legionella* at will must have continued to dog him over the weekend. I prayed his delay in getting help wouldn't cost him his life.

I escorted Donna to ICU and led her to the door of the isolation room where the staff had put Michael. There I helped her to don the protective clothing, followed her in, and stood behind her as she gazed down at her husband. His chest rose and fell to the rhythmic hiss of a respirator, his body full of tubes and lines, and his every sign of life wired into a tiered bank of monitors behind his head. Her tears flowed silently as she hesitantly ran her gloved hand through his hair, but she remained erect standing at his side. "You can leave me alone with him now, Earl," she commanded softly, the steel in her voice catching me by surprise.

Looking back as I left ICU, I saw she hadn't moved. She remained motionless in that lit chamber, the beginning swell of her pregnancy suggested by the green gown enveloping her. Off to the right, I could see a similar room, only dimly illuminated, where the form of Stewart Deloram stirred and turned in a restless sleep. How many more glass coffins would there be? I thought angrily, cursing the monster that had done this.

I roared out of the parking lot at St. Paul's and headed for UH with one objective. I was going into the hospital and I was going to find what Michael had discovered. I didn't care if I had to jump the security guards, break a window, or smash locks. Pussyfooting around had cost too much. As for fear of running across the Phantom, heaven help him if I did. I was in a rage.

The storm hadn't let up any, nor had my speed. Once more the car rocked as I flew through water-clogged streets and screeched around corners. Occasionally under a street lamp I saw my spray fly up to the front steps of the old gray stone houses that hugged the sidewalks in this part of town.

Thankfully part of my brain continued to serve me rationally. Halfway to UH I had a better idea than committing a B&E. Driving one-handed, I fished out of my coat pocket the telephone number that I'd made a point of getting earlier that evening, though I never expected to be using it so soon. I flicked on my overhead light so I could see the numbers and quickly punched them into my cellular. It took about a dozen rings, but finally Williams's sleepy voice boomed out of the receiver, "This better be good."

"Dr. Williams, it's Garnet. We've got a serious situation here, and I need your help."

"Now?" he queried. I could just imagine the expression on his face.

"Yeah, now. I haven't got time to explain how or why, but I've got reason to believe the infections that killed Phyllis Sanders were deliberately inflicted. Most likely two other nurses where she worked were similarly infected with *Legionella* in the last six months. One of them died. Three days ago, as you know, the ICU doctor treating Sanders inexplicably contracted what we presume is *Legionella*, and an hour ago I resuscitated my best friend, a doctor in my ER. He's in septic shock, also presumed to be from *Legionella*. His only risk factor was poking around UH to try to find out how the other infections got started!" My frustration and anger had exploded out of me as I talked. I paused for breath and drove, straining to see through the windshield, listening to the silence my outburst had provoked on the other end of the connection.

"Have you been drinking?"

"Christ!" I screamed at him, almost losing control of my steering. "I am not some weirdo," I yelled at him. "You ought to know that from being in St. Paul's just one day." How hospital personnel react to a doctor on his or her own turf always gives a pretty quick and reliable take on a physician's reputation, for better or worse. "Did anyone besides Rossit and Hurst imply anything but a favorable impression of me?" I wasn't above arguing shamelessly on my own behalf, hoping he hadn't run across a few of my other enemies. I was desperate for his help. Overhead a roll of thunder drowned out the sound of the rain on my car.

He chuckled. "Actually, it was those two turkeys trying to bad-mouth you that added most to your credibility."

I felt a glimmer of hope.

"But what in the world makes you think such a wildly improbable story could be true?"

"Because the three nurses had a habit of being malicious to patients, and I think there's someone at UH who's taken a deadly exception to their cruelty."

"What?"

I again imagined his incredulous expression from the tone in his voice. "Because there's a history of someone punishing punishers in that place, but never this lethally," I answered. "Look, I don't expect you to believe this without evidence, but Michael Popovitch found something in the last few days that convinced him we're up against a serial killer. He didn't have time to tell me what it was before he arrested, and I must get at those same files he was looking at."

"But how can I—"

"By calling the security guard at the front door, then saying that you're in charge of the CDC investigation of the hospital and you suddenly need this additional information. Order him to let me in and give me whatever I want."

"That will never work."

"It won't work if we wait until morning. Security would make me go through channels once all the regular staff are in. But if you make the request tonight, when the night guards are alone, we might pull it off."

"But I told you I'm not even part of the hospital infection group—"

"You also told me the only way through a situation like this was bluff," I shot back. "*Big, bold-faced, lying bluff!* Now was that little speech also just some of *your* bluff, or are you for real?" I held my breath, one-handed my way through more small lakes forming over the road, and waited for his reply.

"I don't know, Garnet," he said over the noise of the spray, "all this is flaky as hell—"

"Listen to me!" I cut him off again. "I looked up some of the papers you wrote. Your specialty seems to be analyzing unusual patterns in the spread of infectious diseases and determining whether a vector—a carrier like a rat, a mouse, or a tick on a deer—is responsible for the spread of otherwise inexplicable outbreaks. I think what we have here is an inexplicable series of infections where the 'carrier' is a serial killer. If you can track down a four-legged vermin, maybe you're perfectly qualified to find a two-legged one so we can put a stop to him. Simply adopt the same perspective you've used to discover vectors in the other bizarre cases you've solved."

There was complete silence for at least thirty seconds. Then I heard him chuckle again. "You impress me, Dr. Garnet. You really impress me. Give me a few minutes to get the security people at UH on the phone and I'll see what I can do. In case this crazy idea of yours works and you actually find something worth looking at, where can I meet you tomorrow morning?"

I told him.

A few minutes later I was in the parking lot of UH. As I listened to the rain drum on the roof and gave Williams some time to work his magic over the phone, I began to make a mental list of what I'd look at first. *Check the charts!* Michael had written. To begin with I'd have to find out what charts he meant. Then hopefully I'd discover the pattern that had led him to believe the Phantom was real. But as I organized my plan it dawned on me that whatever that pattern was, it mustn't have revealed the killer's identity. Otherwise, he'd surely have scrawled a name on the note he'd been so desperate to write.

I glanced at my watch and decided it was time to go. Williams shouldn't have needed more than five minutes to succeed or fail in his bluff. I glanced up at the forbidding building I was about to enter and thought seriously about taking a tire iron out of my trunk and carrying it under my raincoat, for protection. As angry as I was, I was still chilled by the thought of going alone into that isolated realm of subterranean corridors where the records were kept. But I remembered the metal detector at the front door, resigned myself to using only my wits for self-defense, and ran through the rain toward the entrance under the watchful eye of the gargoyles.

Williams had bluffed as promised.

"Yes, Dr. Garnet, we've been expecting you. It must be pretty important for the CDC to bring you out on a night like this." Of the two guards on duty, it was the one with more stripes on the sleeve of his uniform who spoke to me. His colleague stood behind their desk, not at attention but not slouching either. To my surprise, they were both wearing surgical masks.

"Who ordered those?" I asked, pointing to their faces after I'd flashed my identity card and signed their book for after-hours visitors.

"No one. It's just this business of checking everyone for infection, and now with two nurses dead, well, we're all pretty nervous. Dr. Mackie insists we're in no danger but has given permission to everybody working here to wear a mask if they feel more secure, for now. Even a lot of the patients have requested them."

They'd clearly overreacted. But as Williams had cautioned on his first day, people weren't always rational when it came to deadly microbes.

"Where do you want to start?" asked the senior guard.

"Administration," I answered. "I'll need the minutes from the last two years of the Infection Control Committee. We'll find them wherever they keep the records of all confidential meetings."

The hospital carried out these proceedings under the umbrella of quality assurance and, as such, records of them were immune even to subpoena by a court of law. The powers that be meant such confidentiality to assure frankness in exposing and correcting mistakes, which they thought to be more important than lawsuits in protecting the health of patients. Nevertheless, if any of this information leaked or got out by accident, individuals could use it in a court case, and so the hospital guarded such documents the most closely of any of its secrets.

But the security man nodded without question, his partner wrote our destination beside my name, and we set off in the direction I'd taken last week when I'd met Janet and Michael in staff health. This time I ended up in the lushly carpeted section of that wing, where the administrators obviously looked after their own comforts, whatever else they did. My guide led me down a hallway paneled with rich dark wood, checked his key ring, and unlocked a heavy double door opening into a large room lined with shelves holding nothing but black binders, rows and rows of them. Each shelf had a sign designating which committee its contents were from, and each binder had a label designating which year's proceedings it contained. In an age of computer hackers, most hospitals preferred to keep a single copy of this kind of material on paper and locked in a vault. The only reason such records were kept at all was that accreditation boards demanded documentation of quality assurance activities. Michael would have access to these as a state accreditor. Williams must have sounded mighty impressive to get me in here.

I quickly found the two volumes I needed, and while the guard looked on, I found the minutes that dealt with the incidents from two years ago. Skimming them and working forward to the subsequent follow-up meetings, I saw nothing substantial that Janet hadn't already told me. I jotted down what I'd come for—the chart numbers of the victims.

After returning the binders to their places, I spotted another shelf containing the minutes for Death Rounds at UH and shivered. My own appointment with that process at St. Paul's for Phyllis Sanders's case was scheduled to begin in about five hours.

After the guard locked up, I had him let me into the record room in the nearby staff health clinic. I'd obtained the numbers of eighteen charts, and if any of them were recently active, they would be on file there. I found two and signed them out. The remaining sixteen should be downstairs in the archives where Janet, and presumably Michael, had studied them.

I found myself tensing as we rode the elevator toward the subbasement. I had to concentrate on keeping my breathing steady, and when we arrived with a definitive lurch, I felt my back dampen with sweat.

The guard stepped out and held the door for me. I swallowed, then forced myself to move. My eyes inadvertently focused on the steel frame of the elevator entrance where my head had been rammed. Once in the corridor, I found myself staring down the well-lit passage off to the right where, in the distance, I could see the darkened entrance that led to the basement of the abandoned asylum. But there was no movement in those shadows tonight.

"This way, Doctor," my escort said, starting to walk in the opposite direction. I turned and hurried to stay beside him, trying not to keep looking over my shoulder. The route we followed was a mirror image of the one I'd taken four nights ago, except this time we arrived at a door marked ARCHIVES at the end of our trek. The guard unlocked it, snapped on a light, and let me into yet another room filled with rows of shelves lined with files, but it was much larger than the other two rooms I'd just visited. The air was hot, the place smelt of dust, and there were plenty of places for someone to be standing unnoticed. Feeling as foolish as if I were checking under the bed, I made the guard wait until I walked up and down each aisle, making sure no one else was there. When he left, I locked the door and stood in the stillness, listening to his retreating steps. I looked around and realized, as Janet had told me, there was no phone. My own cellular was back in the car, as usual. Out of habit, I never brought the thing into a hospital to avoid the risk of scrambling a monitor or resetting a respirator. The faint sound of the elevator doors closing in the distance confirmed I was on my own.

I shoved away all thoughts of someone creeping up to my door and focused on finding the remaining charts. As I located them, I spread one out after the other on a large table and flipped through each dossier to entries dated approximately two years ago. It was an easy matter to locate the clinic visits I was looking for.

There were three types of events.

About ten of the victims had reported explosive vomiting with no other symptoms or signs to explain a cause. They were all isolated incidents, each had occurred shortly after they'd eaten a meal in the cafeteria, and in each case no one else who'd eaten the same food had reported any problems. Some were nurses, some were orderlies, some were technicians, and they'd all worked in different areas of the hospital.

There were five episodes of an acute syndrome involving dizziness, sweating, tearing, slowing of the heart rate, urgency to urinate, nausea, abdominal cramps, and small pupils. Again a variety of people with different jobs were involved, but this time they all worked in physiotherapy or rehabilitation.

The third grouping of cases were brief, solitary hallucinogenic experiences in three nurses from the psychiatry department. The three occurrences were months apart, and none of the subjects had a history of mental illness or drug abuse.

I leaned back in my chair, stretched my arms and legs, and once more felt the ache of too little sleep. But my mind was revving. This was familiar turf for me—basic toxicology. Janet was right. Some agent or other had made these people sick, and while any alert physician could make an educated guess, it was routine work for an ER doctor to look at the signs and symptoms and figure out exactly what those agents could be.

The ten cases of explosive vomiting suggested an obvious cause. Ipecac—a rather tasteless syrup that we formerly administered to overdose patients in order to induce vomiting—could have been added to a sauce or gravy poured over the victims' food. Even though we hardly ever used it anymore, it could still be found in most hospitals. A few of the victims had actually expressed the suspicion something had been slipped into their meal, but the attending doctors had mostly concluded it was mild food poisoning, viral gastritis, or malingering.

The three psychiatric cases I thought could be explained by a mild short-acting hallucinogenic. Psilocybin, a form of mescaline, or peyote, its naturally occurring precursor, came to mind. Though I rarely saw overdoses of these substances these days—they weren't usually found on the current much deadlier menu of street drugs— they could be obtained in special places, such as on university campuses. Both substances existed in pill or powder form, they both had a bitter taste that might go undetected if mixed with something like strong coffee, and they both weren't usually included in an initial drug screen. Given the perpetual pot of heavy-duty caffeine found on most psych wards, it wouldn't be hard to slip a dose of either substance to an unsuspecting victim in a cup of that particular brew. I'd want to ask these nurses if anyone had offered them a coffee shortly before they'd hallucinated. The notes indicated that all three had raised the possibility they'd been given something. One of the examining physicians had written *Hallucinogen?* on one of the nurses' charts but hadn't pursued it. Several other doctors put the next two episodes down to stress.

The complex syndrome that had afflicted the physio and rehab workers was in fact the most straightforward of all. The symptoms and signs brought to mind an acronym we teach the residents—SLUDGE BAM—made up of the first letter of each symptom and sign produced by organic phosphate, or insecticide, poisoning. Not all the signs were there—they wouldn't be in a mild exposure—but enough were to make the diagnosis: Salivation, Lacrimation, Urination, Diarrhea, Gastritis, Esophagitis, Bradycardia (or slow heart rate), Airway distress, and Miosis (the clinical term for small pupils). The attending physicians recognized this possibility in the differential, or list of probable diagnoses suggested in their notes, and had explained the episodes as accidental exposures to an unknown source of pesticide. Checks of the work area, however, had failed to turn up any trace of organic phosphates. I made a note to visit these people while they were on the job.

Most victims of accidental insecticide poisoning I'd treated in ER had absorbed the stuff through their skin. One woman had simply sprayed her bathroom floor, then walked on it in her bare feet. Perhaps there was something in the routine of workers in physio and rehab that exposed their skin to this type of contamination.

At first I found it puzzling that the examining doctors had given so little credence to all the victims who'd suggested they'd been attacked, but a glance through previous entries in their charts suggested why. The majority of them were frequent visitors to the health service with nonspecific trivial complaints—fatigue, dizziness, vague aches and pains—that on investigation never turned out to be significant. In short, the Phantom's victims seemed to also have in common the trait of malingering—not the basis for a lot of credibility. I remembered my own suspicions about Phyllis Sanders. What was it her son had said about her? *She never minimized anything.*

I glanced at my watch. It was 3:00. My usual limit of staying alert easily on an overnight shift without having to fight off sleep was around 4:00. After that I could be jolted awake by a hair-raising emergency but wasn't mentally fit for much else. Tonight, however, I was charged with energy. Instead of chasing shadows I was finally faced with puzzles that I had the expertise to answer. These charts and their two-year-old secrets were like manuals outlining how the Phantom had carried out his deeds. Until now he'd managed to keep those means of attack hidden, just as he still succeeded in keeping his means of infecting people concealed. It was the Phantom's trademark, his key to invisibility. If no one knew an attack had been made, there was no attacker; if no one knew a murder had been committed, there was no murderer. By exposing his means from two years ago, I'd breached that cloak of anonymity a little, given him form, and brought him a bit into existence. In other words, I'd gained a step on whomever I was pursuing.

But it was a step on an old trail. As tantalizing as these records were—no doubt Michael had recognized everything I had—they contained nothing beyond what had happened back then. Certainly they weren't the files that convinced Michael this same creep had found a way to wield deadly organisms, one of them previously unknown, with stealth and specificity. He had to have found something more, some bridge between the previous attacks and the recent infections. The pattern he mentioned must have been in other charts somewhere else. If I was going to make Williams a believer, I had to find those charts.

I got out of my chair, groaned as my knees and back lodged their own protest against no sleep, then started pacing to loosen up and better think what to do next. The silence of the place magnified the sound of my shoes on the linoleum floor.

I'd interview all these people as soon as I could if they were still around, I thought. The two whose active charts I'd found upstairs would be no problem, but the fact that the other sixteen files had been out of circulation long enough to have been put back in the archives, especially after showing a pattern of frequent visits, might mean those people no longer worked here. I returned to the table and started making a list of the eighteen names, addresses, and telephone numbers. Not wanting to stiffen up again in the chair, I wrote standing up. As I worked, the ancient pipes running across the ceiling gave an occasional clank. The scratch of my pen across the notepaper provided the only other sound in that deserted place.

Once, reaching for another chart, I inadvertently pressed my weight against the table and caused it to shift. The screech of its metal legs scraping across the linoleum sounded like a blast on a trumpet and made me jump so abruptly that the file flew out of my hand. Christ, I thought, decrying my own skittishness, let me finish and get out of here.

While I continued to scribble, I began to think where I might ask the guard to let me look next. Janet had said the sort of cruelty that this group practiced was hard to prove and not often reported. But what if that wasn't entirely true? Perhaps some of their victims had complained, were on record somewhere as having done so, and might be well worth talking to. I'd at least get a gauge as to the degree of anger they felt toward their punishers, perhaps even a sense of whether that anger could be motive enough for revenge. But there was another even more likely possibility to be explored. Who had these victims complained to? Was there someone in the process of hearing such complaints who'd decided to administer a little rough justice on his or her own outside of official channels?

Either way, if anyone had ever leveled charges against any of the people on the list I was compiling, their personnel records would probably contain a copy of any such complaints and the name of the patient who had complained. That's where I'd ask to go, the personnel department, I decided, rushing to finish with the second-to-last chart and feeling ecstatic at the sensation of finally making some headway.

If I wasn't so sensitized to sounds in the eerie silence of that subbasement or if I hadn't been so on edge, I might never have heard the familiar distant hum. It came more through the walls and overhead ducts than through the air. It was so far away that for the first few seconds my mind processed it out as an unimportant noise. Only when it ended and was followed by the faint distant rattle of the doors sliding open did I realize the elevator had come back down.

I felt a wave of alarm sweep through my stomach, then tried to reassure myself. Perhaps it was only the guard doing rounds or coming to check on me. I stood absolutely motionless. Maybe someone needed an old chart from this very room for a patient who had just arrived in ER.

But no steps came my way.

I quietly walked over to the door and listened. Still nothing.

Okay, I thought, forcing myself to breathe slowly. The elevator may simply have come down empty, sent by someone who had gotten off at a higher floor but also pushed the subbasement button by mistake.

Maybe. I wanted to grab my list and get the hell out of there. I tip-toed back to the table; added the final name, address, and telephone number; and returned to the door jamming my notes into my pocket.

There wasn't a sound outside. I turned the lock as slowly as possible, but it opened with a loud click. I froze, ready to twist it shut again if I heard the approaching thud of running footsteps. Nothing came. I pulled the door open a crack and peeked out. Thankfully I was at the end of this particular corridor, so even with the sliver of a view I gave myself, I could see enough to tell no one was there.

I stepped out and made my way toward the first intersection. Holding my breath when I got there, I slowly looked around the corner and down the next hallway. It was also empty. I turned left and crept along, passing two more intersections with equal care. When I got near the long corridor where the elevator was located, my real trepidation began. Even though I was at the opposite end of where the passage led to the basement of the old asylum, I couldn't help but imagine that the figure I dreaded seeing was out there waiting for me. My heart raced faster than ever and my breathing once more quickened. I pressed my back against the wall and prayed that the lights wouldn't go off again. I don't know how many seconds I was standing there, rapidly loosing my battle with panic, when I heard something—something so faint and far off I wasn't sure it was real.

It was whimpering—a steady, repetitive whimper. It was coming from down the corridor that I was bracing myself to enter. While I listened, it kept getting farther away until I could barely hear it anymore. Torn between fear and my determination to see what it was, I forced myself to look.

A hundred yards away near the far end of the long passage I could see the back of a person in greens pushing something. Even from that distance I could make out two horizontal white straps tied behind the person's head, indicating a surgical mask. The whimpering was the sound of squeaky wheels on a supply cart of some sort.

I let out my breath, once again feeling foolish at having become so alarmed at a simple noise. Probably an orderly getting something out of storage, I thought. I stepped into the hallway and started for the elevator.

Then the figure in the distance abruptly turned right without looking back and entered the tunnel leading into the asylum.

Chapter 13

I froze in midstep. Why would an orderly go in there? The place was posted off limits. It was hardly a suitable location to store supplies. My thoughts raced ahead unchecked. Was it the figure who'd attacked me? Maybe even the killer himself? After poring over two-year-old traces, had I suddenly stumbled on him returning to his present lair? Or was it simply someone ducking into the deserted tunnel for a cigarette? The nonsmoking nineties had driven nicotine addicts into back doorways among the garbage pails in most hospitals that I knew of. A dark tunnel on a cold rainy night would be a luxury.

Whoever he was, he'd either presumed he was alone or didn't care. Either way, he didn't know I was here, and I felt a heady rush of excitement. The advantage was clearly mine. If this was the creep who'd put Michael in ICU, then maybe I could take him by surprise, hunt *him* down and crack *his* skull. The prospect rekindled my fury and abated my fear. Damn you to hell, I thought bitterly as I started for the ominously dark entranceway up ahead.

I needed a weapon. There was nothing in the hallway. I quietly opened a few of the doors as I went, looking for something, anything I could wield. Nothing. As I passed the elevator doors, now closed again, I saw the overhead indicator light read *SB*, telling me the car was still there in case I needed a quick getaway. There also had to be stairs somewhere, but I hadn't seen them.

I continued along the hall, still searching for something to protect myself with. But opening door after door, I found only furniture or stacks of boxes which I hadn't time to explore. I was about forty yards from the tunnel entrance and was increasingly careful not to make any noise.

I came up on an alcove full of pails, mops, and cleaning supplies. I found a wooden push broom and settled on the handle, unscrewing it from the brush. As I crept the rest of the way to where the dark passage led off to the right, I took some practice swings with the hardwood stick and was satisfied I could certainly whack my quarry's head enough to stun him.

At the junction, I paused before turning the corner and listened for the squeak of the cart. I heard nothing, nor could I detect the tell-tale smell of tobacco. Only the pungent odor of damp earth seeped into my nostrils. Nevertheless, if I'm wrong about this, I thought, I'm going to give some poor slob one hell of a Smokeenders program. I got my staff ready, holding it up over my shoulder to swing like a bat, and stepped around into the center of the passage.

The lamps from the corridors behind me sent light about twenty yards into the darkness. No one was there. I moved to the far wall, pressed against the rough cold stone of the century-old construction, and crept forward. I usually swung a baseball bat left-handed—once a year at a charity game between the staff and the residents—and needed my back against this side of the tunnel to get a good shot at whoever came at me.

Yet again I neither heard nor saw anyone.

As my eyes got used to the dark, I could see enough to continue farther up the passage, but I knew there would soon come a point where it would be pitch black. What then? I was beginning to have second thoughts about my impulse to come up here.

I proceeded about another thirty yards when I saw something glinting dimly up ahead. It looked like a barrier of some kind, stretched across the entire passage, from the roof to the floor. A few more steps brought me close enough to see it was made of heavy wire mesh, like the fencing around a school yard or tennis court but with much smaller openings. It was held in place against the dark stones of the ceiling, walls, and floors by a lighter-colored cement, suggesting it was erected in a more recent era. In its center was a door-size gate, also made of mesh, and kept closed by a heavy U-shaped latch. There was no lock, and when I lifted the catch, the gate swung open with barely a creak. It was obviously kept oiled. Now why the hell was this barrier put here? I wondered, stepping through.

I kept going forward but was rapidly running out of light. Finally I had to stop, barely able to see my own hand in front of my face. I stood in the dark and held my breath so as to hear better, but not a sound came from the darkness up ahead. For all I knew, the figure was familiar with his way around the massive old building and

could be anywhere. One thing I was certain of. This was no one slipping off for a smoke.

The air here was perceptibly cooler than before and felt slimy
against my skin. There were more odors now too, the metallic hint
of damp rock joining the moist earth smells wafting toward me. I
once again imagined the basement rooms with dirt floors where they
used to chain inmates to the stone walls. The reminder of those poor
souls left me chilled to the bone.

I also began to feel foolish standing there with my broom handle.
Even if I were idiotic enough to press ahead, I could fumble around
in the dark all night in this place and still never find him. But I'd be
damned if I was about to turn around and go home. At the very least
I might find some answers, such as who'd bashed me into the elevator and the reason why. But far more important, if it was the killer, I
wasn't going to miss my chance to stop him here and now. There
would be no more glass coffins if I could help it.

I turned and looked back the way I'd come. The light from the
distant entrance gleamed off the rough-hewn walls and stone floors
like moonlight on water. It shone through the wire mesh, throwing it
into a shadowy relief, making it appear softer, like a web strung over
the way out. But the sides of the passageway, where the floor met the
walls, remained in shadow, and as far up the tunnel as I was, that
space was ink black. I could lie there, undetected, and wait for whoever it was to come back. I'd then be behind him as he walked
toward the light. When he stopped to open the gate, I'd be in a perfect position to jump him.

Or I could stay hidden and follow after him until he reached the
corridor where I'd at least see who it was. If I knew him, chances
were no surgical mask would keep me from identifying him. If he
spotted me and ran off, I'd give chase. If he attacked, I'd be ready.
I'd also have better justification for splitting his scalp open.

While I thought about these next moves, I realized my initial fury
was giving over to a colder, more critical, far more effective anger.
Obviously clobbering whoever it was without warning ran the risk
of letting him come up with some cock-and-bull story about why he
was down here. I might even end up giving him a chance to charge
me with attempted murder. I certainly had no real proof that whoever I'd seen come in here was the killer. Hell, apart from Janet, poor
Michael, and maybe Williams, no one else even thought there was a
killer.

I crouched down and felt the surface of the cold stones. They weren't outright wet but damp enough to be hard on my joints as well as my muscles. I stretched out facedown, managed not to groan, and tried to fit the bony parts of my hips against uneven hollows in the rock wall at my side. I'd keep the white of my face shielded by my arms as he went by. My stick was in my right hand.

I lay there listening to the absolute silence, figuring I'd have no trouble hearing his approach, with or without his cart, but I'd have to breathe as silently as I could to avoid detection when he was beside me. I glanced at the luminous dial of my watch, easy to read in the total darkness. It was a few minutes after 4:00. I was ready.

I awoke with a start. The first sensation I had was of total pain the second I tried to move. I wasn't sure at first where I was. Something scrambled over my right foot, tugging on my trousers. Then I remembered everything and bolted upright. I exhaled a loud groan as all my muscles shot into spasm, and in the dim light I saw the humped outline of a large rat scurrying about my feet.

"Shit!" I screamed kicking at it with both feet, then frenetically propelling myself backward.

It shrieked, either in surprise or rage at being disturbed, and scuttled off into the darkness. I hadn't made contact enough to hurt it any and wondered if it would charge back at me. Keeping my eyes fixed on where it had disappeared into the black passageway, I backed up to the gate, let myself through, and slammed it behind me. I now knew what the barrier was for—to contain the rats.

I was shaking—from revulsion of that thing crawling over me while I slept, from being bone cold and stiff, from my muscles recoiling into spasms every time I tried to use them. My teeth were chattering, and besides everything else I really had to pee. I managed to get my wrist steady enough to read my watch. It was a few minutes after 6:00.

Mist had replaced the rain but it was still dark when I raced back to St. Paul's. My driving hadn't improved any, and my mood was as foul as my breath.

I'd blown a God-given opportunity to put a face on this nightmare and was furious with myself.

At the entranceway to that accursed tunnel, I'd stood around as long as I could, freezing, hopping from one foot to another, and wondering what to do. Was he still somewhere up there? Or had he already gone back out, passing me in the dark as I lay sleeping? Possibly. But in the silence he probably would have heard my breathing, unless it was muffled by my head being facedown on my arms. Had he instead left the asylum through some other unguarded exit—an unlatched window or unlocked door known only to him? Maybe he needed a way to come and go without security knowing he was in the building.

I shot through the remaining pools of water in the street, sending great cascades arching away from the car all the way to the sidewalk. Despite an overnight scouring from the storm, the stone fronts of the houses remained stained and shabby in the passing glow of my headlights.

The meeting I'd arranged with Williams was to have been at 6:00 in my office. I'd intended to explain why I thought a serial killer was infecting people and hopefully to show him some specific leads from a night of going through records at UH. Now what he'd hear was how I'd armed myself with a broomstick, followed some orderly pushing a cart into an abandoned asylum, and then fallen asleep! I took my rage at my own stupidity out on yet another puddle, roaring through it and scattering it into a million droplets.

I had hoped if I could at least create the suspicion in Williams's mind that the infections were caused deliberately, we could then use Death Rounds to sound the alarm together—convince some members of the meeting that Michael had been attacked, show them his note which I still carried in my pocket, and get them to consider that something deliberate and sinister was behind the infections.

"Bloody pathetic," I muttered, given how hopelessly naive that idea seemed now.

I spotted Williams's big four-by-four parked near the entrance to ER as soon as I pulled into the doctors' lot at St. Paul's. When I got closer, I saw the big man himself was waiting in the driver's seat, pouring himself a coffee from a large thermos. He eyed my car suspiciously for a few seconds after I pulled up beside him, probably recognizing from my vehicle that I was the *jerk* who'd cut him off Friday. Nevertheless, he saluted me with his cup when I got out, smiled, and started to step down from his much higher cab. I inwardly winced when I saw how immaculately dressed he was in a blue blazer, a white shirt with crisp-looking cuffs, and a hand-painted tie of the kind I never even bothered to price when I went shopping.

My own outfit—the slacks, shirt, and sports jacket I'd spent the night in—were smudged and wrinkled from lying on the stone floor.

The bottom of my right pant cuff was torn where the rat had pulled it. Even though I'd tried to brush my teeth with my finger in the first washroom I'd found back at UH, my mouth still felt like a toilet. I needed a bath, a shave, and a change of clothes, and I hadn't time to get any of them.

Williams looked me up and down in astonishment when I walked up to him. His eyebrows arched; his nose wrinkled. "Decided to look our best for the ordeal, have we?" he commented wryly.

"Come on, we've got to talk," I said, turning toward emergency. My watch told me Death Rounds started in twenty minutes. The trouble was, I wasn't sure I could convince Williams even if I had twenty hours.

In my office Williams sat across from me and poured us each a coffee from his thermos while I called ICU and asked about Michael.

No change—still shocky, on a respirator, and unconscious.

Then I dug out an electric razor that I kept for the times I worked overnight in ER and started to explain the connection between three nurses with *Legionella* and the so-called victims of the Phantom from two years ago.

By the time I got to my being attacked five nights ago in the sub-basement, half my stubble was gone, and Williams was frowning hard enough to send furrows all the way up to the front of his shiny, immaculate scalp. The furrows deepened during my résumé of what I found in the archive charts and my speculation about the probable agents used in those first attacks. When I told him I'd followed someone into the abandoned asylum a few hours ago, it was enough to make him lean forward, massage the grooves in his forehead with his free hand, and mutter, "Jesus Christ!"

I'd no idea whether he believed me or thought I was crazy.

Nevertheless I barged ahead with the rest, including how I'd stu-pidly fallen asleep lying in wait in the dark. As I talked, I ran my fin-gers over my chin feeling for any patches of whiskers I'd missed with the razor. Unable to find any, I pressed the off button, putting an end to the buzzing, and in the silence between us, outlined what records at UH I thought we should go through next. When I stopped speaking, a glance at my watch told me we were ten minutes from the start of Death Rounds.

Williams remained motionless in his chair, staring at me with a fixed look of incredulity. I found his silence unnerving but said nothing. I figured this decisive man wouldn't keep me waiting long for his verdict on whether I'd have his help.

As he sat there thinking, I took out a bottle of aftershave lotion to splash on my face. If I dumped the whole lot over my head, I thought, it wouldn't be enough to hide the aroma from the rest of me. I reached into my office closet and found a crisp white lab coat to pull over my soiled clothing.

"How did you know about the three nurses and those other workers being cruel to patients?" Williams suddenly demanded. My back was turned to him and his voice caught me off guard.

I hadn't mentioned Janet's role in perceiving that the Phantom was active again. Nor had I admitted that it was nothing more than my faith in her ability to see what others had missed that formed the foundation of my early suspicions. But I decided to go for broke and risk winning him over by being as candid as possible. "My wife's an obstetrician and gynecologist at UH. She realized her patients all had trouble . . ."

While I explained I watched his eyes, again looking for some hint as to how I was doing. I got none.

He leaned back in his chair when I finished, studied me some more, then asked, "And neither you nor your wife attempted to report this idea?"

"Of course we did. No one believed us. No one wanted to."

"Do you have any suspicions about who this killer might be?"

My mind flashed on Rossit, on Hurst, on the powerful interests behind the amalgamation. "Not really," I answered. My speculations, though disturbing, were so nebulous that I figured I'd lose Williams by even mentioning them.

He rubbed the angle of his jaw with his little finger and again seemed to consider me from head to toe. "Well, I can see why no one listened to you," he commented after a few seconds. "Your story sounds crazy."

I felt a resurgence of all my pent-up fear and frustration. "Goddamn it!" I blurted out angrily. "I'm sick of these sanctimonious scientific blinkers you guys wear. My best friend's upstairs, maybe dying. He scoffed at our warning too—"

"Hey!" he commanded sharply. "Hold your horses. I didn't say *I* didn't believe you. I said your story *sounds* crazy. You already won me over last night when you suggested I analyze the *Legionella* cases as if an unknown vector was involved. Maybe it's a killer; maybe it isn't. But you were right about one thing: I would consider a carrier in any other outbreak where it wasn't clear how a bug was being passed around."

His measured response took a few seconds to register. Then came a surge of hope that he might become our ally in this. If Williams gave our case any credibility at all, help could be at hand. "You mean you think you can convince the CDC to investigate what's behind these infections," I asked, "including the possibility that they were deliberately inflicted?" We'd finally have a chance to launch a proper hunt for this murderer.

"With that story?" Williams gave a derisive laugh. "No way! But I've got an idea how we can get them to go over that asylum with a fine-tooth comb. It might flush out the character you're looking for or it might not, but it'll be a hell of a lot more effective than creeping around the place in the dark with a broomstick."

My expectations thudded back to earth. The disappointment must have shown in my face.

"Hey, come now," he said, pushing himself out of his chair. "There's no time for sitting around and becoming discouraged. We don't want to get the crowd at Death Rounds doubly angry at you by making them wait. And when we get there, stride in fast, try and sit away from the others, then keep your legs under the table. After all," he chided with a wink and a grin, "who's going to believe someone with B.O., dirty trousers, and a shredded cuff?"

Despite, or maybe because of, the absurdity of my position, his ribbing made me laugh. "Yeah, my mother would be shocked! Imagine, not having had a bath or a change of underwear before I head off to save my career and stop a serial killer."

But the wisecrack didn't ease the increasing tightness in my gut. The specter of the killings and the attempted killings had so dominated the last few days that I'd repeatedly shoved any fears I had for my job into the background. Yet I had no illusions about what lay ahead. This was undoubtedly Hurst's most determined attempt to unseat me, and I'd never been at such a disadvantage or felt so targeted. Nor could I shake my suspicions, vague as they were, that he and Rossit were somehow involved in the murders and that they wanted my credibility in tatters in case I found out enough to try to expose them. But figuring it pointless to reveal such nebulous fears to Williams, I instead kept faking a bravado I most definitely didn't feel. "Being a fancy dresser like you might impress the hell out of your ducks, Dr. Williams, but it'll take more than hiding my scruffy outfit to keep the likes of Hurst and Rossit from ousting the likes of *me*. Now, if you were to pick up *those* two birds for banding and a botulism check, then release *them* back into a swamp somewhere, that would get them off my back for a while."

His grin widened into a wicked smile as we marched out of my office and started toward the pathology department.

In the basement corridor the number of residents clutching cups of coffee and scurrying alongside us didn't help my apprehension any. It was a sign that attendance at the session would be good. On rounding a corner, I saw a clutch of people outside the entrance to the seminar room, some of them carrying in stacks of folding chairs. I instinctively slowed. "Quite a lynch mob," I muttered.

"Relax," Williams said quietly, putting his hand against my back and gently urging me forward. "Most people are probably here to find out why this case caused such a stir."

Inside the long narrow room about twenty people were crowded around an extended central table and another group was hastily arranging a second ring of folding chairs against the wall. Some of my own staff approached me to inquire about Michael, most of them having been told about his admission as they passed through ER.

More than a dozen people were gathered around a huge silver coffeemaker parked in a corner on a steel cart. The rich aroma from its steaming contents was tinged with a hint of formaldehyde fumes. These were emanating from seven loosely covered Tupperware containers spread out along the center of the big table. Through their translucent sides I could see the dark shapes of what would be Phyllis Sanders's major organs—lungs, heart, liver, spleen, kidneys, brain, and a flat coil of something that I presumed was intestine—all marinating in a cloudy brown fluid.

Williams nodded toward the far end of the display. There sat Rossit holding a gavel, ready to chair the meeting, his eyes fixed on me. To his right was Hurst, also staring my way while leaning back in his chair, his arms folded across his chest, and the corners of his mouth giving the slightest suggestion of a smirk. Like a malevolent Mona Lisa in drag, I thought angrily. Beside him was Baker, the hospital lawyer. All three were dressed in dark suits. There wasn't a noose on the table in front of them, but the scene reminded me of the quickie saloon trials depicted in old westerns.

Halfway down the table I also recognized the woman from the CDC's hospital infection group who'd given me Williams's phone number. She, too, was watching us. Free of her former protective gear and sporting a crimson pantsuit, she stood out in the midst of all the white coats and was almost as stylishly dressed as Williams.

But when I nodded hello, she scowled, jumped up, and strode over. "What are you doing here, Douglas?" she demanded frostily, facing Williams and ignoring him. Without giving him a chance to respond, she added, "I was designated to detail this wrap-up."

"Just making myself available, Doris," he answered curtly, "in case there were any complaints about how I handled the first few hours of the operation. Believe me, I don't want your job."

She flushed, appeared about to speak, then abruptly spun away and returned to her place at the table. Obviously turf was an issue even within the prestigious halls of the CDC.

"Everybody's going to be fighting to grab a piece of the fame from this case," Williams lamented, shaking his head as we found two empty chairs against the wall. "Even if we had some decent evidence to support your claim about a phantom killer, which we don't, it would still be hard as hell to make Doris or anyone else back off from their rush to publish and get them to seriously consider the story."

His gloomy prognosis left me trying to tuck my grotty-looking pants as far out of sight under my seat as I could while I surveyed the room and cast about for some better strategy to make people listen.

As expected, I recognized a few staff members with whom I'd had blowups in the past. More reassuring was seeing Susanne and one of our rookie nurses sitting against the wall opposite me. Susanne nodded to me, but the pale, young blonde woman at her side sat motionless, her unblinking stare riveted on the Tupperware. From her frightened expression, I figured she was the nurse who'd ignored Phyllis Sanders's complaint of orthostatic dizziness, there to confess her mistake and face her reckoning, just as I was. It didn't seem to be making it any easier on her that the ultimate responsibility and blame for sending the woman home fell on me.

Seeing Cam dart into the room jolted these gloomy thoughts out of my mind. He strode over to Doris, shook hands, and bent down to talk to her. Uh-oh, I thought, hoping he hadn't already discovered my entry into his confidential records. Maybe he'd shown up only to report on the screening results from University Hospital. But as he talked to Doris, her scowl returned and she nodded toward Williams and me. He returned my gaze, then strode over to tower above me. His blue eyes were blazing, and he didn't look happy.

"Security told me you were snooping through the minutes of my Infection Control Committee last night!" he challenged, his angry voice loud enough to make people around us stop talking and glance up at him. At their abrupt silence Cam looked around nervously and seemed to become aware of the scene he was starting to create. He moved his mouth closer to my ear. "I was also told you'd been in the archives until an hour ago," he continued in a fierce whisper, his fury now sibilant but clearly undiminished. "I went down there. I saw the files that you were looking at! I already warned Janet to stop trying to dredge up that Phantom nonsense. But for you to pretend to be from the CDC, violate our security, and breach confidential information—that's enough to at least charge you with unprofessional conduct, if not criminal trespassing." He was literally spluttering, his fists clenched between us, his red face inches from my own.

"Hey, Cam, ease up," I protested, instinctively recoiling. While I'd expected him to be annoyed at what I'd done, I certainly wasn't prepared for him to be this angry. "I was there to find—"

"You're no better than a lying thief—"

"Dr. Mackie!" interrupted Williams in a whisper loud enough for half the room to hear. He leaned over and placed his huge hand on Cam's forearm. "Dr. Garnet didn't impersonate a CDC official. I ordered him in."

Cam jerked his arm free and retorted aloud, "You no longer had any authority over this case, Dr. Williams! I'm particularly appalled that you'd betray your fine reputation by aligning yourself with the garbage ideas . . ."

While he ranted I felt increasingly dismayed to see him so upset. He was visibly shaking, and under the glare of the fluorescent lights I could see particles of perspiration glistening in the pores below his blond hairline. What could be making him react like this? There was nothing so startling in his Infection Control Committee records that Janet hadn't already told me. Perhaps it had been my going through the medical records of the Phantom's first victims that had set him off? But why should he be so outraged about that?

Some people in the room were growing quiet again as his angry words once more started to attract attention. "Settle down, Cam!" I implored under my breath. As baffling as his behavior was, the last thing my credibility needed here was a public spat with the man.

But the sound of my voice made him worse. His blue eyes grew so dark that I feared for a second he might actually try and grab me. Instead, he again leaned close to my ear and warned, "If you think

I'm going to let you or Janet undermine University Hospital and harm me or my department by dragging up those old Phantom stories—"

"Cam!" I interjected again, determined to put an end to our scene. "Michael Popovitch was admitted last night in septic shock from what we presume is *Legionella*. Just before he went into respiratory arrest, he scribbled this." I reached into my shirt pocket and pulled out Michael's cryptic note about the Phantom.

Cam frowned at the unfolded piece of paper as I held it before his eyes, took it out of my hand, then turned pale. "Oh my God," he muttered.

"That's why I went through those records, Cam," I pressed as gently as I could. "I was trying to find what Michael saw."

But he looked at me with such a blank expression on his face, I wasn't sure he'd even heard me.

At that moment Rossit slammed down his gavel and brought the meeting to order.

Chapter 14

The people who'd been waiting outside found seats while some other latecomers tipped the large coffeemaker to try and dribble the final dregs into their styrofoam cups. Conversations throughout the room died down. A few more residents rushed in and found places where they could lean against the wall.

Rossit began, "We will open this special Death Rounds with a particular welcome to our distinguished visitors from the CDC, Drs. Doris Levitz and Douglas Williams."

Williams nodded his acknowledgment to the greeting. Doris Levitz flashed the room an icy smile, pointedly ignoring Williams.

Most of the people who'd been watching Cam and me were now paying attention to the proceedings. A few had exchanged puzzled looks and whispered together before shrugging and turning toward Rossit. But Cam remained standing, staring at Michael's note.

"I also wish to welcome our colleague Dr. Mackie from University Hospital," continued Rossit. "The unfortunate case we will examine today has touched both our institutions."

At the mention of his name Cam gave a start. "Right," he answered, then vaguely looked around. He walked stiffly to where some of the medical students were perched along the top of a counter. They made an opening for him.

The practice in these sessions was that the residents present the case. Rossit gave the floor to the young man who tended to Phyllis Sanders on her first visit. He stood and, reading nervously from prepared notes, related the apparent benign findings of both his clinical exam and the many lab tests he'd ordered. He then put her initial chest X ray up on a viewing screen, answered a few questions from the staff doctors about its negative readings, and sat down.

Rossit glanced at Hurst, turned back to the resident, and asked, "Tell me, Doctor, why did you order all these tests if you figured this woman wasn't very sick?"

The resident flushed. "Well," he started, "she kept insisting I check her more carefully, that she was sicker than I thought."

"Obviously she was right!" snapped Rossit, with a wave to the containers on the table.

The resident started at the callous remark. There were a few chuckles in the room, while others gasped. I felt myself bristle.

"Tell me," Rossit continued, "what was the attitude to this patient on that day?"

The resident's mouth hung open. "Pardon?" he asked.

"You heard me," persisted Rossit, his voice cold. "We all know how a demanding patient can be taxing on the staff of a busy ER. I want to know how the nurses and doctors reacted to her."

"I don't know how to answer that, Dr. Rossit." The resident's voice was strained. He looked in my direction, his eyes wide with alarm. Rossit's reputation for savaging doctors included stories of how he occasionally ripped into residents. There wasn't a sound in the room.

The little man leaned forward. "Did you consider her a GOOMER, Doctor?" he asked snidely.

I went molten. "Now just a goddamned minute, Rossit!" I bellowed, leaping out of my chair. GOOMER was a despicable acronym used by cruder members of my staff, sometimes, inexcusably, even by doctors, in referring to troublesome patients. It meant Get Out of My Emergency Room, and I loathed the term. Unfortunately, the residents inevitably learned it on the job, and some thought it cool.

Rossit flew back in his chair in exaggerated surprise at my reaction. Hurst made a pyramid with his fingers in front of his lips, but I caught a glimpse of his snide smile. The rest of the upturned faces around me simply looked dismayed.

"Would you care to add to that comment, Dr. Garnet?" asked Rossit, eliciting another round of chuckles from those in the audience who were fans of this kind of spectacle.

I cursed myself for getting suckered into a stupid outburst and tried to recover some shred of dignity. "I'm sorry for my loss of self-control, Dr. Rossit, but the term GOOMER is contemptible, and anyone working in my ER is taught to despise both the phrase and the attitude it stands for." I managed to keep the tremor in my voice appropriate, but inside I was raging. "I also wish to point out that badgering the residents is no longer an acceptable way to teach!" Attack me, you prick, if you will. Hell, I'm the guilty one. But leave my students alone!

I heard a few murmurs of approval as I sat back down. Rossit shrugged, and we moved on.

At his invitation the young nurse beside Susanne stood up, introduced herself as Miss Johnston, and haltingly recounted the fateful moment when Phyllis Sanders got out of her ER bed, complained of being dizzy, and was wheeled from the department. While Rossit listened attentively, Johnston kept glancing over at him, her apprehension obvious. When he was about to ask questions again, Susanne leaned forward, cleared her throat loudly, and glared at him. He paused at the sound, eyed her warily, then gently explained that he simply wished Nurse Johnston to clarify a few details for him. It seemed even he knew one of the basic rules of medicine—never piss off the nurses.

Turning back to Susanne's protégée, he managed to elicit a piece of information that I was curious about.

"Phyllis Sanders was an experienced nurse," he commented. "Did she protest that her orthostatic dizziness was important and should be checked out?"

Nurse Johnston flushed. "Yes."

"And what did you do then?" There wasn't a hint of judgment in his voice.

The young woman swallowed, looked over at me, and answered, "I told her that Dr. Garnet was one of the best physicians in the hospital and that she could trust his judgment." Her voice quavered. "I also assured her that if he said it was safe for her to leave, she could go home without worrying about anything." At that point her tears flowed down her cheeks. She reached for a tissue and dabbed at her eyes. "Sorry," she muttered.

She sat down and Susanne put a comforting arm around her narrow shoulders. The silence in the room was like ice.

Rossit let it hang there for what seemed like an eternity. Hurst studied the people across from him, his mouth completely hidden behind his fingertips.

"Now for the return visit," said Rossit somberly.

The story of the resuscitation went by like a bad dream. Referring to our ER record, Rossit made it a point to note that Michael had stepped in to take over the intubation. "Was there any particular anomaly in her airway that made it a difficult procedure for you, Dr. Garnet?" he asked.

I shook my head, answering, "No," choosing to ignore his insinuation that I'd flubbed a key step in the resuscitation for no good reason. I knew that he was deliberately trying to chip away at me, but there was nothing I could do about it. I would only make things worse if I rose to his bait and tried to defend myself.

Rossit took it on himself to outline Sanders's clinical course in ICU. Up to the point of her death, he'd measured her lab values every few hours, and his review of these results reduced her dying to a process of numbers. "By the time we got her, death was inevitable," he concluded. Here I had to agree with him.

Next Rossit turned the session over to Len Gardner, who flipped open the Tupperware containers and began explaining his autopsy findings. He started with Sanders's lungs, demonstrating features unique to the destructive process of both *Legionella* and staphylococcus. I'd no need to view any of it again.

My eyes wandered instead to the other specimens—Sanders's liver, spleen, kidneys, intestine, and brain—in which I could see abscesses.

". . . hematogenous spread by septic emboli," Len explained, switching on his slide projector to show us death at the cellular level.

A feathery pink-and-blue dotted image of normal lung as it appeared under a microscope filled the screen at the far end of the room. Len then clicked the slide carousel forward and portraits of the little killers themselves appeared—slim red-stained rods for *Legionella*, bulky blue clusters of "grapes" for staphylococcus. The most telling image of all came next. It revealed clusters of staphylococci pouring through a tear in the lining of a small airway and flooding into the underlying lung tissue. Closer inspection showed the damaged area was already teeming with rods of *Legionella*. "It's a two-step process," explained Len. "*Legionella* prepares the way; staph ends the day," he added, putting the deadly serious teaching point into a silly rhyme, which none in the room would ever forget.

The next few slides demonstrated over and over where each of these organisms had visited other tissues in other parts of Sanders's body. They flashed by like snapshots taken of a pair of travelers at different stops on their voyage.

The room broke into applause at the end of Len's presentation. "He's terrific," said Williams, his huge hands contributing greatly to the show of appreciation.

I sat there thinking that the Phantom had virtually slaughtered her from within, cell by cell, organ by organ. I glanced over at Rossit and Hurst. They looked relaxed and unconcerned, occasionally whispering together and smiling. If either of them was involved in the killing, it was hard to imagine they could show such indifference before so graphic a display of the victim's remains. Cam on the other hand was transfixed, his expression grim, his eyes locked on the table as Len recovered the lineup of entrails in their containers.

While Rossit introduced Dr. Levitz to reveal the culture results, my attention remained on Cam. His behavior had me completely baffled. When Janet had told me he'd scoffed at her suggestion about the Phantom, I'd assumed she'd encountered the same scientific skepticism we'd initially run up against in Michael. But Cam's reaction this morning was clearly a lot more than that, and I had no idea why. I also didn't know how I could continue my search for what Michael had discovered at UH if Cam made good on his threat to report me for last night's visit. Even if he didn't go to the extent of pressing criminal charges but said anything at all about it to his CEO, I'd be lucky if I could get shown the way to a washroom in his hospital, let alone be given access to yet another roomful of confidential records.

Levitz began her introductory comments concerning VanA genes, the conjugation process, and inhibitory strains, but for me the words quickly became a buzz.

Perhaps Janet could carry out what I'd intended to do myself— check the personnel files of the people on the list I'd compiled in the archives and look for the names of patients who'd made complaints against them. But would Cam try and stop her too?

If you think I'm going to let you or Janet undermine University Hospital and harm me or my department by dragging up those old Phantom stories . . .

If she did agree to go on searching through charts, she'd have to make sure Cam didn't know about it.

As I watched him sitting with the medical students, he stole another look at Michael's note, then crumpled it up and dropped it in a nearby wastebasket, pointedly scowling at me as he did so.

You can't simply toss this away, Cam, I thought, feeling annoyed at his gesture and wondering all the more why he was so determined to keep us from *dragging up those old Phantom stories.*

Levitz continued to drone on in the background about organisms exchanging genetic materials in someone's intestine.

I tried to stop myself from rushing to conclusions about Cam's motives the way I had with Rossit and Hurst. Unlike those two, he certainly had no reason to be linked to the Phantom. I also knew Janet thought the world of him, and often I trusted her judgment of someone more than my own. In deference to her, I decided not to speculate about a man who was both her colleague and friend. It felt more comfortable to give him the benefit of the doubt, until Janet or I found out what was bothering him.

At that moment Levitz delivered her punch line. ". . . a confirmed superbug, a vancomycin- and methicillin-resistant staphylococcus . . ."

All around me were gasps and exclamations of surprise. "My God!" "Why didn't they tell us?" "Are we safe?"

Rossit and Hurst immediately joined Levitz in uttering assurances about the negative screening results.

"Why were we lied to?" someone yelled.

"To avoid panic," boomed Williams at my side, adding his voice to the other three giving reassurances and calming people. With his help the uproar gradually subsided, and Rossit slowly reclaimed control of the meeting.

"Dr. Levitz," he began, "I'll ask you in your capacity as a representative of the CDC to pronounce on the last issue of this case. It's our policy in Death Rounds to assess if the death under review was preventable or not."

Without hesitation and pointedly not looking in my direction, she answered, "The only way we can stop this organism is through prevention. This woman's staph infection might never have gotten a toehold in her lung had *Legionella* been diagnosed properly, then treated aggressively during her first visit, and the CDC feels our report of this case must signal that message to other physicians everywhere in the country. Accordingly, unless studies into the organism's aggressivity categorically prove otherwise, our write-up in the *Mortality Morbidity Bulletin* will stress that the initial attending physician might have averted the woman's death if he had acted appropriately."

I felt she'd cut my windpipe. No amount of mental preparation could take away the actual blow of being judged responsible for a preventable death in front of my peers. But she'd done worse than that. It seemed I was going to be made an example of—turned into the CDC's poster boy—for letting the bug of the decade into the United States.

For the next few seconds I sat immobile, feeling my face burn and sensing every eye in the room turned on me. I felt Williams's large hand press on my arm and heard his voice declare something loudly to those around us, but I wasn't paying attention. While he talked, I stared straight ahead, not wanting to face anyone I knew, certainly not anyone who worked with me or whose opinion I cared about. I started to resent Williams's prolonging the ordeal by talking on and on. Why didn't he just shut up, I thought, so everybody would leave and I could run the hell out of here?

But he didn't shut up, and despite my trying to tune out everything around me, some of what he was saying filtered through.

"I think you're all missing a piece of a bigger picture here," he insisted. "If you count them up—this patient Phyllis Sanders, Drs. Deloram and Popovitch from St. Paul's, and two other nurses from University Hospital who I've been told were diagnosed as having *Legionella* earlier this year—you've got a concentrated pattern of *Legionella* infections in a group of five otherwise healthy hospital workers that hasn't been explained. Dr. Rossit, you and your colleagues have got a responsibility to look at this group as a whole."

I noticed Cam's face immediately crease into a frown at the mention of the other cases at UH.

Rossit seemed caught by surprise. "Oh," he said, "of course, if you—"

"Good! Now here's what I think," Williams cut in. "The first three cases seem related to University Hospital. Even Dr. Popovitch's infection may have been contracted there as he's been doing an audit on the premises since last week. Perhaps there's a source in the place that's been overlooked."

The effect of this comment on Cam was electric. "Wait a minute," he protested, his eyes growing dark with fury again. "I've personally supervised two extensive screenings of every water delivery outlet in that hospital. You can't just fly in here and smear—"

"Hey, Dr. Mackie, I'm sure there's no *Legionella* organisms where you've looked. It's where you haven't looked that I'm worried about."

"What do you mean?" demanded Cam.

"I've had a report that some of your staff at UH go into the abandoned asylum. Maybe for a smoke, maybe for legitimate purposes—I don't know the reasons why. The point is, I'm sure there are reservoirs of stagnant water throughout that place. If your people are entering those premises on a regular basis, that could be your source."

From the astonished look on Cam's face, I could tell the idea had never crossed his mind. "Well, I'll be damned," he muttered.

"What do you think, Dr. Rossit?" asked Williams, turning to address the chairperson.

"Me? I think it's a very perceptive observation and the place should be screened from top to bottom immediately." From the gleam in his eye I suspected he thought trouble for Cam at UH was good for him and St. Paul's.

Even Hurst chimed in. "I wholeheartedly agree with Dr. Williams's and Dr. Rossit's endorsement of the search."

"Dr. Levitz, what's your opinion?" inquired Williams. "After all, it is your call."

His deferral to her authority was astute. It put her back in charge, and her smile indicated she seemed to appreciate the gesture. "Of course it has to be done," she replied. "We should make it a priority recommendation."

"Very clever," I muttered to Williams out of the corner of my mouth. "All of it's very clever."

Rossit adjourned the meeting, Doris scribbled something on a pad, and Cam eyed me angrily before following everyone else out of the room. While I didn't have a clue why he remained so hostile, his reaction to Williams's suggestion was in obvious contrast to Rossit's and Hurst's enthusiasm for the idea. Obviously for those two, a search of the Phantom's domain held no fear.

After the meeting I refused to talk to anyone, even Williams, and instead retreated to my office for refuge. I didn't lock the door, but I sure as hell wasn't encouraging any visitors. I had too much work to do twisting paper clips into pretzels.

I knew I wouldn't be fired from my position as chief today. I wasn't even named in Levitz's final pronouncement, nor would I or the patient be identified in her published report. That's not how these things were done. But Hurst had the verdict he needed. In spite of the confidentiality of Death Rounds, whispered conversations afterward *would* name me and help shape the hospital's own collective judgment on the part I'd played in Sanders's death. Time, along with the inevitable gossip surrounding the *MMB* article, would do the rest. When my annual review for reappointment by the board came around in a few months, Hurst could simply refer to "that unfortunate business in ER," and everyone would know what he meant. He could then add something about St. Paul's not being able to afford a hint of scandal or incompetence involving the chief of emergency if its ascendancy over UH was to be assured at this critical juncture in the amalgamation process.

I shuddered, recalling other power struggles in which I'd witnessed the careers of colleagues summarily derailed by similar asides.

My torn cuff caught my eye, reminding me I hadn't showered or changed yet. Glancing at my watch I was surprised to see it was only 8:25. Death Rounds had lasted a little over an hour. The ordeal had felt like an entire day's work.

In the end I hadn't any idea how to counter Hurst's probable strategy to get rid of me. Nor had I any clearer grasp of whether it was part of a larger conspiracy by him and Rossit to cover up their involvement in the killings. I had to admit, though, that their relaxed demeanor in front of Sanders's remains and their eager acceptance of a search of the asylum weighed against the idea. In fact, their behavior was so contrary to what I would have expected, it crossed my mind that perhaps the two of them were simply playing their usual dirty hospital politics after all. Rossit wanted the chair, Hurst wanted rid of me, and they made a deal to help each other get what they wanted. That was simple enough to withstand even Janet's skepticism. But I still couldn't entirely put the darker possibility out of my mind.

As for Cam's behavior, I again refused to let my speculation about him go any further until I talked to Janet. Her perspective would keep me from straying into nightmare scenarios. Thinking of her, I immediately remembered she didn't know about Michael yet. I knew no matter what I said she'd be horrified and would once again blame herself for instigating a hunt for the Phantom without having anticipated the possibility of a backlash. Michael's grave condition only confirmed that this maniac, despite some twisted mission to avenge cruelty, would kill any innocent who threatened him with exposure.

I called locating at UH and, while waiting on the phone for Janet to answer her page, toyed with the idea of delaying telling her that I'd gone back to the archives. I knew she'd be furious with me for going in there alone, especially after she learned what happened to Michael. But I quickly realized I had to warn her about Cam's reaction to that visit. He might assume that she'd put me up to it and tear a strip off her the same way he had torn one off me.

I decided definitely not to tell her about following someone into the asylum. For that bonehead play, she'd kill me herself.

The receiver clicked in my ear. "One moment please, Dr. Garnet," said the operator. "I'll connect you with the nurses' station in the case room."

After more waiting and more clicks, a woman's voice answered, "Case room."

"Hi, it's Dr. Garnet. I'm looking for Janet. Is she busy?"

"Oh, I'm sorry, Dr. Garnet, but she's down in emergency. I'll transfer you—"

"No, don't bother. Just tell her to call me as soon as she's free." I wasn't going to break my news to her while she was in the middle of some case.

"No, Dr. Garnet, you don't understand. She's in emergency as a patient. She signed herself in this morning because she woke up with a cough and a bit of fever. We were a bit surprised because she didn't sound too bad when she called in to transfer her cases—"

Whatever else the woman said, it was to air. I didn't even hang up the receiver before I darted out the door.

Chapter 15

The emergency department at UH was one of the areas the hospital had renovated recently. Countertops and work spaces were pleasing curves, the color scheme blended soft pinks with pale greens trimmed by gray, and plants were everywhere. The effect no doubt made the people working there feel better, but it didn't do a thing for my fear. Nor did the sight of everyone wearing surgical masks make it easy to stay rational.

Still breathless after running in from the parking lot, I said to the clerk at the receiving desk, "My wife, Dr. Janet Graceton, is here. Can you tell me which bed she's in?"

"Oh yes, Dr. Garnet, she's already been transferred to ICU, but if you wish to speak with the doctor who saw her—"

"No thanks," I uttered, spinning around and heading toward the elevators. Here, as in my own hospital, ICU was on the fourth floor. But when I got into the main corridor leading to the elevators, I saw a crowd of people already waiting in front of the large brass doors. I took the stairs instead.

I kept telling myself that Janet had to be okay, that if she'd contracted *Legionella* it was in the early stages yet, that we'd be starting the treatment early the way we had with Stewart. But what if she also had the other, the staph? "Please, no, not that. Not that!" I pleaded to myself as I pounded up the stairs.

Behind me I heard the door that I'd just gone through fly against the wall with a bang. "Dr. Garnet!" came an echoing shout accompanied by the sound of whoever it was running up the steps after me.

I leaned over the railing and saw it was someone in isolation garb. The instant he looked up I recognized him from his close-cropped blond hair, even with his surgical mask on. Already in a state of near panic over Janet I groaned out loud at the prospect of another encounter with Harold Miller. "Look, Mr. Miller, this isn't really the time to talk to me. My wife's just been—"

"I know, Dr. Garnet," he interjected, jogging the rest of the way up to where I was standing. "When I heard she was in, I did the sputum cultures on her myself. I've been helping out with the screening program here, so I was around—"

"You've seen her? How is she?" I almost grabbed his shoulders. He was a head below me, standing one step down.

"That's what I wanted to tell you, not to worry. She looked how my mother must have been that first visit, you know, not too sick."

I felt a jolt of anger. If he was going to start putting me on the defensive about his mother again, I was past being empathetic about it. I turned away and continued on up the stairs, hoping he wouldn't follow.

But follow he did, and his insistence on talking as he kept pace behind me set my nerves on edge. "I wanted to tell you, Doctor Garnet," he went on, "that I don't think anything could have saved my mother, even if she had been diagnosed properly at the very beginning, given what the second organism turned out to be."

I couldn't quite make out if he was blaming me or forgiving me, or even if I'd heard him right, but I remained focused solely on getting to Janet. "Mr. Miller, please, not now," I told him as nicely as I could, speaking to him over my shoulder without slowing down. We were passing the second-floor landing.

"I'm just trying to apologize, Dr. Garnet, for accusing you the way I did!" he practically shouted from a few steps behind.

There was something desperate in his voice that stopped me. When I turned to face him, I found the pain in his eyes above the edge of his mask hard to look at, and I immediately regretted my initial abruptness. "Mr. Miller," I stammered, "please excuse me for snapping at you, but we both have great personal problems at the moment and—"

"That's why I wanted to tell you now, Dr. Garnet, so you wouldn't have to worry about me and be wondering what I was going to do. You've got enough pressure on you, given the scare of the outbreak and now with Dr. Graceton's falling ill. I want you to know I realize you were up against an unstoppable organism that had never been encountered before. I even understand better now about your missing the *Legionella* prodrome."

Some of his words sounded a little rehearsed, as if he'd written certain phrases out and then memorized them to use on me. But however clumsily he was going about it, he seemed determined to put me at ease—a gesture that was as surprising as it was magnanimous—even if it was not something I had time for at the moment.

I forced myself to stand there and listen, despite my wanting to get to Janet. After all, I reminded myself, although I hadn't seen a notice, it was likely he'd only just buried his mother on the weekend. Janet herself would blast me if I showed the smallest sign of cutting short any effort on his part to make peace. She had predicted that he would soften and that his hostility would subside while I'd remained skeptical. I certainly never expected an apology. I didn't deserve one.

He seemed to relax as it became evident he wouldn't have to chase me anymore. His choice of words became less stiff. "Dr. Mackie explained to me that sending my mother home had been an error in judgment, not outright negligence on your part, and that I shouldn't try to damage you in court." He stopped for breath. "Everything I've learned about you since tells me you're a first-rate doctor. That's all I wanted to say. I know you want to see Dr. Graceton, and I won't hold you up a second longer. She's also tops in my book. If there's any need of more laboratory work for her, it would be an honor if you'd let me handle it personally. When it comes to testing procedures, I'm known for not hurting patients. That's one of the reasons I was named chief technician. Dr. Mackie's a real stickler about us not hurting patients."

Without another word he turned, descended the stairs, and went out the ground floor door.

I should have been relieved, but I felt guiltier than ever. The whole time he was talking, beyond the sound of his insistent way of speaking, I kept being reminded of his mother's voice. At first I wasn't sure what it was they had in common—a pattern of inflection, certain rhythms of speech, shared phrasings—but I found it annoyed me. Then I had it. There was a certain tone that the two of them shared. In him it was only a hint, a vocal ghost of what had been a blatant trait in his mother. I probably would never have picked it out in his speech at all if I hadn't met Phyllis Sanders first. But what I'd heard an echo of was her whining, the note of discontent that ran through everything she said, her means of announcing her disappointment in life, her way of implying the question *Are you going to disappoint me too?*

Disgusted with myself, I resumed my climb to the third floor. In the face of a difficult and generous deed by her son and in the light of what that same resentment of mine might have cost his mother, I still had enough spite in me to dislike even a reminder of her voice.

As I ran the rest of the way to ICU, I had a fleeting thought about Cam's speaking to Miller on my behalf. Maybe, after having gone to the trouble of defending me, he felt betrayed by my breaking into his files, and that was why he was so angry this morning. But my preoccupation with Janet quickly shoved aside any further questions about his strange behavior.

The isolation rooms in ICU were identical to the glass coffins at St. Paul's—elevated, situated against an end wall, and brightly lit compared to the subdued lighting throughout the rest of the unit. They also appeared small and claustrophobic, and as I approached the only chamber that was occupied, I felt my stomach knot. Through the windows I could see the backs of half a dozen residents wearing protective gear crowded around the bed, blocking my view of Janet. But nearing the door, I could hear her well enough. "Please stop, stop it," she sobbed, then her plea exploded into a retching cry followed by gagging, coughing, and the rasp of stridor—the rattling wheeze of indrawn breath through an obstructed windpipe. The sound sent a chill through me. Something must have blocked her upper airway.

One of the residents uttered, "Christ! Get some atropine."

"What's happened?" I demanded from the doorway, frantically grabbing a gown from a pile on a cart and reaching for a mask. But as I pulled them on none of the residents answered me. Instead they started barking out panicky orders to each other and remained bent over the bed where I heard Janet continue to cough and struggle for breath.

"Turn her on her side!"

"Suction her!"

"It's laryngeal spasm. She needs atropine!"

"Tell me what's going on!" I shouted as I strode into the room still pulling on a pair of surgical gloves.

A nurse turned from the bed and tried to block my way. "Sir, you aren't allowed in here right now," she snapped at me, placing the flat of her hands on my chest and pushing.

I brushed them off. "Like hell I'm not," I snarled, shoving by her. "I'm Dr. Garnet, her husband."

"You are not a doctor here!" she cried out in a shrill voice.

Ignoring her, I slid between the residents and saw Janet lying on her side, her face practically purple, and her entire upper trunk and neck straining to draw a breath. A thin plastic suction catheter dripping with saliva and vomit lay hissing on the covers in front of her. Scattered across the bed were unused culture bottles, swabs, and slides. My alarm rocketed. These dolts must have been trying to suction her trachea for a sputum sample. The muscles in her larynx and vocal cords had responded by locking into a protracted spasm and cutting off her airway. She might even have aspirated vomit into her lungs.

Fighting back my own panic, I reached for her neck. It was bulging with strands of tendons and webs of muscles as she struggled to gasp in a breath. I managed to palpate the pulse of her carotid artery, but I could count two seconds between each beat beneath my fingers.

Through clenched teeth I ordered the nurse who'd tried to bar my way, "Get me two milligrams of IV atropine stat!"

She simply stood there.

"Move, you idiot!" I screamed at her, beside myself with fright.

She flinched, then turned toward a set of open shelves at the head of the bed where there were labeled trays of different drugs in single-dose vials.

Janet's eyes were bulging at me. I didn't know if she could see, but she grabbed at the front of my gown while her entire body bucked rhythmically in her continuing struggle to draw a breath. I clasped her hands to my chest. They were cold and slippery with sweat. "Janet, it's Earl. I'm going to give you something to restore your airway. Just a few seconds more and you'll be breathing."

The nurse slapped two small brown vials down onto a nightstand and glared at me over the top of her mask.

Fuck you, I thought, turning for help to the residents instead. "Get me a ten-cc syringe and twenty-two needle filled with normal saline," I snapped at the young man on my right. To the woman beside him I added, "You get the crash cart ready and prepare to intubate, in case what I'm about to try here doesn't work." I spun around to face their colleague on my left, "You draw up ten milligrams of midazolam and a hundred milligrams of succinocholine. We may yet have to sedate and paralyze her." They jumped to obey. After the mess they'd made, it obviously mattered little to *them* who I was, as long as I saved their patient and their asses.

More hideous rasping noises continued to come from Janet's throat—the sound of air sucked through an opening in the vocal cords no bigger than a slit. We probably had another thirty seconds before she'd start to seize. Cardiac arrest would follow. Right now she was still conscious and in agony.

"Hold her firmly and keep her head steady," I told the three remaining residents, "but don't hurt her, you hear me!"

"Yes, sir," they mumbled in unison under their masks.

Janet's eyes widened even further with panic as they pushed her down and grasped her head between their hands.

"I'm here, Janet; this will help you," I reassured, trying vainly to sound calm. Inside I didn't know if I could do what I had in mind. Fear of failure was constantly present in any race to win back an airway or recapture a heartbeat, but the terror of losing Janet jangled my thinking, unsteadied my hands, and corroded my nerve.

Atropine would reopen her airway by blocking the neuronal pathway that was keeping the larynx in spasm, but the IV route took time. A resident handed me the syringe that I requested, the inch-long needle glinting under the ceiling lights. I squirted out a few ccs of saline, snapped open the brown vials, and drew the atropine up into the cylinder. Then I grabbed an alcohol swab from the nightstand and, to the gasps of the residents, ran it over the front of Janet's larynx. I was going to inject directly into her neck. I'd never treated laryngospasm this way before, but I'd put needles into the trachea to freeze it for intubations of head trauma cases and I'd shoved atropine down endotracheal tubes during cardiac arrests. I couldn't think of anything that would work faster.

"Janet, if you can hear me, close your eyes, love!" I commanded, my voice shaking as I located the landmarks of the cricothyroid membrane—the thin "window" covering the opening where access to her windpipe would be easiest—and brought the needle point up, pressing it against the overlying skin. She seemed to stare at it and increased her efforts to break free. "Hold her," I yelled.

They steadied her movements, and I shoved the tip of the needle hard enough to penetrate her skin, pulling gently back on the plunger as I advanced the point. A tiny stream of bubbles flowed up into the cylinder indicating I was through to her airway. I angled the needle toward her larynx, pushed the plunger as hard as I could, and yanked out the emptied syringe.

Ten seconds passed. Her movements grew feebler and her eyes, still open, fluttered up under her lids.

From the resuscitation cart I grabbed a black rubber ventilating mask, connected it to an oxygen outlet, and pressed it to her face. I squeezed the attached bag in an attempt to force air down her lungs, but there was resistance against my hand. It meant her larynx was still closed.

Another ten seconds passed. Her eyes were nearly shut, her skin was blue, her limbs were starting to jerk.

"Get ready to sedate and paralyze her," I ordered, but my own voice sounded far away while my panic continued to mount. If she seized, her teeth would clamp together and her body would start heaving with convulsions so powerful that we'd break her bones if we tried to hold her down. We'd only be able to intubate her after the drugs or the severe lack of oxygen broke off the pulsing muscle contractions. That might take more than a minute, enough time to put her into cardiac arrest.

I squeezed the bag once more. Again the resistance remained so firm I couldn't budge my fingers. Then I felt a release, the bag responded to the pressure of my hand, and I saw Janet's chest rise. I squeezed again and again, each time pushing oxygen more and more easily through her opened airway and into her lungs. Over and over I ventilated her, watching her skin quickly turn back from blue toward pink. Soon she was stirring, moaning, and shoving the mask away as she rapidly resumed breathing for herself. She coughed repeatedly, but didn't expectorate much. When I listened to her chest, she was wheezing, but the sounds were distributed uniformly, probably from the infection, and there was equal air entry into the bases of both right and left lungs. It would take an X ray to be sure, but I didn't think she'd aspirated.

When she finally stopped choking enough to speak, she looked at me incredulously and croaked, "You put a bloody needle in my neck!"

Tears came to my eyes as I laughed to keep from crying. "And you scared me half to death," I said, leaning over and putting my arms around her.

The residents shuffled nervously and the nurse looked on disapprovingly. I ignored them all. They'd account to me later, I swore, but I didn't give a damn for anything at that moment except to feel Janet against me. Yet I was also thinking like a physician. Her breathing was still labored, presumably from her developing pneumonia. While I held her, I reflexively checked the IV, making sure her movements hadn't dislodged it. I noted the label on the overhead bag read *Erythromycin*. I was resetting its flow rate with one hand when I saw Cam standing at the door watching us all.

He was wearing protective gear, but his eyes above his mask were dilated and dark with rage, exactly as I'd seen them earlier this morning. For a second I thought it was the sight of me again that was making him furious, but he swung that fierce gaze toward the residents, "What the hell have you been doing to Dr. Graceton!" he screamed at them.

The bunch of them seemed to flinch, but one in particular averted his eyes and tried to edge behind the others. Cam must have seen the movement as well, because he immediately singled him out. "You! Tell me what happened or I'll suspend the lot of you and make sure you never set foot in this hospital again."

The young man froze, and the others moved away, leaving him standing alone in front of Cam. His face reddened above his mask all the way to the upper tips of his ears.

"Well?" demanded Cam, towering over him.

"I thought we could do a simple aspirate with a small catheter," he began to explain, sounding plaintive. "I did it all the time on patients in recovery during my anesthesia rotation—"

"Those patients are already sedated and intubated!" roared Cam. "What the hell made you think you could do the same to an alert patient?"

"None of us had experience with midazolam to put her to sleep, and I figured without her intubated we shouldn't freeze her gag reflex—"

"Jesus Christ, lord save us from what you call thinking. And the rest of you did nothing to stop this genius from nearly killing Dr. Graceton?" he yelled, turning to the others. "How dare any of you stand by and not attend to a patient's pain before an invasive procedure—any invasive procedure at all—you understand me! You damn well don't hurt patients. I've half a mind to put tubes down your throats and let you experience what you just put Dr. Graceton through. Disgraceful! The lot of you are on probation as far as I'm concerned."

Now all the residents flushed crimson above their masks. Some grew wide-eyed while others glared furiously at the one who'd performed the suction.

"You don't go near a patient of mine without discussing it with me first," continued Cam, his voice lower, but his tone as hard and unforgiving as ever, "and you don't write an order without it being countersigned immediately by a staff person. In forty-eight hours you bozos will present what you did here today to a special grand rounds on laryngospasm in front of all your colleagues in our residency program. Now get out of my sight!"

They filed out of the room without looking at each other. Some were so dazed they had to be reminded to remove their gowns and masks at the door while the others flung their clothing into the disposal bin and stomped off. The nurse quietly tried to follow them, but Cam wasn't finished with her either.

"Hold it," he told her brusquely. "You've got some explaining to do as well. What were you thinking of, letting those clowns proceed the way they did? They were obviously in over their heads. Who even ordered a tracheal aspirate?"

She stopped moving toward the door and turned to face him. I only now took a real look at her. She was dark-haired with a few strands of gray, tall, and as far as I could tell rather slim looking, but whatever physical attributes she had hidden under her costume, I'd already decided that her disposition was nasty. A name tag over her left breast told me we should call her Miss Brown. "It's your own policy, Dr. Mackie," she replied in a sweet singsong tone that sounded belligerent.

Cam exploded, "Doing tracheal aspirates on unmedicated patients is not my—"

"Getting proper sputum samples is, especially since we've had so much trouble with infected personnel lately. I saw a note in her chart saying the sputum sample they got in ER was scanty."

It was Cam's turn to go beet red. "*Legionella*, as you should know better than anyone, Miss Brown, doesn't produce much sputum." His voice vibrated with the same barely controlled anger I'd heard him direct at me this morning. "My guidelines for getting proper sputum samples are meant to be applied with clinical judgment."

"I'm only a nurse, Dr. Mackie. It's not up to me to know which rules you want used and when—"

I felt Janet lift her head off my chest. "That's a crock, Cam. I told her that Harold Miller had taken samples in ER and that the scanty sputum was to be expected. She refused to listen." Even weakened by what she'd been through, Janet's tone had the scalpel-sharp bite she saved for unpleasant truths.

"Why, Dr. Graceton," the woman protested, "you can't expect to give orders when you're a patient—"

"But I can give orders, Miss Brown," bellowed Cam, "and since you're so good at following rules, here's one for you. Until I can haul you into a morbidity review about what you did here, you're no longer to have anything to do with nursing Dr. Graceton. Come with me, and I'll arrange it with your supervisor! By the time I'm through with you, you'll never work in an ICU again!" He stormed from the room, practically ripping his protective clothing off at the door before heading to the nursing desk.

Brown flashed a murderous look at Janet, then followed after Cam. She flung her own gown, mask, and gloves on the floor beside the designated bin.

"Jesus Christ" was all I could say. I'd seen bungling before—what the residents had pulled was the sort of near disaster that happened from time to time, unfortunately, in a teaching hospital—but Nurse Brown was outright scary. She deserved everything that Cam had threatened her with, if not outright dismissal. The residents would probably learn from this. What Cam had in mind for them made it unlikely any of them would ever screw up doing tracheal suction again. But I doubted any amount of disciplinary action would ever make Brown into the sort of nurse I'd want near Janet, me, or anyone else.

Yet seeing Cam once more fly into a rage, even over a serious infraction, I was left feeling ambivalent and uncomfortable about him. He was a chief in this hospital. He knew a public blowup could badly disrupt a critical-care unit and interfere with the staff's calm and concentration. No one was immune to being angry—I'd also wanted to scream at both Brown and the residents—but his performance only added to my doubts about his tendency to lose control. My first impulse was to transfer Janet away from the bunch of them.

"Janet, let me get you out of here and to St. Paul's, where I can assure you no one like Brown or these residents will get near you."

"You'd deliver me to the hands of Gary Rossit? No thank you."

The recollection of him sitting beside Hurst at Death Rounds and grinning up at me flashed through my mind. "Of course not," I quickly agreed. "Being around him is totally out of the question. But whoever the Phantom is, you're vulnerable here. I can get someone else—"

"Stop it, Earl!" She leaned back out of my arms and looked me in the eye, a stern expression crossing over her face. "Stewart Deloram wasn't safe at St. Paul's, and I told you before, running away is not an option." She took a breath, as if to continue speaking, then seemed to change her mind. She put her head back against my chest. "As for the residents and nurses," she added, sounding a little softer, "I'm sure Cam will make certain there won't be any more screwups by them. Besides, it's my infection that's got me scared now. Despite Stewart Deloram doing well, I don't know how bad I'm going to get, and I want Cam taking care of me."

I continued to stroke her hair and cradle her against me, glad she couldn't see the tears that I felt brimming in my eyes. Her straightforward admission of yet another of my fears—that no one knew for certain how ill she might become—nearly made me lose the puny grip I'd managed to keep on my emotions.

As I clung to Janet, I looked through the glass in the front of her room and watched Cam standing in the nurses' station with his back to me. The overly tall man was engaged in an animated conversation with Brown and another nurse who I presumed was the supervisor. Whatever I thought Brown deserved, I continued to be troubled by the way he kept waving his hands about while stabbing at the air between them with his index finger. Obviously he was still beside himself with fury. The image of his face at Death Rounds, distorted with rage and inches from my own, wasn't hard to recall. I'd given him the benefit of the doubt then. It was altogether something else to suddenly have him as Janet's physician now that she'd been attacked. Even when he was focused on the residents, I'd felt disturbed by being in such close quarters with him.

Perhaps it was the shock of having had to resuscitate my own wife, perhaps it was having seen my best friend put near death not twelve hours earlier, perhaps it was the frustration of not being able to prove this killer even existed, certainly it involved my instinct to protect those I loved above all else—whatever the blend of reasons, it was a potent fuel for a rush to judgment.

In a flash any inclination I had to be balanced and fair was gone. Suspicions that I'd tried to keep in check resurfaced with a vengeance and images I'd tried to suppress or explain away flew to mind—Rossit and Hurst glibly chatting before the remains of Phyllis Sanders, the powerful business group ringing Hurst as he manipulated his way through the amalgamation meeting at St. Paul's, a shadowy figure creeping up on Janet.

"Do you have any idea who might have gotten close enough to infect you?" I asked through clenched teeth trying to keep my voice steady and my stomach down.

"No," she replied meekly. "I've been racking my brains about that. To give me *Legionella*, whoever it was would have had to make me inhale a contaminated mist or spray, but no one's been near me and me alone with anything even resembling an aerosol. At other times, when I'm in close quarters with staff members doing procedures, I'm wearing a mask, gloves, and a gown." She paused and after a few seconds added, "It's so frustrating, knowing that sometime in the last few days I must have come face to face with the Phantom!" Then she started to cry.

I was ready to kill whoever had attacked her.

Turning from the window and nuzzling my head against hers, I asked, "Does Cam always get as mad as he did just now? I've never seen even a hint of that kind of temper whenever I met him with you." Thinking the unthinkable was no longer out of bounds.

She sighed, then took a few seconds to answer. "Don't judge him too harshly. He's fanatical about kindness to patients, the way we all should be, but for him, well, it's a special cause."

I felt a chill run through me.

"What do you mean a special cause?" I persisted, finding it increasingly hard to keep my voice even.

"It's personal, Earl," she replied, "something he once told me in confidence that he doesn't like talked about. It's got nothing to do with the Phantom, trust me." She was no longer crying, but she still sounded shaky. I don't think she suspected the impact her words were having on me.

The chill became a prickle of dampness on my back as I recalled some other words Harold Miller had said at the end of our conversation on my way up here. At the time I was so desperate to see Janet I'd hardly paid attention. *Dr. Mackie's a real stickler about not hurting patients.*

I considered very carefully what I was about to say. "Janet, I know that you don't think I'm good at speculating and that you have a great deal of confidence in Cam, but his behavior this morning at Death Rounds was bizarre." I paused, waiting for her protest at even a hint of my being about to speak negatively of her friend, but I felt her body stay relaxed against me. Cautiously, I continued, "He was furious that I went into the archives last night and looked through all the old charts of the Phantom's first victims—"

"You what!" she exclaimed sharply, pushing herself away from me again. She immediately began coughing.

I quickly tried to explain. "Yes, I went through those files, Janet. I had to. After Michael was admitted—"

"Michael?" she croaked, barely able to find her voice as her coughing spell continued. "What do you mean Michael was admitted?" She was sitting bolt upright now.

Damn! In all my concern for her I'd forgotten she didn't know about Michael. I certainly hadn't wanted to spring the news on her like this. I reached for her hand. The gesture made her look doubly alarmed. "Janet, we admitted Michael last night in septic shock from what I'm sure is *Legionella,*" I told her, watching her eyes widen. "There's no sign of staph, but as of this morning he was still unconscious and on a respirator."

She uttered a little cry. For the next few seconds all she said was "Oh no" over and over while her horrified expression grew until her blanched face looked like a silent, openmouthed mask. "But how?" she finally demanded. "Where?" Her voice was high and tremulous.

"Any time we got near any organisms in the lab we were in protective gear. Cam and Miller made sure of it. They're both adamant about that kind of thing, especially now. Oh, why did I get him into this!" she wailed.

I took her back in my arms and rocked her.

"What about Donna?" she asked.

"Shaken but holding up when I left her last night."

Between more of her coughing bouts, we sat in silence, hanging onto each other. I wanted only to let her rest and comfort her, but comfort her with what? My thoughts continued to rage with questions about Cam, and I was increasingly convinced she'd be in danger if she stayed here. But without hard evidence I was unlikely to budge her belief in him.

"Janet, about Cam," I began again, "you've got to listen to me. I swear he's covering up about the Phantom." This time I pressed ahead, not wanting to give her the opportunity to interrupt. "Not only is he trying to keep us from drawing attention to the attacks from two years ago, but when I got Williams to instigate a search of the asylum, he seemed most unhappy about that as well. You tell me, if he's not got something to hide, what's he afraid we'll find?"

Janet lifted her head from my chest and gently cradled my face in her hands. "Will you listen to yourself?" she said softly. "I know that it's because you love me and that you're frazzled by the fact I've been infected"—she took off my glasses, kissed me on my forehead above my mask—"and having had to rescue me from those doltish residents must have scared you silly." She kissed me again, this time on my eyes, then brushed her lips across my ear while moving her mouth closer to my neck. "Will you listen to yourself?" She brought her head up, still clasping my face in her hands, and, staring me right in the eyes, said, "Come on, get off Cam's case."

Before I could sputter an answer, I was startled by the sound of someone clearing his throat behind me.

"Earl, you've got to let her rest," said Cam from the entrance to the room. Sitting on the bed holding Janet, I'd been facing the other way and hadn't seen him return. He was already in clean protective gear; that meant he must have been putting it on just outside the door while we were talking. His voice was polite, but his presence filled me with anxiety. As I stood up and looked at the man who had become such a dreadful enigma to me, I wondered how much he'd heard of our conversation.

"I'm sorry, Cam," I protested, making no attempt to hide my hostility, "but I need to talk with her, and under the circumstances—"

"It's okay, Earl, Cam's right," Janet cut me off. "You should go now and let me sleep. Kiss Brendan for me." She was giving me an order. She pushed herself away and lay back on her pillow. I was disturbed by how drawn she looked.

"That despicable nurse won't bother you anymore, Janet," Cam told her, speaking very quietly. "I've arranged for only our best ICU staff to take care of you from here on. Anything medical I'll do myself, that is . . ." He let his voice trail off and looked sideways at me. "That is, if you still want me as your physician," he concluded, turning his eyes back toward her.

"Of course, Cam," she said, sounding surprised but shooting me a warning glare, making it very clear I was to stay silent. "Who else would take care of me but you?"

Cam glanced over at me again, and my stomach writhed like a bunch of cold snakes. But I stood there saying nothing, racked by confusion about what to do as much as gripped by panic. He in turn seemed to relax a notch and stepped closer to the bed. "That's settled then," he said, taking Janet's hand in his.

What if I confronted him, I wondered, tried to scare him off by throwing all my suspicions at him here and now, even without proof? How would he react?

"I now order this beautiful woman to sleep," he was proclaiming with a warm smile, "which is an important step in getting her back on her feet." He'd reverted to the pleasant self-confident tone I was used to hearing when he'd kept me laughing at dinner parties.

While Janet's returning smile revealed how comforted she was by this brilliant physician's physician, I felt warning bells going off throughout my head telling me to be very, very careful. Since she was staying put, if I opened my mouth and threatened him, I might end up placing her in more danger than if I kept quiet. Perhaps I'd already said too much if he'd eavesdropped on most of what I'd been saying to Janet before he came into the room.

He straightened to his full height, gave her a friendly wink along with a final pat on her hand, and then turned toward me. As pleasant as his expression seemed, his eyes were hard as blue ice. "Now Earl," he said quietly, gesturing to the door, "how about meeting me in my office after my clinical rounds, say, about eleven? I think you and I should have a chat about what happened at Death Rounds this morning."

Chapter 16

I needed proof that Janet would believe, even if it pointed to Cam. I figured the best way to get it was to pursue my original plan—go back through the confidential files of University Hospital and find whatever Michael had discovered. Even if *the pattern* hadn't told *him* who the killer was, that same evidence that had convinced him there was a killer could perhaps point Janet and me toward a name. Except now I'd have to somehow do an end run around Cam to get to those files.

I decided to take my problem to the top, and in Janet's hospital that meant I had to go down to the third floor and meet with Reginald Fosse, the CEO. His office was housed in the plush confines of the administration wing.

While walking from ICU to the stairs and descending one flight, I worked out the details of what I would say. By the time I was striding over the thick carpets, my torn pant cuff flapping, I'd concocted a scheme made up of a bit of blackmail, a touch of bribery, and a whole lot of bluster.

Reginald Fosse had diplomas for a master's in business administration and a master's in health-care administration hanging on his wall, but no M.D. As such he was part of the managerial breed that has taken over the running of hospitals in the United States during the past ten years. This group has served shareholders in publicly traded providers of health care well, but its impact on the health of the nation has been less clear. Every hospital it kept out of bankruptcy hasn't necessarily been a victory for the sick, especially when it did it with disastrous money savers such as the ill-fated one-day-obstetrical-stay policy for a delivery. Janet had fought against that loopy idea, and Fosse, to his credit, had listened to reason before state legislation forced him to.

He was a pleasant enough looking man. The top of his head was balding, he had a few strands of white hair that he kept combed over it, and his midriff bulged over his belt. But the grandfatherly wire-rimmed glasses he wore perched on the end of his nose made him seem comfortable with his middle age and his smile was full of warmth. He'd agreed to see me right away and expressed his concern about Janet, obviously having already been informed of her admission.

A hospital CEO who is not an M.D. must rely on doctors for advice on medical issues and can end up feeling at a disadvantage against the brightest and best clinicians in the place. Nevertheless, smart CEOs will recruit the support of these doctors to obtain the soundest advice possible on medical matters, while keeping their own council for managerial decisions. Too often, however, out of insecurity, a nonphysician manager will try to exert his or her authority by battling doctors and blocking anyone with clinical competence from gaining too much political influence. These CEOs tend to surround themselves with wimps and weaklings and reap the inferior caliber of advice appropriate to such circles. Over the years, from Janet I'd learned Fosse leaned slightly toward this latter school of thought. As I took the chair he offered me in his sitting area, I thought of a way I might turn the tendency against him.

Looking around, I found it hard not to admire the man's office. The room was big, the rose-colored rug under my feet was thick, and his windows were full sized, though almost all I could see through them were the other wings of the hospital, a patch of the grounds, and beyond that, curling tar paper on the rooftops of nearby houses. His dark mahogany desk was about as large as the entire floor space in my own spartan work area back at St. Paul's.

The photos hanging beside Fosse's two diplomas showed him smiling and shaking hands with a variety of people, none of whom I recognized. In most of them he was also holding up an oversized check with lots of zeros behind the first number, donations, presumably—often the only way to finance innovative programs, new construction, or state-of-the-art equipment now that the profits of Health Maintenance Organizations went more to Wall Street than into patient care.

I thanked him for his concern about Janet and then in twenty minutes told him everything I knew about the Phantom: the events from two years ago, the *Legionella* infections of the nurses, Michael's infection and his note, and Janet's infection. Without other doctors around to inform him that I was crazy, my fantastic tale seemed to overwhelm him. During the telling of it he leaned more and more off the edge of his seat, and when I made it clear that I feared more attacks, a sheen of perspiration appeared on his scalp that turned his hairdo into a series of wet strings. I then implied that while I didn't have any evidence that I could take to the police, I'd have to report Michael's illness and all that had happened here to the state accreditation board, so they could name a replacement for Michael. Even if they didn't believe a killer was on the loose, I explained, once they learned of the infections, they'd be officially obliged to redo their accreditation.

By the time I finished with him he looked thoroughly frazzled as well as frightened.

"But why couldn't we continue the search informally, the way Dr. Popovitch was doing for Dr. Mackie?" he blurted out after a few seconds. "If someone's doing the hideous things you claim, we can't wait for outsiders to get going on the problem. At least it would give us a chance to get at whatever Dr. Popovitch discovered and to see what we're up against." His tone was almost pleading, and while I'd no doubt his main priority was preventing further infections, I suspected he was also thinking a lot about damage control for his hospital's reputation.

I continued to set the hook. "Of course, that was my first preference," I told him, "provided we moved quickly, but Dr. Mackie has adamantly refused even to consider the possibility that someone is infecting personnel in your hospital. He's left me no choice."

Fosse blanched anew at this piece of news. "He's what?"

I told him about Cam's reaction to my having tried to look at the files in the archives, without revealing my suspicions about Cam.

"Jesus Christ!" he exclaimed after removing his glasses and rubbing his eyes. He looked increasingly troubled as I talked and didn't even question how I'd gotten access.

"May I make a suggestion?" I figured it was time for the bribe. "Since I'm going to be around here a lot on account of Janet, why not let me continue to go after the files Dr. Popovitch found? I'd be discreet and could report solely to you. You'd have to overrule Dr. Mackie, of course, but I don't see you've got any choice."

His worried expression shifted into a mask of cool neutrality. Since he wasn't a doctor, I guessed he'd never cross a physician as important as Cam without having at least some M.D.s from his own hospital lined up on his side of the argument. "Well, Dr. Garnet," he began while the muscles in his face squirmed, "I appreciate the offer, but it's a difficult time for you—"

"I know how you can get another of your chiefs here to whole-heartedly back the plan," I interrupted. I let him stare at me a few seconds, just to whet his appetite, before adding, "I'll do anything to stop this killer, because until he's stopped, I'm convinced Janet's life is still at risk. Trying to convince the police or anyone else that he exists is hopeless unless I find whatever Dr. Popovitch discovered." I wanted him to know what was at stake in case Cam tried to intimidate him into backtracking.

Finally, having suitably prepared him, I offered what I felt certain neither he nor the chief I had in mind would refuse. "Here's what I propose. Tell your chief of emergency, William Tippet, that I'll support his being named the new joint chairperson of emergency medicine in return for his granting me temporary privileges in his department and appointing me to do a special audit. He can call it something vague, such as a joint project comparing mortality rates of ER cases common to both our hospitals. Unofficially he can play it down and say it's really just a courtesy, meant to give me something to do while I stay near Janet. That should keep my poking around from raising too many eyebrows and would give you the reasons you'd need to counter any howls of protest from Dr. Mackie. It won't fool him, but he won't be able to give you much heat either."

Fosse looked interested. I knew William Tippet would jump at the chance to be overall chairperson. Wild Bill's longtime insecurity around me would make the opportunity to finally prevail irresistible to him. And Fosse himself would much prefer one of his wimps to be chairperson of a key department like ER. At this stage, neither of them would have any idea Hurst was in the process of dumping me anyway.

"I'll speak with Tippet," he said after a few seconds. "Where can I reach you?"

I gave him my numbers. While I was shaking hands with him at the door to his office, I asked, "By the way, do you know of any reason why Dr. Mackie should be so defensive about the Phantom story?"

"No, not at all," he replied without hesitation.

His answer had seemed straightforward enough; his eyes certainly hadn't flickered from my own, nor had his voice changed in tone. But in the last half hour it was the first time this institutional politician had said anything to me without at least a few seconds hesitation. If he weighed the truth so carefully, might his answer at the ready be a lie? In any case, I didn't believe him.

I descended to the first level basement and headed toward Cam's office, which was located near the labs. As near as I could tell, with all the twists and turns in the hallways, I was directly over the subbasement wing where I'd spent the night. Unlike the subbasement, however, this level had been renovated, and the corridors were wide and well lit. I was five minutes early for our eleven o'clock chat.

CENTER FOR BIOLOGICAL INVESTIGATIVE STUDIES declared a large wall-mounted sign in gold lettering at the entrance to Cam's domain. Beside it someone had pasted up a more modest *Labs,* written by hand on a piece of cardboard. The pompous version probably hadn't made it clear that this was the right place to hand in a lowly sample of pee or give a specimen of blood.

The rooms I walked by were each as big as a three-car garage, and in every one of them was a labyrinth of scientific equipment bedecked with flashing lights and endless displays of digital readouts. HEMATOLOGY, BIOCHEMISTRY, VIROLOGY, CYTOLOGY, and BACTERIOLOGY read the signs over each doorway. These various areas of expertise would together determine the thousands of individual clinical measurements done here daily—the levels of sodiums, potassiums, sugars, proteins, red cells, white cells, and dozens of other ingredients in the human body—that would help quantify the diagnostic mysteries of the more than eight hundred patients lying in the beds upstairs. Through the open doors over the hum of the ventilation system I could hear the casual chatter of busy lab workers, mingled with the incessant summons of beeping monitors, warning buzzers, and timing bells. Along the corridor where the air didn't circulate as well, my nose tingled with a stinging aroma of unrecognizable chemical reagents mixed with the familiar scent of coffee. Occasionally I got a whiff of an all-too-recognizable stench, such as the one that emanated from a string of carts loaded with half-filled urine cups.

I also noticed that here hardly anyone was wearing a surgical mask, as opposed to the way a majority of personnel were in the rest of the hospital. Probably Cam's influence, I thought. He'd made a point of not wearing one himself once we left Janet's room. "If we don't act rationally through all this and encourage others to do so by example, we're in danger of ending up with outright panic," he'd declared overloudly in the nurses' station, making sure they heard him before he walked out of ICU.

Down here the only people I saw through the various lab windows wearing masks, a usual precaution when working with potentially airborne agents, were either working directly with fluids that might splash or plating organisms onto petri dishes under ventilating hoods in the bacteriology lab.

Through yet another open door I saw into a classroom and caught sight of Harold Miller taking nasal swabs from about a dozen people in housekeeping uniforms. Another thirty or so were lined up waiting in the hallway outside. UH was clearly carrying out its commitment to screen every single worker in the hospital.

In fact, the entire place was a superb testimony to the competence and exemplary leadership of Cam. It was impossible to reconcile the man in charge of these works with the monster I'd been making him out to be. Yet, on seeing all the technical prowess under his control, I couldn't help thinking that if anybody were able to find a way to use microbes as murder weapons, perhaps Cam could here.

I paused outside his closed door and focused on how I intended to handle myself. Whatever he had to say about what happened at Death Rounds, I'd be trying to get a sense of whether he was lying. If the chance came, I'd press him about why my poking into the business of the Phantom upset him so, but I'd have to be careful on that topic. He'd obviously be upset enough when he learned that I'd already been to Fosse behind his back. It might enrage him further if he realized I'd then come down here to try to catch him out. Above all, I had to make sure my feinting with him didn't precipitate a further attack on Janet.

He was waiting for me.

His office was both spacious and luxurious, equal in every way to Fosse's. It was paneled with dark wood, lined with wall units of bookshelves, and carpeted with rich blue broadloom. In one half of his large room was a sitting area, as there had been in Fosse's, defined by a couch and matching easy chair. Occupying the other half was a desk that looked about the size of the CEO's, but behind Cam's, tastefully positioned off to one side, was a potted tree. Natural light came in through a long narrow line of windows at the level of the ceiling, about the only clue we were in a basement. Thin-slatted Venetian blinds dressed up the effect, and track lighting gave the room a soft illumination that was easy on the eyes. The final result seemed to be the hospital's way of stating, "You are honored as a world-renowned physician."

"Have a seat," he said, casually indicating the couch. He walked over to a wooden hutch, slid open a panel door to reveal a small fridge and a row of glasses. "Would you like a Coke, or can I have my secretary get you a coffee?"

"Nothing, thanks," I said, far more coldly than I intended.

He stopped in midreach for a glass, turned to look at me with no trace of a smile left on his face, and slowly closed the door to his minibar without taking anything for himself. "Right," he said, his own cool tone seconding mine and making it clear we were both finished with niceties.

He came and sat on the arm of the easy chair beside the rather low couch where I was sitting. The higher perch made him tower over me. I wondered if he had deliberately designed his seating arrangement to achieve this effect as a way of intimidating troublesome colleagues. I'd read somewhere that Lyndon Johnson used to pull that trick.

"You really went over the line last night, Earl," Cam began. "Here I defend you to Miller, and you return the favor by sneaking around behind my back. Why didn't you come to me? After all, you—"

"Janet came to you, remember? You wouldn't listen."

He grimaced. "Look, I'm willing to allow you were distraught over Michael and influenced by that crazy note of his—"

"Crazy!" I interrupted, leaping to my feet and forcing him to look up at me instead. His mouth dropped open in astonishment.

"I'll tell you what's crazy," I continued, practically yelling. "It's you continuing to ignore Janet's warning that these infections are connected to the Phantom business!" So much for being careful, I thought, as I let fly my anger.

He started leaning back from me as I brought my face closer to his. Give him a taste of his own tactics was all I could think; I bored in on him until I was inches away. "Then Michael got infected, and now Janet's been infected, yet you still don't seem to get it. Worse, you continue going around like she and I are the enemy for pursuing the one idea that might get to the bottom of what's already a nightmare."

Cam's face flushed. "Now wait just a goddamned minute!" He got to his feet. He was taller than me again.

"No, you wait just a goddamned minute! This is about people's lives, Cam, patient's lives, Michael's and Janet's lives. Speaking on behalf of patients, I have to be professional. On behalf of a friend I can be as nasty as it takes, and on behalf of Janet, I'm going to be *your* worst nightmare!"

I was screaming up at his face and couldn't stop. Fear, lack of sleep, the possibility he had infected Janet—all combined to drive my rage way over any point where I could control it. Hell, after days of frustration and stalking shadows, I suddenly didn't want to control it.

He stepped away, his expression quickly reverting from anger back to openmouthed shock.

I pressed in on him. "You want to charge me with trespassing, you go right ahead. I'm past it all, Cam! I don't give a fuck anymore for your reputation or mine or either of our hospitals.' Got that?" I stabbed the front of his chest with my finger. "I only care now about keeping Janet safe and bringing down this killer, no matter whom I have to talk to or how loud I have to scream!"

His face had drained to white. I'd backed him up against a wall loaded with plaques, citations, awards, and degrees. A cautionary voice from deep within me said, "This is crazy," but I was beyond caution, not even capable of listening to what was left of my own reason.

"So tell me, Cam, what are you really up to? You were livid that I saw the records from the Phantom's first attacks. They're quite something, aren't they? I even figured out how he did it. He's real, Cam. As real as can be!"

"This could jeopardize Janet!" insisted that inner voice, sufficiently loud this time to snap me out of my tirade. I stood for an instant, breathing hard and fighting to regain my self-control. My outburst was anything but what I'd planned; for a few seconds I think I was probably as close to losing control as Cam was at Death Rounds, but I was rational enough to realize something. My anger had given me a momentary edge on him. I quickly decided I'd test my suspicions even further and throw some more of them in his face to see what he did. Afterward I'd do whatever it took to protect Janet.

"So I have a warning for you, Cam," I continued, "just like you had one for me this morning. Explain to me right now why you seem so determined no one investigate the Phantom—what you're afraid we'll find—or you're liable to end up being investigated yourself."

He reacted as if I'd punched him in the gut. His color drained even further to a dusky gray that was alarming to look at. I felt I'd hit a bull's-eye.

"Well, which is it going to be?" I continued. "Do I yell my head off about the Phantom, the infections, and you trying to cover it up until someone somewhere listens, or do you level with me?"

If I got any closer to him, it would be indecent. I spun away and walked over to the hutch where I slammed open the wooden door, grabbed a Coke out of his fridge and pulled the tab off the can without looking at him. I took a swallow and felt the cold liquid run all the way down to the pit of my stomach. The sensation reminded me I hadn't had breakfast yet. I glanced at my watch. It was 11:10.

When I did turn around to face him, the one word to describe him was *deflated*. His eyes, usually so fierce, looked as faded as denim. He moved away from the wall, eyeing me warily. "You've got it all wrong, Earl. You've certainly got me wrong." He sounded shaken and was circling around me, putting the couch between us, as if he were afraid I might spring at him. "I admit I went over the top at you before Death Rounds. Let me apologize for that. I should have been more understanding." He was almost pleading. He extended his hand tentatively, reaching over the back of the couch, like an opponent at the end of a tennis match reaching over the net.

I figured it was a good time to push for answers. "Why were you so enraged that I was looking at those charts?" I demanded. "You've seen them. You've got to know that those people were all attacked by someone."

"I didn't want stories about the Phantom starting up again." He started to withdraw his hand, then pointed it at me. "Don't you realize the panic that could cause? It would have been bad enough to have rumors that someone was spreading *Legionella*. And now, after our scare about the superbug, a story like that would be catastrophic." He spoke quietly, but the urgency of his tone was impossible not to hear. An act? Maybe not. Panic was a legitimate concern, as Williams was forever stressing.

"Why were you so furious about the asylum being searched?" I demanded, letting my impatience sound while paying close attention to the expression on his face.

There was a flash of the familiar blue in his eyes. "I was furious that you had probably been spreading tales about the Phantom to Williams—you must have told him something fantastic or he never would have helped you get into those records—but again I apologize for my anger. You had Michael's note and, well, I can see why you did what you did, but that doesn't make it right." His voice sounded strained and he seemed ill at ease, remaining behind the couch while shifting his weight from one leg to another. If any of this behavior was because he had something to hide, I really couldn't tell. For all I knew, it could mean he had to take a leak.

"You still don't accept," I persisted, "that the Phantom is responsible for the infections."

He shook his head. "No, I don't accept that notion at all." He took a deep breath and said, "Look, Earl, there's no point in our battling over this. We're on the same side. Won't you please accept my apology for being so angry with you about the archives and let it go at that?"

"I'd like nothing better, Cam, except you haven't explained a thing."

He sighed, then moved around in front of the couch, and sat in the low seat he'd initially given me. "At least sit down, Earl. We have to talk about Janet. If you can't accept my apology, do you want me to withdraw from her case? I can suggest a number of excellent members on my staff who could take care of her, but I still would prefer she remain under my—"

"Before we talk about Janet, answer me this." I was determined not to let him shift the topic away from the Phantom. "Do you think those people whose charts I saw last night were attacked or not?" I remained standing, looking down on him.

He grimaced once more, then answered, "Yes, I believe someone was doing something to those individuals, but that has nothing to do—"

"And do you think those individuals were chosen because they'd been cruel to patients?"

He swallowed." Really, there's no point in this—"

"Answer me, damn it!"

He looked up and seemed to study me. "Yes," he said after a few seconds. Then he added, "All those individuals had questionable reputations for their work with patients. None of them ever had anything proven against them, but they shared a tendency to generate a lot of complaints from people in their care, just as Janet told you."

"So someone was punishing the punishers?"

"Yes," he admitted, after a second's hesitation.

The silence between us then was total. I felt a wave of exhilaration, like I'd gained yet another step on that two-year-old trail, then wondered if I'd bullied him into acknowledging the existence of the Phantom back then, or had he his own reason for suddenly leveling with me, at least about that? His expression was neutral, telling me nothing.

I kept pressing. "How can you admit there was a Phantom yet not see that Phyllis Sanders and those two other nurses, so Janet tells me, were exactly the kind of punishers he was singling out two years ago?"

His eyebrows arched at the mention of the other nurses. He sighed in exasperation. "I knew Janet would tell you all about Brown, just as she told me about the trouble her patients had with Sanders and the OR nurse."

Brown? Janet hadn't told me anything more about Brown. Good God! I thought. Did he mean Brown was one of the Phantom's *Legionella* victims. One had survived, I remembered, and if I recalled correctly, she'd been from ICU.

"But it isn't relevant," continued Cam, "because I keep coming back to the same starting point. There's simply no way these bugs can be selectively made to infect individual people." He slammed his fist into his palm as he made his point. He was sitting more erect, becoming aggravated again.

As surprised as I was over his remark about Brown, I didn't have time to dwell on it. As soon as I saw I was starting to shake him up, I honed my attack and went after him even more forcefully. "Because you say it can't be done doesn't mean somebody hasn't found a way!"

"Christ, Garnet, I give up with you," he exclaimed, pushing himself up off the couch and starting to pace in front of me. "You're obsessed with this!"

"Then what did Michael find?"

He continued to stride back and forth, waving his arms. "I don't know what he thought he found. Hell, he was sick, out of his head. Let me be blunt." He came to rest standing behind the couch again. "I know bacterial organisms better than you do," he said pointing once more at me. "When I say it can't be done, I mean that everything science has discovered about these organisms says it can't be done."

My anger surged. "Maybe you'd be a little less scientifically pure if it were someone from your family in ICU," I shot back at him.

This time his eyes ignited into blue fire. "You have nothing to teach me about having someone in ICU!" he snapped. "I know a hell of a lot more about that kind of pain than I hope you ever will." He leaned across the couch toward me again, but unlike before, he kept his hands gripped onto the cushions, like talons. I could see the tendons in his fingers straining into the material.

A loud knock on the door broke the silence as we glowered at each other. Before Cam could answer, Miller stuck his head into the room. "Doctor Mackie, I'm sorry to interrupt, but could I see you for a minute?" As he asked the question he was already in and closing the door behind him. I wondered if he'd heard us arguing.

He walked over to where we were standing, his surgical mask hanging loosely around his neck and his eyes showing the same tormented expression I'd seen earlier. He nodded toward me. "Excuse me, Dr. Garnet, I won't take a minute." To Cam he said, "The bacteriology technicians tell me you're organizing a search of the asylum for *Legionella*. I'd consider it a personal favor if you'd let me be in charge of the team."

Cam frowned. "But Harold, you should be on leave. I know you want to help, but in this case, follow my advice and go—"

"Please, Dr. Mackie. I'm better off at work than sitting at home thinking about her."

I turned away and took a few steps over to the wooden hutch, ostensibly to find a place to toss my empty can of Coke, but I felt uncomfortable eavesdropping on his pain.

While he made his case for staying on the job, I tried to tune out the conversation a bit more by studying a collection of photos on top of the hutch. They were of a man and a boy doing various outdoor activities—skiing, biking, canoeing—but over a period of years. While the man was consistently an older version of Cam, the boy aged through a series of shots from being a child to becoming Cam as a young man. There were no recent pictures.

"You're sure, Harold?" I heard Cam ask from behind me, his voice sounding full of doubt.

"Believe me, all I want is a chance to find out how she got infected," Miller answered forcefully. "By the way, who thought of searching the asylum?"

Without hesitation Cam said, "Why, Dr. Garnet here had something to do with that suggestion. I really missed the boat not thinking of it myself. Maybe he also has some advice about what you should be looking for in there?"

He hadn't sounded sarcastic. When I turned to face him he stared at me rather impassively. There was no longer anger in his eyes. If anything, he looked sad. He added, "In fact, maybe he'd like to do the search with you."

I nearly stopped breathing. "Pardon?" was all I could say, not believing what I'd heard. I studied Cam's face again for some hint that e was toying with me, but his steady gaze revealed nothing but that strange funereal stare.

Miller on the other hand, looked astounded. "Dr. Mackie, with all due respect, it's dirty work in there, getting water samples from rusty pipes and crawling around some of the spaces we'll have to go through—"

"Of course, that's up to Dr. Garnet," said Cam, not taking his eyes off me.

What was Cam doing, proving he had nothing to hide or daring me to come and find it, sure that his cloak of secrecy could withstand even my scrutiny? But if he was so secure with his ability to escape detection, why had he been so upset about my going through the files? He never would have aroused my suspicions if he hadn't made such a big fuss in the first place. Once more I studied him.

"What about it, Earl?" he prodded, his expression still neutral and indecipherable, except for his somber-looking eyes. "Would that make you feel better about Janet—pursuing what infected her?"

I didn't know what to say. "All right" was all I managed to answer. My insides were in turmoil as I still tried to figure out what he was up to.

"Okay, Harold," said Cam, turning to his protégé and putting his hand on the young man's shoulder. "I know you'll do the most thorough job possible, though personally I think you're pushing yourself too hard right now." He paused, then very softly added, "Maybe it's fitting that you and Dr. Garnet hunt down the organism that took your mother."

Harold still appeared stunned at having me thrust on him. At first he didn't say anything, looking from Cam over to me.

"Harold?" repeated Cam.

"Yes!" replied Harold with a start, seeming to snap out of whatever he was thinking. "You're right. Maybe it is fitting."

Cam asked, "When do you think you'll start?"

Miller was suddenly all business. "We'll have to coordinate with someone from the engineering department. We'll need plumbers, diagrams of the water system, extension cords and lights—I don't know what all. Also, our own day shift is strained to the limit with screening everyone in the hospital. I thought we could ask some of our people to work a double shift and go into the asylum during evenings."

Cam nodded his approval, then asked him, "Can you be ready by this evening?"

"I don't know. I've personally got another hour's worth of screening scheduled, but I could start organizing a team right after that's finished. I suppose it's possible we could get started tonight."

Cam turned to me. "Will you be around, Earl?"

"Sure," I answered, unable to believe I was volunteering to spend another night in that hideous place. Harold continued to look unenthusiastic about the prospect of baby-sitting me, but he took my phone numbers and told me he'd call at the end of the day when he knew what time we'd start. He then thanked Cam and left.

Cam stared at the closed door for a few seconds. "How do you think he's handling it?" he asked, turning toward me.

Before answering, I noticed he was frowning and seemed much more troubled than he'd revealed while Miller was with us in the room. "I don't know," I answered tentatively. "Grief is such an individual thing. He seems driven to work during what should be his period of mourning for her."

Cam grimaced. "*Driven*—that's the word for it. The poor boy's acting like he's determined to track down the infection that killed his mother by himself. I swear he's cultured more people here during the screenings than any other technician on staff at UH. He even wanted to lead the team we sent to check out his home where his mother lived with him, but I insisted on doing that job myself." Cam shook his head. "I just hope I'm doing the right thing in letting him take on so much." The gentleness in his voice was almost fatherly.

Feeling especially sheepish after our fight, I said, "Uh, Cam, I appreciate your having spoken to him on my behalf. He met me on my way in to see Janet. It seems he's not blaming me so much anymore, thanks to you."

Cam seemed pleased. "Good! It's important he get beyond that."

"You also made quite a gesture, including me in the search. I appreciate—"

"I did that for Janet's sake," he said with a dismissive flick of his hand. "The one good thing that came out of your going to Williams was that he saw what I'd missed. His suggestion about checking the water outlets in the asylum was brilliant. After Death Rounds I went immediately to our CEO and got him to authorize it. That's what I was doing before I learned Janet was admitted and saw you in ICU. Maybe now you'll be convinced I didn't oppose the search, only your crazy stories."

This time it was my turn to stare openmouthed at him. I'd presumed he'd announced the search because it was forced on him. Un-

ess what I'd just heard was an act, he actually seemed hugely enthusiastic about it.

He sighed. "It's my hope, Earl," he continued, surprising me by
speaking very slowly, very gently, "that if you believe I've nothing
to hide, then maybe you'll not prevent me from taking care of Janet.
She's going to need good care, Earl, and I think I can give it to her.
But if you and she do decide to transfer to another hospital, please do
it quickly, before she's too ill to make the trip. Another measure I
strongly advise you to do is to put your baby on a prophylactic dose
of erythromycin. Infants are in the vulnerable group, and even
though person-to-person spread without an aerosol isn't suppose to
happen, we still protect those at risk. Obviously he's been in close
proximity to his mother. You and the nanny should be okay, but,
well, with the unexplained spread to Deloram, Popovitch, and now
to Janet, maybe you should protect yourselves too, until we make
sure we're not up against some new pattern of natural transmission."

I found it hard to process all the information he was giving me. He
sounded kind, caring, and empathetic, but his eyes were saying
something else. I felt transfixed in their blue glare, like a rabbit in
front of an oncoming truck. "Cam, wait a minute—"

He waved away my attempt to speak. "There's just one thing you
must agree to do. Abandon your talk about the Phantom and give up
your hunt for whatever you think Michael found. I can't have you
stumbling around and possibly setting off rumors. If you give me
your word on that, I won't report your unauthorized entry last night.
After the drubbing you took at Death Rounds today, that's the last
sort of trouble you need. What do you say?"

I couldn't say anything.

He looked at his watch. "You'll have to excuse me. I've got a lecture
to give that started fifteen minutes ago. Make yourself comfortable
here and think over my offer. Let me know what you decide about
Janet as soon as possible."

With that, he was gone from the room.

Chapter 17

Well, well, well, I thought. That *was* about as subtle as being hit by a truck.

Like me, he obviously wasn't averse to a bit of bribery and blackmail, but I had to think I was better at it. The real question remained. Was he a monster reeling me in, or was he an honorable man trying to do what he thought was right for Janet, for his department, and for his hospital? In the final analysis I had no idea.

My stomach rearranged itself a few more times, then clamped back down on the cola I'd treated it to five minutes ago.

I'd found nothing that would persuade Janet that Cam shouldn't be trusted. She'd be furious about his crude attempt to blackmail me and would have no qualms telling him to his face that he was pigheadedly wrong about the Phantom. But she'd buy his excuse that he was frantic to keep rumors from panicking the hospital. Cam himself could claim, "I explained everything to him, gave him carte blanche to explore the asylum, and he still won't believe me." Janet was then likely to invoke her often-used marital right to consider me a part-time dolt and blast me for continuing to suspect the man.

What's more, she might be correct.

I had to wonder if my judgment wasn't skewed by lack of sleep and if I wasn't stirring up nightmares about the man for nothing. Being surrounded by Cam's gallery of personal photos and testimonials didn't make me feel any easier. It somehow seemed doubly offensive to be sitting in his own sanctuary and sullying it by thinking evil of him. If he was innocent, he had a perfect right to be outraged by my sneaking into his files. I knew that Janet would say I was off beam to call his reaction over the top, especially after he'd tried to help me with Miller.

My back and legs hurt even from sitting still, while my head started throbbing and reminded me I'd better get to bed. If I wasn't careful, I thought, I might end up snoring on Cam's couch. I forced myself to stand up, groaning loudly as I did.

Maybe all my suspicions were wrong, I continued to muse, even the ones about Rossit and Hurst. But that vein of thought immediately led once more to the hideous possibility that the killer was a complete stranger.

Hoping to settle my stomach and find something for my headache, I wandered over to Cam's minibar and checked if he kept some antacids or acetaminophen stashed with the cans of pop. I had to settle for a club soda. As the bubbles tried their best to be my breakfast, I ruminated once more about the killer being a man or woman I didn't know. The roots of his or her motive, however twisted, would be beyond anything I was aware of or could ever hope to figure out, and his or her identity perhaps impossible for me to ever uncover.

The thought made me shudder. I could never protect Janet against such an anonymous menace, even if I was with her twenty-four hours a day. Anyone—an orderly, a resident, a nurse—could slip her something during the routine maintenance of her IVs. The possibilities gave me the creeps—injected potassium to stop her heart, short-acting paralytics to stop her breathing, a syringe full of air through her intravenous line to block the flow of blood to her lungs—but this killer would probably use his trademark: completely resistant staphylococcus. I didn't know how he had infected Phyllis Sanders without her knowing it, but I knew how I could do it to a woman full of IV lines as she lay sleeping. I'd inject the organism directly into her bloodstream. Once more an image of that shadowy figure from the subbasement spiraled into my mind, except this time he was creeping up to Janet's bedside. My stomach lurched toward my throat.

I marched over to Cam's desk, my resolve on fire. I'd join in the search of the asylum tonight if I could, but getting the files that Michael had found remained my top priority. If going through the asylum did manage to flush out whoever I'd seen down there, without those records and the supposed proof they contained that a murderer was at work, I wouldn't be able to turn him over to the police; officially there were no murders to charge him with. For the moment, everything depended on Fosse and Tippet not being able to refuse my offer and Cam's being kept ignorant of it until it was a fait accompli.

Nor could I let Cam report me for unlawful entry. One whiff of that kind of trouble and Fosse wouldn't have anything to do with me. I had to let Cam think he'd cowed me into backing off.

I scrolled a piece of printer paper out of Cam's desktop computer setup and wrote:

> *Dear Cam,*
> *Sorry for the misunderstanding, and thank you for your*
> *helpful suggestions about prophylactic erythromycin for*
> *Brendan. As for Janet, she has absolute faith in you, and*
> *I know of no better physician to get her through this*
> *ordeal.*
> *   Earl*

If only it were so simple, I thought. I knew Cam would decode my carefully chosen words and know I was still suspicious as hell. Maybe that wasn't such a bad thing. The balance between his thinking I'd acquiesced, yet knowing I was onto him might be enough to keep him in check for a while if my worst fears about him turned out to be true.

Then, in case my powers of subterfuge and intimidation weren't all I hoped they were, I dug out a yellow pages from one of his desk drawers, looked up a private security company, and arranged for a uniformed guard to be at the door of Janet's room twenty-four hours a day.

Out in the hallway I passed by the classroom where Miller was still busily screening staff members seated at a row of desks. As he moved from person to person—hunching over each of them, culturing and plating, rhythmically getting the job done—he seemed to keep everyone relaxed, and none of his subjects ended up wincing with tears running out of their eyes as had many of the people I'd cultured.

I found myself wondering if he should be trying to work off his grief. Doubtful, I decided, thinking like a clinician. Frenetic activity wasn't always the best solution to mourning. It could delay his coming to grips with his mother's death and actually prolong his sense of loss. Perhaps I'd have a chance to talk to him tonight about it, during the search.

I was about to walk away when I thought, Better make sure we don't give the Phantom advance warning we're coming. "Mr. Miller," I called into the room, "could I have a word?"

He looked up from where he was about to take another culture. "Sure," he said, walking over to the doorway carrying the partially open packet of swabs.

"I wonder if you could avoid broadcasting the search of the asylum and ask the other workers you recruit not to mention it as well."

"Oh?" he asked, cocking his head.

I quickly invoked a little more authority. "To avoid panic," I whispered. "Dr. Mackie says we must avoid panic at all costs."

He quickly nodded in agreement. "Of course. Good idea. I'll call you when we're ready."

He turned back to his work, and I scooted upstairs to ICU. I had questions for Janet regarding Brown . . . and Cam.

"You aren't starting to pin motives on Cam now, are you, Earl?" Janet demanded crossly.

She was coughing more than before and beginning to wheeze loud enough that I could hear the high-pitched mewing sound without a stethoscope. But she wasn't too sick to immediately sense what I was up to when I started asking her about Cam's special cause.

"No, not at all," I lied. "Now how about answering the question. Or perhaps you'd like to explain what Cam meant when he said, 'I knew Janet would tell you all about Brown.'"

She started at the mention of Brown. "Earl, I swear, if you've embarrassed me by insulting Cam with one of those conspiracy theories of yours—"

"Do you want me to ask him myself?" I interrupted.

"You wouldn't dare!"

I made a move toward the door. "Watch me!" As much as I'd expected her not to take my suspicions seriously, I felt too tired and frayed to be very patient. I was also bluffing; I didn't intend to stir him up about anything right now.

"My God!" she declared, her eyes widening. "You seriously doubt him?"

She could only see the upper half of my face over the top of my mask, but it must have shown her enough to make it clear I was deadly earnest.

She immediately stopped sounding angry and implored, "Earl, whatever you're thinking about him, I know it's out of fear for my safety, but he's not capable of hurting anyone—"

"Janet, just tell me how Brown figures in this and explain why kindness to patients is such a special cause for Cam. I'll make up my own mind about what it means." Not meaning to be as curt as I sounded, I tried to soften my tone. "We can't afford anything less than the same critical thinking you'd apply to a medical problem."

She gave me a puzzled look.

"You know what I mean," I added. "You're refusing to do a complete differential on all the possibilities of who this killer is."

She started at the reprimand. The allusion to a physician failing to consider all the diagnostic possibilities when attacking a clinical problem was a low blow. But after another coughing spell, she reluctantly agreed to tell me what I wanted to know.

"She's the ICU nurse who survived the Phantom's attack of *Legionella*."

So I was right, I thought, yet the revelation remained startling.

Janet continued. "Today's little effort, I'm sure, began as payback for my trying to nail her in the past about her little games and ordering her away from my patients. Except this time, she was stupid enough to make those residents mess with an airway and got herself in way over her head."

I couldn't believe what I was hearing. I remembered Cam had said she should know the sputum would be scant. "You mean what happened was deliberate?"

"I doubt she meant to put me into laryngospasm. She certainly never nearly killed anyone before. She's always been just a petty tormentor, and, as I told you, she probably didn't realize that the residents would bungle things so. Wanting me to choke and retch my guts out during an uneventful tracheal aspiration would be more her speed. It's ironic. I couldn't put her out of business for what she did with my patients, but what she pulled with me got so out of hand it will probably finish her, certainly in ICU as Cam said, if not altogether as a nurse at UH."

I was speechless. "She could have killed you! If any part of this was deliberate, she should be charged with medical assault!"

Janet started coughing, then only partially recovered her voice. "Think about it, Earl," she rasped. "This was a classic example of how Brown and the others like her got away with their nasty crap, though never with anything so lethal. But even here she did nothing more than show a note about scanty sputum written by someone in ER to the residents and then inform them of the ID directive about proper culture samples. We may know what she was really doing, but who can prove it, let alone have her indicted for it? Even in the morbidity review, Cam will probably only get her charged with a major error in judgment. But at least it will be enough to label her officially as trouble and keep her out of critical-care areas. Even if she isn't fired now, she'll finally be on such a short leash her days here will be numbered."

Her days may be numbered, period, I thought. Messing with someone when they were helpless was indeed liable to make people very angry if my own anger was any gauge.

"Why didn't *you* stop the residents?" I asked Janet as gently as I could. I still found it hard to believe how any of this could have happened. "You're not known for being overruled easily."

I saw her bristle. "Because," she answered icily, "I didn't catch on at first that it was Brown who'd put the residents up to it." After a few seconds of cool silence she added, "Besides, I was determined to be a good patient and do what I was told, not act like a doctor and get special treatment. When I did start to protest, the resident who wanted to suction me kept insisting that he'd done it this way before and that he'd be in and out before I knew it. It sounded wrong, but I'm a gynecologist, not a respiratory specialist. It was only after that catheter was down my throat that I realized they didn't know what they were doing."

I knew what she meant. Doctors invariably have a hard time finding the right distance to take either from their own care as a patient or from the care of a family member. Being too close and interfering could be as much a disaster as standing too far off and ignoring well-honed instincts that something's wrong. The dynamic was hard on the treating doctor as well. The physician's physician had to be a very special breed.

"And what about Cam's cause?" I asked as unobtrusively as I could. That I suspected her friend was, I knew, painful to her. It would be even harder on her to tell me anything that she knew would add to those suspicions.

I watched her expel a long breath and lean back on her pillow.

"His father was a hemophiliac," she began matter-of-factly, but in a hoarse whisper that was painful to listen to. "The man actually worked in this hospital as a lab technician. You can imagine how Cam grew up, witnessing the man suffer with crippling bleeds into his joints that sometimes only morphine could ease. Once Cam was in medical school, he learned the true extent of his father's pain when he saw firsthand the incessant needles and invasive procedures all hemophiliacs are forced to endure. Besides, remember the attitude about giving narcotics to these people back then. It was pretty judgmental, and most hemophiliacs had to put up with a lot of insinuations that they were faking pain to get a fix."

I knew exactly what she meant. I'd witnessed that kind of ignorance even in my own ER. What kind of impact could it have had on a son, knowing that his father was subjected to the indignity of having to prove again and again he was in pain?

"I think Cam became a director of laboratory services precisely because of his father," Janet continued. "I suppose he sees it as a chance to make sure that, at least in his domain, no one suffers the sort of unnecessary pain that was inflicted on his dad."

"Is his father still alive?" I asked, remembering the lack of recent photos back in Cam's office.

"No," Janet answered solemnly. "Like so many hemophiliacs in the early eighties, he became infected with HIV from improperly tested blood products. He died about ten years ago."

It all made terrible sense. "Janet, do you realize what you're saying?" I asked, my throat so dry I could barely speak.

She pulled back from my chest and looked at me with a hard blue stare that outdid anything Cam had fired my way in the last few hours. "What I'm saying, Earl," she said, her cutting tone sounding through the hoarseness, "is that the experience turned him into a fine and caring doctor I trust with my life. He is not some twisted fiend hell-bent on revenge, and if you had any sense of intuition of your own, you'd know I'm right."

The only sense I had was that it was pointless to argue with her.

Minutes later I was advising everyone in the nurses' station that I'd arranged for a security guard to be at the entrance of Janet's room and that he'd be logging anyone who went near her. I didn't give them any reasons and got more than a few raised eyebrows, but nobody protested out loud. I also gave strict orders that no one, not even Janet, was to send the guard away. After our talk about Cam, I didn't have the nerve to tell her what I'd done to protect her.

Half an hour later I was in ICU at St. Paul's looking at Michael through the window of his isolation room. As alarming as it was again to see him so helpless, I was also appalled to see that Gary Rossit had taken over his care. He was in the cubicle inserting a long thick needle under Michael's right clavicle to serve as a conduit to his central venous system.

The nurses assured me the little man was hovering over Michael like a mother hen, then gave me a brief synopsis of the treatment he'd ordered. It seemed complete and included rifampin, the second-line antibiotic used in patients desperately ill with *Legionella*—the same one that he'd lambasted me for suggesting in Sanders's case.

Michael's most recent chest X rays—taken about an hour ago—were up on a nearby viewing box beside the ones done last night when he was admitted. The whited-out areas were clearly larger, indicating the infection was spreading. I blocked out images of lungs in Tupperware that tried to crowd in on my thoughts.

The nurses found it reassuring that as of yet his sputum hadn't turned copiously purulent. "It may be too early for staph," I told them, while thinking it may already be too late for my friend.

I turned back to the cubicle as Rossit threaded a plastic catheter into Michael's subclavicular vein. Two residents watched with rapt attention a set of fluorescent green numbers and curving lines appearing on a small overhead monitor. These were the pressure readings that confirmed the tip of the catheter was gliding through the right-sided chambers of Michael's heart and into the large pulmonary artery leading from the heart to the lung. Rossit could now determine Michael's huge fluid requirements in the presence of septic shock and hydrate him properly without overloading his circulatory system.

As far as I could tell, Rossit was making Michael one of his master efforts. The most aggravating thing about enduring the little man's bullshit over the years was getting a glimpse of what a good doctor he could be when he pulled out all the stops, then seeing him revert to his nasty one-upmanship once he'd pulled off yet another of his miracle saves.

But today there was another possible explanation for Rossit's attentiveness. If he were involved with the killings, he might be hovering over Michael to assure his death at the first opportunity.

Rossit caught my eye through the window and quickly turned away. Whether the reaction of a man guilty of murder or simply that of a creep who had loaded the dice against me at Death Rounds this morning—either way he didn't seem happy to see me. Fresh from my showdown with Cam, I was primed to take on little Gary.

I put on a protective outfit and stepped into the room. "Dr. Rossit, I'd like a word in private, please." Turning to the residents, I asked, "Would you two gentlemen excuse us?" My tone of voice made it an order, not a request.

They quickly left, taking only seconds to discard their gear at the door.

Rossit eyed me over the top of his mask. "Look, Earl, about this morning—"

"Shut up, Rossit! I just got back from admitting my wife to ICU in University Hospital. She's also been diagnosed with *Legionella*, and I'm in no mood for your crap!"

"Your wife!" he exclaimed. From the part of his face I could see, his shock seemed genuine enough.

"Surprised, are you, Gary?" I shot back. "I wonder. Because I think someone deliberately infected her, just like someone probably deliberately infected Michael and Stewart Deloram. Now I'm not sure why Stewart was a target, but I think Michael and Janet were attacked because they were trying to expose whoever had also infected the nurses from UH. Am I going too fast for you, Gary, or do you know this already? Stop me if you do."

I was standing over him, making him look up at me, and I felt a glint of satisfaction at seeing his pupils widen ever so slightly. I was scaring him.

"Earl, for God's sake, what are you saying—"

"I'm saying I'm going to expose this killer. In the meantime, nothing further had better happen to Janet or Michael, is that clear?" I refrained from my urge to tap him on the top of his head with my fingernail.

"You can't be serious," he protested.

"What I'm serious about, Rossit, is that you better be at your healing best with Michael here. I'm going to be double-checking every molecule of stuff you put into him, and there damn well better not be any suspicious incidents. Got me?"

This time I did poke my index finger into his chest, then spun around and strode out of the room. I didn't look back as I discarded my gear into the bin at the door.

"You're crazy, Garnet," I heard him shout from behind me, "certifiably bonkers, crazy!"

I called the same security company and made identical arrangements for Michael's room as I had for Janet's. The nurses were just as puzzled as their colleagues had been at UH, but once again I gave orders, not answers. I signed out for the rest of the day and headed home to sleep. It was 2:00 P.M., but I was fighting to keep my eyes open and knew I wasn't safe to see patients in ER. On my way out I stopped at the hospital pharmacy to get Brendan, our nanny, and myself some erythromycin.

As I stood at the counter and waited for the pharmacist to prepare the medication, I wondered about my own chances of being attacked by the Phantom. Michael and Janet had done little more than discreetly look through old records, yet that was enough to provoke this killer. I'd just confronted the two people I suspected most and practically accused them of murder. Even if I was wrong about Cam or Rossit, it was a pretty good bet that if this maniac was close enough at hand to have known what Michael and Janet were up to, he'd know what I was doing as well. I tried to convince myself that, unlike Michael and Janet, I was sure to be ready for any move he made against me. But I also decided it was time to finally tell Williams about my list of suspects, short as it was, just in case things didn't work out the way I hoped. After all, he was the only other person left standing who was suspicious enough about the infections to take over the hunt. I'd phone him tonight, when he was back in his hotel.

In case things didn't work out the way I hoped—I cringed as I thought of the phrase. It was one I sometimes used to prepare a patient for the possibility of death.

Brendan was asleep when I got to the house, and I resisted picking him up and rocking with him. The Phantom could add making me afraid to touch my own son to his list of victories.

After I showed Amy, our nanny, how to give him his medicine—the banana-flavored liquid looked a lot easier to down than the big red-and-black capsules Amy and I had to cope with—I spent time explaining to her that Janet was stable and the medication for us was simply a precaution. She looked worried and asked a lot of questions about *Legionella*, but most of those questions were about what early signs she should watch for in Brendan.

My long overdue shower came next. I turned the nozzle on full and stepped into the heat, steam, and noise. For something like a second, enveloped in the force and feel of the water pounding down on me, my mind washed itself free and gave no thought to the gathering dangers outside.

Finally, sitting on the side of my bed, barely able to stay awake, I phoned ICU at University Hospital and learned from one of the nurses that Janet was sleeping, her condition no worse.

"By the way, the first of your guards is here," the woman added. "He's big, I'll grant you that."

"Good," I replied sleepily.

"And your wife's hopping mad at you about it."

Muffy jumped up beside me as I put down the receiver and lay back, ready to surrender my mind to sleep for a while. Tonight, I thought, if Miller kept his team quiet, we might grab the shadowy figure prowling around in the asylum and put an end to the need for guards.

Lingering on, the image of that dark shape trespassed into my dreams. I was chasing it through dark passages lined with stone walls and floored with earth. However fast I ran, the form ahead disappeared around corners and turns in the endless maze. Some of the passages must have come back out behind me, because soon, whoever I was hunting was behind me, and I was running for my life.

The ringing wouldn't stop. It went on and on, louder and louder, piercing the blackness and hurting my ears. I knew it would go away if I waited long enough, yet every time it sounded, I got pushed closer to opening my eyes. One more ring and I'll take a look, I promised, but I let three more go by. Finally my eyes did open, and all I saw was black. It was night, and the luminous dial on the alarm clock read 9:10. I flailed around with my hand, found the phone, and managed to get the receiver end to my ear. Cam's voice startled me awake.

"Earl, get over here as fast as you can!"

I was instantly on my feet. "What happened to Janet?" I believe I yelled the question.

"It's not Janet," he said quickly, his voice tremulous. "I think I found what Michael Popovitch discovered. You were right all along, but I have to show you, and I want Williams here as well. Do you know how I can reach him?"

I switched on the bedside lamp, found my jacket where I'd dropped it, and fished out the paper with Williams's number.

Once I'd given it to him, he ordered, "Meet me in my lab!" then hung up without waiting for my reply.

Twenty minutes later, at 9:32, I sped onto the grounds of University Hospital. Despite my recent practice at driving fast through waterlogged streets, it took me five minutes longer than what Janet boasted was her usual time to make it in for a delivery. I'd spent the difference at stop lights, fighting the impulse to run the red. While waiting at one intersection, I'd called my answering service. Among the messages that had piled up over the afternoon was a request I call Mr. Reginald Fosse as soon as possible.

Through the tall trees and thinning fall leaves overhead I could see the lights of the massive building and its various wings spread wide and high into the darkness. The floodlights placed around the bases of the great stone walls made each of the sections appear separate and suspended in the mist, almost floating, like a huge cube ensnared in the surrounding branches. It was a wonder Fosse's fund-raising efforts hadn't capitalized on the eeriness of the place to turn it into a theme park by night that reverted to a major teaching hospital by day.

I found a parking space beneath the gargoyles. Though it wasn't raining, the mist was thick enough to leave particles of water on my windshield, and the air was so cold that I could see my breath. Huddled in my overcoat, I hurried from the car toward the entrance. I kept trying to fathom what could have caused such an about-face by Cam. And what had suddenly made him enough of a believer that he'd gone off in search of what Michael had found in the first place? Whatever had happened, I still didn't trust Cam and was glad that he'd called Williams to join us.

It was after visiting hours, so security once more made me sign in at their desk. Since it was the evening shift, the guards weren't the same as on the previous night, but like the others, these two were also decked out in surgical masks. The one checking out my ID said, "Oh, Dr. Garnet, you'll need us to let you into whichever records department you'll be requiring."

"Pardon?" I said, not understanding.

"Your special audit for Dr. Tippet," he explained, sounding a little puzzled, probably at my own show of surprise. "I presumed that's why you're here. We received the memo from Mr. Fosse late this afternoon saying we were to give you whatever access you needed."

"Oh, right," I acknowledged. Wouldn't it be ironic, I thought, if the hard-won access was no longer necessary? "Actually, I was called in to see Dr. Mackie tonight," I explained. "I'm to meet him in his lab."

His eyebrows shot up. "So that's where he rushed off to. Christ, he was on his way out of the hospital around six when he came over to our desk, asked to see our sign-in book. After glancing through it, he ran for the elevators." He leaned forward and whispered, "Is

there a problem? I hope there's not more people from the hospital
with that deadly infection. I heard one of the doctors from here came
down with it this morning." I could hear the fear in his voice. "Could
someone carrying that bug have signed in here and exposed us?"

"No, not at all," I lied. "I'm sure that business is under control by
now." But I was thinking, what would Cam have wanted with the
sign-in book? I finished writing *Bacteriology Lab* as my destination
and rifled back through a few pages but couldn't see anything in today's entries that I could imagine being of interest to him. Shoving
the ledger back toward the guard, I figured I'd probably find out
what it was in a few minutes from Cam himself. One thing I noted
before closing the page was that Williams hadn't arrived yet.

It wasn't until I got off the elevator in the first level basement and
started down the deserted corridor toward the labs that I realized
what I should have thought of earlier.

Perhaps Cam hadn't gone off searching for what Michael had
found after all. What if he had absolutely nothing to show me and
had lied about it to bring me here? I slowed my steps and involun
tarily looked over my shoulder.

Lighting in the wide hallway in this part of the hospital was
bright, and the shiny floor gleamed for as far as I could see. No one
was in sight. Apart from the receding noise of the elevator as it re
turned upstairs, there also wasn't a sound, and the quiet of the place
made me feel uneasy. I stopped walking when I reached Cam's
elaborate sign. Standing beside the words BIOLOGICAL INVESTIGA
TIVE STUDIES, I stared ahead into the complex of laboratories where
he was waiting for me.

We wouldn't be entirely alone, I told myself. There would be a
least one lab technician on duty for emergencies, perhaps more than
one if the caseload upstairs in ER was heavy. Plus Miller should be
about somewhere, preparing to go into the asylum; only that minute
did I remember he was supposed to have called me.

But staring down the long passageway that led into the laby
rinthian series of rooms, I didn't see a single figure come out of any
of the doors or hear anyone talking. Perhaps the technicians were
upstairs in ER, I thought, taking bloods. As for Miller, perhaps he
was also somewhere else in the hospital, lining up the electricians
and plumbers he needed. Or maybe he'd gone ahead to start the
search without me. He certainly hadn't seemed too keen to have me
along. In any event, it was possible I'd end up alone with Cam down
there after all.

Do I go back upstairs and wait for Williams? What if Cam hadn't even called him? Telling me he was going to phone him could have been another lie, said to reassure me just enough that I'd agree to come and not be too wary when I went into his lab.

I instinctively moved to press my back against the wall and kept an eye in both directions. The stillness of the place was increasingly oppressive, and I began to feel stirrings of the same panic I'd nearly succumbed to one floor below in the far more claustrophobic confines of the subbasement. I was thinking perhaps I should get the security guard to accompany me when the silence was abruptly broken by the sound of a phone ringing far off in the labs.

Someone calling for a technician, I thought. One of them might be somewhere down here despite the place appearing deserted. I swallowed and began walking toward the persistent trilling.

I passed by the doors to hematology. The lights were on, but no one replied when I poked my head in and called, "Hello!" I only heard the gentle murmur of machines. I got the same result at bacteriology. The sound of the phone continued to come from a room farther down the row of departmental signs. I reminded myself that during evening hours back at St. Paul's I'd often had to let it ring forever before getting an answer, but nevertheless I felt more than wary as I continued along the corridor. Up ahead was the bacteriology lab.

When I got near, unlike in the other rooms where the lights were on, I could see only blackness on the other side of the glass door. This wasn't unusual. Unless a life-threatening infection was in process upstairs, no one would be doing cultures or plating Gram stains at this hour. But the ringing phone was clearly behind this door. I turned the knob. It was unlocked.

I pushed it open and looked inside. "Hello?" I said to the darkness, feeling like an idiot—a very scared idiot.

The only sound besides that incessant ringing—much louder now—was the soft hum of the ventilating hoods. I could see the illuminated digital settings for temperature and humidity control above a row of incubators on the counter nearest to me. At the far end of the room was the blue glow of a computer terminal someone had left on. The noise of the phone was coming from near there. The back of the room was black as pitch and nothing at all was visible in those recesses. I felt around the inside wall near the door but couldn't locate a light switch.

The ringing kept on. Was it Cam, calling to tell me to meet him somewhere else? Or had he been suddenly summoned upstairs for some emergency? My alarm rocketed as I immediately thought of Janet. Maybe he was phoning me about her. I quickly made my way toward the sound of the phone, using the blue light of the distant computer as a beacon. Once I got near the screen, I found the receiver easily enough by the glow. It was a single line and had no indicator lights.

I picked up. "Hello, Dr. Garnet here!" My voice sounded overly loud as I broke the quiet around me.

At the other end of the connection was only silence.

"Hello?" I said again.

Nothing. Then I heard a whisper, a breath more than a voice, but coming through the silence of that open line, the soft words were as distinct as the chill that went through me.

"Look around you!" I heard whoever it was command, followed by a click and the annoying buzz of a dial tone.

I practically dropped the receiver as I turned and got ready to run. I wanted out of there.

But something caught my eye that stopped me cold.

Two words were now blinking on what had been a completely blank computer screen a few seconds ago.

I stared at them.

This time the chill up my back was like a shot of electricity.

They read, *Janet's Dead.*

I screamed.

I would have run to ICU, but my legs felt like water.

The phone. I grabbed the receiver, my hands shaking, and punched in the number I already knew by heart.

"ICU," answered a nurse coolly.

I felt so nauseous that when I opened my mouth to speak I gagged.

"It's D-Dr. Garnet!" I managed to stammer. "Has something happened to my wife, Janet?" The effort nearly made me vomit.

"One moment, Doctor," she said coolly, and put me on hold.

"Oh my God," I kept saying, feeling the burning liquid rise to the back of my throat. They've gone to get a doctor to give me the news was all I could think.

I heard the phone receiver click. The shapes in the dark room swirled, and I had to support myself with a hand on the counter.

"Hello, Dr. Garnet?" came the woman's voice I'd heard a few seconds ago. "Janet's the same, sleeping but coughing, and when she's awake, her chest is uncomfortable. But she's certainly stable. Did someone tell you otherwise?"

I couldn't talk.

"Dr. Garnet?" she asked again.

"Thank God" was all I could manage to say. "Sorry," I added, and hung up, too rattled to explain. I looked back toward the computer screen, feeling gutted by the impact of those hateful words.

It was blank again.

I ran to a nearby sink and threw up.

Why was Cam doing this to me? was all I could think after I finished heaving. He *must* be insane, bringing me here, then putting me through that kind of terror. But he'd no longer be able to deny it was him. Yet he had to know that, must have wanted to reveal himself as well as traumatize me. Why?

I finished rinsing out my mouth and could think only of getting to Janet, but I saw there were now more words on the screen.

This time I felt like heaving the monitor against the wall. "Fuck your mind games!" I yelled at it, not even wanting to give him the satisfaction of reading them.

But I did.

Look in the microscope, and see how she'll die!

"Son of a bitch!" I exploded, reaching for the phone to call security. Maybe they could trace what terminal these messages were coming from or at least be a witness to what I was seeing. I told the guard only that I needed him urgently.

But when I looked back at the screen, it was blank again.

If Cam had appeared in front of me at that moment, I'd have ripped his face off. I started to pace, feeling more enraged by the second yet impotent to do anything. How dare he play with my deepest fears!

Striding back and forth I caught sight of a tiny light from one of the back counters behind the incubators. It was screened from the door, and I hadn't noticed it when I first arrived.

I immediately knew what it was and felt sick with fear again.

I was looking at the reflector light of a microscope left on, and I was sure it was the next item of this loathsome show-and-tell game.

"Damn you!" I cursed aloud. Once more I wanted to walk away and not submit to his terror by doing exactly what he intended me to do. But once more I succumbed. I made my way through the dark to that tiny light. My eyes were adjusted now, and I could make out the counters enough to maneuver around them. I came up to the binocular eyepiece, leaned over to look through it, and saw what I'd been dreading.

The field was filled with blue-colored cocci in clusters resembling bunches of grapes.

When I looked up, I noticed a petri dish sitting off to one side of the microscope. In the ambient light of the reflector lamp I could make out that the growth medium was abundantly spotted with the gray rings of bacterial colonies. Even though they were covered by a transparent lid, and my mind told me they probably weren't airborne, I found myself holding my breath and backing away. But not before I'd read the sticker label applied to the lid that indicated these bugs were growing vigorously in a soup of nutrient well laced with both methicillin and vancomycin.

If that label wasn't a lie, the petri dish was loaded with the superbug.

All I could think of was Janet, and Len Gardner's macabre rhyme from Death Rounds: Legionella *prepares the way; staphylococcus ends the day.*

"Oh my God." I moaned. She could be infected with both after all. Her sputum might not be purulent yet simply because it was too early. "No, please no!" I continued to murmur. The untreatable organism might already be spilling through breaks in the lining of her airways and setting up to destroy her lungs, exactly as the autopsy slides had demonstrated.

I could hardly breathe.

By the time I staggered back to the computer terminal, I found yet another message waiting for me.

> *You have seen my work.*
> *I'm forced into the open.*
> *The punishers will be punished all at once now.*
> *It's incubating in fifty who deserve it.*
> *More will follow.*
> *Evacuate the innocents before it's too late.*

PART THREE

Sepsis

Chapter 18

I didn't move, couldn't even drag my eyes from the screen. My ears seemed to amplify the sound of my own breathing, and I felt my tongue catch against the dry insides of my mouth when I tried to swallow. I don't know how long I had been standing there—seconds? a minute?—staring and not wanting to believe what I was seeing, when I sensed someone behind me. I started to spin around, my hands reflexively drawn up in front of my face, and nearly screamed when I saw a figure walking toward me in the dark. Then I heard a familiar voice.

"Is that what Mackie found?" Williams asked.

"Son of bitch, you scared me!"

"Whoa!" he said, stopping while still a few feet away. "Man, are you ever jumpy. Why are you in the dark anyway? Turn some lights on and maybe you won't be so skittish. What the hell's this?" He moved closer to the computer. The blue light bathed his head in a dark glow that accentuated his broad cheeks, furrowed eyebrows, and curved down mouth. The result turned his expression into a frowning mask of polished dark wood. "Oh my God!" he exclaimed as he read. "Where's Mackie?"

"I don't know." My mouth was so dry I could barely speak. "He actually called you?"

Williams quickly straightened from peering at the screen. "He said he thought you were right all along, that the *Legionella* infections were deliberately inflicted. But this? 'It's incubating in fifty'? C'mon! Is the message for real, or is someone stringing us along?"

"You tell me. It appeared after I got here." I quickly related what had happened when I arrived, trying to keep my voice steady. He hadn't heard about Janet's being infected by *Legionella* and was visibly shaken by the news. I didn't accuse Cam outright, but by the time I told everything else, his absence was becoming more peculiar by the second.

Williams glanced at the colonies of bacteria in the petri dish, then looked in the microscope. "So why isn't Mackie here?" he demanded.

"Guess!" I snapped.

The harshness of my response made him start. He looked up from the binocular eyepiece, clearly puzzled. After a few seconds he said, "You're not suggesting . . ." As his voice trailed off, his face seemed to work in slow motion. His jaw sagged, his eyebrows rose, and his forehead molded itself into a maze of wrinkles. "Jesus Christ! You seriously think it's him?"

"Let's just say I've got a lot of unanswered questions about the man's behavior since this morning." Williams's expression grew more astonished as I explained my suspicions.

"Holy shit!" was all he said at first. He began to pace and repeatedly rubbed his hands over his scalp. Finally he said, "I have to tell you, Garnet, I've got a few problems with the idea of Mackie's being the killer. For starters, why would he suddenly contact us, terrorize you about Janet in particular, and in effect reveal his murderous crusade, especially after being so successful at keeping both it and his identity hidden?"

It was a troubling question. "I don't have a clue why," I admitted. "But if part of his reason was that he wanted to single me out for an extra dose of panic by threatening Janet, I've got to tell you, it worked."

"I'll grant you this. If Mackie doesn't walk in here pretty damn soon, what you've just suggested will sound a lot less off the wall than it does at the moment. But you haven't a shred of proof—" Williams broke off and glanced at his watch. "Damn!" he muttered, starting for the phone. "It's less than fifty minutes until the shift change at eleven o'clock, and that means we have to decide right now whether we let people go home. No matter who's behind this, we've got to assume these bacteria are what he claims they are until we can do confirmatory tests. If we act promptly, we'll have at least half the hospital workers effectively in quarantine. Keeping the workers who are here now and not scaring off the night shift before we can grab them as well will be tricky if not outright impossible."

While continuing to talk with the speed of a machine gun, he picked up the receiver and punched in enough numbers for long distance. "As far as patients, visitors, and families of workers—"

"Wait a minute," I interrupted. "How can you even consider keeping people in the hospital with a killer on the loose? He's already threatening to infect more victims. In fact, you may end up locking him in here with us."

Williams's hand froze over the phone. "Jesus!" he said, aghast, staring hard at me. "I hadn't thought of that. We'll have to protect them somehow. But there's no question we need the quarantine—" He stopped and spoke into the mouthpiece. From his side of the conversation I quickly learned he'd reached Doris Levitz at her home in Atlanta.

I was left eyeing the colonies in the petri dish. We needed confirmation fast whether they were for real. A simple Gram stain would tell us immediately if they were staph. But a culture with sensitivity studies would take two days, and without that kind of proof, no one would believe that we were dealing with a fully resistant strain of staph. What if we were to confirm which antibiotics were in the culture medium? Identifying drug levels was a routine procedure for a big city ER, and I knew that within the hour we could at least verify whether these bacteria were growing in a soup of methicillin and vancomycin. Nobody would ignore that finding.

But staring at the small gray patches on the dark brown agar made me imagine similar colonies teeming with microbes all along the lining of Janet's airways, ready to follow the *Legionella* into the tissue of her lungs. Or what if he was yet to plant them in her and was on the way to her room at this very moment? "Shit!" I raced over to a wall phone with more than one line and called ICU.

"Has Dr. Mackie been in to see Janet?" I blurted out as soon as a nurse answered.

"Why, no, Dr. Garnet. Not since this morning." It was the same woman I'd spoken with ten minutes earlier. "Is something wro—"

"Please let me speak to the guard I hired! Have him take the call from her room." While waiting for them to get a phone to her cubicle, I thought, They must think I'm nuts. When he picked up I told him there'd been a new threat and ordered him not to let anyone near Janet, Dr. Mackie included. Then I hung up.

Williams was still talking with Levitz.

" . . . we'll need the National Guard as well as the police," he said, "and certainly every available city and state public health official. You've got to get the CDC to give us a hot-zone treatment for this place, Doris! That means the mayor's office and the city's entire disaster response team will have to keep the community under control."

My head swam listening to him, and I slumped against the

counter, staggered by the implications of locking up an entire hospital. Everyone would have to be in isolation from everyone else. University Hospital would be rendered a prison. Thousands of us—orderlies, clerks, technicians, nurses, doctors, and patients—would be gloved, masked, and gowned.

"Here's the kicker, Doris. His message says *More will follow.* This creep's liable to be in our midst, moving about, selecting victims, trying to punish the punishers and anyone else who gets in his way, so don't tell me I'm overreacting . . ."

The questions multiplied. It seemed such an illogical move—Cam's declaring himself so openly if he intended to continue killing in secret—yet this madman, if anything, was logical in his tactics. For Cam to be the killer, there had to be a reason why he would set up what we'd found here, call us in, and then choose to disappear. What was I missing?

"Besides, Doris, we don't even know how long we have before the first cases might hit!" Williams was yelling now. "What do *you* propose we do for the people already incubating the damn bug? Hell, Garnet's wife may be one of them. By the time we got the results of culturing everyone again the way *you're* insisting, we could have a pile of corpses and be doing autopsies. I warn you, unless we quarantine everyone now and wait until those who get it die, we haven't got a chance to keep the organism within these walls—"

He broke off when he glanced my way. He'd said nothing I couldn't figure out for myself, but his blunt statement of it jacked up my fears for Janet until the effects of panic and adrenaline were all I could feel. From the way he was staring at me, my fright must have shown in my face.

"Call me back when you've got confirmation for the quarantine!" Williams barked and slammed down the receiver. His own face sagged, and into his eyes seeped a terrible look of pain. "I'm sorry, Earl, I didn't mean that to be as hard as it sounded. I had to shock them. They were talking about waiting for a forty-eight-hour confirmatory test."

"Help me find some way to protect her," I demanded, barely able to keep my voice from shaking. "The CDC has to know everyone in the world who's working on resistant staph. E-mail them all—anyone who's published anything about the superbug over the last year. Maybe one of them's found new answers that aren't published yet. The old answers—salves and soaps—can't be all there is." I hated the pleading in my voice. I'd heard it so often from patients and families who couldn't accept there was nothing more to be done.

He just stared at me, shook his head, and turned his palms to the heavens. "I'm sorry, Earl; I don't know what to tell you." He sounded unsure and hesitant, the authoritative tone I'd grown used to as he'd taken command over the last few days completely gone. "That sort of update we do all the time. I'll make sure that Doris rechecks for new replies, but as of last Friday, when we first got the call from St. Paul's, there was nothing hopeful in the pipeline. Certainly no new antibiotics will be ready for at least two years. A group in Denver is trying to develop a vaccine; the idea is to produce antibodies against the toxins by which staph does its damage to human tissue—"

"A vaccine! Listen, if it's life or death—"

"Earl!" he interrupted. "They're barely starting to test it on mice. Even if they had it ready for humans, remember, it's a vaccine! It would take at least two weeks before it started being effective. Anybody infected now . . ." his voice trailed off.

I felt my anguish for Janet grow so profound and dark that I couldn't move.

Williams turned away quickly, but not before I glimpsed a glistening in his eyes that I thought was tears. He obviously found it as difficult as I always did to tell hard truths.

"Dr. Garnet?" called a familiar voice at the door.

I turned and saw Reginald Fosse coming toward us. His worried expression gave his face a whole new set of creases. Behind him was the security guard I'd summoned.

"Dr. Mackie isn't here?" Fosse asked. "He phoned and said he'd found the evidence you were after. Scared the hell out of me!"

It was hard not to notice the man was dressed in a cowboy outfit.

He saw us gawking at him. "I was in the middle of a fund-raiser," he quickly explained, pointing to a card pinned to his left breast pocket which read *Buffalo Line Dancer Society—HOOFERS FOR HEALTH DOLLARS*. "And you are?" he asked, stepping up to Williams with his hand outstretched.

Williams introduced himself, showed Fosse the message on the computer screen, and began to explain what he intended to do about it.

I took the guard aside. He didn't know how to trace E-mail, but he did manage to give us light, finding the switch that had escaped Williams and me. He reluctantly agreed to check all the offices in the other labs to see if any computer stations were left on only after receiving multiple reassurances that he wouldn't "catch something" simply by looking around "down here." I assured him he'd be fine but didn't ask him if he had a habit of being vicious to patients.

By then the way Fosse's color was draining from his face, leaving it a shade whiter than lard, I knew he'd understood there'd be no more hoofing for the moment. "Quarantine? Police? The mayor!" he shrieked at Williams." What the fuck are you talking about, 'quarantine'?"

Williams towered over the pudgy middle-sized man between us. "What I mean, Mr. Fosse, is that if those threats you just read are carried out, your whole hospital may be ground zero for what could be the worst institutional outbreak since before the advent of penicillin, and, like in those times, we've got dick all to fight it with!"

At that moment Harold Miller walked into the room.

Fosse's back was to the door. "Why, this could be a prank," he was saying, gesturing at the screen.

Williams exploded. "Testing the specimen we found in the petri dish—" He stopped himself on seeing the young technician standing in the room. He took Fosse by the elbow, whispered something to him while nodding toward Miller, and led the administrator over to the microscope.

I quickly walked over to where the young technician was standing. He was wearing a jogging outfit, much more modest than those worn by Williams, and his close-cropped hair was wet, as if he'd just taken a shower after a workout.

"Dr. Mackie left a message on my answering service about an hour ago," he said in a low voice. "It said he'd found out something about the *Legionella* infections." He eyed the two men arguing and whispered, "What's up with them?"

I shrank from telling him. Not only would he learn that his mother's death was murder, but hearing that Cam might be involved would probably be equally devastating to him. From what I'd witnessed this morning, Cam had seemed to be a father figure as well as a mentor.

"We've got a problem on our hands. Someone's threatened to use microbes against certain personnel in the hospital" was all I said, promising myself that I'd take him aside shortly and level with him. Even in ER I needed a moment before breaking bad news to find the right words, and I was usually a lot less rattled there than I felt now. That Cam's display of caring could have been a sham was bad enough. That he might have comforted the son after murdering the mother was heinous beyond telling.

"A threat? What kind of a threat?" he demanded, growing excited.

"Actually it's good you're here," I continued, ignoring his question. "Find a quiet phone somewhere and call in as many technicians as you can reach. I'll explain later, but we're going to have to mobilize a huge operation in the labs tonight and, among other things, start a massive rescreening program." I spoke as rapidly as possible so as not to allow him room for questions. "By the way, what happened about searching the asylum? I never got your call."

Miller frowned at my evasions. "The earliest I could get a team organized was for tomorrow morning," he replied, glancing over to where Fosse, now red-faced, was gesticulating and speaking in terse whispers to Williams. When I still didn't explain what they were fighting about, Miller's expression became an outright scowl, but he left to do what I'd asked.

" . . . just a petri dish and a microscope slide," Fosse persisted, no longer keeping his voice down once Miller had gone out of the room. "I repeat, how do we know it isn't some hoax rigged up to scare us?"

The CEO's ongoing denial infuriated me.

But Williams handled him. "Pay attention, Reginald!" he snapped. "I'm going to teach you what it means to have fifty men and women wandering around your building with the superbug growing in them."

Fosse looked increasingly alarmed as Williams, already towering over him, drew closer. "Staph in particular gets around by touch," he continued. "It likes to live on hands, under fingernails, in groins, and up noses." As he talked, he ran his right thumbnail under the fingernails of his left hand, crudely gestured with the thumb at his own crotch, then wiped it across the opening of his nostrils.

Fosse's mouth dropped open at the unseemly routine.

But Williams wasn't finished with the lesson. He held up the extended thumb until it was an inch from Fosse's face. Fosse cringed, snapped his mouth closed, and pulled his head back.

Williams kept him cowering like that a few seconds, then softly asked, "Now are you really willing to go home, kiss your family good night, and tell them all's well?" He brushed his thumb across Fosse's lips.

Fosse shrieked, ducked under Williams's arm, and started to back away. "Now ju-just a minute!" he sputtered, spitting out and wiping his saliva away with the back of his hand. Looking wildly from Williams to me, he declared, "You two can't bully me like this! I insist we get Dr. Mackie here."

"Earl," Williams said, "I've no more time to argue with nondoctors." He made the last word sound like an epithet.

Fosse reacted as though he'd been slapped. "How dare you speak—"

"Whoa! Settle down, both of you," I ordered.

"Are you going to tell him what you suspect about Mackie?" Williams asked, his voice coldly neutral.

Fosse released Williams from his glare and turned to me. "What does he mean?" he demanded, his hostility unabated.

I hesitated a moment before replying. Not understanding why Cam had abandoned his secrecy increasingly bothered me. Without that, I knew, I didn't have a good grasp of what had happened tonight. Maybe the man in front of me had the answer. "Mr. Fosse, why was Cam Mackie so defensive about my looking into the matter of the Phantom?"

He flushed an even deeper shade of red, then stammered, "I . . . I told you, I've no idea—"

"When I asked you in your office today, I think you lied when you said you didn't know. I want you to level with me now!"

"Oh, God! Cam couldn't do this—"

"Why was he so goddamned uneasy?"

"Look, I don't want to discuss—"

"Tell me!"

Fosse swallowed. "Why is it important? After all, a great man's reputation is at stake."

"Could he have been afraid I was about to stumble onto some proof he couldn't deny, something that would make it so obvious he was responsible for the infections that he knew he could no longer hide his guilt?"

"No! It was nothing like that. They were simply old rumors, never proved—"

"What was he afraid I'd find?"

Fosse swallowed a few more times. Then he seemed to slump. "All right," he said, taking a big breath and letting it slowly run out of him. "Two years ago, because of what happened to his father and because of his well-known abhorrence of anyone being cruel to patients . . ." Fosse paused for yet another large intake of air, ". . . there were whispers by some that he might be the one behind those events attributed to the Phantom."

Whispers from two years ago. As startled as I was at the revelation—it certainly could be the reason that Cam hadn't wanted me dredging up stories about the Phantom—I doubted the old rumors would have been enough to make Cam give up his cover if he were the killer. But they were enough to make *me* walk back to the phone and pull an end run around my own confusion, Fosse's protests, and all the institutional denial a place the size of University Hospital could muster. Let the professionals sort it out, I decided as I called the police to report that a death threat had been made against my wife.

"What are you doing here, Dr. Garnet? Is Janet okay?" asked a group of case room nurses who were on their way to work.

I was back in gloves, mask, and green gown again, waiting at the front security desk for the homicide detective I'd spoken to. It was 10:40, and already people on the night shift were arriving. Despite my outfit—Williams had declared that as of now everyone in the hospital must put on protective gear—some of the women who worked with Janet had recognized me as they flashed their identity cards to the guards.

"She's the same," I told them, "and thanks for asking. I'll give her your regards." I'd detoured through ICU on my way to the main entrance. Janet had been sleeping, but I'd hastily skimmed through her chart and grilled her nurses until I'd satisfied myself that for the moment there were no beginning signs of staph. Yet there was no lessening of my panic, knowing full well it could be too early to tell. I also knew that my only chance of stopping the organism was to figure out how he'd put it into her if he had, and, if possible, how to get rid of it before the infection started. If Phyllis Sanders's course was typical, I had very little time to do so. It had at least been reassuring when the private guard told me that so far no one had even tried to get anywhere near Janet.

Her case room colleagues didn't hide their quizzical looks at my costume as they hurried on their way, and I was glad they hadn't time to ask questions about it, which I didn't want to answer. They'd find out soon enough, once everybody from the night shift was safely inside.

The detective who was on his way to take my report was the only cop I knew personally in Buffalo. I'd managed to convince the police dispatcher who'd screened my call, after a bit of an argument to track him down for me. Within minutes, much to that dispatcher's surprise, Detective George Riley of homicide had agreed for me to be patched through to him.

"Hi, Doc," he'd said sleepily. "This can't be good news."

I'd helped him last year during the investigation of our former CEO's murder. I had mixed feelings about the man. He was as much a bureaucrat as a detective—always protecting his ass against his superiors—but he'd listened to me when none of the other investigators had, and I figured I needed that kind of help right now. After hearing only the brief description that someone was trying to kill Janet and perhaps others with a deadly bacteria, he'd sounded incredulous but had agreed to come at once.

As I stood there waiting for him, the stream of workers, mainly nurses, continued to file into the building. They remained relaxed as they passed the security guards, obviously still unaware that they were walking into a quarantine.

Even before I'd left the lab, Doris Levitz had phoned back confirming the CDC agreed to throw its weight behind the measures that Williams had demanded, and Fosse had succumbed to the inevitable. On my way up the stairs there had been an announcement on the PA that all staff currently on duty would remain at their posts during shift change and that supervisory personnel were to assemble in the auditorium at midnight for further instructions. "The hospital has been ordered to remain on standby, pending further information about a possible external disaster," declared the carefully worded announcement. Speculation was probably going on right now about what to expect—a plane crash, a bus accident, a bombing somewhere—yet I doubted anyone would guess immediately that they themselves were the potential victims and that they were about to become prisoners. The minute they were told to put on protective gear, however, suspicions would skyrocket. But it was after the midnight meeting when they'd finally be told about the Phantom that I expected all hell to break loose.

The security guard who'd come back from checking the offices whispered to me that he'd already been ordered to have his men position themselves at the exits of the building and not let anyone leave. Before hurrying off, he also advised me that he hadn't found any open terminals but that Mackie's unit was still warm.

I moved closer to the front doors and relished the cool night air on my forehead. Wearing the gown over my clothing felt hot, and the mask, as usual, was stifling. But it was thinking of Cam and what lay ahead that had my brain on fire. The one question—why would he admit now that he was the killer?—continued to plague me as I readied myself to report him to the police.

I inhaled deeply, trying to pull through my mask traces of the cool air that were drifting in from outside. The extra puff of oxygen didn't give me new answers. The only reason I still came up with was that he must have figured I was about to stumble onto something current which would reveal he was guilty of causing the infections.

A porter pushed a cart stacked with surgical gowns, boxes of gloves, and masks up to the security desk.

Getting ready for the party, I thought grimly.

All the officials Williams had summoned and anyone else not slated for quarantine would now have to enter and leave the hospital in exactly the same way we entered and left the room of an infectious patient, putting on protective gear before stepping into the place, and discarding the outfit into bins on leaving. The process would be a giveaway as to what was going on. At the moment, thankfully, I didn't see anyone so much as glance at the supplies parked off to one side.

There was still no sign of Riley. "Come on," I muttered, growing increasingly impatient. I restlessly leaned against one side of the door frame, then the other, and watched the security guards checking ID. Anybody missing his identification badge had to sign in, just the way I'd had to, as any visitor would, before the guards let him pass.

The sight of those people writing in the book reminded me about Cam's glancing through it earlier that evening and then running back into the hospital. Watching a nurse hastily start adding her name to tonight's page, I wondered about what had set him off. I certainly hadn't seen anything very telling in the few pages I'd skimmed through. Yet three hours later he'd called us all and started his show rolling.

Then I thought, *Sign in, just as I'd had to, as any visitor would,* and felt a prickle of excitement run up and down my back. My God, could it be that simple? I quickly stepped over to the desk, grabbed the book from the startled nurse, and flipped back to the pages covering Saturday and Sunday.

There in front of me was what Cam must have seen.

Michael had inadvertently left an itinerary of the rooms where the guards had let him in to look at records this past weekend. Every department, every room, every place was listed with his signature beside it—*Archives, Personnel Records, Administration, Vault for Confidential Minutes, Staff Health Records, Laboratory Services, Microfilm Repository*. I could follow his route.

My excitement mounted even more as I wondered if that's what Cam had done. Had he followed Michael's "trail" and discovered it led to evidence that he knew would expose him? Michael might not have discerned who the Phantom was from what he'd found, but Cam could have felt threatened enough to think he'd been *forced into the open*.

Then my mind leaped to the most tantalizing possibility of all. Anything that had so convincingly overcome Michael's skepticism about a phantom infecting people must have laid to rest his biggest objection to the idea: not knowing how it could be done. Had he found out the killer's method? That could be key to saving Janet's life, to saving many lives, perhaps even Michael's own if it wasn't already too late.

I started to tremble, trying to decide what would be the fastest way to proceed. If Michael had signed for anything in each department he'd checked, there might be an individual record on-site. Or, perhaps, the clerks who'd come to work this morning would remember whatever documents they'd found left out for refiling. I could barely contain my eagerness to get started.

"Doc, Doc," a voice said repeatedly from behind. "Doctor Garnet!" It took Detective Riley several tries before he penetrated my racing thoughts.

"Whoa, Doc, you're losing me. Begin at the beginning, and take your time."

We were back in the lab, seated at the desk where the microscope was located. I was in such a rush to go after my new leads that I was having trouble relating the events of the last week in a way that Riley could follow.

He was a large man, and looked uncomfortable stuffed into a gown, mask, and gloves. Under the lights I could see perspiration forming on his forehead below the line of his thick dark hair. I'd had to help him pull everything on before we'd come down here, and knew his clothes were damp to begin with from the fog outside. Sitting there, ready with his pad and pen, he dwarfed the lab stool, its spindly legs much shorter than his own.

I settled myself down and tried to explain my story in a more logical fashion. I could hear Fosse on the phone across the room calling the hospital leadership personally—chiefs and board members—insisting that they come immediately, saying only that they'd be told about the crisis when they arrived at the midnight meeting. I knew the board members would be allowed to go home again, but the chiefs would be walking into the quarantine where they'd be held with the rest of us.

I managed to lead Riley through everything, from Phyllis Sanders's infection, through the history of the Phantom, the events in the subbasement, the subsequent infections of Deloram, Michael, and Janet, and the happenings tonight, including what I'd just discovered about the sign-in book at the security desk. "Those records could save lives," I stressed, "but we've got to hurry."

He immediately called security and ordered them to seal the rooms that Michael had visited.

I kept the rest of my account factual and, at Riley's request, omitted for the moment any mention of the various suspicions I'd had about Mackie, Rossit, and Hurst. But by now Cam's failure to show up made it almost impossible not to speculate out loud about his being involved. When Riley himself finally raised the question, Fosse, between calls to his board members, protested from his side of the room that he still couldn't believe it.

Throughout the rest of my statement, Riley took occasional notes and frowned repeatedly but interrupted only when he needed explanations about the bacterial organisms involved. When I came at last to showing him the message still on the computer, he whistled, then commented, "Jesus, Doc, your story is one hell of a lot more than a threat against your wife! I'm way over my head on this one."

"I know, but believe it or not, I was having trouble getting the CEO here to move on it," I explained, nodding toward Fosse but keeping my voice down. "I called you because I could at least report the threat against Janet myself. Things seem to be moving better now."

At that moment Williams appeared in the doorway and motioned to me to join him. He, too, was masked, gowned, and gloved and had been with Miller and his techs running tests on the contents of the petri dish. "We did a Gram stain on the colonies and confirmed they're definitely staph," he told me, "and we've detected the presence of both methicillin and vancomycin in the growth medium of the petri dish. To put it bluntly, the organism's practically marinating in the drugs, and it's still flourishing like hell."

The grim news was nothing more than I expected. I took him completely by surprise, however, when I told him about the sign-in book and what I expected that lead to give us.

"Fantastic," he replied, his eyes lighting up.

"But we'll need more doctors," I told him. "It took Popovitch two days to review all that material—what about the other ID specialists on staff here?"

"Already called in—to help out with the quarantine—but we can switch them to going through records. They're familiar with the *Legionella* cases, so they should be able to spot anything that Popovitch was able to see. But I'll need your help at the meeting before you join them."

"Hey! That search could save lives—"

"Listen! There's going to be one hell of a squawk about what needs doing here, and there's a whole lot more lives at stake if we can't make this quarantine work. I need someone local with credibility who will back me up."

"But I don't work at UH."

He winked at me and shrugged. "So? You're the *only* Buffalonian I know with credibility who'll back me up. That means you still get the job." His eyes flicked over to where Riley was now standing beside the stool. "Who's he? The dick you called?"

"Yeah," I answered rather absently, not at all pleased to be pulled from the search. "He's from homicide. I imagine he'll want to talk to you."

I introduced Williams to the detective, and as I anticipated, Riley asked Williams how seriously he took the threats against Janet and the other personnel in the hospital. I watched Riley's eyes widen as Williams outlined the full extent of a hot-zone operation.

While the two men talked, I overheard Fosse discussing the situation with the mayor and the chief of police in what must have been a conference call. He was requesting that every available officer be used to surround the hospital. The police were to arrive without lights and sirens and take up their positions in the dark with as little noise as possible. He then had a similar conversation with the governor, asking for the National Guard to be on standby.

By this point Williams and Riley had fallen silent and were listening along with me to Fosse's end of the conversation.

"We've allowed the evening staff one phone call each to advise their families they won't be home," he was explaining, "but haven't told them why yet, only that we're preparing for an emergency. I expect the shit will hit the fan in a few minutes when we start giving information and announce the quarantine. We'll be in much worse trouble by morning when the city wakes up. What we'll do with the day shift I've no idea yet, and once the media gets hold of the story, I don't know how we'll handle it all."

At that point all of us started to put in our two cents worth and, at the end, Fosse reversed his request to the governor. I heard him settle on a thousand troops, the first of them to arrive by dawn.

Never was there any mention of how much force either the police or the soldiers should use if someone panicked and made a run to escape the hospital. But Riley brought it up. He leaned over and whispered, "If any poor bastard does take off, what the Christ are we supposed to do—shoot him?"

"Sorry, Janet, but something's happened, something big. I'm here with the police."

Her eyes shot open and she groggily pushed herself up off her pillow into a half-sitting position, then shielded herself from the light with one of her hands. "What?"

She sat stock-still as she learned of the threats against her and the hospital, her face a porcelain mask. She remained almost as inscrutable on hearing of Cam's disappearance. When I told her Fosse's revelation that Cam was once suspected of being the Phantom, she declared, "Those rumors must have been pretty few and far between. I never heard them." Her tone was like ice, but she was suddenly blinking more, and I knew she was fighting back tears. Yet as I described the other extraordinary events cascading into place around the hospital, she seemed to bring even that subtle giveaway of emotion under control.

When I finished, she stared at me in absolute silence, her gaze now unblinking. Only her glistening eyes and her pupils widening with fear or anger or both continued to betray the depth of her turmoil. The quiet went on long enough to make Riley squirm. I could hear his leather shoes squeak behind me on the linoleum floor. Finally all she said was, "Cam couldn't do this."

"Why do you say that, ma'am?" the detective asked.

She looked at him as if he were an idiot for questioning her. "Because, I know the man," she replied softly, as softly as the cutting sound a scalpel blade makes in flesh. "He isn't insane, he isn't a killer, and he would never even imagine something so monstrous as what's happening here." She looked at me. "Earl, I swear I don't understand why he's disappeared, but if you've ever trusted my instincts, trust them now. It's not Cam! If the police waste their time pursuing the wrong man, it's exactly the sort of thing that the real Phantom would count on, especially if he intends to continue killing!"

While Riley questioned Janet further, I went back downstairs and met Williams scurrying off to his meeting.

"Coming?" he asked, though it sounded more like an order.

"No, I've got something to do down here first." He started to frown. "But I'll be along in just a few minutes."

"Good," he snapped, his forehead unwrinkling. "By the way, the police have formally taken over from hospital security. They've already found out that between six and nine tonight Mackie had several security guards let him into some of those same rooms and departments that Popovitch visited. It also seems Mackie was in such a hurry that every place he went he left anything he looked through in a pile for refiling." Williams started to turn toward the stairs. "I've briefed the ID group as best I can about what they should keep an eye out for," he said, speaking over his shoulder as he rushed away. "Don't be late!"

"*Best I can* my ass," I muttered, resenting Williams as he disappeared through the stairwell door. "Best for Janet would be to put *me* in with the ID group right now."

I found Miller in a classroom where he was briefing his technicians on what would be required of them tonight. Telling Janet about Cam had been difficult enough, but I knew her mettle. Steeling herself for whatever had to be faced was her nature. How Miller would take what I had to tell him, I had no idea.

I interrupted his session, asked if I could have a private word with him, then took him far enough down the hall that no one would overhear.

"In better circumstances I'd wait until you had an hour to spare and take you to an office where you could sit down, but there's no time. What I'm going to reveal to you may start to become common gossip in twenty minutes, as soon as Fosse and Williams begin their meeting, and I don't want you to find it out by chance. Brace yourself, because I'm afraid the news is bad." I took a breath, and told him everything in a rush.

Despite my attempt to prepare a few phrases beforehand, the words I said sounded hard and distant, as though they weren't my own. They seemed instead like fragments from some terrible story told by someone else.

"Cam Mackie's disappeared . . . he might be behind the threat to the hospital . . . somehow caused all the *Legionella* infections . . . may have infected your mother with the two organisms that killed her . . ."

As I spoke, I kept thinking I must be ripping him apart.

But Harold Miller reacted with silence, exactly as Janet had done. His stillness was uncanny, as though he had brought every cell in his body to a standstill and focused himself entirely on listening to how his mother had been destroyed. He didn't get angry, he didn't cry, he didn't even show astonishment. He seemed to absorb what I was telling him the way a black hole absorbs light.

I placed a hand on his shoulder to comfort him, but his muscles felt like bundles of high-tension wires vibrating under my fingers. I cast about for something to say that might soften the impact of what I'd just hit him with. "Janet doesn't believe he's done any of it. She's convinced it's all the work of someone else," I told him, not fully understanding why I did. I suppose I felt if he knew someone else had believed in Cam, still believed in Cam, he might feel less singled out for betrayal.

"Do *you* think he murdered my mother?" was all he asked, as though he couldn't process anything I'd said after that single revelation.

"I honestly don't know what to think," I admitted. "Some of what happened tonight doesn't add up, even though I confess I've had terrible suspicions about Cam myself. But Janet's adamant he's innocent, and her instincts are disturbingly good."

He looked at me with that dreadful torment in his eyes which I'd grown so used to seeing. "Thank you for telling me this, Dr. Garnet. You've no idea what your and Janet's efforts to get at the truth behind my mother's death mean to me. Not many people would do as much." His voice trembled, the sound of it resonating with strain. His vocal cords must have been stretched tight as a drum.

We talked a few more minutes. He kept the forced steadiness in his voice from cracking, and his attempt to comfort me after I'd given him such devastating news suggested a remarkable inner strength on his part. But during our brief conversation, I recoiled from the darkness and pain I felt simmering beneath the surface of his disciplined manner.

He excused himself, explaining he had to get back to his staff. As I watched his powerful shoulders recede down the hall, I could still sense the extraordinary strength I'd felt in them. He was like a volcano ready to erupt.

A ripple of alarm ran through me. I'd been so concerned about the anguish he'd feel when he learned his mother had been murdered, I never thought what he might do about it. I hoped to hell he didn't find Cam before the rest of us did.

Chapter 19

One of my patients once gave me a brutal insight into the bond between healers and the sick. "Doc, it's a matter of risk. I have it. You don't. You can empathize or sympathize as much as you're able, but at the end of the day, it's me who does the suffering, maybe even the dying, while you never have to agonize about getting out of here alive. None of you can know how I feel."

I glanced at my watch as I hurried upstairs. It read 12:20. By now everyone at Fosse's meeting knew exactly what it felt like to wonder about getting out of here alive.

The hospital sounded like a hive that had been poked with a stick. In the stairwell I could hear running footsteps echoing down at me from the floors above. Doors slammed in the distance. On entering the corridor I heard murmured conversations coming from inside a long row of offices. Phones were ringing. When I crossed the main foyer and headed toward the auditorium, I saw two uniformed police officers at the entrance, struggling into protective gear. Some of Fosse's invitees were scurrying along with me. In our gloves, masks, and surgical gowns, we looked like latecomers to some bizarre midnight costume ball.

All of us could hear the yelling up ahead well before we got to the auditorium. Two shifts of supervisors, all the chiefs, and a complete turnout by the board members shouldn't add up to more than a hundred and twenty people. But it sounded like Fosse had ten times that number in there, and all of them angry.

Those with me seemed hesitant to go in. I stepped up, shoved open the doors, and saw pure bedlam. Williams was up onstage with Fosse, and both men were desperately calling for quiet. Below them was a herd of people, all of them in protective gear, milling about the front of the stage, yelling.

"No way!"

"I'm outta here!"

"This is the United States, asshole!"

Scattered throughout the auditorium were a few dozen people who weren't joining the crowd. Up against the far wall I saw Riley, huddled with three gray-haired men. They were all staring incredulously at the scene in front of the stage. One of them turned and tapped Riley on the shoulder, motioning him to lean his head closer so they could talk. Through the gaps between the back ties of the man's gown I could see flashes of his dark blue uniform.

People in the crowd, still bellowing, started to turn and head toward the door where I was standing. A hundred and twenty people wasn't a huge number, but as a substantial portion of them approached, they looked like a mob to me. Over the tops of their heads I saw Williams's and Fosse's eyes grow big as saucers.

"Wait!" yelled Fosse.

The wild bunch was no more than twenty feet from me now and seemed pretty determined to walk out and defy the two men's authority. Riley's comment flashed through my head. *What are we going to do—shoot them?*

I hoped no police were in position yet.

I grabbed a chair, stood on it, ripped off my mask, and thought of the most outrageous thing I could say. "Hold it! I'm contaminated," I screamed.

It was as if I'd cracked a whip over every head. The group froze, and within seconds their angry shouts trailed off until there was complete quiet in the room.

I seized the advantage. "Some of you know me. I'm Dr. Earl Garnet, and my wife, Dr. Janet Graceton, is admitted upstairs in ICU with a diagnosis of *Legionella*, thanks to the creep you've just been told about."

The people closest to me pressed back against the rest of the crowd. "Get by him!" someone in the back murmured. "So what if he's infected? We're wearing protective gear!" yelled someone else. It would be seconds before they'd all start pushing their way through the doors behind me.

"Think of the people you're going home to!" I shouted. "They're not in any protective gear." They kept edging toward me. "Some of you may already be carriers. Forty-eight hours, that's all it would take to be sure you're safe—both for yourself and anybody you touch. For God's sake, act rationally like the health professionals you've always been."

"Why should we sit around and let some maniac infect us?" demanded a man near the front.

"Right!"

"Exactly!"

"Let's go!"

They surged forward.

"I know which of you he's going to kill, even which of you he may already have infected!" I yelled.

That stopped them.

"What!"

"You're kidding!"

"How can you know he's already infected some of us?"

They still sounded hostile as hell, but they remained where they were.

"I also know how we can stop him," I added. Seeing the lot of them ganged together in isolation dress had just given me an idea. "If you'll all take your seats again," I suggested, replacing my mask and stepping off the chair, "then I'll tell you exactly what I think we can do."

Fosse looked at me with a skeptical stare when I climbed up on the stage.

"This better be good!" Williams muttered through his mask.

I stepped up to the podium and began speaking without even waiting for people to take their seats. I knew my hold on them was tenuous. "For reasons I haven't time to go into now, we know this killer has a very specific agenda. All his victims are what I would call punishers, colleagues who enjoy being cruel to patients." I quickly outlined the type of abuse involved. "If we isolate them immediately, confine them all to a specific high-security ward, then I think we'd not only have taken any current carriers out of circulation, we'd also have a good chance of preventing him from infecting any others for the moment. It's only an initial measure, but it would at least keep us safe for tonight and give us time to organize a better plan."

At first no one spoke.

Then came murmurs of disbelief.

" . . . out of his mind . . ."

" . . . nuts . . ."

" . . . why would anyone kill over delayed pain meds . . ."

A woman glared up at me from the front row. "Supposing what

you say is true, and from what you've told us so far that may be supposing a lot, do you know these 'punishers' by name?" she demanded sarcastically.

"No, but they know who they are, and I'll lay you odds so does everyone who works with one of them."

"Why would they step forward or agree to be locked up?" called out a man in the back row.

"The best reason in the world—self-protection. Turning themselves over to us would be their best bet to keep from being killed. Of course, if any of them don't see it that way, I'm sure their colleagues could be persuaded to hand them over. Who wants to be near a potential target?"

"They could run," he persisted.

"They could already be infected," I shot back. "Without our help to decolonize them, they're dead. The CDC also has the means to pull in any experimental therapies that might exist against this bug, in case decolonization doesn't work." I knew I was resorting to *bold-faced lying bluff*, but if I didn't tempt the punishers into coming forward by offering them false hopes, I doubted they'd step up and identify themselves in exchange for salves and soaps. "Cooperating with us is their only chance of surviving if this killer's already got to them," I declared without batting an eye. I'd lost a few of my scruples during my battle with the Phantom.

More questions poured out, and Williams started helping me answer them. My ideas outraged some, brought on the derision of others, but no one left the room. The longer they discussed a plan about how to curtail carriers and prevent more killings, I figured, the less likely they were to cut and run. But it was disaster planning raised to the level of a jazz riff. I kept making up answers as they asked questions, throwing out solutions without a thought, afraid to stop in case the first hesitation would cause doubt and the whole scheme would collapse around me.

Maybe it was the result of too much coffee, too little sleep, or a whole lot of wishful thinking, but shortly after 2:00 A.M. even the lawyers in the crowd—there seemed to be a disproportionate number of them on the board of UH—were giving their cautious approval to what we'd come up with.

"Put it this way," one of the lawyers said, "by the time we get through the screaming with the civil liberties types, you folks will have your forty-eight-hour culture results. We've got enough stalling power to give you that."

We'd first concentrated on immediate measures for everyone already in the hospital—steps that were intended to get us through the night and into the next day. All staff would be screened immediately and remain quarantined on the wards where they worked. They in turn would screen all the patients on those wards. The cultures would not only be processed by the labs at UH but by every bacteriology facility in the city; this would provide resources enough to test everyone immediately and simultaneously. Those at risk for being targets, the punishers, would be rounded up and placed in separate wards; Fosse would open a wing for them that had been closed as a cost-cutting measure. They'd remain there under protective guard until all cultures were proven negative or until those who were already infected became ill. While waiting, the high-risk group would be offered prophylactic erythromycin and the sort of decolonizing procedures Williams had suggested back at St. Paul's— bactericidal soaps, mupirocin ointments up the nose, and nasal lavages. To reduce the risk of spreading the superbug into the general population of the hospital, anyone who did fall sick in that ward would be cared for by those who remained well, minimizing the need for additional personnel to go in and out of that particular quarantine area.

It was the Phantom's perfect irony, I thought—punishers taking care of punishers.

Throughout all this talk, Riley had been joined by more and more gray-haired men. The surgical gowns hid their rank, but each new arrival seemed to bring the ones already there to attention, and I could imagine the ever-increasing amounts of gold braid under the already bulging sleeves of their protective wear. The last of these men to enter the room stepped up to the podium, introduced himself as the deputy chief of police, and assured us that University Hospital was now surrounded with enough police officers to prevent anyone who refused to cooperate from getting through their lines.

Left unsaid, again, was how they'd stop anyone who tried.

He then explained that each supervisor would be accompanied back to his or her ward by two police officers. More could be summoned in an instant if the so-called punishers didn't agree to come along to the wing that Fosse had designated for them.

We even managed to convince ourselves that we could avoid transferring out the patients, for the moment. While new admissions and emergencies would be directed to other hospitals as of now, in the morning Fosse would stress to the media that these safeguards were precautionary measures only, that the patients already here would be perfectly safe, and that staff using reverse isolation techniques would continue to care for them. The "threats," he would emphasize, were only against specific hospital personnel, all of whom had been taken off duty and placed in isolation for their own protection.

Planning for beyond the morning was more problematic.

". . . direct the day shift away from UH to alternative quarantine facilities . . ."

". . . what about separating out the punishers from this group as well—they're most at risk to be carriers . . ."

". . . live-in contacts of all our staff should be screened, maybe quarantined . . ."

". . . contact all workers who are at home before they start coming in. Instruct them where to report . . ."

". . . we'll need a communications team. Some clerical staff will have to be called in to help us here . . ."

The strategy slowly took shape, the amount that needed doing outside the hospital being clearly greater than what we had to accomplish within, with one exception.

"But the killer may be locked in quarantine here with us," protested a young nurse in the front row. Her lone voice brought absolute silence to the room.

Then someone else asked, "Do the police know anything about who's doing this or how he's managing to infect people?"

"The police are investigating," Fosse replied coolly.

The evasion prompted someone to yell, "There's a fucking maniac on the loose, Fosse. We've got a right to know when the police think they'll nab him."

"Right!"

"What are the police doing about this psycho?"

"How the hell can you say it's safe for any of us to stay here?"

Noisy shouts of agreement and demands to be told what the police knew continued to come from everywhere in the room. Unruliness was threatening to erupt again when Riley got a nod from one of his superiors and hopped up on the stage.

"Hold it!" he yelled, his hand up to the group as if they were oncoming traffic. "I'm Detective Riley and am leading the investigation into who's responsible for the threats made against people in your hospital. We've got two jobs to do here. One's in your hands—to keep everyone safe from this bacteria. Mine's to nail the creep, as Dr. Garnet so appropriately called him. I also think Dr. Garnet's plan is the best way for the moment to keep everyone safe from this killer. Within the confines of your own wards, you'll immediately know if an outsider has entered your area and we can grab anyone who shouldn't be there in seconds. I suggest the sooner you get back to your floors and get organized, the quicker we'll make it impossible for whoever's doing this to get to you. To answer your question about what we are doing to apprehend him, we've called up every available police officer in the city to work on this case and have even alerted the FBI, requesting that they check their national files for any individual or group with a history of terrorizing hospitals. As for pursuing local leads, we intend to start interviewing your staff in groups, floor by floor, tonight."

He must have had a lot of practice in settling down a crowd. A low rumble of mutterings rolled through the room, then once more voices of reason replaced voices of rage.

". . . what if we also move the staff that is here now away from UH, once outside sites are provided for everyone not yet in quarantine. That would take away the killer's hunting ground . . ."

". . . pull all our staff from patient care immediately . . ."

". . . It'll take days to round up enough staff from other institutions to replace them all, but if the patients knew we were working toward that end, they might be reassured enough we wouldn't have to move them at all . . ."

"Where's Dr. Mackie? Why isn't he here by now?" someone called out from the middle of the audience. I recognized him as one of the department heads at UH but couldn't recall his name.

Fosse answered without hesitation, the lie at the ready. "We haven't been able to locate Dr. Mackie to inform him what's happening yet."

The meeting was then adjourned, and everyone started to file out the door. Out of the general noise I heard one voice murmur, "Doesn't this sort of remind you of that Phantom business two years ago?"

"It's not how the Phantom infected all those people that I'm asking you about. I want to know how *you two* would do it," Riley demanded. He'd asked Williams and me to stay behind in the auditorium for a few minutes. While Williams was half sitting on a large table at the far end of the stage sipping a coffee, I was leaning against the podium, and the detective was pacing the distance between us. All three of us were squabbling over the best way to stop a killer.

"Shit!" growled Williams. "How *he* did it or how we'd do it, what's the difference?" He kept glancing at his watch, making it obvious he had far more pressing things to do. "I told you; we don't know."

I also had no time for whatever distinction Riley was trying to make, its usefulness escaping me entirely. I was already angry that the meeting had delayed my own attempt to discover Michael's find.

"Look, Riley," I began, trying to keep my impatience from souring what little civility was left in the room, "I told you before that lives may depend on our figuring out how he plants the staph organism on his victims. What little time we may still have to use that information is running out fast. If either Dr. Williams or I have any new ideas, we'll page you immediately—"

"No, you look, damn it!" Riley interrupted. "*Catching* this creep will save lives. Mackie's nowhere to be found in the hospital, and we had no better results when a dozen of my men searched the asylum. Unless this Phantom of yours is so stupid that he's hanging around waiting to get caught, the only way we'll get him is if you two help me learn how he works. I've got to know what he thinks, what he needs, and how he has to prepare in order to strike his victims. With information like that maybe I can anticipate his moves and ambush him."

"But that's why you've got to let me at those records—"

He cut me off with an impatient wave of his hand. "I've got a man checking regularly with that group of ID specialists who are down in the archives. They keep saying it's slow work. Hell, your friend took two days to find whatever it is we're after. I need information right now!"

"So?" said Williams. "Your little pep talk doesn't change the fact we don't know how he does it. And every minute you keep us here, the greater the chance this quarantine will fall apart."

The sides of Riley's jaw muscles bulged against the ties of his surgical mask. "Let me tell you how cops work, Doctor," he replied through what sounded like clenched teeth. "When we don't know how a crook has done a job, sometimes we go to the scene and figure out a way to do the crime ourselves."

Williams snorted, "Well that explains a lot."

Oh, Jesus! I thought. "Come on, Douglas! We're all tired and scared. We don't need to start snarling at each other."

"Sorry," he said immediately, "but I have to get upstairs." He stepped away from the table. "And I'm afraid I've got to bring you with me. You did a fantastic job of settling people down here tonight when I wasn't able to, but that was just a preview. No one on the floors is going to take the news that they've been slapped into quarantine any better. We're both going to have to run all over the building talking down reactions just like the one you saw here. We blow it, and there'll be a major stampede out of the hospital."

"No!" I started to object. "You can't keep me from the chart search—"

"For Christ's sake, Earl," Williams snapped, brusquely silencing me, "get the priorities straight!" Before I could say anything in reply, he spun around and laced into Riley. "As for you, Detective, I know you've got to be as scared as I am about what can happen if a few hundred people charge that police line. We also both know that despite orders not to hurt them, all it takes for a disaster is one nervous rookie who unholsters a gun, or a panicky citizen who struggles too long in a choke hold. Even a worse possibility, Lord help us, is that someone does get safely through and carries the bug into the city. By the time we'd track down anyone who was a carrier, who knows how many times he or she has picked their nose, then reached out and touched someone."

Riley put new levels of stress on the ties of his mask. "All the more reason, Doctor, to give me what I need now," he insisted in a quiet voice, showing remarkable restraint. "Those people upstairs are going to be a whole lot easier to keep in line about the super-bug if they expect we're about to nail this—how did they put it?— 'maniac.' You got a pretty good preview of that reaction as well!"

Williams crossed his arms in front of his chest, still gripping his now empty cup, and glared at Riley. From the eyes up he looked anything but happy, yet he stayed put.

Riley continued. "As I was saying, solving the same problems that the crook had to solve in order to carry out his crime can put us on a similar wave length."

Williams groaned.

Riley stepped up to within a foot of him and became even more pedantic. "Occasionally it makes us do the same as the guy we're after—walk where he walked, touch what he touched, that kind of thing. Who knows what traces of himself he left behind—a hair, a torn fingernail, a shoe print even. The point is, when we can get that close to where our quarry's been standing, sitting, climbing, and so on, there's no telling what we'll discover about how he committed his crime." He was eye to eye with Williams. "Now let's get to work. As you can see, you're not the only one with things to do tonight!"

Williams let his exasperation show by heaving a huge sigh. "Your little game won't change the fact that we don't—"

Riley pivoted to face me. "How would *you* get the bugs?" he snapped.

"What?"

"I said, how would you get this super bacteria he's using?"

"I couldn't," I answered. "It would take some kind of skill in recombinant DNA techniques." Concentrating on what Riley wanted became difficult as Williams's grim warning about hysteria spreading throughout the hospital began to work on me. Any fleeting optimism I had that we might get control of the situation suddenly seemed stupidly naive.

"Is there anyone here or at the university who could do that kind of work?" pressed Riley.

I turned to Williams. "Is there?"

He continued to glare at Riley. "Not that I'm aware," he replied. While his gaze transmitted a thousand volts of fury, to my surprise he actually sounded resigned to sitting through the exercise.

It was Riley's turn to exhale with exasperation. "Try to focus on how you'd do it with what's at hand," he instructed, catching us both in a stern glower that probably only cops were licensed to use. "Stick to what's here, what's done as a matter of routine in the hospital. This guy's bamboozled the lot of you with these bugs for a long time and used them to commit two murders without anyone knowing. That suggests his method was simple. Most brilliant crimes are. The more complex schemes tend to fall apart."

Williams leaned back against the table again, cocked his head, and said, "Okay, I'll play your little game, since that seems to be the only way you'll let us out of here. If I were this creep and I wanted to make a superbug without getting too fancy, I'd think about using the natural way—conjugation. Bugs lying around together in a tube of shit—now that's pretty low tech." He crumpled his styrofoam cup and flung it the width of the stage into a cardboard box full of refuse.

Then he gave me a sly wink and cracked, "Trouble is, I'd have to hang around a lot of assholes waiting for the product."

Riley exploded. "Goddamn it, Williams, if you don't start cooperating, I'll slap an obstruction—"

"We're wasting time!"

"I'm warning you, obstruction of justice . . ."

Williams's smart remark had set off an idea. I tuned out his wrangling with Riley and quickly thought it through. After what was admittedly a brief analysis, I began to feel in my bones it was an idea that could work. "Oh my God!" I exclaimed, my excitement erupting.

Williams and Riley immediately stopped arguing and stared at me. "What?" asked Riley.

"You're right, Douglas. Conjugation—Cam could use it!" And so could Rossit, I thought fleetingly, rushing on with my explanation. "Just plate MRSA and VRE in the same petri dish and let them grow together. Keep growing the mix over and over, until sooner or later, it happens. The two organisms exchange genetic material . . ." My voice trailed off. It was so simple—so sick-in-the-pit-of-my-stomach, chillingly simple.

"Jesus Christ, Garnet, that's it," exclaimed Williams, slamming his hand on the table and jumping up out of his slouch. "Routine screening for MRSA and VRE could have given Mackie the organisms he needed to start with."

"What do you mean?" demanded Riley.

Williams ignored him and kept right on talking to me. "Suppose you or I were culturing someone with MRSA. What's to stop us from keeping a swab on the side and culturing up our own private stock of the organism? We could do the same while working up a carrier with VRE. We'd have the ingredients."

Turning my way this time, Riley insisted, "Explain, damn it!"

I was pumped. My mind raced through the next steps of how it could work. I picked up where Williams left off. "Plate the two organisms on a culture dish together. Let them grow side by side. Then add a dose of vancomycin. If any staph bacteria survived, he'd know that his MRSA had acquired the VanA or VanB gene from the resistant enterococci and that he had the superbug. It could take a lot of tries, but sooner or later, he might find that it had happened. All that'd remain for him to do would be to plate more and more cultures of the surviving staph organism, and presto, he'd have his supply—enough superbug to infect this whole hospital."

"Jesus!" repeated Williams. "He could do it in a couple of petri dishes slipped in among the hundreds done here daily. Or even if he had kept it off-site of the lab, he could hide a supply out of the way and wouldn't require much more than an incubator like the ones kids use to hatch baby chicks. The whole setup's at the level of a school science project."

"He could move it around on a cart," I added, thinking about my encounter in the subbasement.

"What about the *Legionella*?" Riley asked. He'd stopped trying to get explanations of the technical jargon. He must have decided he'd finally gotten Williams and me on too good a roll for him to keep interrupting us.

"Same way," answered Williams. All his hostility toward the detective vanished. It had been replaced by the exuberance of discovery. "Screening. Water supply sites are notorious for harboring that bug; we find it even in hospitals that claim they're clean."

I remembered Michael's telling me the same thing—a week ago back in my office when he'd insisted that he come here to investigate the source of the nurses' infections. It seemed a lifetime ago.

"It wouldn't be impossible to find a contaminated water source," Williams continued, "confirm it by special culture, then let the organism multiply in samples of the water. As long as he kept them from being heated past seventy-seven degrees centigrade—that's the temperature *Legionella*'s killed at—he could end up with a super-concentrated solution of the stuff by simply letting his specimens sit around, not too hot, not too cold."

"One more question," Riley said. "Why go to the trouble of making the superbug? Why not be content with killing people by using *Legionella*?"

It was a good question, but I was able to answer it without hesitation because once having climbed inside the Phantom's way of thinking, it *was* possible to see things from his point of view. "*Legionella* offers a chance to be treated," I said with unseemly excitement. "The superbug is a sentence to certain death. If the purpose, besides killing, is to increase the terror of the victims, what's more horrifying than knowing that you're going to die within days, and that you'll die choking? If your purpose is to panic an entire hospital, hell, the choice is obvious. *Legionella*'s scary. The superbug's the stuff of nightmares."

I caught Williams staring at me and nodding in agreement. His eyes conveyed incredulity as he admitted, "I'm amazed we managed to figure out so much!" He even apologized to Riley. "That's a hell of a neat trick you have there, getting people to know what they think they don't know," he said in a very sincere tone, then couldn't appreciate why Riley and I were laughing at him.

But not even Riley had tricks enough that we could solve how the Phantom managed to infect people with these bugs.

The three of us were headed upstairs. We were hurrying along the corridor leading away from the auditorium when I asked the detective what he figured were the chances of picking up Cam in short order.

"If he's alive, not bad."

"What?"

None of us broke stride, but Williams matched his step to Riley's and mine, placing the detective between us. "Explain," he said curtly.

Riley answered. "Right after you and I first talked, we sent a patrol car over to his apartment. He's not there of course, but his bank books and passport are. He lives alone, yet seems to be friends with a lot of his neighbors, so we had a nice-sized group, including his landlady, telling the officers that they hadn't seen him tonight. As I said, he's also nowhere to be found in the hospital. If your theory's right and he is the killer, then he's hiding out somewhere not too far away, probably getting ready to pounce. That's still *our* number one theory as well—we've issued a warrant to bring him in for questioning—but it will take more than theories before we can convince a judge to let us do a real search of his rooms, his office records, his car—"

"Then why did you say he might be dead?" I asked.

"Dr. Garnet, you should listen to your wife. She knows how to look at all the possibilities, not just one or two. After we talked awhile, she began to wonder if he hadn't been framed."

"What?" I felt the snakes in my stomach spring to life and start coiling into knots.

"Consider it," Riley said. "Mackie, if he's innocent, may have found something, just as he claimed, which revealed not only that there was a phantom at work but also who it was. His sudden disappearance could have been engineered to keep him quiet."

"Jesus Christ!" The notion demolished every thought I'd had about the man. I was speechless. The possibility of *his* being set up had never occurred to me. I looked across at Williams. His frown was headed into the front half of his scalp. I guessed he hadn't included the idea in his differential either.

We were entering the main foyer. Our shoes clacked on the marble, startling the two security guards at the desk. I could see a uniformed police officer standing at ease outside the glass doors.

Riley went on talking. "Your wife also remains convinced that until tonight Mackie was steadfast in his conviction that the infections couldn't be deliberate, so, like Popovitch before him, he must have found something that changed his mind. Dr. Graceton had an interesting suggestion, too, about why he might have been so defensive about the Phantom—besides his fear that you'd resurrect the previous rumors. What if back then he dropped his investigation into those events simply to let those same rumors die out as quickly as possible? Wouldn't he feel guilty about doing so? The point she's making is that the man could be entirely innocent of being the Phantom, and you would still have struck a nerve in him when you started to poke about in the archives."

"You and Janet seem to have had quite a talk," I said.

He ignored my comment as we hurried along. "The one thing your wife and I are in complete disagreement on is whether the murders are connected to the amalgamation of your two hospitals."

My surprise at her telling him that theory must have shown in my eyes.

"Oh yes, she told me your suspicions, all right. Except she's pretty skeptical about them. But I have to side with your idea; half a billion budget is a lot of motivation for anybody to do anything. Don't you worry, we'll look into this character Rossit, and of course Hurst; I remember *him* from when we were investigating the murder of your former CEO. As far as all those captains of industry on your board, well, I can tell you for a fact that taking care of business in this town can get pretty rough."

"Except they wouldn't destroy the spoils of their victory," I said without thinking. The realization had just popped out, unbidden, almost before I'd known the thought was in my head. Riley and Williams were looking at me sideways, puzzled expressions on their faces. I quickly explained. "Hurst and his friends would want UH left intact so they could dominate it."

"Maybe not," Williams countered. "At least not if they didn't want to share the half billion."

Riley and I both looked sideways at him.

He explained while all of us kept up the brisk pace, "Some hospital mergers I've witnessed actually abandon one of the two institutions and create a single superhospital. If UH crumbles, then St. Paul's becomes the biggest show in town. How far would your board, Hurst, and guys like Rossit go to win that kind of prize?"

By the time we finished chewing over that possibility, we'd reached the third floor by elevator and were in the corridor passing some windows overlooking the grounds. Williams rushed on ahead toward the nearest ward, but Riley paused to look outside and I paused with him. I could see human forms reflecting the unmistakable glint of badges. Here and there police officers wandered into lighted areas where the amber glow of sodium lamps illuminated the little white plumes of their frosty breath. For about a second these wisps would drift along before dissipating and blending in with the haze of gray fog that filled the night. Farther back in the darker areas under the trees I caught the reflected glimmers of blue and red above the occasional gleam of white paint, the pattern repeating itself over and over—police cars.

Standing there, I found myself wondering if the Phantom was again out there somewhere, beyond the circles of police, past the mist, gloating once more over the impact of his work on the hospital. But was it Cam, forced out in the open, the advantage of his invisibility ripped away? Or was it Rossit, as an agent for Hurst and his board, executing the takeover that Williams had suggested? Or was it someone else, as Janet thought, who still evaded me, the master controller, his invisibility assured because he'd just offered us Cam as a scapegoat . . . with my help.

Williams and I had no method as we attempted to calm people and keep everyone rational. We simply made it up as we ran from floor to floor, pleading the same arguments we'd used on the fly earlier in the auditorium and at St. Paul's last week, coaxing, cajoling, intimidating, and when that didn't work, we called the cops. We tried to teach a few of the clinical chiefs the things to say, hoping they'd exert some leadership, but they were too rattled themselves to be of much use. They stared at me blankly as I implored, "For God's sake get a grip. If we don't settle people down, someone's going to bolt and inadvertently carry that organism out of here. At least help us get everyone cultured."

Armed with a specific task, these "leaders" seemed to collect their wits enough to get working, but I found myself fuming at them for their feeble performance. It was clear the kind of weak leadership Fosse had encouraged.

Everywhere Williams and I went, we initially met panic, defiance, and anger—what we'd seen in the auditorium but tenfold. Physical scuffles broke out as some nurses tried to storm out of their wards. Orderlies had to restrain their own colleagues. Hallway shouting matches woke up the patients who soon learned enough fragments of what was happening to become panicky themselves. Fosse at least had had the foresight to cut off outgoing phone lines. But then the already explosive mood was fueled by outraged men and women screaming that they'd been foiled in their attempt to contact families, lawyers, and even the media.

The dynamo that came to the fore in the crisis was Harold Miller. He was everywhere, leading his small army of technicians into each and every ward, starting them off collecting cultures, then demonstrating the technique as he got the rest of the staff screening one another and the patients. Culturing and plating throughout the night, he was always explaining what he was doing, was always reassuring his subjects, and was forever offering little courtesies. More than once I saw him help people tie their masks back on or provide them with a fresh one instead. He, more than anyone, got us through the culturing that had to be done during those early hours.

The worst was rounding up the punishers. Some who were too frightened to resist stepped forward and begged our protection. Others were turned over to us.

"Looks good on you, Rachel!" a rather grandmotherly looking nurse screamed at a frightened and much skinnier, younger colleague who was being led away.

"You goddamned bitch, I'll get you for this!" Rachel screamed back. The rest of the nurses on the ward and some patients who'd been wakened by the ruckus promptly booed and hissed Rachel as she was paraded off the floor. It was certainly rough justice, and probably a few innocents were rounded up with the guilty. I winced when it occurred to me how many lawyers would be employed indefinitely sorting out what we were doing tonight.

At one point during the evening I was asked to see three nurses who had complained of flulike symptoms, but on examining them, I found that none had a postural drop in blood pressure or the biochemical changes consistent with a *Legionella* prodrome, and none of them had findings suggestive of a staph infection. They asked about antibiotics, and I told them, "Medically it's not indicated. But if you think you might be a target of the person making these threats . . ." I let the suggestion hang there.

When they vehemently denied they were "like that," I assured them again that they needed no medication, but the encounter reminded me to take the second capsule of my own prescription.

Through all of this, I kept racing back to ICU where I'd look up Janet's latest vitals on her chart and would check with the nurses that they'd seen no sign of her cough turning purulent. Despite there being no change in her condition and the guard at her door reporting that no one had tried to approach her, I'd run back to the floors haunted by my own proviso—*it's early yet.*

By 4:00 A.M. an eerie lull had settled over the hospital. Eventually, again paralleling what had happened in the auditorium, most people had settled down, started cooperating, and wanted to do what was best for themselves and their families. Culturing was mostly complete. About seventy people were under special protection. Apart from some individuals who tried to get by the guards, and a few who actually made it to the grounds before they were stopped by the police, the quarantine was intact.

To say we couldn't have hoped for better was true, but it was more an admission of how precarious the best we could hope for was. With the morning shift due to arrive within three hours unless we diverted them elsewhere, we all knew we were teetering toward worse.

I paused in front of the same window Riley and I had looked out of a few hours ago. The fog was thicker now, but I could still distinguish the shapes of police officers on patrol. The area under the trees, however, where I'd caught glimpses of their cars before, was so thick with shrouds of gray that not even the overhead sodium lamps could penetrate the gloom. Yet I could tell something new was happening out there. Through the panes of glass in front of me the persistent guttural growl of diesel engines made itself heard— the kind of noise I'd have expected from heavy equipment at a construction site.

The National Guard was moving into position.

Chapter 20

Fifteen minutes later Williams reached me by phone. "The ID guys have found something," he said curtly. "They're in archives."

When I walked in the door of that familiar room, I saw a half dozen men and women standing with Williams in front of three tables that had charts spread over them. A tall gray-headed man was directing his comments mainly at Williams. While he spoke, a few of his colleagues were sipping from coffee mugs, having untied the bottom of their masks so that they could lift them up each time they drank. A large silver thermos sat on one of the tables in their midst. The aroma of the fresh brew was tantalizing, but no one offered me any.

Riley stood off to one side, and if the way he was giving the ties to his mask a good stretch test was any indication, he was obviously unhappy. When he saw me enter, he walked over and whispered, "These guys mean well, but frankly, between you and me I don't think they'll find squat. They're too . . . too . . . well, doctorish. They're looking for medical inconsistencies, not murder."

I held a finger up to my lips, signing he should keep quiet, and focused on what was being said.

". . . Dr. Mackie had left out a few hundred charts sorted into different piles," the elder physician was explaining to Williams, gesturing to the tables.

"A few hundred!" exclaimed Williams. His frown shot into previously unfurrowed territory.

"We figured he couldn't have gathered so many without help, so we called the clerks who work here."

Behind me on a table was a phone that had a yellow *Buffalo P.D.* sticker on it. I thought about how much more comfortable I would have felt if I'd had that with me when I was here the other night.

". . . They told us Dr. Mackie had stormed in around six P.M., catching them just as they were leaving for the day. He had with him records from our own Infection Control Committee and had marked on them three lists of charts which he insisted the clerks pull. We discovered the first list was for the charts of patients who'd been screened after being exposed to Phyllis Sanders in the ten days before she became ill. He'd then sorted those into piles arranged according to which patients she'd cared for on the last day before she left on vacation, on the second to the last day, the third last, and so on. The second list was, we found, for the charts of patients exposed to Brown during the ten days preceding her *Legionella* infection. He'd arranged them the same way and repeated the procedure with the charts of patients who were exposed to the OR nurse prior to her pneumonia. Remember, these two nurses had also left on vacation a few days before their illnesses."

"That's interesting," said Williams. "How did you guys see all that?"

The older man reached for a chart on a nearby pile, flipped it open to some blue-colored pages, and pointed. "We found the pattern by looking at entries in the nurses' notes for each file. But that's all we got." He handed the chart to Williams and continued, "What I hoped to see was a single nursing act that Sanders and the two others had each performed during the days when they would have been exposed to *Legionella*. I thought perhaps we'd find they were infected during a specific procedure. Unfortunately, all the nursing procedures listed in these charts were routine—dressing changes, monitoring vital signs, administering medications—and nothing stood out. Cam must have been after something else."

Williams flipped through a few pages, then closed the file and handed it back. "Then we'll keep looking through these for that something else," he said. "I'll stay and help you."

There was a murmur of appreciation from the others sitting around the room. One of the women in the group stepped up to Williams. "Is it true that Dr. Mackie's a suspect . . ." At that point her voice lowered beyond what I could hear.

When I turned to look at Riley I could see he was anything but pleased with the results he'd just heard. He leaned over to me, his eyes wide with alarm. "You see, Doc! They found nothing, just like I told you. You've got to get me more than this, and I mean now, or your Phantom's going to get his chance to deal out another round of infections like he threatened." He sounded both frustrated and more than a little desperate. "Why aren't *you* checking out some of the other places Dr. Popovitch visited?"

I knew exactly where I'd start.

"Mr. Fosse, what got Cam Mackie off the hook two years ago when he was suspected of being the Phantom?" I asked. We were in his office. I'd dropped by to advise him I'd be working just outside his door, revisiting the vault where confidential minutes were kept, then going into the human resources department. I'd thought it wise to let him know I was there, not that he heard noises and figured the Phantom was back. Before leaving I'd decided to ask about Cam.

"Two things, really," Fosse answered, leaning back in his chair, "though one raised a few eyebrows. The whisperings about him started to pretty well die down when an attack occurred while he was lecturing out of town. What made people suspicious again was that there was another attack two weeks later, also on a day he was away. That caused a few nasty comments about the timing of the two occurrences being a bit too convenient for him. But the gossip ultimately ended when, after those two episodes, the events stopped entirely. Everyone eventually assumed the Phantom business was over and put it behind them."

"Was anyone else a suspect at the time?"

"No," Fosse answered with a shake of his head.

At that moment his phone rang. He was soon engaged in a conversation about the plans to receive the day shift at a number of outside facilities, and I stood up to leave while he was ticking off his orders.

". . . have our eighty supervisors each call twenty of their people at home from lines that are still open in administration. Tell them that there's been a threat but the situation's under control, and then direct them to where they're to report. I'm expecting all my chiefs momentarily, to further discuss strategy for the people here . . ."

That was one group I didn't want to get stuck with again, I thought as I scurried out the door.

The vault full of confidential minutes now had a strip of yellow police tape across it, making it necessary that I have both a security guard and one of Riley's men get me through the door. Once in, I retrieved the volumes containing the minutes of Cam's Infection Control Committee. They were, as I expected them to be, in their proper place on the shelf, since Cam would hardly need to look up records of his own meetings.

I hadn't paid much attention before to the order in which the Phantom's different methods of attack were used, but I quickly checked now which type of attacks had occurred when Cam was out of town. On both occasions the symptoms had resembled a SLUDGE BAM syndrome, the result of organic phosphate, or insecticide, poisoning. In fact, from Cam's committee minutes it was easy to see the overall chronology of the attacks. There seemed to be two phases. Provoked psychoses and incidents of induced vomiting were intermingled in a haphazard fashion over an initial period of four months. But then, the Phantom's activities had ended with a consecutive string of five insecticide poisonings, including the last two, for which Cam was away.

I leaned back in my chair and thought about the pattern: five insecticide poisonings in a row—three while Cam was in town, followed by the two when he was away—then no further activity from the Phantom for two years. The sequence certainly intrigued me.

At first I wondered if Cam had developed the insecticide method of attack after perfecting the other two techniques, then got an accomplice to carry it out a few more times during the out-of-town speaking engagements. But the alibi occurring twice was too clumsy, and Cam would have known it was. Fosse had probably put it mildly when he said the pair of convenient coincidences "raised a few eyebrows." So why had those last two attacks been timed like that?

I thought for a while longer. Complex scenarios suggested themselves, again involving accomplices, but none of them rang true. The Phantom's brilliance at keeping himself invisible went totally against the notion of his resorting to sharing his secret with someone else and rendering himself vulnerable to being exposed by that person.

Frustrated by the vagueness of it all, I pushed out of my chair and started to pace. One thing that struck me clearly, as an ER doctor, was how significantly more dangerous the insecticide poisonings were—potentially lethal in fact—compared to the effects of ipecac or a short-acting hallucinogen. Vomiting or seeing things for half an hour almost seemed appropriate tit for tat against the kind of petty cruelty the Phantom had singled out for punishment. After all, the cruelty, though vicious and inexcusable, wasn't a killing offense.

Even Janet had insisted her ordeal at the hands of the residents hadn't at all been typical of what Brown, and presumably the other punishers, had usually indulged in.

It felt strange to be even commenting on appropriateness when referring to the acts of a maniac. Yet switching to pesticides was a definite escalation, taking the punishment to a level where it could kill, even though the crimes remained minor. If such an irrational step-up had a logic to it, I couldn't figure it out, and I finally concluded the reason must be buried in whatever madness drove this psycho.

No other revelations leaped off the pages at me. Before leaving, I quickly flipped ahead to more recent entries in the minutes and located the sessions that had investigated both Brown's *Legionella* infection and that of the OR nurse who'd died. I learned nothing new from the committee's conclusions but scribbled down the chart numbers for each nurse's medical files. I wanted to go through the cases myself.

I paged the same guard-cop tandem I'd had before and got by more yellow tape to enter the personnel department. It was actually a set of offices—I counted nine in all—behind a main entrance door. Eight of the rooms were evenly divided on either side of a long hallway. The ninth, located at the back of the complex, was the largest and contained the files. I made my escorts wait while I verified no one was lurking anywhere, even looking into a large oak armoire full of coats which was by the main door. When I checked the file room I could see that Cam had evidently skipped these records as well; there were no folders lying around to indicate that he'd been here before me. But I knew from the sign-in book that Michael had, so I sent the two uniformed men away, both of whom seemed amused by my skittishness, locked myself in, and got to work.

I stuck to my plan and, using my list, dug out the personnel files of the Phantom's first targets from two years ago. Six had already left the employ of the hospital, but their files were kept, as were all hospital records—even those of the dead—for the possible eventuality of legal action. Of them all, I found that only three had ever had official complaints leveled against them and that none of those complaints had resulted in disciplinary measures.

The alleged infractions were exactly the sort of petty things I'd come to expect—one complainant reported being repeatedly roughly handled during dressing changes, another told of being verbally abused whenever she requested her pain medication, a third had been ridiculed for wetting the bed after her requests for a bedpan had been ignored. All three accused nurses had denied any intent of wrongdoing and were let off without so much as a reprimand. Obviously Janet was right about the cruelty being hard to prove, and it certainly was clear why most patients wouldn't even bother to report it.

The absence of so much as a nasty note in any one of the other fifteen files put to rest my earlier idea that the Phantom had encountered all eighteen punishers as a result of formal complaints being brought against them. I nevertheless wrote down the names and addresses of the three patients who had filed charges, in case I wanted to reach them. I was curious to know if they'd also discussed their problem informally and off the record with someone outside normal disciplinary procedures—someone to whom other patients might also have complained about a punisher rather than pursue the matter through proper channels.

But it was when I started paying attention to dates again that I got a big surprise. The three complaints I'd been looking at were made several months prior to the first attack by the Phantom, and the three people named in those complaints were his first targets.

I felt a prickle on the back of my neck.

What's more, each attack occurred within weeks of the hearings into those complaints—hearings that had failed to take disciplinary action against the punishers.

Like electricity on a rheostat, the prickle grew to a tingle.

I couldn't explain much else I'd encountered tonight, but I felt I was looking at what had sparked the creation of the Phantom. The sudden clarity after so many vague leads began to make me feel heady.

The membership of the disciplinary committee was included with the rulings, but I didn't recognize a single name. That didn't diminish my excitement much. I already knew the Phantom was operating outside this committee, and even though the proceedings were suppose to be confidential, if UH was anything like St. Paul's, confidential proceedings usually leaked like the Titanic.

"What have you got?" said a familiar voice from a few feet behind me.

I jumped a foot and screamed as loud as I could. Whirling in midair, I saw it was Williams. "Jesus Christ!" I roared at him.

His eyes wrinkled merrily at the corners, the result of a smile which his mask kept me from seeing. Obviously he was amused at his effect on me.

"Will you stop doing that?" I asked him crossly. "How did you get in here anyway?"

"The door was open," he said casually. "Fosse told me where you were."

"What do you mean the door was open? I locked it."

His eyes became a little less merry. "Sorry, but I found it open. Maybe you didn't do it right."

"Bullshit I didn't do it right!" I exclaimed, striding out of the room and down the hallway toward the lock in question. I was halfway there when in burst Fosse, looking wide-eyed above his mask, followed by half a dozen other people in protective gear. One of them was holding a brass lamp upside down, waving the base in the air like a club. "What happened?" Fosse demanded, breathing hard as he pulled up. "We heard a horrible scream."

"That was me," I said curtly, glaring at Williams.

The large man immediately said, "Sorry," then explained what had happened and apologized again, especially to me, for having upset everyone. But while he continued to settle Fosse and the chiefs down, I stepped over to the door and verified I indeed knew how to set the lock properly.

"Someone unlocked this door while I was working in here," I said over my shoulder. The group quickly fell silent as I turned back to them and added, "Maybe whoever it was sneaked in, then left, or maybe the person's hiding right now in one of those rooms behind you." I'd spoken coolly, looking past them toward the eight darkened doorways on either side of the long corridor.

"Shit!"

"No!"

"You're kidding, right?"

The bunch of them reflexively drew together, forming a circle with their backs to the center.

"We'd better look," said Williams quietly, no trace of the jokester in his voice now.

He moved toward the first door, slowing as he approached it, then slipped his hand around the edge of the frame. When the light snapped on Fosse and the others followed behind like a timid posse, the one holding the lamp in the air at the rear.

It was hard not to laugh as they repeated this procedure before they peeked into each room. I started to feel a little foolish at having been a bit too spooked by an unlocked door. I found myself staring at the armoire beside me, almost embarrassed at wanting to look in it again, especially after having endured knowing glances from the guard and the cop when I'd checked it not forty minutes earlier. I'd make sure Williams and his bunch were at the other end of the hall where they couldn't see me when I stole a look this time, I decided. I was probably going to take enough of a ribbing as it was when the little search I'd sent them on came up empty.

I was looking left toward the passageway, leaning forward a little, checking to see that the others were out of sight when I stepped up to the heavy wooden doors and pulled on the latch. The panel exploded open with such force that he must have had his leg raised at the ready to kick it out. The full weight of the wood smashed into the right side of my head, then my upper body, throwing me against a desk that was behind me. All I saw coming out of the cabinet was a raised lab coat held up as a screen before it was thrown roughly over my head like a sack. I was immediately squeezed by a pair of arms pinning my own down. I tried to yell but all my breath had been knocked out of me, and I couldn't see because of the coat over my head. I felt myself yanked to my feet, then one of the arms let go, only to return and deliver a hard punch right into my solar plexus. If there'd been any air in my lungs to begin with, it would have roared out of me with a bellow and brought the others running. As it was I doubled over, making little more than gagging noises muffled by the coat over my head. I couldn't breathe in and lost even more air when I started to gag on my vomit. I then felt him grab me by the scruff of the neck and yank me forward, still bent over. I've been here before, was all I had time to think before I smashed head first into something very hard.

Except this time I didn't lose consciousness. He probably hadn't been able to get me up to speed and the coat had blunted the blow, but I nevertheless collapsed into a gasping choking ball. By the time I got the coat off my head, the door leading out of the complex was closing, its motion slowed by an overhead arm attached to a pneumatic cylinder. I was halfway to my feet when Williams came trotting up the hallway, the lines in his forehead furrowed into question marks. The noises of an oak door against a skull or a fist hitting a gut weren't all that loud, but I guessed it had eventually been enough to get his attention.

"Get him," I croaked, still doubled over as I pointed toward the door just when it clicked shut.

The large muscular man was out of the room like a shot. Even with the carpets I could hear his steps pounding down the corridor as he gave chase. I staggered over to the doorway. "Call security," I rasped at Fosse, who'd finally made it up from the rooms in the rear. His "leaders" hung back about twenty feet behind him. "And Detective Riley, fast! Tell him the killer just ran out of administration."

I was now breathing a bit, but not well. At least I didn't think I was going to vomit any more.

I got to the door, more or less erect, and started after Williams. He was just exiting the far doors that led out of administration and into the rest of the hospital. Whoever we were chasing was already out of my sight. I started to jog, my breathing quickly becoming more labored and disgustingly noisy. By the time I got to those same doors, even Williams was nowhere to be seen. I stepped into the outside corridor, hoping that the linoleum floor there would amplify the sounds of running feet enough for me to tell which way they'd gone. Nothing. I located the nearest stairwell and threw open the door just in time to hear the clatter of quick echoing steps coming from way below me. They were suddenly cut off by the noise of a door slamming.

I started down.

Two floors below was main, or ground, level. I stuck my head out the door of the landing and listened. There were no sounds of running.

At the first level basement, it was the same. This creep must have led Williams into the subbasement, I thought, feeling my fear mount as I headed down that final flight. I didn't know how quickly Fosse was getting reinforcements organized, but I was sure he didn't know which direction Williams and I had taken once we were out of administration.

I braced myself as I opened the door and prepared to step into that oppressive corridor. But I wasn't prepared for what awaited me. The subbasement was in complete darkness . . . again.

Chapter 21

"Williams!" I yelled.

There was no sound.

"Williams!" I screamed.

Still nothing. I was standing in the stairwell, holding the door open, letting the light from behind me flow into the blackness of the passage in front of me. I didn't have a clue what part of the subbasement I was in; I hadn't seen any stairs the other times I was here.

I kept hoping to hear the sounds of guards or police on the stairs above. "Can anybody hear me?" I yelled up into the silence. "We need the police down here!"

No luck.

Maybe whoever it was had led Williams back to the upper floors by another staircase or had gotten far enough ahead of Williams to jump on the elevator, wherever that was; I still didn't have my bearings. All he'd have to do then, presuming he was in protective gear, was step out on any floor and become one of the fifteen hundred other people now wearing masks, gloves, and gowns.

I'd just about convinced myself I could return upstairs with a clear conscience when I heard a moan coming from far up the dark corridor.

"Williams!" I cried once more. "Are you all right?" No answer, not even another moan. "Shit!" I muttered, looking for something to jam the door open. I ended up using one of my shoes for want of anything else. I then removed its mate and once more resorted to gripping it by the toe, ready to use its heel for a weapon. As prepared as I'd ever be, I peered into the darkness up ahead and went creeping toward where I'd heard the plaintive sound.

I tried not to think of what the Phantom might have done to Williams. I tried to think even less about his waiting by Williams's body, using the moan to lure me to the same fate.

I kept to the center of the hall for as long as the light behind me illuminated my way. Then I turned a corner and was unable to see a thing. "Williams!" I called again. As before, no answer. But I reasoned he couldn't be too far off if indeed it was he who had made the sound.

I pressed ahead, my right hand feeling along the wall, the shoe ready in my left, the darkness absolute.

Twenty feet later I literally fell over him.

"Damn!" I exclaimed, going down hard on my knees. But I frantically started feeling with my hands, finding his feet, his legs, rapidly working up to his neck. I palpated around for his carotid artery. He had a pulse. I supported his head between my hands and brought my ear up to his mouth. He was breathing. But when I reached his bald scalp, even through my gloves, I could feel the warmth and slipperiness of blood—a lot of blood. "Oh Christ," I muttered.

I found the laceration by feel. I could slip my fingertips into it. It was deep, about two inches long, and on the front part of his forehead. He must have turned to face his attacker just before he got hit with something. I gently slid the end of my index finger across the bottom of the wound, feeling for any depressions in his skull or jagged edges of bone. There were none, but that didn't mean a non-depressed fracture was ruled out.

The main problem was hemorrhage. I couldn't feel any pulsing of an arterial bleed through the latex of my gloves, but any cut to the scalp could bleed heavily. I wadded up a corner of my surgical gown into a makeshift pad and pressed it firmly against the laceration. I prayed I wasn't pushing pieces of skull into his brain.

There was nothing else I could do except try to stop the bleeding. I couldn't drag him out myself and at the same time keep his head and neck stable, his airway open, and his laceration properly tamponaded. As it was, I could still feel his blood flowing through my fingers despite the pressure I was applying. "Help!" I screamed, hoping someone on the stairs would hear me through the door I'd left open. "Help me. I've got an injured man here!"

Sooner or later my cries had to attract someone—had to, damn it! But no reply came.

Then, from away in the darkness far up the corridor, as softly as a breath, I heard what made my blood run cold.

Laughter, a low, easy, rolling chuckle—distorted by the walls, it echoed toward me and was as chilling as ice. Then it ended, cut off by the distant sound of the elevator doors closing.

* * *

Riley assured me his officers had found us in less than five minutes, but as I sat there in the dark, it felt like hours. Williams had even started to come to before they'd run up to us, but I hadn't let him move. Once we got him to ER and into the capable hands of Wild Bill Tippet I could see the laceration, though bloody, was a pretty routine affair that would be made right by a bit of sewing. A subsequent CT scan confirmed there was no fracture or evidence of underlying hemorrhage in the brain.

"Do you think I'll have a scar?" inquired Williams, eyeing the needlework in a mirror before a dressing was put on it.

Tippet fluttered around us the whole time like a nervous hostess— I always seemed to have that effect on him—and reassured me endlessly that the only reason he'd missed the midnight meeting was that he'd felt he should stay with his troops in ER. "Keep them calm, that kind of thing," he kept insisting, talking at double speed. He actually seemed deflated when I admitted I hadn't noticed his absence. But I did notice now that he was wearing two surgical masks instead of one. I suspected his own fear of being in close contact with possible carriers from other parts of the hospital was the real reason he hadn't shown up.

I didn't hold his fear against him. Everyone was frightened and growing more so by the hour. I think that's why I didn't tell anybody, not even Riley, about the laughter. I'd no intention of scaring any of them any more than they already were.

But I couldn't protect myself from remembering that sound. It had seemed so unforced, as though my cries for help had been a source of real amusement to him. This Phantom might claim to be avenging past cruelties, but that laugh was as sadistic as any I'd ever heard.

I did tell Riley about hearing the elevator go up.

Nevertheless, he made his men search the subbasement and walk through the asylum again. As I expected, they found nothing.

"You sure there's no place someone could hide?" pressed Riley when his team reported back to him. We were standing outside ER, waiting for Williams. "Sewers, passageways, septic tanks?"

The men winced, and I saw one of them wrinkle his nose under his mask. "We didn't see any sewers or septic tanks," one of them answered, "but we went into everything a man could easily fit through. Besides, why would he bother to hole up there anyway?"

The officer gestured toward his gown and tugged at his mask with his glove. "What with our costumes, I've never seen a better place to hide in plain sight."

"Not if you're already well known," snapped Riley.

I interjected. "That's the point. It couldn't have been Cam. I already told you I heard him take the elevator. That meant this guy *did* go upstairs to hide in plain sight. Like you said, Cam couldn't have done that and counted on going unnoticed. He'd have had to stay well hidden somewhere else."

Riley spun around to face me. "If you're going to go running after a murderer, Doctor, which by the way, nearly got your friend Williams in there killed, when are you going to learn to consider all the possibilities?" He was fuming, as usual his jaw muscles bulging under the straps of his mask as he pretended to give me a second to come up with an answer. "Think, Garnet! Mackie could have sent the elevator upstairs empty, as a ruse, then tiptoed off in the dark and retreated to his hiding place. Now for God's sake, leave the physical pursuit of this maniac to me and concentrate on tracking down what your friend Popovitch found. I've got enough to worry about besides baby-sitting you!" He swung his fierce stare back to his men. "And one of my many worries, gentlemen, is whether you did a thorough search, given your obvious attitude that he wouldn't be there anyway."

At 6:30, still stinging from Riley's rebuke, I was back in the auditorium, alongside Williams and Fosse, facing the same group of supervisors and chiefs who had been here not four and a half hours ago. This time even Wild Bill Tippet had shown up, double masked of course. Only the board members were absent; they had presumably gone home to bed.

Williams, up and about with a dressing on his head, elicited a little self-congratulatory cheer from the audience when he announced, "Good job, everyone. You've kept the quarantine intact so far." But the mood quickly became somber again as he reviewed the arrangements to eventually relieve them of their duties taking care of patients and transfer them out to external quarantine facilities. "I doubt anything will happen before the end of the day. With the load we've already put on surrounding hospitals and medical personnel, it will be a while before we find enough staff to replace you and free up enough spaces to receive you."

As the meeting broke up, I heard someone mutter, "Where the hell's Cam Mackie? Shouldn't he be here?"

Somebody else quipped, "Maybe he's hiding in the fog, with the army." The guy got a halfhearted laugh from his colleagues.

Though Fosse had blocked outgoing phone calls, no one, it seemed, knew how to block E-mail. At 8:00 A.M. every electronic media outlet in Buffalo began reporting that they had received an anonymous message containing a threat against University Hospital. Bulletins followed about the place already being surrounded by both the police and the National Guard. Within minutes parts of the actual text were being read on air by a half-dozen radio stations.

I have infected the staff with a bacteria called staphylococcus which I've made completely resistant to all known antibiotic treatments. This organism can be transmitted to patients by touch, and once it penetrates the body, is unstoppable, resulting in certain death. The first fifty carriers will become ill in the next twenty-four hours. Protect your loved ones. Evacuate the patients.

At that moment all our plans to save UH came crashing down.

Ten minutes later an assembly of media trucks, reporters, and TV cameras had rushed in to take up positions outside the army and police lines. Beyond them was an ever growing gallery of people— hundreds of them, some still in dressing gowns, some with children, and more arriving by the minute. The gray morning light had thinned out the fog enough that I could see all the way to the edge of the grounds. Past that point the newcomers seemed to materialize out of the mist.

What I couldn't hear or see from my vantage point—the third floor window I'd been at previously—I learned from the cacophony of all the radios and TVs around me.

". . . increasing numbers of people here, all of them calling out names, presumably those of loved ones inside, whether patients or staff . . ."

". . . we are trying to confirm that a terrorist has contaminated University Hospital . . ."

". . . while we have no casualty numbers yet in this fast-breaking story, we've learned that it could be a disgruntled employee who has released bacteria into the water supply . . ."

People near me huddled in small groups, watching and listening to the various broadcasts, their expressions showing more alarm by the minute. I could see all our work to keep people calm coming undone before my eyes.

"It's not true," I started to protest. "They've got it wrong, all wrong!" But the more I implored them to stay calm, the more it seemed the newscasters pumped up their fears, and the more panicky some of them became.

On the TV screens cameras had zoomed in on patients at windows holding up signs written on sheets saying GET ME OUT OF HERE! SAVE US! HELP US! The effect on the crowd was electric. A roar went up outside that I could hear through the glass in front of me and over the nearby TV and radio noise. The sound quickly organized into a chant. "Get them out! Get them out!" The rows and rows of people weaved back and forth in the mist for a few minutes, seemingly undecided, then surged forward, pressing in on the lines of soldiers. The reporters were caught between the two and didn't seem to know in which direction to point their microphones and cameras.

"Get them out! Get them out!" The cry became a cadence for the mob's advance.

The troops started to back up, but rifles were unshouldered and pointed upward, over the heads of the oncoming men, women, and in some cases kids, probably in their teens. I could now hear the cries of the officers. "Steady, men. Steady!"

The inner line of police had linked arms, and more officers were standing firm across the parking lots in front of the hospital as the soldiers backed toward them. Gone were the police hats; they'd been replaced by helmets. And the ranks of officers held their riot sticks out in front of them.

"Get them out! Get them out!"

Most everyone around me grew still as we watched the nightmare unfold below us.

"Someone do something!" murmured a woman at my side.

The lines drew closer together.

"Oh, God! Stop them!" cried a man standing behind me.

From down the hallway came a shriek, "That's my husband! And my son!"

The PA overhead howled with electrical interference, then boomed, "Your attention please, everyone! For the sake of your families outside, settle down, move away from the windows, and take down those signs! This is Dr. Douglas Williams, of the CDC. I'm about to be patched into every radio and TV station out there, and my voice will be carried over the PA systems on their mobile units . . ."

As if to give credence to his claim, the excited chatter of the commentators from all the nearby portable radios and screens suddenly gave way to his voice, and Williams was speaking at us from hundreds of sources. More electronic howls filled the air outside, and the man's message rolled over the grounds like the word of God.

"Everyone stop! Stop now. Your family members and friends in University Hospital are safe. Look up! They've moved away from the windows because they don't want you to rush the hospital and endanger yourselves."

While he talked, the TV cameras zoomed in on the now dark panes of glass, showing that no one was standing directly behind them. As they held there, new signs began to appear: STOP! DON'T DO THIS! WE'RE OKAY!

The chanting down below was diminishing. Most faces in the crowd were upturned, and people had stopped moving forward. The inner lines of soldiers and police stood fast.

Williams's voice continued to work its miracle. "First of all, no one is even infected yet. We are simply doing cultures on everyone . . ."

As I stood by the window I began to breathe again. It looked like we'd dodged another bullet . . . well, another rocket.

But another one was already on its way.

"Dr. Garnet," said a nurse at my elbow. "I was sent to get you." She led me away from the window. I didn't like the look in her eye. "About a dozen people in the special quarantine ward seem to be coming down with *Legionella*," she told me in a hushed voice.

I scribbled a message to Riley. *Get more men on the door to special quarantine. It's starting!* I gave it to the nurse who had found me and told her it was for his eyes only.

The wing Fosse had opened up contained two wards, each with twenty rooms, four beds to a room. I noticed a few newcomers were being led to these quarters. "Day people," explained a nurse. "They weren't contacted in time to be directed elsewhere."

Even through my mask I could tell the place was beginning to have the odor of too many people not having had a shower. Fosse would have to arrange for changes of clothes and toilet articles to be brought in for everyone here as soon as possible. Civility often started with a bar of soap.

Two members of Cam's department who hadn't been in the archives had already confined the suspect cases I was to see in three rooms at the end of a corridor. As I got near, no one had to tell me that their symptoms included diarrhea.

"We're sorry to call you, Dr. Garnet," said the younger of the two physicians after they'd both introduced themselves, "but we know you've seen the only other case involving both organisms—the Sanders woman—and, well, the whole situation is so bizarre we wanted your opinion, to make sure we weren't overdiagnosing anyone."

They weren't. While none of the twelve was very ill yet and they all had flulike symptoms similar to those of the three nurses I'd seen last night, they also demonstrated postural hypotension and the slightly abnormal blood results—namely low sodiums and albumins, with slightly elevated white cell counts—characteristic of early *Legionella*.

None of them could believe something so serious could begin so benignly. Over and over I heard, "Except for a bit of dizziness when I stand up and the occasional runs, I don't feel that bad, Doctor." But they were scared. "Will I be all right?" they kept asking.

"I'm certain you will," I kept saying.

Some studied my eyes, and I'm sure they saw the lie. My dread of what would become of them in the next twenty-four hours was so strong that they couldn't have helped but sense it.

After examining everyone, I huddled in the corridor with the two ID specialists. I knew there was nothing I could tell them about the conventional treatment of *Legionella* or staph that they didn't already know. What they wanted from me were my observations on how these particular *Legionella* and staph infections varied from the norm. "Smokers will get it the worst, of course, but even the young ones could be in trouble. The usual age ranges don't seem to apply," I advised them.

The older of the two—I estimated he was about my age—raised a skeptical eyebrow. "That's hard to believe." His junior colleague flushed above his mask. I suddenly sensed that there was a dispute between the two men and I'd been called in as a third opinion.

"Look, I'm just telling you what I've seen," I said to the skeptical one. "Like you, I can't explain how these people are being infected."

The younger specialist whistled. "Man, however this creep's doing it, he must be giving them a hell of a dose over a protracted period of time—"

"What else?" the older man asked me, cutting off the speculation of his younger colleague.

I answered quickly, not wanting to get drawn into their fight. "Even to know whether the oral erythromycin we started them on last night has some attenuating effect, we'll have to wait and see. However, I think you can expect the IV treatments they're on now to work well with the nonsmokers, as far as the *Legionella* infections are concerned. But staph remains the real problem for them all. The first sign of it will be their sputum turning purulent. At that point, they're terminal."

While I wrote my clinical notes—the other staff confined to the ward had prepared charts for each of their sick colleagues—I could tell the nasal lavaging had begun. Gagging noises started coming from the direction of the rooms I'd just left, and as I endured the sound, it was all I could do to keep myself from retching.

No sooner had I walked out of the ward and headed for the exit than a figure ran toward me from the opposite hallway. "Dr. Garnet," yelled an unpleasantly familiar voice. "Wait, please!"

She came right up to me and grabbed the front of my gown. Her eyes looked frantic. "Please, Dr. Garnet, I don't belong here. They didn't reach me at home in time to direct me somewhere else. Now that I'm here, they say I've got to stay. You've got to make them let me out!"

I reflexively put my hands on hers and tried to pull them off me. "Really Miss Brown, this is not appropriate. Whatever you think, this is for your own safety—"

"Safety!" she shrieked. "I just found out that whoever's doing this—some are saying it's the Phantom again—has already tried to kill me once, that he gave me my *Legionella* infection. I've got to get away. He'll get me again, I know he will!"

"Miss Brown!" I said as loudly and as sternly as I could without actually yelling. "Get a grip on yourself, and think. He can't get you with *Legionella*. It has a way of granting immunity, through your white cells, and you're protected. But he's also got a staph organism that no one can treat, and your safest place right now is here. Remember, you got ill last time when you were on vacation. We don't know that he didn't infect you outside of the hospital. In this ward you're under guard."

"No, please," she persisted, holding my hands in a viselike grip,

"I'm sorry about what happened to your wife. Please, it was an accident. I never meant that to happen. I never ever wanted that!"

All at once I felt so angry that I had to use every ounce of self-control I possessed not to tell her how much she disgusted me. "I told you, get hold of yourself!" I was shocked by the hardness that I heard in my own voice. Over her shoulder I saw Miller and his team of technicians being allowed past the guards and into the hallway where Brown and I were standing.

I don't know if he heard much of our exchange, but he stepped over and said, "Hi, Dr. Garnet. Quite the job, isn't it?" His mask couldn't completely hide the pouches that had formed below his eyes from lack of sleep, but there was no evidence of fatigue in his voice. "Can I be of any help?"

I nodded at him, then suggested, "I'm sure Nurse Brown would appreciate it if you did the screenings on her yourself." I released her hands and stepped away. She looked from me to Harold Miller, her fear still very evident in her eyes.

Miller stepped over to her, took her by the elbow, and gently said, "I'll be glad to. Come, we can do it over here on this bench."

While I discarded my protective gear at the doorway in exchange for a clean set, I watched Miller carefully help the woman off with her gloves and begin culturing her left hand. She nervously raised her right fingers to her mouth and started biting on her nails. He shook his head and pulled her arm back down in her lap. I could hear him talking quietly as he worked, and though I couldn't make out the words, he must have been saying the right things, because I thought I saw Brown's shoulders relax a little.

I quickly ran to ICU and again checked on Janet. Once more her vitals were stable and her sputum remained nonpurulent, but this time I sensed all the nurses were more guarded in their replies to me. I knew why instantly. Lurking unspoken among them was the knowledge that today or tomorrow, as the pneumonia ran its course, they'd know whether Janet had also been infected with staph. They were instinctively taking their professional distance from both of us, preparing themselves to have the clinical objectivity they'd need if the worst happened. Janet was awake when I went into her cubicle.

"From the eyes up, you look worse than me," she said hoarsely, then started coughing uncontrollably.

I ran through the night's events, but not wanting to frighten her more, I left out the attack on me and Williams. Fosse had had the telephone lines reestablished, so we then called Amy at home. She was desperate for word of us, having watched all the TV coverage, but we settled her down with multiple reassurances that we were okay. When she held the receiver up to Brendan, we made tender noises at our son and listened to his happy babble, escaping for a few blissful minutes the nightmare that had trapped us. After hanging up, the feeling of being cut off from him hit me like a weight. From the desolate expression in Janet's eyes I knew she was battling a similar feeling. I don't know who broke into tears first, but we held each other for what seemed like a long time before either of us could stop.

"Call and check on Michael," Janet quietly ordered me when we'd both dealt with our sniffles in the aftermath.

I punched in the number for St. Paul's intensive care unit and endured the usual wait for someone to pick up the phone.

"ICU," answered a woman's voice.

"It's Dr. Garnet. I'm calling to inquire how Dr. Popovitch is doing."

"One moment please," she said coolly and put me on hold.

Oh Jesus, I thought. Janet immediately sensed my alarm. "I'm on hold," I whispered to her.

The phone clicked. "Earl, it's Stewart Deloram speaking."

My fear reached the screaming point.

"Stewart, why are you there?"

"I'm half back in the saddle, helping out a bit," he said quickly. "But I'm afraid I've bad news. Michael's sputum became purulent overnight. We've done Gram stains of course, and the only glimmer of hope is we can't see staph. The pus may be debris from parts of the lung where the *Legionella* has knocked off the circulation, but in any case he's not doing well."

The words thudded on me like rocks at a stoning. I could barely speak. "Does Donna know?" I asked. Janet's eyes widened in panic on hearing the question. "He's alive," I whispered, covering the mouthpiece for a second.

"Yes, of course. She's handling it very well."

There was nothing more to say. Stewart was initiating the routine to prepare the family for death.

"Stewart, I'm glad you're there," I told him, then hung up before he could ask me anything about the situation here.

This time Janet and I didn't cry. I think we felt too emptied by the shock. We simply held each other and rocked.

* * *

Williams had prevented a riot, but he hadn't managed to defeat his greatest nemesis—panic. Despite his best attempts to get everyone to stay rational—the media, the crowds of people outside, and most of all the politicians—he couldn't convince them that the isolation procedures and the plan to replace our own staff with outside personnel were measures enough to keep the patients safe.

It was a little after 10:00 when I found him standing by the same window I'd been looking out earlier. He was slumped against its frame, shaking his head, and staring at the scene below. "The mayor and governor folded to the pressure," he said forlornly without turning his head. "They've ordered the evacuation of the patients."

Below us was the largest number of ambulances I'd ever seen parked in one place. The drivers were lounging against the doors, chatting and waiting—all of them wearing masks, gowns, and gloves. Farther out a few dozen army trucks had been backed up to the edge of the parking lot, their tailgates down. Those drivers were also in protective gear as they relaxed, sat around, and in some cases even snoozed in their cabs. The media and crowds had pulled back toward the outer edge of the property. Half hidden in the mist, they stood quietly observing us, waiting for our next move, like a chorus fallen momentarily silent but still ready to offer its commentary.

"We're to start moving out the patients at 10:30," Williams informed me as he walked away.

Once the word was given to get ready for the evacuation, the patients had gotten more nervous, not less. During the hurried preparations, I saw masks half tied, gowns left open at the back, and gloves not pulled up properly over the ends of sleeves. If by a remote chance one of the evacuees had already contracted the superbug, these half-assed measures wouldn't be much protection against it being spread around once he or she got outside.

Those who could walk milled about the exits while waiting to leave, some pushing their own IV poles. Those who weren't mobile sat in wheelchairs, orderlies standing at the ready. Staff had transferred the bedridden to stretchers and would roll them to the backs of the waiting trucks. It looked like the starting line for a bizarre race.

Williams had told me that hospitals all over the county were making isolation facilities available to receive our transfers; even military installations had opened up. Off-duty medical personnel from other institutions, called in to take over, would care for the patients we'd be sending them. The staff of UH, including those not in the target group, were meant to remain in quarantine here, until the culture results cleared them to leave.

At 10:30, floor by floor, they started out. Despite shouted orders to go slow, the people who could walk inexplicably rushed to get downstairs, crowded into elevators, or tried to pass the person in front of them as if a few seconds longer in the place could be fatal. The ones on wheels were at the whim of their drivers. The whole process was as frantic as if someone had cried, "Abandon ship!"

I was asked to join with other physicians to assess high risk patients in critical-care areas—unstable cardiacs, patients in shock, those on respirators, the list was endless—and pronounce on their suitability for transfer. It didn't take long to see that in some cases the trip would kill them. On the issue of no risky transfers being made the physicians stood firm. ICU here would remain fully operational, security would be provided around the clock, and nobody would be allowed near any of the remaining patients without an order countersigned by two other doctors. Acute resuscitations would only be done by the two intensivists on site. In other words, no one could come close to a patient on his or her own initiative and slip them something.

We were also told there'd be no replacement of our ICU staff by outside people. The other hospitals were so overloaded by our patients—both the ones we'd sent them and our share of the new emergency cases that came in daily from all over the city—they no longer had personnel to spare.

Janet insisted on staying.

"ICU will be one of the safest places in the city," she said sadly.

I told her that she was probably right but that I was keeping the private security guard at her door, just in case.

I watched the final stages of the evacuation from what had become my usual vantage point on the third floor. Lines of patients were still winding their way across the grounds to the waiting trucks and ambulances. Overhead I could hear the sounds of helicopters, the staccato of civilian rescue craft mingled with the unmistakable wall-pounding window-rattling thudding of a large Blackhawk provided by the army. The fog had lifted enough for them to transport the sicker cases.

We'd lost. He'd won.

Patients, not doctors, nurses, or any other kinds of staff, were the true lifeblood of a hospital. It was patients who gave the hospital its purpose, its mission, its reason to exist. As I watched from my spot high above, they streamed out the doors, the long lines looking like rivulets of fluid flowing away from the sides of the wounded institution. In my mind I heard his terrible low rolling laugh, and I couldn't help thinking that just as I'd seen him destroy Phyllis Sanders from within, cell by cell, I was seeing him exsanguinate University Hospital, bleed it out, patient by patient.

The only person I knew who had reason to hate this place so much was Cam Mackie.

Chapter 22

I kept having to steel myself for what lay ahead.

Just as the fate of Janet and Michael would be decided within the next forty-eight hours, so too would the outcome of the detainees at University Hospital. Some of those already infected with *Legionella*, if they were carrying staph, would be dead, while others would know they were dying. Others still would be told they were carrying death, even though they were not yet ill, and would be kept from leaving. Although the vast majority would ultimately go home, their cultures negative, the dreadful uncertainty affected everyone and hung over the hospital like a fearful shroud.

Meetings were hastily called to flesh out how the dying would be handled. How much should we tell them? Did they want a final visit with their family members? Should we allow them to touch? Could mothers hold their children one last time? Should we then culture the family members and hold them in quarantine? What about counseling? I saw people coming out of a planning session. Their eyes were huge and white in dark sockets.

Overhead the Blackhawk pounded the air with its rotors as it came and went, carrying away six stretchers at a time.

And all the while we struggled with how to stop the killer from infecting more victims.

"You have to figure out how he does it," Riley kept demanding.

But no one could.

While Williams and the ID specialists continued to search for the unifying link in the archive files, Riley ordered me to visit every other department that Michael had been let into. "But take one of my men with you," he added, glaring at me like a stern parent.

Even when Doris Levitz and her group from Atlanta finally arrived in the early afternoon, Williams managed to persuade them that their most pressing priority should be to help out with the work going on in the archives. I saw his point. Those files involved the largest amount of data to be gone through, and unlike Riley, I hadn't dismissed the importance of what we might find there.

Every few hours I continued to call ICU at St. Paul's. Michael remained in limbo, connected to life by a respirator, hovering near death. Deloram still clung to hope because he couldn't find staph in the debris he kept suctioning out of Michael's endotracheal tube. After I hung up, I remembered to take my third pill of erythromycin.

I checked in with my own ER and found out from Susanne that they were coping. I answered her questions about UH as best I could, but when she asked if Janet and Michael would be okay, my own fears were so near the surface I found it impossible to answer. The Blackhawk was thundering overhead on yet another of its trips, and I used the noise as an excuse to end the call, claiming I couldn't hear.

I then joined in the paper chase and spent the afternoon tracking down what Michael had looked at. The Blackhawk continued to come and go, its sound making itself heard everywhere I went, including the basement. By evening, after about two dozen trips, I heard it no more.

The ID specialists were repeatedly called away to the special isolation ward as more nurses and orderlies developed signs of early *Legionella*. I learned from Williams that there were another ten cases and that some of the infected women I'd seen in the morning were already showing evidence of severe respiratory distress.

"Purulent sputum?" I asked.

"Not so far," he answered.

During the evening Cam's disappearance increasingly became the subject of whispered conversations throughout the hospital. From the fragments I heard, half the gossipers thought he was the killer, while the other half were as adamant as Janet about his innocence.

I made calls to ICU at St. Paul's almost every hour now. Nothing had changed, but I felt certain I was on a death watch.

By 10:00 I could no longer keep my eyes open and had a cot put in Janet's ICU cubicle beside her bed. After yet again checking her chart and grilling the nurses to confirm there'd been no change in her sputum, I fell asleep holding her hand.

Michael lived through the night. I called St. Paul's as soon as I woke up, using the phone at the nurses' station so as not to disturb

Janet. But his condition was otherwise unchanged from yesterday evening.

I showered in the surgeons' changing room, switching my over-ripe clothing for OR greens and putting on clean protective gear. Another day in the dungeons, I told myself after grabbing a coffee and heading into the subbasement. The pleasure of the caffeine was doubled by the brief respite from the mask that I enjoyed each time I lifted it to drink.

Though it was only 7:00 A.M., I found Williams in the archives explaining to Riley what his group had found after working all night.

"... it wasn't something the charts had in common that *was* there. It was something that *wasn't* there."

Riley nodded at me as I joined them. Williams went on speaking. "Each nurse had participated in a sterile procedure on a patient sometime during their last few days at work."

"I thought you said all the stuff they did during that time was routine," Riley said.

"We did. What wasn't routine was that on each occasion, the sterile procedure had never been ordered by anyone."

Now he had Riley's attention. "Go on."

"The procedures themselves were varied. A dressing change, a culture of a suture site, a bladder catheterization to obtain a sterile specimen. But in each case there was never an order for the procedure entered on the patient's chart. Nor was there any clinical evidence of a suspected infection according to the doctor's notes on any of the charts."

"How could unordered things be done to patients, and no one catch on?" asked Riley.

Williams explained. "These procedures are so ordinary, a nurse wouldn't even check a chart to see if there was a request."

"Wouldn't the person asking have to be a doctor?"

"No, anyone in the care chain—another nurse, an assistant nurse, a medical student—could catch the targeted nurse, say that a culture or a dressing change was to be done on so-and-so, and ask the nurse to help. Even a porter might turn up with a requisition and claim the lab had sent him to pick up a sterile urine specimen from the lady in room such and such—that they'd lost the one from a few days ago. A nurse would oblige."

"What if someone did notice there was no written order?"

"Mistakes aren't common, but mix-ups do occur. Sometimes the old joke about getting the enema meant for the person in the bed next to you isn't far from the truth. Occasionally the confusion has serious consequences, like medication being given to the wrong patient. But on the level we're talking about, these procedures are very benign, common as dishwater, and, apart from the bladder catheterization, wouldn't cause any upset even if the patient knew they'd been done in error. What's puzzling is that these procedures all required the nurse in each case to don protective gear. Their contact with the killer must have occurred when they weren't protected.

Riley's eyes widened. "One of those nurses, Brown, is alive. Does she remember anything about it?"

"Unfortunately no, but we only talked with her briefly. Perhaps you'll want to spend more time questioning her. As I said, though, with the procedures themselves being so ordinary, it's unlikely a nurse would remember doing one or another. We even called the patients. They couldn't recall such minor events either; this isn't surprising given everything else that was probably done to them while they were here."

"But the person initiating the procedure could be with the nurse he'd targeted while that procedure was being done?"

"Like we said—another nurse, a resident, a porter waiting for the specimen—anyone of them could be in the room and none of them would have their presence recorded on the chart."

"Can either of you think of how someone could use those procedures to infect the nurse?" Riley asked us.

"Unfortunately, not yet," Williams answered.

I simply shook my head.

Riley remained excited, despite our failure to furnish him with the killer's technique. "I can get my officers to go over old duty rosters and question everyone present on the wards when those unauthorized procedures were done," he declared. "With exact times and dates, it's just possible someone might remember something!" He looked over at me. "Did you get to those other areas where Popovitch had been?"

"Yes I did," I answered. "It turns out that Cam had been there as well. He'd left Nurse Brown's chart out in staff health, and in the repository where they keep former records of the deceased, I discovered he'd left out the old charts of Sanders and the OR nurse. But I didn't find anything as dramatic as what Dr. Williams came up with."

"You didn't disobey me and go back there alone?" Riley snapped, his eyes suddenly clouding over.

"I had one of your men posted on the door, as you ordered," I reassured him. I reached under my gown, slipped my cellular phone out of my pocket, and held it up for him to see. "Besides, I can always dial nine-one-one."

Williams laughed, but the scowl on Riley's face only deepened. Since the attack on me and Williams, Riley had been adamant about precautions for our security. He would have been even less pleased to hear what I hadn't mentioned—that his man had been repeatedly called away to help his colleagues settle the frequent disputes that we'd seen breaking out all over the hospital. Not surprisingly, with the patients gone and nothing to occupy them, many of the staff were finding the wait an unbearable strain, especially those confined to the wards where the *Legionella* cases were breaking out. There was also trouble involving a few people with previously unknown drug or alcohol dependencies, and some particularly nasty encounters occurred when some of them started going into withdrawal. Whatever the cause, squabbles sometimes became physical and required the intervention of many police officers at a time. I'd finally sent Riley's man to fetch the portable from my car, just in case I needed help fast during one of the frequent times he was away. Since ICU and the isolation wing were the only parts of the hospital still functioning, I'd felt it was safe to use the device this far from those places.

"Please continue," Riley said.

"Everyone here thought it was blind luck that two weeks before contracting her pneumonia Phyllis Sanders had been screened for staph and found to be negative. My own wife commented on how fortunate that was, because it meant the hospital only had to screen the OB patients and newborns who were on the ward during that two week period. What's odd is that when I checked the charts of Brown and the OR nurse, they also had negative screening results dated two weeks before they contracted *Legionella*."

"What's the significance of that?" Riley asked.

"The fact they were screened is not unusual. With MRSA's being a problem in a lot of hospitals these days, such screening is common. But the timing for all three, I think that might be more than coincidence."

He sighed. "Can't you just tell me what it means?" He was starting to sound impatient again. Being forced to rely on medical experts for information rather than doing his own investigative work seemed to be driving him crazy.

"I wish I could. A clerk named Madge in staff health who was called in to help was pretty talkative after she'd ended up sitting around doing nothing all day. Through her I was able to check out the whole process by which screening is carried out. I wanted to see how it could be used to target three specific nurses at precisely two weeks before each left on vacation, but frankly I'm mystified. The whole operation is so loose—wards are done randomly and many people are involved in the taking of specimens—that I've no idea how the killer could have manipulated the routine so precisely. Maybe your men could interview Madge and find something I missed."

Riley didn't say anything at first. While Williams had given him a lot to think about, I felt that I'd been less helpful.

But the detective apparently thought otherwise. His eyes shed the defeated look they'd had five minutes ago. "Thank you, Dr. Garnet," he acknowledged with a nod. "I'll talk to Madge myself. Maybe I can get her to tell me how *she'd* go about setting up a screening timed to a specific nurse's vacation." He gave me a wink and added, "You know my method." Turning to Williams, he asked, "What are you going to do now?"

"Continue checking these charts," Williams said, patting one of the stacks on the table beside him. "Sometimes lab requisitions are initialed by whoever does the test. We're hoping the Phantom may have slipped up and shown a requisition to his target as a way of getting her to do the procedure."

After Riley left, I asked Williams, "Are there new cases upstairs?"

"Yeah, seven more were diagnosed with *Legionella* overnight—five orderlies, a doctor, and yet another nurse. His range of victims is wide."

"What about purulent sputum in the cases from yesterday?"

"None," he answered. "It's still too early."

Purulent sputum developed in four of the nurses before midmorning. Six more followed the same course early in the afternoon. I heard later that they all knew what it meant without being told. Throughout the rest of the day whispered accounts about how they were doing kept coming from the ward and were relayed throughout the hospital.

". . . emotionally, she's taking it amazingly well, simply asking for a priest . . ."

". . . desperate with fear, but who wouldn't be, knowing you're going to die?"

". . . can't accept it at all, raging one minute, sobbing the next, unable to get her breath . . ."

We heard that all of them were deteriorating medically—agitated from air hunger, plucking at their nightclothes, wracked with wheezing while coughing despite frequent treatments with bronchodilators and high concentrations of oxygen. The descriptions gave me visions of Sanders.

Statements of wishes were hurriedly obtained from them regarding what resuscitation measures they wanted performed once they stopped breathing. Some were adamant: "No tubes down my throat." Others couldn't face the issue and became hysterical when it was raised.

Husbands were told their wives were dying; wives were told their husbands were dying. Counselors quickly met with family members to try to prepare them for visits. Staff explained isolation procedures in hastily arranged meetings. "Of course families can touch, except infants and the very elderly," a doctor or nurse would say, "provided you accept that you'll be screened and kept quarantined in your home afterward."

The reports of what was going on became more disturbing as the afternoon drew to a close.

The plea heard most often from the victims was, "Don't let me die alone."

"I beg you, sedate me, sedate me, please," one of the nurses had sobbed, "so I won't break down in front of my children."

No one wanted to risk bringing infants into the hospital. Fosse ordered arrangements made instead so that families could carry their babies across the grounds and approach the outside windows of the isolation wing. Nurses and orderlies took mothers in wheelchairs or on stretchers to the ground floor and allowed them to take off their masks so they could try to smile at the tiny bundles held up to them on the other side of the glass. Two nurses had to support one woman as she leaned forward to catch a glimpse of her little son while her husband lifted him toward her. She bravely managed to smile down at him for a few minutes, then collapsed completely, racked by sobs and wailing, "I want to hold him. I want to hold him." Cleaning crews standing by to resterilize the place couldn't bear to watch.

The two ID specialists I'd met on the ward yesterday shared identical expressions now, no difference of opinion evident in their haggard, haunted looks. They both kept joining us in the archives during the intervals when nothing further could be done medically, and counselors, along with men of God, had moved in to replace them at the bedside. "I can't stand it on that floor," the middle-aged one confided, "but hunting the bastard who did this helps keep up my nerve to go back in."

The outbreak of purulent pneumonias only increased my vigilance over Janet's progress . . . and my despair. During ever more frequent visits to her I kept fighting back images of what those families were going through a few floors away. Nor did I want to speak about them with her. Their agony was so close at hand and could so easily become our own that I couldn't bear to acknowledge it. Rather I made small talk, called home with her to speak with Amy and Brendan, or simply held her hand.

I brought her news of Michael each time I came. If I stayed with her for more than an hour, she wanted another update before I left. I made those calls from the nurses' station, not to put her through the agony of hearing a one-sided conversation as before. But it was still hard on her. She would watch me through the window of her cubicle for my nod that he was still alive.

Afterward Janet and I would huddle together, helpless in a modern ICU and left to praying that we'd all be passed over by the contagion in our midst.

What kept me searching through records was my certainty that Michael had found proof of how the Phantom infected people. I'd also begun to suspect from our own piecemeal progress that *the pattern* which had revealed this proof to him might not be found in some single set of charts or solitary collection of records. Rather, I thought, it could be the kind of pattern that emerged only after he'd looked at a lot of sources and gathered together observations from all of them.

Around 10:00 that evening, after making no further breakthroughs with the charts in archives, I took a new tack. If Cam was the killer, then what had been done to his father in this hospital was the sole reason behind the vendetta. Could his targets have had a direct link to the way his father had been treated here? Perhaps Phyllis Sanders had been his nurse. Perhaps Brown as well. She was young, but might have been involved just before the man died. In the later pictures of Cam with his father that I'd noticed in his office, Cam had appeared to be in his mid-to-late twenties. I presumed that meant his father had died around ten years ago.

The man's chart, I speculated, could hold a list of the intended victims. Not only would we then know who needed special protection, but we could also be ready to grab Cam when he came for those whom he hadn't yet infected.

"It's worth checking," Williams agreed wearily when I told him my idea. "We're not getting any further here."

I figured Mackie senior's record would be stored on microfilm in the repository with all the other dossiers of the long dead. Security and the police said that they'd let me back in but they couldn't spare a man to stay with me right then.

"Fine, I've got my phone," I told them. I'd also noticed on my previous visit that the door to the room had an inside bolt, probably from the days when a photographer worked on-site processing film and didn't want to be disturbed.

Once I got inside, it took me a few minutes to figure out the index system, but in no time I was spooling the chart of Mr. Stephen Mackie through the view finder. It was a sobering experience. The entries were a record of one man's encounter with one of the great scandals of U.S. health care and with the plague of the century.

Page after page documented his ordeal with hemophilia, the record showing repeated visits to ER for treatment of painful bleeds into his joints. On each occasion he had received an IV administration of cryoprecipitate, a preparation of the clotting factor he lacked which was collected from the blood of multiple donors, and on each occasion he'd had to fight for adequate treatment of his pain. The nursing notations made me wince. *Suspect patient is exaggerating complaints of discomfort: try placebo saline*. In other words, they'd injected simple salt and water, subjecting him to hours of agony before giving him the morphine he'd needed. These entries went on into the eighties and continued through the years in which thousands of hemophiliacs like him had been infected with AIDs through cryoprecipitate prepared from contaminated blood. The policy of paying individuals to give blood, which always encouraged indigents and street people to donate and lie, was never wise, but it was outright negligence to have continued the practice long after word was out in the streets that "Slims" or the "Gay Plague" also was occurring in mainline drug addicts.

Cam's father, I read, was diagnosed in 1985, after a bout of pro-tracted fever, diarrhea, and weight loss. At that point he was forced to stop working in the labs, and his visits to ER increased. His course was typical and quick—treatment then was primitive, limited to drugs like immuran—and he fell victim to the ravages of previously rare infections that became a familiar litany to physicians from the mid-eighties on: bizarre pneumonias caused by a protozoan organ-ism called *Pneumocystis carinii*—treated in those years with tetra-cycline and Septra but never completely defeated—or lumps of other protozoa in the brain, a condition called toxoplasmosis gondii, which produced seizures as they ate into the neuronal circuitry—again diminished by toxic drugs that I could barely pronounce, and again never completely eradicated.

Each event took a piece out of him, left him farther down the slope toward death. Here too the nurses' notes were telling, to his credit. *Patient cheerful, optimistic, spent time chatting with his son.* A few days after one such entry he died—3:10 A.M., Monday, August 31, 1987.

I'd found no signature of Phyllis Sanders or Brown or any of the other names I'd been keeping an eye out for. My idea was wrong. But I'd learned a lot about Cam's father and liked all of it. I also had a good idea of the forces that had shaped Cam, but whether it was for the better, as Janet believed, or for the worse, I still didn't know.

I was returning the roll of microfilm to its receptacle on the shelf reserved for *M*'s when my eye caught another name on the index card posted for that section. *Miller, Mrs. Phyllis Sanders.* Below that I read *Miller, Dr. Carl.*

It took me a moment to realize what I was looking at. The chart of Phyllis Sanders was still on the table where I'd been looking at it yesterday. It wouldn't be microfilmed. Then I understood. When she'd resumed the use of her maiden name after her husband had died, they had made a new file, the one I'd already seen. In effect, she'd buried the medical record of Mrs. Carl Miller alongside her dead husband's. I wondered if it had helped her bury the memories of living with an alcoholic.

The silence in that room was absolute, befitting a record hall for the deceased. Not even overhead plumbing dared to disturb the stillness.

I felt drawn, almost morbidly compelled to know more about the woman who'd become such a nemesis in my life. My impulse to look at the record made me uneasy, as if I'd caught myself wanting to find something in her past that, if I learned it, would explain or excuse my inexcusable reaction to her. But I wasn't in the habit of trying to hide from my mistakes. Part of the psychological price of going to work in ER every day was learning from my errors in judgment and living with having made them. I'd like to believe my compulsion to look at her record came from another impulse, a need to understand her, to do her the justice of seeing beyond what I'd found so annoying about her. It was a service I owed her, maybe even one I owed myself.

Spooling through the clinical notes of an alcoholic's wife is predictably agonizing. Her depression, her anxiety, her need for ever-increasing amounts of antidepressants and tranquilizers—the entries read like an Al-Anon brochure. She too had had many visits to ER—for sprains, bruises, and even for a few black eyes—all the events accompanied by improbable explanations of clumsiness, tripping, or walking into a door. Social workers had interviewed her several times about whether she was being subjected to physical abuse at home, but she'd adamantly denied it.

One therapist had interviewed Harold in his mother's presence when he was around ten years old. Questions about his eating, sleeping, and performance at school had gotten pretty ordinary answers. The interviewer noted that Harold appeared well cared for, that he answered inquiries forthrightly, and that he appeared to be appropriately affectionate with his mother. This interviewer then documented asking a question of Harold about whether he was prone to accidents. Both he and his mother denied this. At the bottom of the page the interviewer had written *No evidence of need for intervention on child's behalf, but FU?*

I spooled ahead, yet as far as I could see, no follow-up had occurred. Had the social worker backed off, because Carl Miller was a doctor on staff, or was there nothing to follow up? Even if there hadn't been legal cause for concern, growing up between Carl and Phyllis Miller had to have been difficult for Harold at best. No wonder he was so awkward.

Phyllis had fewer visits to staff health after that and no more visits to ER with suspicious bruises. Had Carl Miller stopped abusing her? It was unlikely, but maybe the threatened intervention of the social worker had frightened him. The chart ended with a minor entry about her receiving a hepatitis B vaccination sometime in 1985. I'd been spooling so quickly at that point I didn't realize at first that her chart was finished, and I overshot into the portion of the film show-ing Dr. Carl Miller's chart. There wasn't much to see in the section I inadvertently looked at—a few scanty notes documenting his visits to staff health dated years apart, occasional blood results showing his worsening liver enzymes, and a few referrals to psychiatry for what had been coded as stress but were probably attempts to get him help for his alcoholism. None of the appointments had been kept.

I knew I had no business looking at his file, but I was tempted to keep going. It was, after all, the subtext of Phyllis Sanders's story. Nothing would excuse the way she'd vented her anger on helpless patients and had become a punisher, but abuse begets abuse.

I brought more of his chart into view.

What I expected to see was a chronicle of increasingly frequent ER admissions for the catastrophes of excessive drinking—GI bleeds, pneumonias, seizures, delirium tremens, cirrhosis—but he must have gone to another hospital for those. What I was looking at was a single ER entry on the night of his death. Like ten percent of alcoholics, he died by trauma—in this case a tumble down his base-ment steps, resulting in a fractured skull. He'd been pronounced DOA in emergency. An autopsy had confirmed the fracture and de-termined that the cause of death from the trauma was a massive intracranial hemorrhage, aggravated by the way cirrhosis leaves drinkers prone to bleeding.

I rewound the microfilm, sending the pages of Carl and Phyllis Miller's epitaph whirling backward in a blur. Looking through their record hadn't entirely been a waste, I thought, depressed by the mis-ery conveyed in those pages. It had certainly increased my sympa-thy for Harold.

Minutes later I'd returned the film to its slot and was out the door going down the corridor when my cellular rang. Surprised, I flipped it open, only to hear Williams yell, "Garnet! He's infected a nurse after she'd been put into isolation."

"What!"

"I'm in with her now. It's not pneumonia; it's a cellulitis of her hand. We got enough pus for a Gram stain; it's staph."

I could hear a woman shrieking in the background.

"Who the hell's that?" I asked him.

"It's her," he answered. "We're trying a cocktail of antibiotics, but I'm not optimistic. She's just heard from the surgeons what has to be done. The cellulitis is in her right hand. The redness and swelling were present locally around her nails when she got up this morning—she noticed it when she went to change gloves—but she's a nail-biter and has irritated them before, so she didn't think much of it. It still didn't bother her too much during the day, but she woke half an hour ago with high fever, marked swelling locally, and lymphangitis present halfway up her arm."

Lymphangitis—blood poisoning they used to call it—is in fact an inflamed lymph duct, or channel, carrying a clear fluid full of white cells, called lymph. The condition is recognizable as a red line that starts at the site of a local skin infection and then extends along the course of the underlying lymph duct, usually proximally, or in this case up the infected limb. You died, lore had it, when the poison reached your heart, which was presumed to be shortly after the red line reached your trunk.

Today we know that people die when the organisms and their tissue-destroying toxins flood from the original site of infection into the bloodstream and seed themselves everywhere throughout the body. Yet we still use the red line as a marker of how the infection is proceeding and as an indication of how it's responding to antibiotics. Prior to the discovery of penicillin, however, doctors used the progress of the line to determine when and where to amputate.

The screaming and sobbing in the background became words.

". . . I knew he'd get me! I told Garnet he'd get me! And now you're going to cut off my fucking arm!"

It was Brown.

Chapter 23

"Don't come up here," Williams insisted. "You're the last person she wants to see."

"How do you know she was infected after being quarantined?"

"We're pretty certain. It's around thirty-six hours since she was screened on arrival, and there's absolutely no growth in her cultures. Somehow he's infected her since then." The screaming started to crescendo in the background. "I've got to go," he snapped, and the connection went dead.

Despite Williams's warning, I was determined to go upstairs and talk to Brown, no matter how much it upset her. The ordeal she faced was ghastly, but with so much at stake and with so few leads, she had to answer my questions.

I continued to hurry through the oppressive passageways, following a set of turns which I was used to by now, and was completely lost in speculation about how Brown had been infected. Cam couldn't have done it by going on the ward in person, I thought as I rounded a corner and headed down a particularly musty section of hallway. His six-foot-five-inch frame would have been too easy to spot. Maybe he'd contaminated the ward—left colonies of staph where people would touch them during the times they wouldn't be wearing gloves, such as when they were showering. There was an article in the *MMB* once, I recalled, that documented an incident in which an MRSA outbreak was traced to a soap dispenser in an OR. And I'd check with Miller, I decided, to find out if there was any way that Cam could have tampered with the specimen after Brown's screening.

I was somewhat startled by the sound of a door slamming somewhere around the next corner. Instinctively I slowed. Down here it didn't take much to crank me up into a full panic. Echoes of that hideous laugh raced through my mind and fed my sudden fear that the lights would go out again.

The repository was located in its own region of this netherworld, away from the archives, so it wasn't any of Levitz's group or the ID physicians who'd been working there. I heard another door close—this time the sound seemed closer—and I thought I could hear approaching footsteps. It could be one of Riley's men doing another search, I thought, but I'd nearly had my head split open twice now, and I wasn't going to take any chances. Tiptoeing, I backtracked, hoping to make it to the repository where the door had a bolt. Whoever had come after me in the human resources department had had a key, perhaps even passkeys. I kept watching the corner as I retreated from it, moving along with my back to the wall. Another door closed, and the footsteps came closer still. I wasn't going to make it to the next turn in the corridor and out of sight before whoever it was saw me. Reaching behind my back I tried one of the doors I was passing. It was locked. I moved more quickly now, less conscious of noise, only concerned about getting away. I tried another door. It opened. I backed inside, found myself in a small room full of boxes, and quickly locked myself in. I stood in the dark and tried to control my breathing as the steps and the sound of doors opening and closing came nearer. Was he looking for me again? Was it merely one of Riley's men after all? I heard the rattle of a nearby handle that was tried and didn't open. The steps then continued, coming nearer, nearer. I was next.

I leaned my weight against the door and held my breath. I heard the knob turn, feeling the movement transmitted through the ancient wood as I pressed on it with my shoulder. The possibility he could probably kick it to splinters if he knew I was in here flashed through my mind. He gave the handle two more hard twists, then walked away.

I let out my breath, hardly able to believe he'd passed me by. My first impulse was to let him get out of earshot and then call Riley on my cellular. Let the police nail him, I figured. Then I thought, what if the police don't get here quickly and quietly enough, and we lose him again? I heard more doors opening and closing, the sound receding each time. I quickly recovered my nerve, took a breath, and as silently as I could, released the lock to open the door a crack.

He was thirty yards away, just rounding the next corner and passing out of sight. But this time he was close enough I could tell immediately who it was, even from the brief glimpse I'd gotten of him. Gary Rossit was prowling the subbasement of University Hospital.

* * *

I felt as if an earthquake had rumbled through my head, toppling all my ideas and suspicions about Cam's being the killer. Dashed as well was Janet's theory—that the Phantom was some unknown figure who'd framed Cam. The sight of Rossit resurrected the notions I'd had about him in the first place—that he was involved in a brutal plan to sabotage University Hospital. The possibility I could have been right all along was almost as big an upheaval to me as seeing him there. But how had he gotten in?

I didn't have time to stand around and try to answer that question. I could hear him making his way down the next corridor as he continued to open and close doors. I decided I'd call Riley as soon as I learned what Rossit was doing or where he was headed and ran on my toes to where he'd disappeared into the next corridor. There I peeked just in time to see him pass from sight into yet another passageway.

I continued after him, wondering if he were after me. Possibly, except he wasn't using much stealth. In fact, all the noise he was making made it an easy matter to follow him. I thought again about calling Riley. But what would the detective grab him for, slamming doors? All at once I had to backpedal in my thinking. Even his being here wouldn't give the police reason to arrest him. For all I knew he might have walked through the front door and signed in. As the chief of the infectious disease department at St. Paul's, he'd certainly have a joint appointment at this hospital, the way I had. Now that I thought about it, given the circumstances, especially with Cam's disappearance, it was perfectly natural he might come in, offer to look around, and see what he could see. When I peered into the next passage, I saw he was past the repository and crossing the far intersection, heading straight into a part of the subbasement I'd never entered before.

Better tag along, I thought.

But I had to wait a while to let him get farther ahead of me in this next section—it stretched into the distance as far as I could see—until I could safely follow from a long way behind and use recessed doorways to hide in. I'd no idea where we were headed, and the manner in which he kept poking around, sticking his head into every room he could, I began to wonder if he had any specific destination in mind. He seemed instead to be searching for something.

Luckily for me the overhead lights were dim and spaced far apart, so I had lots of shadow to cover my moves while I skirted along the wall from doorway to doorway. Here and there rows of boxes were stacked to the ceiling, affording further cover when I needed it.

As we progressed in tandem through this lengthy tunnel, I kept looking beyond where Rossit was peeking into yet more rooms until eventually I could make out where the passageway ended—against a larger door than the rest which was illuminated by a solitary lamp hanging over its portal. Between it and where I was standing in one of the shadowy spots, there was very little light and many more piles of boxes, but if I didn't want to be seen when he started back, I figured I'd better get into a hiding space now. Although Rossit was short, his torso and arms had always given me the impression of considerable strength, and I didn't savor the idea of his finding me down here while I was spying on him. I even wondered if I hadn't already had a taste of how powerful he was two nights ago when I'd had my own arms pinned, my gut slugged, and my head rammed into a door.

I found a dark area behind one of the nearby stacks of boxes and crouched down, still keeping an eye on Rossit making his way toward the end of the passage. When he arrived in front of that final door and reached for the handle, I figured he'd give a quick look, like he'd already done to a few hundred other rooms down here, and then return toward me. Watching him slowly push it open, I got ready to hunch over in the shadows. But instead of simply glancing in, he stood at the threshold a few seconds, then stepped inside, leaving the door open behind him. I waited for about a minute, watching, thinking he'd come out any second. He didn't.

Overhead some pipes clanked. Otherwise the place was completely quiet. I began to feel cramped staying in one position and tried to shift my legs to make them more comfortable. As I waited, an ever so slight hint of something pungent and overripe penetrated my mask and invaded my nostrils. Probably a rat had died behind the boxes I was kneeling beside.

Suddenly from the room Rossit had gone into I heard a creaking noise, like rusty hinges. Then there was silence again. Was there another door out of there? I kept my breathing slow and shallow so I'd detect the slightest sound that might indicate he was still inside.

Nothing.

The pipes overhead clanged especially loudly, making me jump, then fell quiet again. I still couldn't hear anything coming from the room. Fearing I'd lost him, I stood up and began creeping very stiffly along the right-hand wall toward where I'd be able to see by the half-open door. The odor I'd noticed before persisted despite my moving away from the boxes and began to cloy in the back of my throat. I was about ten feet from the entrance when I heard a soft noise. I froze in midstep.

It was a scraping sound, muffled, not anywhere near, but definitely coming from the other side of that door. It kept repeating, as if someone were pushing something. My first thought was that there might be containers somewhere in that room similar to the many boxes that lined the hallway and that Rossit was moving a bunch of them around for some reason. When the scraping continued, I crept another five feet until I could see partly through the doorway. A ceiling light inside revealed a medium-sized storage area filled with stacks of storm windows and more piles of boxes. In my line of sight against the far wall, though partially hidden behind yet more boxes, was a long table half covered with a white sheet that had been folded back on itself. Visible on the table was a large metal cube of some kind, about two feet square. Beside it I recognized racks of test tubes, bottles, and stacks of petri dishes. Parked in a corner of the room, also half hidden behind some containers, was a small supply cart.

My pulse rocketed into triple digits. Son of a bitch, he's brought me to his lair! I tried to keep my breathing steady. The scraping continued to come from somewhere behind the door, and I could hear Rossit grunting now as he worked. But I couldn't see him. Whatever he was dragging around in there, it was heavy. That odor still hung in the air, and though it wasn't perceptibly stronger, its persistence began to make it repulsive. I stopped breathing through my nose but knew the scent was continuing to fill my mouth. It remained there a few seconds, nearly beyond the range of my sense of smell, but not completely. Soon I began to detect traces of it again as the aroma seeped up the back of my throat and floated into the posterior regions of my nostrils. Since my first anatomy lab nearly thirty years ago I was sensitized to even a hint of that distinctive stench, no matter how many flowers they put out in a funeral parlor or how high they turned up the vents at the autopsy lab.

It was time for the police. I readied myself to tiptoe down the dark hallway behind me. I'd phone Riley as soon as I was far enough away to be out of earshot, probably when I'd locked myself safely in the repository. The cops could then come and collect Rossit, the lab equipment, and, I knew, much worse. But I'd barely taken a few steps when the scraping noises from deep in the room abruptly stopped. In a flash I feared he'd heard me and was coming. Reflexively I ducked behind some of the nearby boxes. No sooner was I crouched down than the silence was ripped by loud retching noises, followed by the thudding of running feet.

I pressed myself back against the wall where it was darkest and huddled into a ball with my face cradled in my arms. I allowed myself a wide enough slit for one eye to peek through. The door flew open the rest of the way, banging noisily against the inside wall as Rossit bolted from the room. In the fraction of an instant he passed under the overhead light I glimpsed vomit streaming from under his mask and down the front of his gown. His eyes were as wide as saucers with black bull's-eyes in them. Then he was tearing away in the semidarkness, his labored breathing loud and full of whimpering sounds, his shoes slapping against the floor.

The echo in the place amplified the noises of his retreat as he got farther away in that long corridor. I got up from my hiding place and watched him go. Silhouetted against the distant light where the hallway joined the rest of the hospital, he gave the illusion of running in place.

It wasn't the behavior I expected from a murderer. Come to think of it, if this was his lab, why had he spent so much time poking his head into all the other rooms on the way to it? Leave the questions to the cops, I readily decided, pulling out my cellular and dialing the security desk. "This is Dr. Garnet," I announced as soon as I heard the receiver pick up. "You know I'm working with Detective Riley."

"Yes, sir!" came the reply. "I've accompanied you myself to the basement."

"Listen up. By no means let a Dr. Gary Rossit out of this hospital, you hear! He's on his way toward you. Stop him, no matter how much he protests. Alert all the guards at the other entrances. Now!"

"Right away, sir!"

"And notify Riley—"

The buzz in my ear told me he'd hung up. Obviously, for him, an order was something to be jumped to. "If only we could get the residents to obey like that," I said out loud, wanting to break the leaden quiet that pressed in on me.

Rossit had passed out of sight and sound, leaving me listening only to the occasional "thunk" of an overhead pipe. I continued to take in air by mouth, but nothing I did could keep away all traces of the telltale smell and nothing would lessen the terrible dread I felt

about entering that room. Nevertheless, I walked up to the fully
open doorway and stepped in.

At first I saw only more storm windows and boxes. Then, looking
over the top of a particularly large pile of cartons stacked in the
middle of the floor, I could see a three-quarter-size metal door set in
the far wall. It was open, but the area it led to was in darkness. I recoiled from looking in. The smell where I stood was already much
more powerful than it had been outside, and mouth breathing left me
actually *tasting* the odor of rot. I needed a few minutes to let my
olfactory senses accommodate to the aroma; pathologists always
taught us never to run from a stink but rather stay in the room a few
minutes and let it become bearable. Sometimes it worked; sometimes it didn't. The trick was to get through the few minutes. I
walked over to the table and tried to focus on the items laid out on its
surface while fighting the urge to throw up.

It was almost as Williams and I had predicted. The large cube-
shaped object was an incubator with a thermostat and a heat lamp. It
was probably intended for hatching chicks and was open on top, but
he'd laid a big cookie sheet over it as a cover. Inside was a rack of
half a dozen shelves—again some kind of kitchen accessory. On
each of these shelves were a dozen petri dishes, every one of them
teaming with bacterial colonies. His equipment looked more like
the stuff of a cooking class than the tools of murder.

I lifted the bed sheet off the other end of the table and discovered
four closed preserving jars full of water. I presumed these were his
supply of *Legionella*. Bundles of culture sticks and collection tubes
were lying on trays, and boxes of gloves and masks were within
easy reach. But when I removed the sheet entirely I found myself
looking at something I didn't understand. Half a dozen surgical
masks were spread out side by side. Near them was a box of thirty-
cc syringes fitted with very small number 25 needles. I picked up
one of the masks, yet couldn't see anything special about it. When I
put it down, however, I realized I had a little moisture on my gloves
at the tips of my fingers. When I examined the other five, I discovered they were all damp as well. Had he spread them out to dry? But
why were they wet in the first place?

I'd have to figure it out later. At the moment I had as good a hold
on my stomach as I was ever going to have, and it was time to get on
with what I'd come in here to do. I walked over to the entrance of
that small chamber. Pathologists must simply have lousy noses, I

concluded as I resorted to holding mine and trying to swallow at what seemed like once every second.

I knelt down and peered into the darkness. The tiny space was barely five feet high at the zenith of a low arched stone ceiling. Braced for the worst, what startled me was that I *didn't* see the corpse I'd been smelling. Instead I was looking at another bunch of large boxes randomly placed about the floor, if floor was the right word. It was nothing but dirt. There was enough light streaming into the cramped space from behind me that I could see where many of these boxes were shredded near the bottom, some of them with holes in their sides the size of a cat. Their contents were probably documents, because chewed strands of paper trailed out from those holes onto the ground like streamers. Were these containers what I had heard Rossit dragging around?

It took my eyes a few seconds more to see the scrape marks where he'd hauled them off an area of darker, coarser earth compared to the gray powdery soil surrounding it. This patch was a few feet wide, and at the far end I could make out a small spot where the dirt was especially roughed up and scattered. Without giving myself time to think about it, I took a breath, went in on all fours, and crawled toward the freshly disturbed ground until I was looking down at what seemed like a shallow depression of mud. There was absolutely no sound in here, and the weight of the whole hospital seemed to press in on me. I gritted my teeth, and tried to push aside the wet dirt with my gloved hand. After letting my eyes adjust again to the lack of light, I could make out that the mud had earth-caked features. The rats hadn't had to dig down more than a few inches to chew on Cam Mackie's face.

I broke into a sweat despite the cold clamminess of that closed space, and when I had to breathe, the air was so putrid that my throat involuntarily seized. Desperate for a breath, I backed out as fast as I could.

He was waiting for me. I had started to get up when I caught a glimpse of his crepe-soled shoes behind me on my left. I tried to wheel around and get my arm up to protect myself. But I was still partially bent over, and the ceiling light was behind him, so all I could make out was a silhouette and the shape of the shovel he was holding in the air like a bat. The instant before he brought it down on my head I realized he was too tall to be Gary Rossit.

Chapter 24

When I next opened my eyes, I was staring at my crotch. My head was lolling on my chest; the slightest effort to raise it sent spears of pain up my back and into my skull. I was leaning forward against some kind of restraints—duct tape, it looked like—around my chest and arms. My hands were bound behind my back, and I was strapped into a chair with my legs lashed together, also with duct tape.

Three strikes and you're out, they say. On this occasion I figured I was out for a long time. The numbness I felt in my hands, arms, and legs and the stiffness I could feel in the parts of me that weren't yet numb were the result, I knew, of being cramped in this position for quite a while.

I tried to take inventory of how badly I was hurt. Definitely some things were wrong. When I tried to look sideways, I could detect a lump that I judged to be the size of a walnut. It seemed to be growing out of my forehead and bulging down over my left eye. That didn't worry me much. A hematoma, or goose egg, always looked worse than it was. More disturbing was a complete lack of sensation on that side of my face, which might mean nerve damage, and that could be permanent. I made a few more painful attempts to lift my head enough that I could see my surroundings. More spasms seared through the upper half of my back from the bottom of my skull, making me wonder if he hadn't also injured my neck. After crying out with the pain a few times, I realized that I was hearing with only my right ear.

The large door to this room was now closed, and my attacker had placed me not too far from the table where he'd cooked up his particular brand of death. As I looked around, I could feel that my surgical mask was much tighter across my face than I was used to, the added pressure against my nose making it hard to breathe. Whoever hit me must have retied it, I thought, but I remained baffled about

310

why he would have. It certainly wasn't out of any concern for my health. I was bothered by the top of the mask biting into my cheeks just below my eyes, so several seconds passed before I realized my glasses were gone. I looked around; they were lying by my feet, smashed.

I noticed something else was gone as well, or at least was barely noticeable—the smell. No mask, however tight, could have protected against that reeking odor. I tried to look behind me, and by peering under my goose egg, I was able to see that the metal door leading into where Cam was buried was closed and sealed with duct tape. Leaning against the wall beside it was a shovel coated with traces of fresh earth. I shuddered. Cam's face, I presumed, had been reinterred. I also saw that some of the boxes that had been piled in the center of the room were gone. Maybe the killer had used additional containers to better cover the grave this time, though I doubted anything would keep the rats away from it for very long.

I'd been so wrong about Cam, and Janet had had him pegged right all along. Like father, like son—Stephen Mackie wasn't just remarkable for the way he'd conducted himself through the hideous ordeal chronicled in his chart. He also deserved credit for getting Cam through it intact—free enough from bitterness that he could make his father proud and become the man and doctor Janet knew him to be. Now Cam lay in the earth, slaughtered. Had I inadvertently set him up to be the Phantom's scapegoat? The question seared into me.

I began coming to grips with the fact that Rossit wasn't the one who'd knocked me out. There was no mistaking that the silhouette I'd seen was the wrong height to have been him. It made sense now, too, his looking into rooms the way he had. He'd no more known where this secret workplace was than I had. What he *was* doing here, I'd no idea, though I wouldn't put it past him to have blustered his way past the guards for no better reason than to grab some publicity for himself. LOCAL EXPERT IN INFECTIOUS DISEASES STEPS FORWARD TO HELP OUT DURING CRISIS was exactly the kind of headline I could imagine him going after. Maybe he'd even figured out as much as Williams and I had and knew what kind of equipment to look for. Damn! If I hadn't kept everybody focused on the asylum, probably Riley's men would have found this place as well.

But they had searched the entire hospital at least once, I recalled, after Cam disappeared. Maybe there'd been no odor then; the rats hadn't yet done their hideous work. Even if the police had looked into that little crypt, they wouldn't have seen the fresh earth with the boxes over it. Another possibility was that they never saw the entrance to the crypt at all. There were sufficient containers nearby to have made a big enough pile that it would have hidden the door altogether. Likewise the table. The police probably had glanced in, seen only boxes stacked to the ceiling, and gone on with their search.

The slightest movement of my head sent new pains coursing through my skull, and I was having increasing difficulty breathing through the tight mask. Had my attacker retied it like this to make it hard to breathe? Or yell?

"Hey! Help me!" I screamed at the top of my lungs. My cry was a bit muffled, but the mask wouldn't keep me from shouting if that's what he was worried about. I doubted he would be, though, when I thought about the chances of anyone hearing me. No one was in the subbasement these days, let alone nights, except those of us going through records. Even then, except for me and my trips to the repository, everyone else was usually in the archives at the other end of the hospital.

But someone who came specifically looking for me might hear. Rossit should have told the police about this place by now. Surely they'd gotten him after I'd called them to pick him up. But where were they? I'd certainly been here longer than the ten minutes or so it should have taken for him to have reached the front door and for them to have gotten back down to this room.

"I'm in here," I screamed, thinking maybe the would-be rescuers had taken a wrong turn, but my little burst of hope that someone was on the way quickly faded in the answering silence. What had happened when Rossit got upstairs? Was it possible he would have not told the police about this place?

I started to feel twinges of panic over what this killer would have in store for me when he returned. I strained my wrists, arms, and legs against the tape, but the more I forced, the more I felt bound by them. My breathing quickened and I began feeling suffocated by the mask. I tried to bend my head far enough to one side that I could rub the bottom tie loose from my jaw with my shoulder, but I only managed to send my neck muscles into their worst spasms yet. I screamed once and then had to hold my upper body completely still to avoid more of the same. I ended up staring directly at the table so laden with death. The sight of it added to my anxiety, and an unbidden thought slithered into my mind. Could he already have infected me while I was unconscious?

Now it was all I could do to keep my panic from going right out of control. I desperately screened the tabletop. Had anything been moved or used? It took me the better part of a minute to realize one of the six surgical masks was missing. The other five remained spread out, presumably left that way to dry. But dry of what? I tried to steady my breathing, but it shot up again as another question raced into my head. Where was the missing mask? My entire body broke out in a sweat as the realization came. He hadn't retied mine. He'd replaced it with the one missing from the table—one that he'd wet with something!

My gaze flicked over the contents of the table for some hint of what that something could be. I stopped at the syringes, then the bottles. This time I knew with the suddenness of a chill. The water! Oh my God! That's how he was giving people *Legionella*. The contaminated water—it was in the mask! The steps raced through my head with terrible clarity. He'd injected it into the inner layers, then let the outsides dry enough so no one would feel or notice the wetness. Once the mask was on his victim, the humidity of exhaled breath—trapped in the nearly closed space behind the mask—would mingle with the contaminated moisture in those inner layers. The result would be moist humid air teeming with *Legionella*, and every time the victim breathed in, he or she would draw the deadly mix directly into the lungs.

With rocketing terror I realized that was why he'd tied my mask so tight—to maximize my exposure!

I'd no idea how long I'd been breathing in *Legionella*. Inhaling the organism in such a concentrated form within such a closed space for an extended period of time would be how he'd achieved the massive exposures needed to infect otherwise healthy adults. I had to get that infested thing off my face!

I bent my head sideways again and despite the searing jolts of pain tried frantically once more to catch the bottom edge of the mask with my shoulder and get it up off my chin. Nothing budged. I looked around for something else I might use to snag it on if I could only rock the chair near it but saw nothing handy at the same height as my head. Then I spotted the shovel. The blade. If I tipped the chair over and somehow wiggled to where it was leaning against the wall, I might be able to hook a corner of that blade onto one of the ties on my mask and rip it off.

Every breath I took felt hot and moist. Thinking of what I was inhaling only made me breathe faster. By sheer force of will I concentrated on what had to be done despite my fear. I initially verified that I could at least rotate my hands and feet enough to manage a few inches of up-and-down motion with both my arms and lower legs. As I prepared to tip myself over, I figured if I got to the shovel, I could possibly get rid of my ties as well as my mask.

I calculated that the best strategy was to land on my side. Flat on my back I'd be like a turned-up turtle unable to right myself; if I went forward, I might land on my face and be knocked out again. I started lurching my upper body from side to side against the tape restraints. At first I got no movement at all, but then I won some leverage by throwing in a little hip action, and in no time the chair was rocking. I kept increasing the size of the arc I was tipping through, wanting to go over toward the left, to be as near as possible to the shovel. But I misjudged, and ended up teetering for a few seconds toward the right, trying to reverse my momentum before toppling in that direction anyway. Crashing to the floor I felt pain explode through my shoulder as I landed on it, and I let out a roar. For a few seconds I lay there with my eyes closed, sure that I'd broken it, but the telltale nausea that accompanies a fracture never came. When the throbbing finally began to subside a bit, I opened my eyes.

And blinked. And blinked again. I couldn't accept what I saw. Refused to. But it wouldn't vanish. He had been lying behind a row of boxes near the table, not so much hidden as simply out of sight from where I'd been placed in the chair. I was looking into the face of Gary Rossit.

That he was dead I had no doubt. There was that unmistakable stillness about him—no breath, no sound, no twitch or flicker of movement in the smallest strand of muscle that always betrays life. His head was toward me, his mask half off, and I could see the purplish color of his skin, suffused with blood that no longer flowed. His eyes, fixed and staring, bulged more than they had in life, and his mouth hung slack in death. His hair was matted with blood at the back, but not a lot. If the bleeding had been the result of an encounter with the shovel, the blow may have knocked him out, but I doubted it had killed him. I couldn't see his neck from where I lay, but his face had all the features of someone who'd been strangled.

He must have been ambushed after he'd run from here, I thought, my mind slowly working its way back up to normal speed.

I'd spoken so harshly of him so often over the years, especially in the last ten days and as recently as a few minutes ago. Yet I felt outraged that he too had been murdered. Whatever I thought of him as a man, he'd had a skill that could save lives, and he'd used it, however it had been twisted up with vicious politics and the perpetual chip he'd carried on his shoulder. In a world where there were those who protected life and those who took it, he'd still been enough of a doctor to put himself mostly on the side of the angels.

I was going to stop the monster who did this, before *he* took any more lives.

The way I was lying put my back to the shovel, which was about twenty feet away. It was going to the longest twenty feet I ever traveled. Using my shoulders and the few inches of up-and-down movement I had in my legs, I managed to make enough pushing motion against the floor that I rotated myself until my head was pointed in the direction I had to go. Then, using my shoulder as a kind of flipper and digging in with the bit of a knee hold I got on the floor, I humped on my side toward that blade, propelling myself, chair included, barely an inch at a time. I hurt everywhere. I was sweating with the strain of each move and breathing hard, always breathing hard and inhaling *Legionella*.

At first I wasn't certain I was even making any progress, but gradually I halved the distance, then quartered it. Each time I heard one of the overhead pipes clank, I was sure it was *him* returning. If by some miracle I got myself untied before he got back, I needed a plan to deal with him. Continually listening for sounds at the door, I kept humping and pushing toward that shovel, all the while figuring what I could do to nail him. Finally I was a few feet away, then inches, then had my head right up against the blade. I couldn't help thinking that it had been in the earth alongside Cam's decomposing body but forced myself to maneuver my right cheek to the top of the steel edge by straining my head away from the floor. I pressed hard into the shovel, hoping some part of the mask would catch or rip, and moved my head down. The steel hurt my skin, but nothing on the mask gave way. Suddenly the shovel shifted, and the handle clattered to the floor.

"Shit!" I exclaimed aloud, to ease my frustration.

I eyed the curved blade now lying on the floor, the handle away from me. I rotated around until my back was to the shovel, and my feet could pin its handle to the baseboard. Then I wiggled and humped some more until I got my bound wrists alongside the blade, got a hand on either side of it, and managed to push the tape binding my wrists up against its edge. Wedging the shovel against the wall, I kept pressing as hard as I could with my wrists, drawing the tape up and down on the semisharp steel. The metal kept scraping my skin, but soon I felt a little separation between my wrists, driving me to work harder and faster until, with a lurch, I felt them spring apart. My upper arms were still bound to the chair, but I could bend my elbows, stiff as they were, and slowly brought my forearms around from behind. By flexing my neck, I managed to bring my hands enough toward my face to curl my forefingers under the bottom straps of the mask. When I had my grip, I wrenched and tore the straps off. The mask now flapped in front of my mouth like a banner hanging off my nose, still attached by the upper ties. A few more flexes and twists of the neck brought me near enough that my fingers could rip the rest of it away, and the hideous covering wafted to the floor.

I took gulps of air like a man who'd been underwater, so much so that I made my head woozy. I had to force myself to once more slow my breathing and started clawing furiously at the tapes around my arms and trunk. Within minutes I had them off, then freed my legs as well.

Of course my cellular phone was gone. Even the erythromycin I'd been taking for two days had been confiscated. I'd no idea what time it was because my watch had been smashed, probably when I'd raised my arm to protect myself. I stumbled over to the door, barely able to move. Knowing full well I was probably locked in, I turned the handle and pulled. As expected, I wasn't leaving that easily. Nor was this door one of the feeble wooden ones I'd hidden behind in the corridor. It was large and metal, and I knew I wouldn't be kicking my way out of here either. Instead I resigned myself to carrying out the plan that I'd come up with while I'd been slithering across the floor. I started to get ready.

Five minutes later I was back in the chair, hopefully close enough to the same place he'd left me in. I'd taken a clean mask from the box on the table and had stuffed the remains of the one I'd ripped off my face into my pocket. I'd returned the shovel to its original position against the wall but had rejected using it as a weapon. I'd first thought of hiding and braining him with it when he came in but had realized he might first open the door a crack, see I wasn't in the chair, then slam it closed, locking me in again for who knows how long. I had to lure him into the room, then get him. Yet if I was in the chair, twenty feet was too great a distance to reach the shovel and take him by surprise. So I'd looked around for an alternative weapon, something closer to the chair and abundant enough in the room that he wouldn't notice one of them was in a little different position than when he'd left. I'd made my choice, had placed it so I could grab it readily, and then had reapplied the duct tape around the front of my legs, trunk, and upper arms.

I held my hands behind the chair, took a final glance around the room, and settled down to wait.

Chapter 25

Someone once said the prospect of being hanged in the morning concentrated the mind. Waiting in that chair, watching the door, and feeling the stillness of Rossit's unseen remains and Cam's nearby tomb, it wasn't hard to think like a condemned man expecting the executioner. Except I doubted I had until morning. Occasionally the pipes clanged, as time passed my arms and legs once more stiffened up, and bit by bit I began to piece together the events of the last ten days in a way that finally made sense.

The initial step was to realize that I hadn't pursued the Phantom, that in reality I'd been subtly led to him and to the connections that had pointed at Cam. Once I accepted that starting point, the rest of what I'd seen and learned since Phyllis Sanders first came into my ER simply flowed into perspective.

Scapegoating Cam, I now figured, had probably been part of the killer's plan from the beginning. I also began to grasp the sweep of that plan—how this killer had set up the execution of punishers and the collapse of University Hospital. But the scheme had started with the business of the Phantom; that whole episode of two years ago had been carefully created for the sole purpose of making Cam a suspect for what was to come.

I once more crawled inside the killer's skin and figured how he'd set it up.

The initial tit-for-tat attacks against punishers who had gotten away with their cruelty were the kind of benign retributions that allowed hospital gossipers to say, "I know it's wrong, but they deserved it." When whispers inevitably turned to who might be responsible, it wouldn't be too shocking a leap to include Cam's name on the list. Probably the killer had waited until those whispers had begun and then had escalated the attacks to potentially lethal events with the use of insecticides. That move would lead gossipers to realize that whoever the Phantom was, he was capable of far more dangerous acts than anyone had initially thought. Afterward came his most ingenious maneuver of all—the *too convenient* double alibi. It would focus speculation on Cam but still leave him off the hook enough that nobody would accuse him openly. Once that seed of doubt about the man was sown, the Phantom's activities were suspended and the suspicion was allowed to lie dormant for two years, until the killer was ready to start his now deadly game of infecting punishers.

As part of his plan the killer had probably meant all along for someone to recognize the pattern of the Phantom at work when the infections began to occur, and all along he'd counted on someone resurrecting the old rumors that would make Cam a scapegoat for murder—mass murder. Except Janet, after recognizing that someone was once again punishing the punishers, had resisted going down the false trail that had been laid out to incriminate her friend. I'd been more obliging.

I'd even offered up other suspects besides Cam on my own— Rossit, Hurst, the entire board of St. Paul's—hell, I'd become a fund of false leads, a voice directing the police to everyone but the killer, leaving the true Phantom free from suspicion, safe from detection.

In that dreary room I anguished that if I'd been more attentive to Janet's instincts, two of the "suspects" I'd fingered might still be alive.

I knew who was going to come through that door. He'd always been close at hand, ostensibly helping, feeding me just enough bits of information to keep me diverted toward Cam. I'd just begun to guess his motive—why he would kill punishers, including one in particular, and then seek to destroy this hospital—when I heard the key in the lock. At the sound I tried to drop my head, slouch forward, and feign being unconscious still, hoping that when he came near enough to check me, I'd take him. But I had to move carefully not to dislodge the duct tape, and he had the door open too quickly.

"Well, well," declared Harold Miller. "Finally awake, are you?" He sounded like a host greeting a guest who'd overslept. He was carrying a tray of culture sticks which he took over to the table. "It's about time, Garnet. After all, I didn't hit you that hard." I didn't answer him, didn't even react. I wanted to size up the best way to make him come near.

"You'll be interested to know I've been busy finishing my 'work,' so to speak."

I felt a rush of alarm. Son of a bitch, I thought, he's been infecting more people. I had to get back and warn anybody he'd been near. "Trying to kill them makes you a worse creep than they ever were," I snapped, hoping to goad him into coming closer.

But he didn't rise to the bait. "Oh, I don't particularly care who I kill to bring down this place. Using punishers as victims was mainly to make it look like Mackie's work. Your arrival here *did* make it necessary to speed up my schedule though," he continued breezily, "but don't worry, I got it done. Even had time for the finishing touches, so to speak, on our star patient in ICU. She was so grateful."

Janet! Oh my God! He'd infected her again. "What have you done?" I cried out. The possibilities tore through my mind like bullets—his infecting her skin, redosing her lungs, slipping the superbug directly into her IV. I felt my head swim, my heart race, my breathing quicken again. It was all I could do to keep from leaping at his neck and strangling him.

"Maybe you've figured out how I've been doing it," he mocked while he puttered with the culture swabs and other screening equipment he'd taken off the tray.

"Damn you to hell, Miller! What have you done?"

He stopped, turned to face me, and leaned back against the table with his arms folded across his chest. "You're not talking very nicely to me. I'm most disappointed, Garnet. I've been looking forward to regaling you with the finer points of my work, not fighting with you." As he spoke, he watched me with those dreadful eyes, but now a fire shone out of the sadness.

I nearly sobbed aloud, I was so frantic. "Tell me what you've done to Janet."

"Some follow-up cultures, as a precaution was what I suggested to her. She agreed, and I swabbed her nasal passages like I usually do when I'm screening people," he replied offhandedly.

"What did you do?" I screamed at him.

He chuckled, easily, hideously. "As I said, I simply screened her."

Screening! The three nurses had been screened before they became ill.

"I had to," he added, his voice suddenly hard. "You yourself told me she never accepted that Mackie was the killer, even after I made you suspect him. Once *you* turn up dead, she'll be a relentless pursuer—too bright and dangerous for my good—so I screened her."

Desperately, I fought to control my panic. I had to get beyond his game of cat and mouse, or he'd go on taunting me with his refusal to

tell about Janet. I grabbed the first idea that came to mind. Seconds
ago he'd sounded inclined to boast. Maybe I could trick him into doing some bragging. Trying not to show even a flicker of fear, as
coolly as I could I said, "I thought so, Harold. You can't tell me what
you did to Janet, because you never got near her—you couldn't
have—not without written orders by two doctors or getting by
a security guard at her door. You may kill me, Harold, but about
her, you're bluffing, and your pathetic mind games disgust me."
Make him defend himself, I figured, and he might blurt out what
he'd done.

I figured wrong.

The impact on him of my defiance was immediate. His eyes darkened, and he started to uncoil from leaning against the table like
some king cobra getting ready to strike.

Oh Christ, I thought, immediately realizing my mistake. I'd been
so desperate about Janet I'd violated the first rule of ER in dealing
with an agitated psychotic. I'd challenged his sense of control.

His powerful shoulders seemed to hunch up. "Listen to me, you
fuck," he shrieked, "or I'll finish you off with the shovel right now!"
His rage so startled me I rocked back in my chair and almost brought
my arms forward to protect myself, thinking he was about to fly at
me. Instead he angrily pivoted and strode over to the shovel. Grabbing it with both hands, he turned and started for me, waving the
blade in the air and eyeing my head like it was a ball on a tee. As I got
ready to leap away from him, I realized in an instant that even if I
made it to the door, he'd nail me in the fraction of a second it would
take to open it.

He stopped advancing about four feet to my side and enough in
front of me that he couldn't see my wrists weren't taped, but he'd
come well within range to finish me with one swipe. Our eyes
locked, and I saw in them a terrible excitement, as if all his pain and
despair had been assuaged by this instant of ultimate control where
he could decide if I lived or died. Even if I didn't bolt, he might
kill me anyway, simply for my defying him. I seized on the one advantage I had left and decided if I was about to die, I'd go down
thinking like a doctor. "Am I feeling what your father made you feel,
Harold?" I asked as gently as I could.

He kept the shovel in the air, but his eyes changed. The fire that so
often appears in the eyes of the insane dimmed ever so slightly. In
ER I always relied on that dimming, as an indicator of how well I
was doing, whenever I had to talk down people who were in Miller's

state of mind. I kept speaking as gently as I could. "I saw your parents' old files. He was abusing you, wasn't he?"

No answer. The shovel remained in the air.

"Your mother didn't stop it, did she? No one from this hospital did either. The one time a social worker from here spoke to you about it, she didn't follow up. Somebody at University Hospital should have known that you'd be too scared to tell the truth, that you'd had to lie, that you'd been made to say everything was fine, that you'd been forced to hug your mother and smile."

The blacks of his eyes began to glow again, but he had a faraway look, as if his fury were being stoked by some distant agony.

"Did your mother frighten you into not reporting your father? Did she say he'd hurt you more, hurt both of you more if you told?"

He seemed to rock back on his heels and leave whatever distant place he was remembering, then focused his gaze once more on me. He nodded but remained silent. Through the transparency of his gloves I could see his hands straining as they kept their grip on the shovel handle. I felt I was dismantling a bomb. If I touched on the wrong memory, his fury could explode.

"The hospital should have pursued their suspicions," I continued, "but it failed you there, didn't it, Harold? Your father hadn't lost his license yet and was still on staff then. Do you think that's why the social workers backed off and went easy on your parents, because both of them worked here?"

This time he spoke. "He gave me a session anyway, even after I did lie, and as usual she just hid upstairs." His voice had changed, had altered to an extent that surprised me. It was free from any hint of his mother's wheedling tones. I was shifting something in his disturbed mind, but if for the better, I couldn't tell. Whatever my impact, I was certain that for the moment my talking to him was all that was keeping me alive.

He kept his grip on the shovel, the blade at the ready.

"What did he used to do to you?"

The question seemed to go by him. He didn't respond at all, as if he hadn't heard it. I'd often seen that kind of reaction in ER as well, when I was after emotionally charged information. From my experience, I knew it was best to let people alone for a moment then, giving them time to wrestle with the pain of recall. As I waited for his answer, I felt I had moved our standoff onto more familiar turf, despite having a shovel held at my head. Eliciting a history from hostile and violent patients—in effect getting them to tell their story—was part of a day's work in ER. But in this case, the questions and their timing had to be exactly right.

"How did he hurt you?" I repeated as gently as I could after what I hoped was an appropriate interval.

The fire in his eyes roared back to life in the here and now. The shovel blade began to move through little test arcs. "He called it punishment," he replied, his voice full of venom but still free of Phyllis's legacy. "Down in the basement was where it happened. He rarely left more than one or two marks on me. Not only did he know how to hurt me so nothing would show, but one of his hits was good for a thousand threats; the fear was the same. Sometimes I felt relief when the blow finally did come; imagining it, constantly expecting it, was more horrible than physical pain." He broke into that chilling laugh. "I think you probably know firsthand what I mean," he taunted, waving the shovel near my face. Then he abruptly stepped closer, still in front of me, and said into my ear, "You know I can and will use it, Garnet." His voice was all at once as cold as the grave, and his eyes, so near mine, continued to glow like a pair of black coals.

Get him now, my impulses screamed. But I didn't know how to decontaminate Janet yet.

He moved back, and my only chance to grab him so far was gone.

He continued speaking from a few feet in front of me. "*I* lived with knowing what he could do, anytime, day or night."

I kept my eyes on the shovel. His hands were now tightening and relaxing his hold on it while he talked. "Sometimes he'd get me out of bed and take me down there—keep me there for hours while he drank and ranted. His specialty was humiliation . . ." His voice trailed off and his black stare seemed far away again. This time his eyes were also filled with a strange incredulity, as if he still couldn't believe what his memory was showing him even after all these years.

In the fullness of his silence I held my breath. I'd no idea what he was going to do. As I watched, his forehead became covered with a sheen of sweat and turned the color of paste. It felt like minutes before he resumed speaking, but it probably had been only seconds. "I used to call for my mother to come and help me, but she just stayed in her room upstairs." His voice had changed again, was thin and little, like a child's. "I think she figured if he had me, he wouldn't hurt her. When he fell asleep, then I could sneak out on my own, but I was always terrified that he'd wake up and come after me again.

The next day *she'd* look me over and say, 'See, it wasn't so bad,' and then start the refrain, 'We mustn't tell. We mustn't tell.'"

He started striding back and forth in front of me, continuing to talk, no longer as a child, his voice hard again. He'd swung the shovel over his shoulder but still gripped it. "By the time I was fifteen, I had some muscle in my arms and shoulders. Do you know what I did to stop him?"

Before I could answer, he'd pivoted and swung the shovel full force at my head!

I'd less than a second to jerk my neck back and felt the cold steel fly by my face. "Christ!" I roared at him. Fright set my heart accelerating. I braced for his next strike and readied myself to jump out of its way.

But he simply stood there staring at me, his gaze coldly neutral. I couldn't tell if he'd intended to finish me off or if the miss was deliberate—a part of the *thousand threats* he wanted me to endure before he finally delivered a killing stroke.

"One swing, Garnet, and it was finally over," he declared softly. The words seemed to float across the space between us. "Used the baseball bat he'd given me for my birthday and hit the home run of my life. On that night, I had peace from hating him. She put him at the bottom of the stairs and made it look like a fall. 'Always good to have a nurse in the family,' she used to say. But if I thought I was free of being frightened or that the hatred wouldn't return . . ."

Oh my God was all I could think.

". . . threatened to turn me in unless I catered to her, doted on her, looked and acted the devoted son. She was obsessed that *I* had to make up for *his* abusing *her* . . ."

He spoke in a rush now, as if pressured to get the misery out.

"As I got older, she tightened the leash. She actually declared my life was hers to control, since without her keeping me safe from the cops I wouldn't have a life."

I still couldn't make a break for it, not with him pacing between me and the door.

"She forced me to try for medical school, expected me to become her new Dr. Miller, said that I was *his* son, that I'd have to reverse the humiliation she'd endured at UH when *he* was boozing and fucking around on her. But I got turned down anyway."

I tuned out his rant and eyed the weapon I'd put within reach, but knew I couldn't get to it as long as he held the shovel.

"I managed to get hospital laboratory sciences. She made more threats about the police to make sure I came to UH when I graduated. Even then I was her slave."

The torrent of words streaming from him was the stuff of delirium. His pace of walking back and forth picked up tempo. The fire in his eyes became alarmingly bright.

"And I wasn't free from hating him anymore. Flashbacks—I was in the basement with him again and again and again—left me so full of hatred that I wanted him alive so I could kill him again and again and again! I wanted that release."

He stopped pacing and stood directly in front of me. The shovel was back on his shoulder, but the two-handed grip hadn't changed.

Anytime, I kept thinking, he could strike anytime.

From the rage I saw in his eyes I figured only a syringe of haloperidol could bring him down now.

Once more I got ready to jump out of the way.

But once again, he fooled me. "The beauty of it, Garnet, is that it worked," he declared in a soft voice.

I flinched I was so startled to hear him speak after being so sure he was about to plant that shovel in my brain. This was his game again, I realized, the *thousand threats* he'd once endured and had now learned how to make, probably liked to make. Sadistic—like father, like son—he'd become what he hated.

"I couldn't be so obvious as to make Mother my first target for the superbug," he continued, his voice dreamy. "I'd tried depositing it on those other nurses first but only managed to give them *Legionella*. Did you know it was a two-step process?" He didn't pause for my answer, neither did his gaze waver from mine. "I timed everything before their vacations so they'd be away from the hospital when they got sick and there'd be less scrutiny to cope with while I perfected my technique. When you told me Mother had staph, though, I had to hide how excited I was. It was fitting she got it first."

He paused, and I held my breath. Whatever demons he was exorcising while he talked, he was skirting around the edges of what I needed to know—his technique.

"I knew immediately you were smart, and maybe a threat—that silly bitch would have to go to your hospital—and I nearly choked when you said right away you thought she also had *Legionella*. At that moment I wasn't at all sure that you'd fall for the Phantom business I'd set up or that you wouldn't see right through the rest of my scheme, so I brought a special mask to St. Paul's that I intended to give you. But luckily for me you'd screwed up on her first visit. That gave me a huge psychological advantage. I gave the mask to Deloram instead, just to muddy the waters." He gave a teasing laugh, the sound of it cold. "You're going to love it when I tell you my secret about the masks. I've become very good at handing one to a colleague after pretending to take it from the regular pile."

Handing out masks to others before putting one on yourself was a point of etiquette doctors practiced without even thinking about it. He could have given one to Michael and Janet the same way.

"Over the next few days, with a few timely hints from me, you began suspecting Mackie just as I'd planned for someone to do. Then I was ready, finally, to infect punishers en masse and bring down University Hospital."

Your technique with staph, damn it! How'd you get them with staph?

He'd slipped into that faraway state again. I didn't move, didn't even blink, not wanting to do anything that would catch his attention and shut him up.

"Doing it drove away the flashbacks," he continued, almost sounding reasonable. "I know they'll probably return, but I can go on with my work somewhere else. Being a chief technician who's had experience with the superbug ought to make me a hot commodity for any hospital in the nation. Wherever I go, I'll be in charge of screenings. Who knows? Maybe picking off a punisher now and then when *he* comes back to haunt me *will* be enough next time."

I wasn't thinking much beyond getting myself out of this room. If I failed, I knew I was dead, either by getting my head smashed or by what he'd infected me with. But it had never once occurred to me that he could somehow walk from here, especially if he killed me, and not be a suspect. That his madness extended to taking this horror to other hospitals left me reeling. Was it possible? The police would eventually find our bodies. Could they actually end up reconstructing a story that let Miller slip away? I didn't see how. Sooner or later someone would surely piece together what had happened like I did, but Miller hadn't made many tactical errors and the mere fact he thought he could get off scot-free meant he'd probably seen a possibility I'd missed.

"You know what's interesting about a swab, Garnet? I can be plating out organisms in the nasal mucosa of my subjects, giving them staph instead of culturing for it, and nobody can tell the difference."

His words hardly registered at first. I was busily figuring how I'd make my move, flexing and unflexing my leg muscles, getting ready, when what he was saying washed over me with the clarity of ice water.

"I keep a special pile of infested swabs with me, ones I've already dipped into my cultures of the superbug. No one notices I seem to have some culture sticks set aside on my tray as I work. I can infect anyone I want with a colony of staph, and it can lie dormant for weeks, until I hand out a dose of *Legionella*."

My first thought was, God help me! He'd infected Brown right before my eyes. My second? That it was definitely time to go!

I leaped from the chair with a scream and then pivoted left. I got a glimpse of the total astonishment in his eyes, then of the shovel starting through its arc toward my head. Already turning, I dropped on one leg and rolled farther toward where I'd left a storm window partly pulled off the rest of the pile and ready to be grabbed. The shovel grazed off my back passing over me as I twirled under it. Too terrified to feel my stiffness, I got to my feet without looking behind me and reached for the window. I got a hand around each side near the bottom of its frame, raised it over my head, and pivoted again to face him.

He was already coming at me, his shovel raised for another strike. He started his swing, but I got the side of the window in the way of the oncoming handle and blocked it. Wood on wood, the blow caused the pane of glass to shatter, some shards of it falling out and showering down around us, the rest remaining in a jagged rim around the inside of the frame. The shovel struck the cement floor with a loud clang. Miller retained his grip on it and immediately started raising it again.

But my window was already in the air. I brought the frame with the sharp glass fragments down around his head at the level of his eyes and pushed as hard as I could.

He screamed as the points found their way into flesh and sockets. The shovel clattered to the floor and he tried to grab the frame with his hands, but he couldn't before I raked it farther down his head toward his neck. Some pieces of glass broke out of the frame and remained embedded in his flesh. Others held firm in the wood, slicing through his mask and lacerating the underlying skin. By the time they reached his jugular, he was pouring blood from his face and had shredded his hands trying to grab around what had become a halter of pointed glass daggers. Screaming and begging "No!" he groped blindly for me, more blood and pieces of latex flying off his palms as he flayed the air trying to find my arms. As soon as I saw his power-ful fingers coming at me, I gave the frame another hard shove, felt the glass go farther into him with a little lurch, and knew I'd punc-tured something. I made a final thrust, then released my grip on the window.

My last push sent him staggering backward. His hands flew to his throat and his scream became a whistling gurgle as he went stum-bling in reverse across the room. The sound told me I'd sliced his windpipe. He crashed against the work table and tipped it toward him as he slid to the ground. The contents fell around him and onto his bloodied head and neck. Even the incubator toppled over, land-ing upside down on his face. He was thrashing, choking, and con-tinuing to make wet, rasping noises through his severed trachea. Blood spurted into the air and gushed over the floor. He clawed wildly at his neck trying to dislodge the frame and the shards of glass that had impaled him. I watched as he inadvertently shoved the incubator away from where it had fallen.

Harold Miller would probably survive his punctured trachea. Even the copious outflow of blood could be stopped if we hurried. But what he wouldn't escape were the contents of the dark brown ooze that was spreading across his skin. The overturned petri dishes had spilled their lethal culture media into his deep and multiple wounds.

Chapter 26

I found both the key to the door and my phone in one of his pockets. He made a weak grab for me as I retrieved them, but lack of oxygen and loss of blood had rendered him harmless. Within two and a half minutes of my call, Wild Bill Tippet arrived with his resus team and went to work on him. Since Miller was a "gusher," Tippet's now being triple gloved, double masked, goggled, capped, and gowned was appropriate.

They intubated, got IVs running, and tamponaded the bleeding sites as best they could. Working around all the embedded glass and infested agar medium was hazardous at best. Then they made a run with him for the OR. Riley arrested him on the fly, reading him his rights while trotting alongside the gurney. When the detective warned his new prisoner that anything he said could and would be used in a court of law against him, Miller, unable to talk but still half conscious, gave the detective a baleful look as if to say *You've got to be kidding*.

In the OR they'd sew up his trachea, repair torn arteries or veins of size, and clamp, ligate, or cauterize the rest, whatever it took to get the bleeding stopped. But from the beginning we all knew we were working on a dead man.

Why bother? Williams best explained everyone's thinking on the subject. "Keep the son of a bitch alive in case we need to know something from him about what he's done!"

I later learned that shortly after they wheeled him out of the OR, they wheeled Brown in, unable to wait any longer before they amputated her right arm just below the shoulder.

I raced to ICU and woke up Janet, quickly telling her only that the killer was Harold Miller, that I'd explain everything afterward, but that right now she must immediately undergo a nasal lavage with bactericidal soaps through the posterior pharynx. Struggling to get her eyes open, she in turn gave a little scream when she saw my battered face. Still half asleep, she proceeded to give her own set of orders, demanding that I immediately find someone in ER to take care of my own problems and that the nurses were to get her a "real doctor" before she'd even discuss the matter of lavages. After a few seconds, however, what I'd said seemed to sink in.

"Harold Miller was the Phantom?" she exclaimed incredulously. "Killed his own mother? Infected all those people? But he was just here less than an hour ago, taking swabs—Oh my God!"

After I agreed to have my lavage done with hers—I'd no idea whether he'd swabbed me as well—she consented. As we gagged and spat together, then applied copious amounts of mupirocin ointment up our nostrils, I prepared myself to tell her Cam was dead.

She took the news quietly, but that didn't mean she took it well. I think she'll probably rage in her soul until the end of her days against the wrongs that led to her friend's dying. Her silence, I suspected, was a reflection of how she'd already resigned herself ever since he'd disappeared to the fact he was dead, though she never said it outwardly. Instead she let me comfort her, then comforted me over and over that I was not the cause of Cam's murder or Rossit's. Afterward we never talked again about how I'd suspected Cam. Strangely, I didn't feel that moratorium was because she blamed me for those suspicions. Rather I think it was her way of telling me that she didn't have to talk about it, that she accepted what I'd done as reasonable and in good faith.

I was having greater difficulty dealing with it all. I kept dwelling on how I could have done things differently. Even Williams and Riley tried to reassure me to the contrary during my formal statement with a police stenographer, but I knew I'd go to the end of *my* days wondering if either Cam or Rossit or both would still be alive had I not thought them capable of murder.

"Intravenous erythromycin and copious nasal lavages," Williams immediately ordered for anyone who'd been screened by Miller and also exposed to a mask he offered.

But instead of running around helping him get everything done, I became a patient tethered to an IV pole, receiving my prescribed intravenous erythromycin to prevent my contracting the *Legionella* that Miller had exposed me to. I kept my cot alongside Janet in ICU but slept fitfully. By 5:00 A.M. I was awake for good. Since I could wander throughout the hospital by pulling my wheeled mast with its dangling bag and plastic tubing along at my side, I slipped out of the unit and squeaked my way down the corridor to where I got a coffee from a vending machine. Then I poked into abandoned rooms until I found a phone to call St. Paul's ICU.

"It's remarkable, Dr. Garnet," the nurse said, "Dr. Deloram's hope about the purulent sputum not being from staph proved founded; the culture's negative. Better yet, Dr. Popovitch's vitals are stronger. His fever's down, and most important, his blood gases are improving. It looks like we might even try to start weaning him off the respirator later today, though that will be a long process."

I found the elevator, rode it down to the ground floor, and pulled my pole with its wheels squealing in protest across the large deserted foyer to the front doors. The guards knew who I was and let me stand in the doorway where I could enjoy the early morning air. I was still enveloped in a mask with my usual protective gear and would be obliged to remain so until several rounds of cultures on me proved negative. But at least the mist felt good on my forehead, and it being Thursday, I could hope to be free of masks and such by the weekend.

Standing below that massive stone facade, I looked up and saw the underside of the chins of the gargoyles. The granite sentinels peered off into the predawn night. I felt like yelling up at them, "The threat is over," but I didn't, of course, and they never wavered in their vigilance. Together, we watched the sun come up.

Late in the morning we discovered that the results from previous screenings had been tampered with. All the current victims now dying from staph pneumonia were recorded as having been negative two days before, which was impossible. We had to start reculturing everyone in the hospital. On the positive side, the prophylactic erythromycin had slowed the emergence of *Legionella* cases. Only five more people developed the prodrome, and the course of their illnesses remained mild.

Ultimately none of the victims Miller had infected with staph during his last round of screenings showed any traces of staph on culture after being lavaged so promptly, including Janet and me.

But the dying wasn't over yet. During the next few days three more of the earliest victims, already severely ill with *Legionella*, died of staph pneumonia. The final death toll from the superbug was thirteen, not including Phyllis Sanders.

Williams's rule of thumb regarding release from quarantine was

"Three negative screenings and you're free." By Sunday morning ninety percent of those who'd been confined were cleared to leave.

The CDC supervised a review and clean-up of every square inch of the hospital.

"We'll eventually give the place a clean bill of health," Doris Levitz said over coffee one morning.

"But will the public?" asked Williams, the front half of his scalp registering his skepticism in multiple wrinkles.

I thought of the gargoyles peering off into the distance and wondered if they would become sentinels looking in vain for the return of patients.

Sunday also marked the day Janet got out of ICU, her *Legionella* in full retreat. I never developed any symptoms at all and was equally grateful that the numbness was gone from the left side of my face. My hearing, I was assured, would be back to normal within a few days.

The hospital had virtually no patients now, and Janet chose a room in OB where she could have the company of some of her colleagues and friends. Since I could be wherever I parked my pole, I also checked into OB, to much teasing by everyone on the ward.

"Who knows," Janet said coyly when we were alone in our room, "maybe nine months from now we'll be back here for real."

We were on the phone constantly with Amy and Brendan, reassuring Amy that we'd both be home in a few days and cooing at Brendan. We wanted to see him so badly, but we wouldn't budge until even theoretical risks from *Legionella* to an infant were well past.

"By the way," Amy told us, "since you haven't been here, Muffy's been sleeping in Brendan's room, guarding him like he was her own pup." Amy held the receiver up to Muffy's ear, and we heard her barking excitedly at the sound of our voices.

I'd continued to check on Michael every few hours and been reassured he was making progress. But I wasn't prepared for the call that came to our room that evening. "Earl, it's Stewart Deloram. I've got someone here who wants to speak with you. Hang on a minute."

I heard rustlings, then I could hear him breathing for a few seconds before he spoke, as if it were difficult for him to get the receiver into position. "Boy," Michael rasped, "that was harder than giving up cigarettes."

On hearing my friend's frail voice, my eyes filled with tears. "Michael, you are amazing! Simply amazing," I told him.

He gave a sound in return that was half chuckle and half wheeze. "Gotta go," he said. "They seem to think I shouldn't talk for long. Better humor them. Bye, Earl."

When I hung up, Janet needed no explanation. My side of the conversation was enough to make her eyes sparkle. We hugged, laughed, and cried, sharing our joy.

That night we slept in the same bed. Despite the narrow mattress and the fact that our IVs kept getting tangled we managed to resume our campaign to keep Brendan from being an only child.

"He says he wants to see you," Williams told me.

"See me! Did he say why?"

Riley answered. "Miller's not saying anything to us, anything at all. Who knows what the creep wants? My advice, Doc? Don't bother. You've been through enough."

It was late Monday morning, and we were having coffee together in the otherwise deserted cafeteria. The area, along with ICU and OB, was one of the few that had been declared clear of staph. As a result, we were free of protective clothing as we sat around and talked, and it felt wonderful, despite the grim business we were discussing.

"I agree with Riley," Williams chimed in. "We've pretty well put together what happened. There's no need to talk to him. He'll be dead in twenty-four hours, anyway."

Undoubtedly he would, I thought, and I might end up wondering about what he wanted to tell me for the rest of my life. "Why don't you two fill me in on what you've figured out," I suggested. I wanted to think over whether I'd see Miller. "For starters, what happened the night Cam disappeared?"

Riley looked at Williams, got the nod to do the honors, and started. "We figured that Miller overheard Cam Mackie when he called you and Douglas. Maybe Mackie even confided to Miller what he'd found in the charts, not realizing that he was talking to the killer. If that was the case, Miller would be faced with a crisis. He already had to know that his mentor was brilliant enough to beat every one of us to figuring out the rest of it. But the fact that Mackie had already zeroed in on evidence of how the three nurses were infected in a matter of hours—evidence so complex, I remind you, it took the rest of us days to find—must have convinced Miller that his own exposure could occur just as quickly. According to our preliminary path report, he probably only knocked Mackie out in the lab, then finished him off by strangling him to death sometime before burying his body. The crime scene investigation will tell us more for sure. That chamber, by the way, was a root cellar at one time."

"We timed it out," joined in Williams. "Miller could have carried an unconscious Cam Mackie to that room, killed him, then raced back to the lab with the samples of staph that he set up for you and me to find. Once his display was ready, he probably used Mackie's office, dialed the number of that single line phone, and waited until one of us answered. When he heard your voice, he started sending those messages. I bet he preferred your getting there first, because he could terrorize you about Janet. Distracted, you were more likely to jump to the conclusion he wanted you to make about Mackie."

Riley took over. "While you and Douglas were figuring out what to do and dealing with Fosse, Miller had time to slip back to his hiding place, bury Mackie, and cover the grave with boxes. Then Miller returned to the bacteriology lab, claiming Mackie had also telephoned him."

I remembered how Miller had looked freshly showered that night when he'd arrived at the bacteriology lab. The thought of him having just washed up after killing and burying Cam sickened me.

"What about the asylum?" I asked. "Was he ever there?"

"Probably," Williams said, "until you spooked him that first night you ran into him. The second time you saw him with the cart, we think he could have been getting ready to move. Given how little equipment he had, it would have been an easy matter—a couple of trips at most."

While refilling our cups from a silver serving pot, I asked, "Did anyone figure out how he used the screening process to set up the targets?"

Riley grinned. "I worked this one out with Madge in staff health." He took a sip of coffee and settled back in his chair, obviously enjoying the chance to show off his discoveries. "Screening is done a ward at a time, but the exact date of each call-up is at the discretion of several people in that clinic, depending on how busy they are. Once a notice goes out, the nurses have two weeks to get their cultures done, at their convenience and without an appointment, either in staff health or in the labs. Madge thinks Harold Miller faked a message from staff health, notifying the floor where his target worked—ICU, the OR, or in the case of his mother, OB."

Riley's use of the abbreviations of our lingo made it hard for me not to smile.

"That started a screening process when it suited him," Riley continued, "shortly before each of his targets was scheduled to leave on vacation. Since the only thing staff health cared about was that every nurse in a high risk area got a minimum number of cultures per year, they'd never be bothered, maybe not even notice that an extra set had been done."

"But the nurses he'd targeted wouldn't necessarily come to him for their cultures," I said.

"The screening itself gave him an excuse to seek them out a few days later and reculture them. 'Bad sample,' he'd say. 'Got to do it over.' Then he'd use one of his swabs contaminated with staph."

Williams joined in. "The timing of the screening was one of the things that tipped off your friend Popovitch. I talked to him briefly on the phone. The other clue was the unordered procedures that required the targeted nurses to get into protective gear, including masks. Like you, he found both those 'coincidences' suspicious. Then he started to figure how it could be done, just as you and I did, but it wasn't until he was being resuscitated, with everyone wearing masks and taking cultures, including from inside his nose, that the exact technique struck him. He sounds like quite a guy. He said that he would have written you a longer note but his residents were impatient to get him full of tubes."

"Amazing" was all I could think to say, remembering how near death he'd been at that moment.

"You know," Williams said, "it astonishes me how well Miller covered his tracks as the Phantom before he resorted to insecticides. I suppose it doesn't matter now, but I couldn't turn up anyone who could connect the ipecac to him. Even his targets from psychiatry couldn't recall if Miller had been around shortly before they'd started hallucinating. We placed him in physio and rehab, though. He was down there a lot around the time of the insecticide poisonings, claiming to need therapy for a sore back. I think I figured out how he did it too. While I was interviewing workers in the department, I observed their routine. They sometimes leave their wet thongs unattended and off to one side while they're in the whirlpool baths with a patient. Miller probably watched his intended victim until he had a chance, then sprayed the target's footwear with domestic pesticide. It's as though he became more visible once he became more lethal, but . . ." The large man shrugged. "Ah, what the hell am I going on for? It's over, thank God."

I thought of a final question. "Riley, could Miller have gotten away with making you think Rossit was the killer, presuming you eventually found both our bodies?"

Riley grimaced. "Think about what nearly happened with you and Miller, Doc. Suppose he'd gotten one good whack at your head before you got him. You both could have died in there. Miller probably thought he'd make it look like you'd strangled Rossit while trying to escape from him, but that the head injuries you sustained in the process were too grave for you to get yourself out of the room afterward. To have set it up, all he'd have to have done would be to smash you into a coma, position you near Rossit, then let his organisms work on you. In time, either they or the results of the head injury would finish you off. When we came on the scene, we could very easily figure that Rossit was the Phantom and that he'd caught you snooping in his lair . . . with a tragic result."

Williams added, "Even if the police found you before you were dead, you wouldn't be in any condition to talk."

We sat in silence for a while, sipping coffee. Whether Miller had that grisly fate in mind for me I'd never know for sure, but it would be the stuff of future nightmares.

Eventually we began chatting about more pleasant things, like going home. We were almost comfortable with each other after what we'd been through together. I'd also noticed how Riley had started calling Williams by his first name. Considering the way they'd been so testy with each other before, I commented on their apparent friendliness now.

Williams smiled. "It turns out we have a common interest in football."

"Common!" Riley exclaimed excitedly. "Doc, you're with someone famous. I only recognized him when I finally saw his face without a mask. This is Spider Williams, one of the greatest quarterbacks in the history of Michigan State. What an arm he had! My dad and I used to drive a hundred miles just to see him play."

"Thanks, sonny," Williams said.

I joined in the laugh—I figured Riley was ten years junior to Williams and me—then left them to their discussion of old plays and long ago victories.

I had something more current to do.

I'd decided to meet with Harold Miller for no better reason than my own peace of mind, an aid to putting the ordeal to bed.

As I approached his brightly lit cubicle midst the dim lighting of ICU, I couldn't help but think of the time when I saw Phyllis Sanders in an identical setting at St. Paul's. Pulling on isolation garb at the door to his room, I watched two nurses ministering to him. One of them fiddled with the dressings around his neck and over many portions of his face. In most cases the gauze was soaked through with reddish brown stains. The other nurse adjusted a pad which had been secured over what should have been his right eye; I'd been told by the residents that it had been removed surgically, there being nothing viable after it had been enucleated by glass during our struggle.

The skin around his head and upper trunk that wasn't covered with dressings was scarlet and puffy, as if he'd been scalded rather than infected. But as soon as I stepped into the room, the smell of the putrefying flesh left no doubt that infection was the underlying process. His coughing was paroxysmal, and rather than use a steel basin which one of his nurses held out to him, he let the resultant sputum roll down his chin. "My head," he moaned. "My head." On his arms and legs were more red swollen areas, some of them also covered by gauze, these too saturated through, but with yellow seepage.

Looking at him, I could think only of the state of the organs I'd seen at his mother's autopsy. It was telling testimony to the destruction that was raging through his own body now. The staph bacteria had obviously been carried from his infected skin into his bloodstream and throughout his body. His lungs would be riddled with cavities of pus, his head pain was probably the result of developing brain abscesses, and further sites of infection were setting up deep within his skin and bone, giving rise to the sores over the rest of him.

As I approached his bed, he was staring off to one side, his remaining eye having the same faraway look I'd seen in the subbasement.

"Harold, it's Dr. Garnet," said one of the nurses.

There was no response. He simply lay there. I leaned over him. "Mr. Miller, I was told you wanted to speak to me."

I wasn't even sure he could hear. But seconds ago he'd been lucid enough to complain about his head. "Does he respond?" I asked the nurses.

"Sometimes," the nearer one said, "when he wants to."

As if to underline her point, he suddenly spoke, but without moving his head or shifting his gaze. "I want to speak to you in private."

The two nurses quickly finished up what they were doing and left.

He slowly turned to look at me. "I obviously don't have much time," he rasped, "and it's hard to talk. I think there's an abscess starting in my throat."

His voice had a slightly muffled tone, as though he were speaking with a hot potato in his mouth, a sure sign of pharyngeal swelling.

"What did you want, Mr. Miller?" I was determined to keep this short and get out as quickly as possible.

"I heard Williams and Riley talking about what you're putting yourself through." He went into another paroxysm of coughing. When it subsided, he said hoarsely, "She wanted to go back to your ER that evening, Dr. Garnet, but I dissuaded her."

"Pardon?" I said, not sure what he was talking about.

"My mother. She told me over the phone she was going to return to St. Paul's and tell you personally about her dizziness—she thought you were so nice and that you'd want to know—but I talked her out of it. If it hadn't been for me, you would have had her at your doorstep a few hours after she'd been discharged, describing her orthostatic drop to you."

I felt baffled, repulsed, and intrigued at one and the same time. But I made no show of my reactions, merely shrugged, then watched intently as he struggled for a deep breath. To my shame, I wanted to hear more.

"And Mackie, he was slated to die," Miller said with difficulty. "Part of my plan to make him a scapegoat, whether you thought he was guilty or not. He had to disappear, to make it look like he'd gone into hiding but was continuing to kill. Except I had to get rid of him that night on the spur of the moment . . . to keep him from exposing me . . . and I didn't have time to get his body to a safer hiding place."

"And Rossit?"

"Well, his opportunism got him to the wrong spot at the wrong time. Of course, if I hadn't left that door unlocked when I ran for a shovel . . . Who would have thought of rats?"

I couldn't listen. It was too morbid. "Look, I don't know what—"

"I murdered them, not you!" he said abruptly.

"Why are you telling me all this?" I was so bewildered by his declarations that I couldn't think of anything else to ask.

But he didn't answer. He simply turned his head, his gaze once more traveling far away.

"Why?" I repeated.

Nothing.

He lay completely motionless, and I saw under the glare of the overhead lights a sheen of perspiration break out over his forehead.

Although it could have been the result of his fever, I suspected it was because Miller was back home, in that basement, with *him*.

* * *

I discarded my protective gear, walked to the door of the ICU, and turned to look at him in his cubicle. He slowly brought his stare back around, his one eye burning into me.

Was he out of his mind? Probably. Had he tried to absolve me? Sounded like it. But it also could have been a con, telling me what he thought I wanted to hear. Why? I'd no idea. Except I could think of little else but him as I stood there. Maybe that was the point of his show—to plant a final hook in my thoughts so I'd never be quite free of wondering about him.

I heard the sliding doors glide open behind me, then close.

"I figured you'd go see him." Riley was at my shoulder. "Did he reveal anything important?"

Important? For the police, not at all. For me, I couldn't tell yet. Perhaps in time I'd sort out whether his last act toward me was noble or in some way malicious. But I doubted that would lighten the load I'd carry for the deaths of Cam and Rossit. "Not really," I finally said.

I stood watching Miller in that chamber until he shifted his gaze away from me, once more casting it into the distance. "It does look like he's in a glass coffin," I muttered.

"Pardon?"

"It's what he said when he first saw his mother in isolation at St. Paul's—that it reminded him of the Snow White story she used to read to him when he was a child."

Riley said nothing at first. When he did speak, he seemed to be choosing his words very carefully. "Doc, what happened to him as a kid was an atrocity, and in my book those two so-called parents are among the worst kind of lowlifes I deal with. But however it started, he's a grown man now—and a killer. That means he plays by adult rules, or else other innocents, like Mackie, pay the price."

My rules as a doctor were so different from Riley's as a cop. Do no harm; comfort always; treat pain; and whenever possible, cure the illness or injury at hand. Those were the fundamentals of my code. I knew that Miller was beyond the help of any measures from that realm, but it felt like such a failure simply to deliver him into Riley's domain and its justice.

"Do you know what that isolation room reminds *me* of?" Riley asked.

I turned in time to see a look of satisfaction pass over his face before he answered.

"An execution chamber."

Epilogue:

Ten Months Later

Mortality Morbidity Bulletin—
Monday, September 1
Update: Vancomycin–Resistant MRSA

A second outbreak of *Staph aureus* resistant to both vancomycin and methicillin has been reported in the United States. The infections occurred in a hospital in Philadelphia and have resulted in six deaths so far. While local health authorities are stressing that there is no danger to the community at large, quarantine measures have been instituted for all staff and patients at the afflicted institution. The first known encounter with this untreatable organism occurred in Buffalo, New York, late last year, but under unnatural circumstances—a deranged individual had acquired the bacterium and was using it to deliberately infect personnel at a university teaching hospital. Although the present outbreak is spontaneous, a CDC spokesperson says that the lessons learned during the previous incident are pertinent to the situation in Pennsylvania. As a result the CDC has created a task force reuniting the physicians and officials who were instrumental in containing the problem in Buffalo and have dispatched them to help out. Unfortunately, fallout from the crisis won't necessarily end once the infections are dealt with by these experts. In Buffalo, even after officials ultimately gave the affected hospital there a clean bill of health, public confidence was so shaken by the prospect of the superbug recurring on its own that the venerable landmark never reopened and most of its staff and programs had to be transferred to a nearby facility. It is feared that the hospital in Pennsylvania may face a similar fate.

The next issue of the *MMB* will focus on what the natural occurrence of this much-anticipated and much-dreaded superbug means for Americans who must undergo hospitalization in the foreseeable future. Our update will include the transcript of a planned interview with the leaders of the appointed task force—Dr. Douglas Williams of the CDC and Dr. Earl Garnet, chairperson of Emergency Medicine at the newly designated St. Paul's University Health Center in Buffalo.

A CONVERSATION WITH PETER CLEMENT

Q. *Peter, you made your debut as a novelist in 1998—with* Lethal Practice. *Would you give us a thumbnail description of your life before* Lethal Practice?

A. Much of my routine was similar to the one I have described for Earl Garnet—working ER shifts, teaching, attending meetings, and keeping the department functional. It's a pretty typical job description for any ER chief—the thrill of working the big cases interspersed with the mundane business of making sure everything is stocked, staffed, and ready for whatever comes through the door . . . twenty-four hours a day, every day of the year.

As with most ER doctors, the rest of my life rotated around the schedule that regulated our shifts. Ask an ER physician to do anything socially and he or she will probably consult this document even before checking with their families or companions to see if they're free. As much as I miss the clinical work and the teaching, I certainly don't miss the hold which that infernal piece of paper had over my comings and goings during the last twenty years. However, since leaving ER to make time for writing, I seem to have fallen under the sway of a new tyranny called "the deadline."

When I wasn't in ER, the rest of my working week was spent tending to my private practice, which I continue to care for today. As much as possible, then and now, I retreat to our country home with my family on weekends.

Q. *What inspired you to embark upon a writing career?*

A. My kids ask me that all the time. "Why write books?" they demand to know—when I could be spending time on really important activities, such as playing with them or doing computer games.

The easy answer is that I thought ER would be a great location in which to set a modern thriller. I have always loved mystery stories told in the first person—especially work by the masters, such as Chandler and Hammett. I knew that by using the immediacy of the device, I would let the reader actually become an ER physician and experience his excitement, his fears, and his doubts. I couldn't resist the fun of introducing someone very evil into this special world and seeing what would happen.

But my young sons don't buy that stuff. I then appeal to their own love of storytelling, and I explain that I share that love. But they reply, "Sure, we all love stories, but why do *you* want to be one of the people who writes them?"

Once, when they were grilling me on the subject in front of one of my friends from medical school days, she silenced them with the best reply I've heard so far. She said, quite matter-of-factly: "Because he has to."

Q. *And why fiction rather than nonfiction?*

A. From nonfiction we learn what has been and what is. In fiction I like how we can play with what might be.

Q. *On the pretext that writers, including novelists, "write what they know," how much of your first two novels is based on your own experience as a doctor in charge of a hospital emergency room?*

A. My job as a writer of fiction, I think, is to create a medical world that is realistic, as opposed to being real. Any doctor doing any writing must protect patient confidentiality above all. That being assured, I made up the medical setting of my stories much in the way we create teaching cases for the residents. In those, no one's medical history is recognizable, but the realities of the problem being observed are accurate. My experiences as a chief exposed me to many of the ethical, political, medical, and economic issues at play in most modern ERs. I then made up fictitious scenarios involving some of those same issues and set their forces loose in my stories. The not-surprising result is that I've received comments from all over America that "it's just like *my* hospital." One way or another, these days we all seem to be looking at variations of the same difficulties in ER.

Q. *ER physician Earl Garnet is the emotional and intellectual center of your first two novels. In what ways is your protagonist similar to—and completely unlike—his creator?*

A. Garnet is married to an obstetrician; so am I. Garnet has a son; I have two. Garnet has a large poodle; our family has two. Garnet and I share a love for a log home on a little piece of paradise in the mountains an hour from our respective cities. One of the things I liked about being chief was that I could hire the best and brightest emergency physicians I knew, and Garnet is a tribute to them.

Am I like Garnet? I certainly identify with his commitment and his passion to be good at what he does, but I'm probably more like a Garnet wanna-be. When I first became chief and announced my intent to hire a physician who was very much of Garnet's caliber, one of my friends in ER gave me an astonished look and blurted out, "You can't be chief over him! He's better than you!"

One thing's for certain: I'm a better doctor for having had the privilege of working with the Garnets of the world.

Q. *The concept of "death rounds" is really provocative. In your novel of that title, Earl Garnet says, "Some doctors shunned the process, but I couldn't have continued as a physician without it." In effect, is this you, Peter Clement, speaking as well? How widespread is the practice of death rounds? And why do some doctors shun it?*

A. That quote is me speaking. I was taught early on that the autopsy was the ultimate tool of quality assurance, and that all deaths, especially the ones we *think* we understand, can teach us

our failings. On a personal level, I always felt I gained an edge
as an emergency physician by subjecting myself to that kind of
review. The next time a similar case came through the door, I
could react to the problem with just a bit more certainty, preci-
sion, and speed.

Most hospitals have some form of morbidity and mortality review—
they're also called M&Ms. Unfortunately, they aren't always applied systematically to all cases, and sometimes these forums are
conducted in an aggressive manner, the physician responsible for
the case being put on the defensive and nobody learning anything
except that it's better to cover up errors to protect your ass.

I always felt the secret to making death rounds work was to keep
the sessions from becoming too accusatory and, if a mistake in
the treatment of a patient was found, to focus comments on how
all of us could avoid making that same error in the future. In most
instances, only a fool would fail to grasp that he or she could have
made a similar slip in a second of inattentiveness, and when a
death was ruled preventable, no one dared point accusingly at the
physician who was responsible.

But the process, even when it's kept civilized, is tough to endure.
A physician who tends to be insecure about his or her clinical
skills in ER is liable to be afraid to face such revealing scrutiny.
Unfortunately, it may be that very sort of scrutiny by peers that
could either elevate the physician's competence and confidence
to a level that would render them safe for ER work—or reveal once
and for all that he has no future in critical-care medicine.

Q. *You chose a pseudonym for your novels. What was the thinking
behind that decision?*

A. Peter Clement is my first and middle name, given to me in
honor of my grandfather. I wrote under this name as a way to help
keep my writing activity separate from my activity as a doctor,
and to establish from the outset that it would be as inappropriate
for anyone to call my place of practice about my books as it would
be to phone Ballantine in New York about making an appointment to see me for a sore knee. At my medical office I have part-

ners, busy secretaries, and phones that are already kept busy by patients trying to reach all of us. A promise I made myself was not to let my work as an author intrude on my colleagues and patients.

Q. *We know that your philosophy (about keeping your real identity secret) has changed recently. How do you account for this about-face?*

A. I never intended to keep my real identity secret, like some kind of "Anonymous." I wanted merely to keep it from being revealed in local media until I could inform most of my patients and get everyone at my hospital accustomed to the idea I was now writing medical thrillers. In particular, I needed enough time to assure my patients I'd still be their doctor.

As it turns out, everyone—my partners, my hospital colleagues, my patients—everyone is delighted with my new career, and local publicity has been tremendously responsive, while at the same time being sensitive to my continuing role in the community as a physician.

Q. *What's the game plan for you—and Earl Garnet—after* Death Rounds?

A. I'm starting to work on a third novel, rebalancing my time for medicine with my time for writing. As for Earl Garnet, I'm sure he'll be around ER somewhere.